Jasper Fforde

Early Riser

HODDER &
STOUGHTON

First published in Great Britain in 2018 by Hodder & Stoughton
An Hachette UK company

I

Copyright © Jasper Fforde 2018

A CIP catalogue record for this title is available from the British Library

Hardback ISBN 9781473650220
Trade Paperback ISBN 9781444763591
eBook ISBN 9781444763614

Typeset in Bembo by Palimpsest Book Production Limited, Falkirk, Stirlingshire

Printed and bound in Great Britain by Clays Ltd, Elcograf S.p.A.

Hodder & Stoughton policy is to use papers that are natural, renewable
and recyclable products and made from wood grown in sustainable forests.
The logging and manufacturing processes are expected to conform to the
environmental regulations of the country of origin.

Hodder & Stoughton Ltd
Carmelite House
50 Victoria Embankment
London EC4Y 0DZ

www.hodder.co.uk

Early Riser

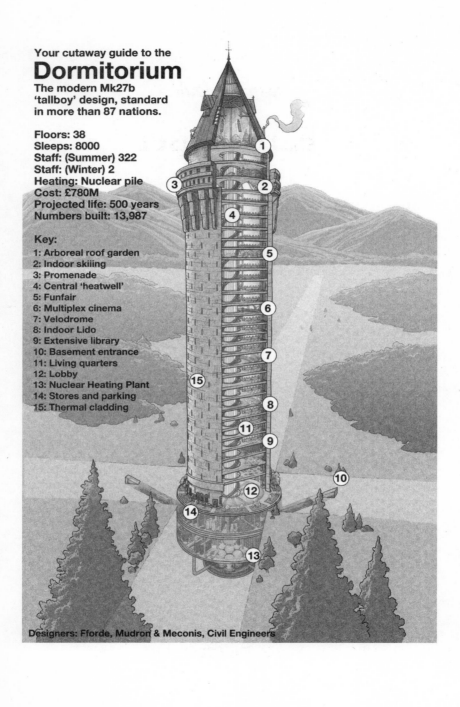

Your cutaway guide to the

Dormitorium

The modern Mk27b 'tallboy' design, standard in more than 87 nations.

Floors: 38
Sleeps: 8000
Staff: (Summer) 322
Staff: (Winter) 2
Heating: Nuclear pile
Cost: £780M
Projected life: 500 years
Numbers built: 13,987

Key:
1: Arboreal roof garden
2: Indoor skiiing
3: Promenade
4: Central 'heatwell'
5: Funfair
6: Multiplex cinema
7: Velodrome
8: Indoor Lido
9: Extensive library
10: Basement entrance
11: Living quarters
12: Lobby
13: Nuclear Heating Plant
14: Stores and parking
15: Thermal cladding

Designers: Fforde, Mudron & Meconis, Civil Engineers

For

Rhulen Marya Ivy Anna Fforde-Gorringe
Made in Australia but inspired by Wales
. . . and who knows a thing or two about hibernation

Mrs Tiffen could play the bouzouki

'... Survivability has increased during hibernation since the introduction of Dormitoria, efficient weight-gain regimes and Morphenox, but superstition and fear remain. The Hib is about rest and renewal as much as about dodging the Winter's worst, and we did our bit to make the oily tar of longsleep seem warm and friendly ...'

– from *Seventeen Winters*, by Winter Consul Lance Jones

Mrs Tiffen could play the bouzouki. Not well, and only one tune: 'Help Yourself' by Tom Jones. She plucked the strings expertly but without emotion while staring blankly out of the train window at the ice and snow. She and I had not exchanged an intelligent word since we first met five hours before, and the reason was readily explained: Mrs Tiffen was dead, and had been for several years.

'It's going to be a mild winter,' said the grey-haired woman sitting opposite Mrs Tiffen and me as the train pulled out of Cardiff Central. 'Average low of only minus forty is my guess.'

'Almost balmy,' I replied, and we both laughed, even though it wasn't funny, not really, not at all.

After some thought, I had concluded that the woman was most likely an actor, part of the extensive Winter Thespian Tradition. Audiences were small, but highly appreciative. Summer players had to make do with the diluted respect of the many whilst Winter Players commanded the adoration of the few.

The train stopped briefly at Queen Street, then rumbled slowly north. It could have gone faster, but Wales has a 75 dB sound limit in operation eight days either side of the Winter.[1]

1. No one knows quite why. Something to do with St David's Day.

'Have you been overwintering long?' I asked, by way of conversation.

'I've not seen a Summer for almost three decades,' she said with a smile. 'I remember my first venue: Hartlepool, Winter of '76, the Don Hector Playhouse. We were performing *King Lear* as the support act to the Chuckle Brothers during their one and only Winter tour. Their gig was packed – almost three hundred people. Never seen that happen before except with the Bonzo Dog Band or Val Doonican, but then they made the Winter season a kind of trademark, like Mott the Hoople and Richard Stilgoe in the old days and Paul Daniels and Take That today.'

Few Summer acts chose to brave the cold – the Winter could be a hard taskmaster. The 1974 Showaddywaddy Welsh tour was a good case in point: the band were first trapped by Hunger-crazed nightwalkers in their Aberystwyth hotel, then lost half their number to an ice storm. Over the next two months their manager was kidnapped and ransomed by 'Lucky' Ned Farnesworth, three roadies lost their feet to frostbite, and their bassist was allegedly taken by Wintervolk. Aside from that, the surviving members thought it was one of their most successful tours ever.

'Never realised how strongly the silence could drag upon one's psyche,' said my companion, breaking into my thoughts, 'and how the solitude can become physically painful. I once went seven weeks without seeing a single soul, stranded in the Ledbury Playhouse during a protracted coldsnap in '78. Colder than the Gronk's tit and for four weeks a blizzard. Even the Villains hunkered down, and nightwalkers froze on their feet. Come the melt the rigor kept them upright – they didn't start falling until they'd thawed down to their shins. For those not with the calling, the absence of humanity can be debilitating.' She paused for a moment before continuing. 'But y'know, in some strange way, I love it. Good for achieving a sense of ... *clarity.*'

Long-time Winterers were well known for expressing their views in this manner – a dark love of the bleakness, and how conducive the solitude was to deep philosophical thought. More often than not, those that extolled the Winter virtues so fulsomely did so right up until the moment they left an overly apologetic note, stripped themselves naked and walked outside into the sub-zero. It was called 'The Cold Way Out'.

'Lobster,' said Mrs Tiffen without relevance to anything, still playing the bouzouki. 'Help Yourself', again, for perhaps the two hundredth time.

Returning from the depths of hibernation was never without risk. If the minimal synaptic tick-over that took care of nominal life functions was halted, you'd suffer a neural collapse and be Dead in Sleep. If you ran out of fats to metabolise into usable sugars, you'd be Dead in Sleep. If the temperature fell too far too quickly, you'd be Dead in Sleep. Vermin predation, CO_2 build-up, calcitic migration, preexisting medical condition or a dozen or so other complications – Dead in Sleep.

But not all neural collapses led to death. Some, like Mrs Tiffen who was on Morphenox – it was *always* the ones on Morphenox – awoke with just enough vestigial memory to walk and eat. And while most people saw nightwalkers as creepy brain-dead denizens of the Winter whose hobbies revolved around mumbling and cannibalism, we saw them as creatures who had returned from the dark abyss of hibernation with most of everything left behind. They were normally rounded up before everyone woke, usually to be redeployed and then parted out, but stragglers that slipped the net could sometimes be found. Billy DeFroid discovered one snagged on some barbed wire in the orchard behind St Granata's three weeks after Springrise. He reported it to the authorities but not before taking its wristwatch, something he was still wearing when he died.

'Seven down,' said the actor, having to raise her voice to be heard above Mrs Tiffen's bouzouki, *'slow to pen a plumber's handbook?'*

'I'm not good with crosswords,' I shouted back, then added: 'I hope the bouzouki playing isn't troubling you unduly?'

The thespian smiled.

'Not really,' she said, 'at least it keeps numbskulls out of the carriage.'

She was right. Today was Slumberdown Minus One, the last full day before the Winter officially began. The train was busy with Mothballers and overwinterers, trying to get to their relevant

Dormitoria or work as status dictated. Several passengers had tried to join us in our compartment but after taking one look at Mrs Tiffen's glassy nightwalker stare they hurried on past.

'To be honest I rather like Tom Jones,' she added. 'Does she play "Delilah" or "She's a Lady"?'

'It would help,' I said, 'for variety's sake. But no.'

The train followed the frozen river up north past Castell Coch, and through the billowy clouds of white vapour from the locomotive that drifted past the window I could see that Winter shutdown was very much in evidence – shutters were closed and barred, vehicles swaddled in layers of waxed hessian, flood sluices greased and set to auto. It was all quite exciting in a dangerously thrilling kind of way. My initial trepidation regarding overwintering had soon changed to adventurous curiosity. Enthusiasm might come, in time, but my sights were set on a loftier goal: survival. A third of first-time novices in the Winter Consul Services never saw the Spring.

'So,' said the actor, nodding towards what had once been Mrs Tiffen, 'harboured?'[2]

'By her husband for five years.'

Most people to whom I mentioned this displayed a sense of disgust; not the actor.

'He must have loved her.'

'Yes,' I agreed, 'he gave everything he had to protect her.'

While Mr Tiffen had regarded his wife as someone with profound neurological issues, we saw her as little more than another casualty of the Winter. The bouzouki playing was merely a quirk, a vestigial memory from a mind that once crackled with personality and creative energy. Almost all of her was gone; only the skill remained.

We pulled into Abercynon station with a hiss. The passengers moved about the platform with commendable silence, easily explained: those now heading for the grateful joy of slumber were too fatigued to celebrate, and those planning to overwinter had only the anxieties of a lonely sixteen weeks to dominate their thoughts. Little was said

---

2. Legally speaking: 'The non-surrender or retention for whatever reason of any person in a Pseudosentient Mobile Vegetative State'.

as the passengers embarked and disembarked, and even the signalman's clicker seemed to have lost its usual sharpness.

'The courts are usually lenient if there's a family component,' said the actor in a quiet voice. 'Mind you, harbouring is harbouring.'

'There'll be no trial,' I said. 'Her husband's dead – and with honour.'

'The best sort in my view,' said the woman thoughtfully. 'I hope for the same myself. What about you? Many Winters under your belt?'

'This is my first.'

She looked at me with such a sense of shocked surprise that I felt quite unnerved.

'*First Winter?*' she echoed incredulously. 'And they've sent you on nightwalker delivery duty to Sector Twelve?'

'I'm not *exactly* alone,' I said, 'there's—'

'—first Winters should always be spent indoors, taking notes and acclimatising,' she said, ignoring me. 'I've lost far too many newbies to be anything but sure of *that*. What did they do? Threaten to thump you?'

'No.'

They didn't need to. I'd volunteered, quite happily, eight weeks before, during Fat Thursday celebrations.

Fat Thursday

'... The length of time humans have hibernated has shifted subtly, mostly due to climatic conditions and advances in agriculture. 'Standard Winter' was adopted in 1775 and fixed to eight weeks either side of Winter solstice. From Slumberdown to Springrise, 99.99% of the population submit to the dark abyss of sleep ...'

— *The Hiberculture of Man*, by Morris Desmond

Fat Thursday had been long established as the first day of serious gorging, the time to indulge in the latest faddy get-fat-quick diets and to take a vow of abstinence from the mass-stealing sin of exercise. Yesterday you could run for a bus and no one would turn a hair, tomorrow it would be frowned upon as almost criminally irresponsible. For the two months until Slumberdown, every calorie was sacred; a fight to keep every ounce. Spring only ever welcomed the mass-diligent.

Skinny Pete went to sleep, underfed and bony
Skinny Pete went to sleep, and died a death so lonely

My job of Assistant House Manager was under the generally amenable and delegation-addicted Sister Zygotia, which made Fat Thursday celebrations pretty much my responsibility. And while leaving me open to perhaps more criticism than usual, it was a welcome break from the day-to-day tedium of running St Granata's Pooled Parentage Station.[3] Basically, Fat Thursday required only three things: enough food, enough chairs, and trying not to let Sister Placentia get her hands on the gin.

Megan Hughes was the first to arrive. She'd spent twelve years at

---

3. Unofficial motto: 'Keeping up the numbers so you don't have to'.

the Pool until she got picked out by a wealthy couple in Bangor. Was married last I heard to someone big in the Mrs Nesbit Traditional Tearooms empire, and was now one of St Granata's patrons: we made a good income selling child offsets to people like Megan, who saw the whole baby thing as insufferably farmyard.[4] It was sort of ironic, really, that she had a career at OffPop – the Office for Population Control – ensuring *other* women were responsibly discharging their duties. Megan and I had not met for a couple of years but every time we did, she told me how much she really admired me when we were growing up, and how inspiring I was.

'Wonky!' she said in a mock-excited kind of way. 'You look *absolutely* marvellous.'

'Thank you, but it's Charlie now.'

'Sorry. *Charlie.*' She paused for thought. 'I think of you and St Granata's all the time.'

'Do you now?'

'Yes. And,' she added, leaning closer, 'you know what?'

Here it comes.

'What?'

'I always *really* admired you growing up. Always smiling through your unhappiness. A real inspiration.'

'I wasn't unhappy.'

'You *looked* unhappy.'

'Looks can be deceptive.'

'All too true,' she said, 'but I meant what I said: inspirational in a sort of tragic way, like you're the failure in the family, but always looked on the bright side of everything.'

'You're very kind,' I said, long used to Megan's ways, 'but it could have been much worse: I could have been born without tact or empathy, and be shallow, self-absorbed and hideously patronising.'

'That's true too,' she said with a smile, laying a hand on my arm. 'We are *so* blessed, you and I. Did I tell you that I got a promotion at OffPop? Thirty-four K plus car and pension.'

---

4.   Offsets were classed as childbearing *avoidance* rather than *evasion* – a subtle, yet legal, distinction.

'That's a huge weight off my mind,' I said.

She beamed.

'You are so *very* kind. Well, mustn't tarry. So long, Wonky.'

'Charlie.'

'Right. Charlie. Inspirational.'

And she walked off up the corridor. It would have been easy to dislike her intensely, but I actually felt nothing for her at all.

Lucy Knapp was the next person of note to walk through the doors. We'd seen each other daily for eighteen years until she left to go to HiberTech Training College. Friendships ebbed and flowed in the Pool, but Lucy and I had always been close. In the six years since she'd left we'd spoken at least once a month.

'Hey,' I said, and we tapped fists together, one on top of another, a sort of secret handshake from way back I-don't-know-when.

Lucy and I were responsible for the dried smear of banoffee pie still stuck to the face of St Somnia on the ceiling frieze overhead, a reminder of a memorable food-fight back in '96. There was even the dent in the plasterwork where Donna Trinket, intent on breaking the ground-floor lap record on roller skates, had come a cropper owing to some recklessly spilt Heinz spaghetti hoops by the kitchens.

'So what's this about you joining Prudential Winter Life?' she asked with, I think, a sense of friendly derision.

'Anything to get me out of this dump,' I replied, 'but it's not like I can *only* sell Hibernational Cover with optional Redeployment and Mandatory Transplant payments – there's also whole-life insurance, term, dental, fire and auto, not to mention frost damage. What do you think?'

'I can hardly contain my indifference.'

'I feel the same way, but, well, y'know, Morphenox.'

I would be expected to work the first ten years at minimum wage, but it would be worth it. Not for the job, of course, which was dull as meltwater, but for the specific perk that went with it: Prudential would transfer my rights to Morphenox across from St Granata's without interruption. I could, quite literally, sleep easy. Despite the strict contractual obligations, lack of job mobility and freedom of choices that it entailed, the career move would be a no-brainer. I could finally get away from here with pharmaceutical privileges undiminished.

'Hey,' I said, 'did you hear that Ed Dweezle danced the Night Fandango?'[5]

'Yeah,' said Lucy, 'I heard.'

Dweezle always had trouble keeping weight on. We used to sneak him part of our food to help him out. I don't know how he'd lasted three Winters on his own once out of St Granata's, but it must have been expensive. Despite being dosed up to the gills on Morphenox he'd entered his fourth Hib way too light and run out of reserves three weeks short of Springrise. He'd nightwalked and been redeployed as a street-sweeper somewhere up north, then parted out eight months later.

'Useful until death and beyond,' said Lucy, 'as the company likes to promote itself in slogans.'

The company to which she referred was HiberTech, who made Morphenox, redeployed any nightwalkers that were suitable and then supervised the transplant potential of each. Their nightwalker policy was neatly – some said perfectly – vertically integrated. There was another slogan:

Everything of use but the yawn.™

I walked with Lucy from the lobby to the Great Hall.

'I'm always uneasy about Pool reunions,' she said. 'On the whole the experience was good, but I didn't like everyone.'

'Rough with the smooth,' I said.

'Shits with the saints.'

We mingled in the crowd and shook hands, hugged or nodded to the other poolers, strictly according to a sliding scale of respect

---

5.   Slang for 'became a nightwalker'. Usual terms were Husks, cabbages, Vacants or deadheads. Revenant was the most polite term, but technically speaking they were in a '*Pseudosentient Mobile Vegetative State*'.

and affection. Williams, Walter, Keilly, Neal, other Walter, other Williams and McMullen were all there and I greeted them warmly. I thought I should say something to Gary Findlay but he turned away on the pretext of more beer from the cooler as soon as he saw me. He and I hadn't exchanged a word since we were twelve, the day his bullying stopped, the day I bit off his ear.[6]

Older ex-residents whom I didn't recognise were mingling freely with the rest of us, as the current residents did with us. Anyone who spent time at the Pool shared a bond, kind of like family. Actually, given the circumstances at the Sisterhood, many of us actually *were* family.

Lucy walked over to pay her respects to the Senior Sisters, who were all sitting on the stage like seven duchesses, holding court. They were giggling foolishly at some small joke, their usual austerity tempered by the triple jollities of occasion, food and, for those not with child, the cheapest sherry that money can buy.

'Our very own Lucy Knapp,' said Sister Placentia as we approached, embracing Lucy but ignoring me as one would a stick of familiar furniture. 'Tell me your news.'

Lucy politely explained to them about her induction into HiberTech's Fast Track Management Scheme whilst I stood to one side. Despite the often erratic levels of care, most of the sisters were generally okay. Without them, I'd have been nothing – infants with lesser conditions than mine were routinely left underweight heading into their first Winter. There were worse Pools than this one.

'*Fascinating*, dear,' said Sister Placentia once Lucy had concluded a potted history of what she'd been up to, 'and what chance you could wangle us an Edward to assist in the kitchens?'

'Next year's model might be an improvement,' said Lucy in a guarded tone. 'I'll see what I can do then.'

Edward or Jane were the default names given to redeployed nightwalkers. With their cannibalistic tendencies reduced by timely snacks and the tattered remnants of their minds ingeniously rewired, they could do simple chores. Too simple, some said, to be useful domestically. The St Granata's over in Port Talbot had an Edward

---

6.   It tasted salty if you're interested, and detached surprisingly easily.

that could wash up,[7] but mostly they were used for strictly repetitive tasks like opening doors, pumping water and digging fields.

'How's it going, Wonk?' came a voice in my ear so suddenly I jumped. It was Sister Zygotia, a particular favourite of mine, despite – or perhaps because of – her eccentricity. She had a fondness for peanut butter and anchovies, used to nail her bedroom door shut during the Winter 'to guard against prowling Wintervolk', then insist that puddings at St Granata's be randomly laced with curry powder to 'better prepare us for life's inevitable disappointments'.

'So-so,' I said. 'The budget for next year is a little tight but we should be all right, so long as the offset payments aren't reduced and we eat meat only once a week.'

'Good, good,' she said in a distracted fashion, then put her hand on my shoulder and steered me to a corner of the hall.

'Look, I don't want to be the bearer of bad news and all,' she said, 'but I am. You should know that Mother Fallopia got wind of your application to the Prudential and, well, she had words with their induction officer. Your application was … rescinded.'

I had to admit I wasn't surprised, but it didn't feel good. Frustration has a smell of its own, like hot toffee mixed with sun-dried mud. I looked at Sister Zygotia, who said she was sorry, and I told her it was fine, really, and I was then relieved to be called away in order to help deal with Sister Contractia, who was taking her door bouncer duties a little more enthusiastically than anyone thought necessary. Sister Contractia liked a good brawl so it took ten minutes to calm her down, sweep up the broken teeth, placate the six people she'd just taken on and clean out the cut above her eye. When I got back, Lucy Knapp was telling everyone about her first overwintering gig at HiberTech, and how she'd actually *seen* a Winter solstice. She showed us the single brass star pinned to her blouse to prove it.

'Did you get sleep-deprivation narcosis?' I asked, parking my frustration in the back of my mind, where it sat with good and ancient company.

---

7. But only plates, saucers, pots, pans and cutlery. Cups, jugs and tankards were a complication too far.

'Once you've shifted your sleep cycle to the late Summer it isn't so bad,' said Lucy, 'but the first season up can be cruel. The only upside was that while you're freezing to death, getting eaten or being press-ganged into domestic service, you could be hallucinating that you were on the Gower Peninsula, sipping mock-banana daiquiris[8] while watching the sun go down from the Worm's Head Bar & Grill.'

Lucy wasn't the only one to overwinter from the Pool, just the most recent. Another Poolmate named Billy DeFroid had been inducted into the Winter Consul Service three years before, and everyone was full of praise up until the moment he was eaten by nightwalkers who had gone pack in Llandeilo. He'd fared better than most. The average life expectancy for a Novice on their first Winter 'boots in snow' was barely six weeks. The Winter wasn't a forgiving place; little wonder newbies spent their first Winter doing paperwork safely indoors.

'So, Lucy,' I said, 'tell us about the narcosis.'

'Quite ... challenging to begin with,' she said. 'I thought my legs were made of chocolate. The colder it got, the more brittle they became. I was worried that if any nightwalkers turned up I wouldn't be able to get away.'

'I've had dreams like that,' said Maisie Rogers who had wandered over, 'running but not being able to escape.'

Dreams. No one who was anyone had *dreams*. Those of us with access to Morphenox happily traded our subconscious hibernational activity for a dramatic drop in stored energy requirements. Morphenox removed the ability to dream, but in exchange gave us increased survivability. For the first time in human history, an individual could realistically *expect* to live through the Winter. 'Morphenox', another advertising slogan went, 'brings you the Spring'. An addendum might read: 'but only if you have the luck, cash or social position to be granted its use'.

'You don't need to wear the whole dreaming deal as a badge of honour,' scolded Megan who had joined us.

We all nodded agreement. Most people who were forced to forgo the pharmaceutical means to ease themselves through the Winter

8. One spoonful of banana Nesquik, equal parts rum and Robinson's lemon barley water.

stayed quiet. It was like wearing a big hat with '3rd Class Citizen' written all over it.

But Maisie, to her credit, was unabashed.

'I'm not ashamed,' she said indignantly, to groans and rolled eyes from all of us, 'and I won't be made to feel ashamed. Besides, dreams are fun and random and at least this way I never get to be a night-walker, lumbering around the Winter, eating beetles and curtains and people and stuff and then ending my days as a spare parts inventory.'

'If you become a Vacant you don't know you're one,' I pointed out, 'that's the tragedy and the blessing – no brain, no torment.'

There were, inevitably, a few downsides to Morphenox: a shocking headache, some fearful hallucinations – and for every two thousand users, one would arise from hibernation as a nightwalker. The 50 per cent of citizens granted Morphenox were the same ones who might end up as drooling subhumans with severe personal hygiene issues and a dismaying penchant for cannibalism. Irrespective, everyone thought it was a risk worth taking.

There was a sudden commotion as the food arrived. We all joined an orderly queue, the conversation rising in pitch with the sense of joyful anticipation. As we waited for the sisters, children and under-weight to be fed first, we chatted about what daft idea self-styled 'sleep extreme' guru Gaer Brills was promoting to fashionable sleepers, and inevitably, who was going to win *Albion's Got Talent*.

'Sleeping in trees wrapped in hessian smeared in goose fat on BMI minimum,' said Lucy, in answer to the Gaer Brills question. 'It'll be raining hipsters all Winter.'

In answer to the *Albion's Got Talent* question, none of us had a clue after last year's surprise winner – Bertie, a sou'wester-wearing dachshund who could tap dance – so the conversation soon changed to a subject currently in the news: tackling a recent upturn in Winter mortality. Moderates suggested baby drives and cash incentives to tackle the increased wastage, while the hardliners favoured barren-shaming, removing all bearing exemptions and axing Child Offset Schemes. Although the population was holding steady against Winter losses, occasional troughs in the childbearing demographic could still cause panic, and right-wing hardliners loved a good panic.

'I heard that lowering the minimum childbearing age would cure the wastage issue in a stroke,' said Megan.

'It would mean redefining the definition of a child,' said Lucy, 'and I'm not so sure that's either desirable or possible.'

'We could always boost the gender ratio to 70:30,' I said.

'Mucking around any more with the numbers is a seriously *bad* idea,' said Lucy. 'I have enough trouble finding a decent date as it is.'

'I say freeze the vast government subsidies awarded to HiberTech,' announced Maisie in her best revolutionary tones, 'and instead of using it to permit Morphenox for the few, establish a workable strategy to ensure that *all* citizens attain target BMI come Slumberdown. We shouldn't embrace Hibernational elitism, we should embrace Uniform Sleep for all – it's fair and just, would increase survivability, lower wastage – and ultimately release the burden of childbearing.'

We all instantly hushed. It was the central tenet and long-stated aim of the once highly respected opposition but now strictly illegal pressure group the Campaign for Real Sleep. They believed that real sleep was the one true sleep, that a pharmacological solution to wastage was morally and fiscally unsustainable, and that humans needed to dream for long-term health.[9] It was a brave or foolhardy person who publicly espoused their views, or even opened up the question for debate. Maisie, on the face of it, was probably brave rather than foolhardy.

'The subsidies are spent chiefly on research to ensure that one day *all* Hibernation is under the protective shell of Morphenox,' said Lucy defensively. 'Don Hector was a genius, but even he had limitations – we'll get there eventually.'

'We only know that because your chums at HiberTech tell us,' replied Maisie, 'it's a mechanism of social compliance. Don Hector didn't make us free, he initiated a class distinction between fair sleeping and foul. We should all be a global hibernating village, equal in sleep, equal in dignity.'

9. RealSleep's unofficial motto was 'What Dreams May Come'.

There was an intake of breath. It was the mission statement of the Campaign for Real Sleep, a sort of rallying cry.

'We shouldn't be having this conversation,' said Lucy, suddenly becoming a *lot* more serious. 'I could get into serious trouble for not reporting you – and Don Hector was a great man who has saved millions through Morphenox.'

'My dormetologist told me there was a new formulation heading our way,' said Megan, 'Morphenox-B. What's the deal with that?'

'And I heard something about Project Lazarus,' I said, my curiosity overcoming my sense of caution.

'If the HiberTech rumour mill could be harnessed,' said Lucy after a few moments of exasperated silence, 'we'd have free power for ever.'

'You didn't answer Megan's question,' said Maisie.

Lucy and Maisie glared at one another dangerously and Lucy's eyelid quivered. I liked her a lot, but she was a loyal HiberTech person, through and through. I think it was an employment entry requirement.

'I don't have to answer Megan's question,' she said, slowly and deliberately.

The exchange was interrupted by some sort of commotion near the door. The guests were parting to let some people through, and that meant one of two things: a celebrity or someone relevant. Or, as it turned out, both.

There were two of them, conversing politely. One was our own Mother Fallopia, tall, elegant, austere, and with a habit so black she looked like a nun-shaped hole in the air. Next to her was a tall man dressed in the white quilted combat fatigues of a Winter Consul. He had a Gold Solstice Star pinned to his lapel that indicated he had seen at least twenty Winters, wore twin walnut-handled Bambis holstered across his chest and carried with him a sense of quiet dignity. He was dark, tall, and had matinee idol good looks. He also looked a little like Euan, Sian, Maisie, Daphne, Billy and Ed Dweezle – but there was a good reason for that.

'Wow,' said Lucy, impressed like the rest of us – indeed, possibly everyone there. 'It's … Jack Logan.'

Jack Logan

'...of all the Winter Service Industries, the Winter Consul was the most dangerous. Few who joined expected to last out the decade, yet recruitment was never much a problem. You didn't find the job, they said, it found you. No-one ever who entered the Winter voluntarily wasn't trying to leave something behind...'

– *Twenty by Seven Solsti and Counting,* by Consul 'Rock' McDozer

Most Consuls sought only anonymity outside the Winter, but a few courted the limelight for one reason or another. 'Wildcat' deLuth over in Sector Nine East was renowned for her capacity for capturing nightwalkers alive – four hundred and sixty-two consigned to the redeployment centres, a record unlikely to be beaten; 'Tangy' Schneider of Sector Nineteen outraged public decency by living with a Winter Nomad when off-duty, and Chief Consul Toccata of Sector Twelve was suspected of resorting to Winter cannibalism more enthusiastically than was considered acceptable or, indeed, necessary.

Jack Logan, by comparison, was the clean-cut, acceptable face of the Consul Service. Sure, there were stories of overzealousness and an eye to commercial exploitation but his record spoke most loudly. The Newport/Port Talbot/Cardiff Region had consistently the lowest levels of wastage, HotPot overheat, Villain incursion and nightwalker outrages of anywhere in Wales. He was genetically Tier One, too – rumour had it that he could charge eye-popping siring fees, but to his credit, didn't.

Logan nodded greetings as he passed, briefly made eye contact, and signed autographs on scraps of paper that were offered to him. We knew he was a long-time patron of St Granata's, but he rarely attended social events.

The initial excitement over, we shuffled along the food queue and picked out some corn on the cob that oozed butter, then helped ourselves to rice and chicken. Large portions, too. It seemed almost thrillingly extravagant.

'What's Jack Logan doing here?' asked Brian, who was behind the counter, serving the food. 'Not the usual, I'm guessing.'

'He's giving Mother Fallopia her twenty-eighth Silver Stork,' said Gary Findlay, who was three places farther up in the queue.

'Well deserved,' said Brian.

Brian had been the venerable sister's twelfth Silver Stork and Gary and Lucy her joint eighteenth. The Sisters of Perpetual Gestation took their pledge seriously. The record was Sister Vulvolia over in Sector fifty-one, with thirty-four. All but nine survived their first Winter and each of them from different sires – but then Sister Vulvolia had a good eye,[10] and took the need for genetic variation seriously.

'Hmm,' said Lucy, picking out a drumstick, 'd'you think Logan will be performing this afternoon?'

It was always possible. Those in the military or law enforcement agencies often had a second career acting out their Winter adventures. Logan's performances were quite sophisticated, with fake snow and wind machines. Once, he featured a real live nightwalker, but that was stopped when he got loose and went on a rampage in the dress circle. A tragic affair, although if it had been the stalls I don't think anyone would have minded.

Once we had stuffed ourselves quite stupid and mopped up the oil and juices with bread rolls, we sat down to get ready for an equal volume of pudding in an hour or two, followed by biscuits and candy floss two hours after that. Anyone who hadn't consumed at least five times their usual calorific intake might be deemed not taking the whole 'bulk up' issue seriously.

We talked some more, catching up on news. What ex-poolers were up to, who had died, then a long procession of do-you-remember-whens that seemed to have become less shocking and

10. It's rumoured that she would often approach potential breeding partners in shopping malls and cinemas, but I've no idea if this is true or not.

more amusing with the passage of time: about Donna Trinket's accident — always a perennial favourite — or when Betty Simcox was
nearly buried alive during a prank that went wrong, or when Joplin
set fire to herself in a prank that went about as well as anyone had
expected — and then, as always, how Dai Powell vanished on his
sixteenth birthday and returned on his twentieth, and no one knew
where he'd been.

'He still has no idea,' said Lucy. 'I asked him again only last week.'

'Kidnapped into domestic service by Villains is my guess,' said
Megan, 'but too ashamed to admit it.'

After the jam roly-poly, apple crumble and bread-and-butter
pudding had been consumed with about two gallons of custard,[11]
Mother Fallopia gave a speech. It was the same old Fat Thursday
stuff that we'd heard before, many times: about how we must all
embrace the virtues of gluttony and sloth as we headed towards the
Winter, and to remember those who had not survived hibernation
last year through not being diligent about their weight, and to
consider a career with the Sisterhood if female, and if male then to
do one's utmost to be a productive member of society and to honour
the Princess Gwendolyn daily and remain loyal to Wales and the
Northern Federation — and so on and so forth. She then announced
her retirement due to a slackening of fertility, and proclaimed she
would be putting the reins of St Granata's firmly in Sister Placentia's
hands, which was met by half-hearted applause and, somewhere at
the back, a groan.

Sector Chief Winter Consul Logan then made a speech, about
how the Sisterhood were more than doing their part to head off
the spectre of Winter wastage, thanked Mother Fallopia for her
numerous confinements and wise and committed leadership of
St Granata's, welcomed Sister Placentia to her new-found position
of authority, then repeated much of what Mother Fallopia had said.
Right at the end he related a short ditty that seemed, at the time,
entirely random:

---

11. Not each, although it felt like it.

*To escort a likely lad from lower Llanboidy with collies and brollies
from Chiswick while Krugers with Lugers take potshots at hotshots is
enough to make mammoths with a gram's worth of hammocks
feel down with a clown from Manchester Town.*

We all looked at one another and shrugged, then dutifully applauded
as Logan presented Mother Fallopia with her Silver Stork. That done,
we returned to the table and the roofing-tile-sized after-dinner mints,
cheeseboard, any leftovers on other people's plates and finally the
serving bowls themselves. Traditionally, Fat Thursday never resulted
in any washing-up.

Several other ex-poolers joined us and we settled down to talk, or
at least, they talked, I listened, my mind still distracted. A cop who
worked in Forensics told us about her job analysing splatter patterns
of messy eating following illegal pantry incursion and food theft.

'It's always out of hunger so they eat on the spot,' she told us,
'and hunger eating is never tidy eating.'

She told us about a Pantry Heist over at the *Cary Grant*
Dormitorium. It was unguarded at the time, having been boarded
up after a reactor shutdown, but stealing pantry was then, and still
is now, an offence carrying the punishment of Frigicution. Most
were blaming Villains, but the authorities decided it was the Campaign
for Real Sleep wanting to retain enough pantry to mount an overwintering campaign.[12] No one with any sense believed them, and
Kiki – RealSleep's nominal head – denied the report as 'utterly
ludicrous'.

'Some said it was the cops nicking stuff themselves in order to
flush out Kiki into denying it,' said someone, I forget who.

'Who is Kiki anyway?' I asked.

'The head of RealSleep,' said Megan.

'I know that. Not the *what*, the *who*.'

'Nobody knows,' said Lucy with a shrug. 'It's not a person, it's a
position. Remove a Kiki and the Vice-Kiki takes over.'

---

12. Staying awake in the Winter requires considerable pantry, a lot of luck, warm
clothes, and several dozen good books.

This was undoubtedly true, as much was run on the Hydra principle, from Royal Families to Winter Consuls to the military to staff at Mrs Nesbit Tearooms. Remove one and another would be waiting just behind. Irrespective, RealSleep had been quiet recently, but like the active-yet-currently-dormant volcano on Skye, no one was sure if that was a good thing or a bad thing.

I left them to their conversation and started to corral the children into tidying up and fetching out the board games and the hookahs as the gathering dusk brought darkness to the hall. Sister Placentia loved a raspberry hubble-bubble when playing Scrabble while Sister Fertizilia tended towards her non-aggressive version of chess where you couldn't take any pieces. Zygotia liked nothing more than a noisy game of Hungry Hippos. Each to their own. But as I was passing Mother Fallopia's office on an errand for Sister Placentia, I noticed a row of people sitting on the bench outside. I asked what was going on and Williams blinked owlishly at me and said that Logan was conducting open interviews for the Winter Consuls.

'*Open* interviews? No preselection?'

'Seems like it. He lost his Novice and needs a new one.'

I thought for a moment. Or rather, I didn't think for a moment. I just told Williams to budge up and then sat down on the bench, heart thumping, and for good reason: joining the Winter Service Industry was risky – little more than suicide, some said – but it did give one access to Morphenox.[13]

'So when did you first consider a Winter career?' asked Williams, who seemed chatty.

'Oh, eight seconds ago,' I replied.

For the 99.99 per cent of the population who slept through, the Winter was an abstract concept. Go to sleep and wake up – hopefully – four months later.

---

13. They used it not during the Winter, obviously, but when they slept – through the late Summer.

There in the Autumn, gone by the Spring.
It's a pain in the arse, this hibernation thing.
Eat like a horse, sleep like a bear,
Maybe live, maybe die — best not to care.

Other than those who worked in the Transplant industry and *had* to brave the Winter, few people opted to face the cold, the vermin, the Villains, the loneliness, the Wintervolk. But with my utterly unrewarding house manager career, limited prospects and the rarity of untrained jobs with Morphenox rights attached, overwintering had suddenly become hugely attractive.

'How about being a Winter Consul?' asked Williams. 'How long you wanted to be one of those?'

'Oh, years and years.'

In truth, given the risks and the usually over-rigorous selection process, *never*. I sat on the bench, trying to keep calm and wondering what I should say. Each interview took about ten minutes and to every applicant that emerged long-faced there was a torrent of questions from the remaining queue. All questions were met with a shrug, the news they'd been rejected, and no clue as to what Logan was actually looking for.

After Williams went in with enthusiasm and emerged looking crushed, it was my turn.

Testing time

'... Hibernational Insomnia or Winsomnia has many causes: some through an abnormality or trauma in the hypothalamus that denies part or full hibernation, others because of Hypnophobia or an inherited disposition towards calcification or muscle wastage. Most choose to be usefully employed during the Winter, but some, the so-called "undeserving awake", prefer to coast through the Winter on the toil and pantry of others ...'

– *Gray's Guide to the Physiology of Hibernation*, XXIInd edition

Mother Fallopia was with Logan in her study, a small, austere chamber that smelled of furniture polish, coffee and photocopier toner. The room had a large wooden desk in the centre, but otherwise comprised mostly filing cabinets and pictures of infants on the walls. It was always unnerving being in here, and not just because of Mother Fallopia and her piercing 'what-have-you-done-to-deserve-existence' look: all the pictures were of the nameless children that didn't make it past their first Winter, and the ones with names who didn't make it past any subsequent. We couldn't ever figure out if the images were for remembrance, an invitation for the sisters to breed better, or because Mother Fallopia just liked pictures of kids and didn't care one way or another.

'You have a message?' asked Mother Fallopia.

'No,' I said, 'I heard the Winter Consul interviews were open to all.'

'You already have a job,' said Mother in a voice like galvanised pipes, 'you don't need another, and believe me, you wouldn't last ten minutes as a Consul.'

I have to admit that I felt an overwhelming desire to apologise profusely and then sneak out, but to my credit, didn't.

'Charlie Worthing,' I said in a shaky voice. 'I'd like to be considered for the post.'

'Let's move on,' said Mother, 'we're wasting time here.'

'No, Prudence,' said Logan, the first time I'd ever heard Mother Fallopia contradicted or someone use her first name, 'we'll see anyone who wants to be seen.'

He turned to me.

'The usual selection process is exhaustive,' he explained, 'but not perfect. I like to find the hidden gems the preselection process has missed. I've seen you about, Worthing, you one of mine?'

'No, sir. I'm a ... surrogacy that turned out wrong.'

'On account of your head?'

'Yes, on account of my head.[14] I was transferred to St Granata's with half of the insurance payout. The rest went to my bios as compensation.'

'Worthing is an insurance write-off,' said Mother Fallopia, 'and one that is still paying off our kindness.'

'I disagree,' said Logan. 'You *were* a write-off. Right now you're a candidate for the Winter Consulship. Each on their merits.'

I liked Logan instantly, and all of a sudden would do anything to work with him, Morphenox or not. He asked me if I saw myself being a career House Manager here at St Granata's.

'No, sir,' I said, now sitting more upright in my chair and ignoring Fallopia's hot gaze, 'I recently applied to join the Winter Prudential.'

'And?'

'Rejected.'

'Reason?'

'Interference ... by a third party.'

I looked at Mother Fallopia as I said it, and she looked away. Logan followed my gaze, and probably guessed what had happened.

'Not necessarily an issue,' he said. 'Qualifications?'

'I can read and write to level 4A,' I said, 'first aid trained, one hundred yards in 14.2, drive, swim and play the tuba.'

'Tell Jack about your D minus in General Skills, Worthing,' said Mother Fallopia, who had not yet given up on her efforts to torpedo my interview.

14. More about my head later.

'It was a D *plus*, actually,' I said, then added: 'Not that it makes much difference.'

'I don't rely so much on exam results,' said Logan before I could go on. 'I was bottom of the class myself. I'm actually after someone with a good memory.'

This was more interesting.

'I came second in the Swansea Town Memory Bee with six hundred and forty-eight random words memorised after only two readings,' I said with a certain degree of pride. It was a record that was still the third highest in the town. Sister Zygotia wanted me to go to the South Wales regionals, but I'm not really that fond of people staring at me.

'Did you know this?' asked Logan, looking pointedly at Mother Fallopia.

'It must have slipped my mind,' she said, 'and I never expected Worthing to be so utterly ungrateful as to apply.'

Logan nodded and looked back at me.

'I need a new Novice with a good memory to train up. Good career path. Exciting too. Lots of challenges. Bit of cash, extra pudding. Medium to high risk of death.'

'What was the last bit again?'

'Extra pudding.'

'And *after* that?'

'Coffee and mints?'

'I meant on your list.'

'Oh – medium to high risk of death.'

'I see,' I said, 'and how's your last Novice doing?'

'She's doing pretty good.'

'She's not,' said Mother Fallopia, arms folded, 'she's currently in an asylum, shouting at the walls.'

'About what?'

'Oh, I don't know,' said Logan. 'Ants or Lloyd-George or buttons or something.'

'And the one before that?'

It was Mother Fallopia who answered.

'They returned her body but without the head.'

'Yes,' agreed Logan reflectively, 'a little mean-spirited, I thought.'

'Nightwalkers?'

'Villains.'

Villains generally lived out on the edge of the ice-fields and often raided nearby towns for pantry and domestic servants. They traded in mammoths as beasts of burden, and dabbled in the stock market, with moderate success. They had their own code of conduct based around ice and honour and good manners and afternoon tea, and would happily kill someone if they disagreed with them – but would often write an apologetic note to the next of kin afterwards. 'Manners,' they were known to say, 'cost nothing.'

'I know I shouldn't ask this,' I said, 'but why did they return her without her head?'

He shrugged.

'Do you know, I'm not altogether sure. We could have asked them once we'd tracked them down, but I wasn't in the talking mood, and, well, it probably wouldn't have affected the outcome. You shouldn't let these small details put you off. Still want in?'

I looked at Mother Fallopia.

'Surprisingly, *yes.*'

'Okay, then. There's a test and it starts right now.'

There was a pause.

'I don't know what you want me to do.'

'That's the test.'

I sat there for perhaps thirty seconds, trying to figure out what he wanted and getting nowhere.

'I told you it was a waste of time,' said Mother Fallopia in a triumphant manner.

'Well, thank you for coming in,' said Logan after a minute had ticked by. 'How many more to be seen?'

'I was the last.'

He shut his notebook.

'Then we're done.'

I felt the despondency rise within me once more, and studiously avoided Fallopia's gaze as I got to my feet, thanked Logan and made for the door. I grasped the handle, stopped, had a sudden idea and turned around.

'To escort a likely lad,' I said slowly, 'from lower Llanboidy with collies and ... *brollies* from Flitwick to Chiswick while ... Krugers with Lugers take potshots at hotshots is enough to—'

I stopped for thought. I'd only heard it once, and wasn't really concentrating. But it had rhymed, and that made it easier. Logan looked at me with interest.

'Go on.'

'—make mammoths with a gram's worth of ... *hammocks* feel down with a clown from Manchester Town.'

Logan nodded.

'That's very good.'

'It was a piece of crap,' said Mother Fallopia crossly. 'Worthing added "from Flitwick" in the middle.'

'I know that,' I said, 'it scans better.'

Logan smiled.

'It does indeed. When can you start?'

'I can start right now. May I ask a question?'

'Sure.'

'Why do you need my memory?'

He stared at me for a moment.

'Because mine's not good enough for what I might need to do.'

He then got to his feet, took my hand in his and pulled me into a Winter embrace. Now I was closer I could smell a mixture of aftershave, dinner and cognac.

'Welcome aboard. Stay close, do what I say and make as many mistakes as you want – just never the same one twice. Got it?'

'Yes, sir.'

He released me, looked at his watch and said that he had to leave. Shockingly, he and Mother Fallopia – Prudence – kissed full on the lips. They embraced tightly, said their goodbyes and he made for the door.

'Walk with me,' he said, and I turned to Mother.

'Thank you for all you've done for me,' I said, trying to be sincere but actually sounding deeply sarcastic. She glared at me in return.

'You'll be back by Springrise,' she said, 'either with tail between

legs or in a zinc coffin. But there'll be no point. Your job will not
be open upon your return. Good luck. You're going to need it.'

We said nothing more, and I followed Logan out.

'Prudence isn't as bad as she makes out,' he said as we walked
towards the exit by way of the back hall. 'What did you do to piss
her off?'

'I wasn't expected to last my second Winter,' I said, 'and my adoption prospects were low, which kind of made me poor value for
money. I'm not sure the insurance payout was actually that large.'

'The Pool can be cruel,' said Logan, 'but they still do an important
job. What's the longest you've stayed up?'

'One hundred and eight hours and twenty-six minutes playing
sleepy phone tennis.'

'How did that work out?'

'Not well.'

I explained that I'd played with the now-dead Billy DeFroid
and Sian Morgan and heard their jeering phone messages once
I'd stirred to wakefulness sixteen weeks later. Billy won the bout
at one hundred and forty-two hours, but his victory was tainted:
Sian was found Dead In Sleep owing to complications arising
from inadequately prepared entry to the Hib, and Billy and myself
were – unfairly, we thought – found guilty of Incitement to
Deprive. I took the six-week community order, but Billy's adop-
tive father paid the fine.

'Not the first time that's happened,' said Logan with a chuckle as
we pushed open the door and stepped out of the building, 'and
certainly not the last. Do you know what kills most people during
the Winter?'

'Villains?'

'Guess again.'

'Nightwalkers?'

'Nope.'

'The cold?'

'It's the *loneliness*. In the Summer it simply makes you glum, but
in the Winter it can be fatal. I've seen strong people collapse inside.
And not metaphorically, I mean *literally*. Like their soul evaporated.

It's in the eyes. They glaze over all dead, like a nightwalker, like there's nothing there at all.'

He wasn't really selling the Winter to me, but I said nothing. He went on:

'The enemy aren't the Villains, womads, scavengers, insomniacs, Ice-Hermits, Megafauna, nightwalkers, hiburnal rodents or flesh-eating cold slime – it's the Winter. To survive, you need to respect her first. What do you need to do?'

'Respect the Winter.' I paused. 'Sir?'

'Yes?'

'What's flesh-eating cold slime?'

'It's probably best not to think about that.'

We stopped at the kerb, where an orange Cosmo was parked. He unlocked it and climbed in, then wound down the window.

'We're done for now. I'm hitting the sack for six weeks, and will see you again at two weeks before Slumberdown. Report to the Cardiff Consulate; we're based right next door to the *Melody Black* Dormitorium – you can get an apartment there. Before that, have a couple of days off. Go to the Gower, see a movie. You might want to finish any long books you've started, wrap up prolonged games of postal chess and deal with any outstanding issues that you think you might regret leaving open.'

'Is it *that* likely I won't survive?'

'Simply a precautionary measure,' said Logan. 'Where possible, I try to ensure I never lose a Novice in the first season. Cheerio.'

The statement didn't *totally* fill me with confidence, but at least I was away from St Granata's, Morphenox rights intact. I watched as he pulled off into the traffic and was lost to view down the road.

I turned around and looked at the old building that had been my home for the past twenty-two years. I thought of wandering in, telling everyone my news and then going out for an extended gorge-crawl at all the local eateries on the seafront – kebab, fish and chips, burger, tofu, kebab – then collapsing, belly distended, armpits bulging, groaning with indigestion at three in the morning, happy and penniless.

But that was no longer an option. My entrance into this Winter would be as something I'd never been before: light.

Cardiff nights

'... Early pulse weapons had required a compressed air reservoir to function, but all modern units use a thermal battery which comprises a detonator to fire the heat source which in turn liquefies the electrolyte in order to generate the high electrical output required. The amperage generated is considerable, but limited to a fraction of a second ...'

         – *A Guide to PVC (Portable Vortex Cannon) Weapons*

'Wow,' said Lucy Knapp when we met over coffee and buns six weeks later. The buns were Chelsea and quite good, the coffee tasted of gritty mud. I'd invited her into the Cardiff Sector House, more to impress her than anything else. She looked around the open-plan offices, identical in layout to every other Consulate in the land, part of the SkillZero protocols. The twin portraits of Don Hector and Princess Gwendolyn XXXVIII looked down upon us in the large entrance vestibule, while the barographs[15] hummed quietly to themselves, the traces indicating that the weather was, despite appearances, actually improving.

'Wow,' she said again once we were seated in the rec room. 'Charlie Worthing, the Novice to Jack Logan. Who'd a thought it?'

'Not me.'

'How has it felt staying thin when everyone you know gets fat?'

'I stopped seeing them after a while.'

'Always the same.'

It was them who stopped seeing me, in truth. As everyone swelled to their target weight to tackle the Winter, all they saw in me was poor health and tragedy. After a month they stopped calling. All, that

---

15. A device used to record barometric pressure. A trace is usually recorded on a piece of paper.

is, except Lucy. She'd welcomed me to the broad overwintering family, and was full of praise and sound advice.

'A good breakfast is key,' she said, 'and well-fitting boots, merino socks and a reliable supply of snacks. Adequate naps are always useful, a tube of Après-Froid – and never underestimate the value of agreeable wallpaper.'

'How so?'

'You'd be surprised how calming a well-decorated room can be. Soft furnishings in pastel tones can be helpful, too, and a collection of soothing chamber music – but on wax cylinder rather than vinyl or tape. Electricity can be tiresomely unreliable and batteries useless in the cold.'

She asked me how the Winter Consuls were treating me, and I said that I was doing their cooking, washing and ironing.

'It was the same with my first Winter with HiberTech,' she said. 'I think it's a form of hazing. In the military you're dumped thirty miles away in your underwear in the snow, in civvy street it's washing up and knitting. Mind you, it's good for team-building, and you'll find it improves your ironing.'

'My ironing doesn't need to improve.'

'*Everyone's* ironing can do with improving.'

She then thought for a moment and asked me to 'keep my eyes open'. I asked her for what, and why, and she replied that as a representative of HiberTech, she had a duty to maintain a good network of intelligence – and I was the only person in the Consuls she knew that she could trust.

'What's not to trust about a Consul?' I'd asked.

She told me: 'Lots' but didn't elaborate, and the conversation had swiftly moved to other matters.

'May the Spring embrace you,' I said, giving her a hug before we parted.

'And embrace you, too,' she said.

I didn't see Logan again until ten days before Slumberdown. The days were now short, the temperature below zero, the snows long established. For the last week there hadn't been a breath of wind, the snow heaped precariously on even the most steeply pitched of roofs. Every now and then I heard a muffled thud as a half-ton of snow slid off and onto the streets below. Drowning isn't the only way water can kill you.

I was leaning on the broad tracks of the Sno-Trac, heart thumping, nervous as hell, looking as professional as I could in my snug-fitting Winter Consul's uniform. Aside from my domestic duties within the Consulate I'd spent two weeks at the Consul Training Academy learning basic survival skills and various modules on the physiology of sleep, dreams, Villains, climate, wind-chill, the H4S radar set and even Wintervolk. The tutors had looked me up and down and there had been muttered conversations behind my back regarding preparedness. Most Novices got a whole Summer to train.

The door to the *Ivor Novello* Dormitorium opened and Logan stepped out, paused, then took a deep breath of the chill morning air. He looked refreshed, and was surprisingly lean – the month's fat contingency I was carrying wasn't something he was willing to carry himself.

'Welcome back, sir,' I said. 'Sleep well?'

He looked me up and down with a quizzical expression.

'Your new Novice,' I reminded him, knowing that the mind can take a while to remap after hibernation, 'I'm—'

'—don't tell me.'

He concentrated hard, then clicked his fingers and grinned.

'Charlie Worthing. The kid with the memory over at Pru's. Yes?'

'Yes, sir. You never did tell me what you wanted my memory for.'

'No,' he said, 'I never did.'

We climbed into the Sno-Trac.

'Do you have my briefing notes?'

I started the engine with a hiss of compressed air then handed him the binder. Logan flicked through the contents as we drove through the empty, snow-draped streets, the drifts piled high against the buildings. In the binder were updated guidance notes from HiberTech as regards nightwalker policy, a list of alerts, missing persons and most-wanted.

'Well, how about that,' he said, 'the bounty on Lucky Ned has been raised to ten thousand euros.'

'Lucky' Ned Farnesworth was one of the more daring members of the Winter off-grid community. He was an unapologetic male supremacist and also indulged in theft, murder, and kidnapping. He was also fond – obsessively, some say – of collecting stamps. Wise philatelists lodged their collections in vaults during the Winter.

'Ten thousand? Is that enough to have his own people turn him in?'

'Not a chance.'

As an example to others, Villains stuffed snitches and turncoats with snow while still alive, a form of retribution that, whilst barbaric, did lend itself to artistic interpretation: the body could be posed in almost any position before it froze solid. Emulating *David* was quite popular, with anything by Rodin a close second. Once, a squabble between two dynastic groups of Villains resulted in the vanquished being made into a very lifelike tableau of *The Last Supper*. It was a popular tourist attraction until they thawed, and for a short time became a best-selling picture-postcard.

We parked up outside the Cardiff Sector House and were buzzed in through the shock-gates where the team were waiting to greet their Sector Chief: Pryce, Klaar, Thomas, Price, Powell, Williams. There would be eight Consuls covering Cardiff including myself and Logan. As little as ten years ago there would have been twenty staff. Budget cuts hit everywhere.

The first day Logan spent settling in and getting up to speed with what was going on, especially as regards long range cold weather forecasts and Dormitoria thermal serviceability. I'd spent the previous six weeks with the team and had learned some of their foibles, both good and bad. It was indeed true they had me doing their domestic errands, but in exchange they regaled me with stories that were designed to both frighten and enlighten: about blizzards thicker than milk that lasted for weeks, of the trees cocooned in ice looking as though shrink-wrapped in glass. Of rain that fell frozen as jewels with a sweet tinkle of chimes upon the rocks, of temperatures so low that mercury solidified in the thermometers and those foolish enough to venture out could be frozen solid in minutes. They told me of snowflakes the size of dinner plates, drifts seventy-foot deep burying villages for weeks on end, of snow-sculptures carved by wind into shapes so jagged and perverse and beautiful they appeared as though hewn by gods.

I listened to each story with a mixture of wonder, fear and incredulity. But despite the Winter's worst excesses, no one who spoke of it did so without a degree of affection.

On the second day we rounded up a confused-looking woolly rhinoceros from the Co-op's car park, and drove it out west beyond the Megafauna fence.[16] Once that was done, we processed the winsomniacs, who ranged from those with genuine medical contrahibernation conditions all the way through to the morally reprehensible sleep-shy: the malingerers, lazy-arses and drug-addled dreamers. Winsomnia was regarded as a national problem, with a national solution – spread them around to share the food and heat burden equally. We packed three off to St David's and another four to Presteigne, then received six from Oswestry.

'I know,' said Logan when I pointed out the pointlessness of it all, 'let City Hall have their fun.'

On the third morning Logan and I went to the ranges, a low building situated on the other side of the river, opposite a bowling alley and KFC outlet, both closed for the Winter. We were there to see how good I was with a Bambi, but we ended up going through almost every weapon there was – from the palm-sized Plinker, which has about the power of a straight punch,[17] all the way up to the Thumper,

16. Megafauna were a perpetual nuisance, but no one ever seriously considered them as anything but residents of northern Europe, same as us. Besides, pizza wouldn't be the same without Rhinozella cheese, and the Autumn mammoth cull generated much-needed food.

17. About 2,500 Newtons from a range of six feet, but reducing in power with distance by the inverse square law.

used primarily for riot control. With one of those on full choke you could knock a dozen people flying from twenty feet.

'A nightwalker can take several large hits before they go down,' said Logan. 'Less in the noggin to scramble, apparently. Ever meet one?'

I told him about the Vacant my old friend Billy DeFroid found caught on the barbed wire in the orchard, and Logan patted the top pocket where his back-up weapon would have been.

'A Snickers twin pack,' he said. 'You'd be surprised how quick comfort food can reorientate their moral compass. I've seen a hunger-crazed man-eater subdued to the mildness of a capybara in only eight Tunnock's Teacakes.'

'They should use it in their advertising.'

'I think they do. Try the Cowpuncher.'

I replaced the Thumper and picked the next weapon from the cabinet, pushed home a larger power cell, pulled the stock hard into my shoulder, flicked off the safety, then squeezed the trigger. There was a momentary high-pitched whine, then—

Whump

The sound made my ears pop and the empty forty-gallon oil drum we'd been practising on was hurled to the other side of the range, badly dented.

'Although nightwalkers are often cited as the most disturbing part of the Winter,' said Logan, taking the weapon from me, 'half of all deaths among the unseasonably awake are caused by panic.'

'Waking night terrors,' I said.

'It's why we never dismiss nightmaidens, Tonttu, Gronk and other Wintervolk as simply Winter myths and legends. To the unseasonably awake half out of their mind with fatigue, imaginary terrors can be just as dangerous as real ones.'

'Sister Umbilica told me the Gronk feeds off the shame of the unworthy.'

'Sister Umbilica says a lot of things,' said Logan, not being as dismissive of the tale as I'd thought. Physical evidence of *any* Wintervolk hovered firmly around the zero mark but the Gronk –

by far and away the least believable – was conversely taken the most seriously.

'You think there is a Gronk?' I asked.

'As I said, dismiss nothing.'

I nodded sagely. The mythical Gronk had many peculiarities, not least a strange mix of a love of Rodgers and Hammerstein musicals and obsessive domesticity – most bizarrely manifested in an apparent desire to fold linen. As a diversionary tactic, superstitious sleepers often left a basket of unfolded laundry outside their house over the Winter, just in case.

'Do you think I could try the Schtumperschreck?' I asked, pointing to the largest weapon in the cabinet. It was originally designed for heavy demolition work and could easily flip a small car, although that close in you'd probably dislocate a shoulder in the attempt.

'Actually, better not.'

'Okay. But hang on,' I said, pointing at a large grey object the size of a rugby ball sitting in the bottom of the weapons cabinet, 'is that a Golgotha?'

The Thermalite Industries 18-B 'Golgotha' was originally developed for blowing railway cuttings through mountains,[18] but once the military heard about it, they begged and begged until they got their own version.

'Yes, it is, and no, you can't touch it. Hang on,' he added, digging in his pocket, 'I need to give you something.'

He handed me an Omnikey made of gunmetal on a leather lanyard. It would be expected never to leave my person, and misuse or loss would carry the penalty of instant dismissal and a prison term.

'Nothing is closed to you, now, Charlie. Not a door, not a car, not a safe, not a single padlock. Use that power wisely.'

I stared at the Omnikey curiously. It had my name engraved on it, and my Citizen number.

'I understand, sir.'

★   ★   ★

18. The first pulse grenade to pack over a megaNewton, they said, but the factory never published specs.

Jasper Fforde

The following day we were inventorying Winter pantry,[19] which is measured in person-days. For the number of people we expected to have awake over the Winter, we had more than enough. Other sectors were less diligent over stores, so pantry was often placed in a vault, and guarded. Grand Theft Pantry remains the only crime to which lethal force might be legally applied, and even this was controversial. Four years ago someone was killed for stealing a packet of shortbread fingers and there was one helluva stink.

Two days after that someone murdered Consul Klaar over in Barry.

She died outside Nightgrowls, a late-to-sleep hangout. Although any force we wielded was mandated non-lethal, by long convention criminals were more likely to suffer an 'inadvertent fatal application of non-lethal force' than to be detained alive, so in consequence, offing Winter Consuls was seen as not just a reciprocal arrangement, but a form of sport. Klaar was well known for corruptly playing one criminal gang off against another and her inevitable demise was revealingly disproportionate in its savagery.

I peered into Klaar's half-track, took one look at her remains and then deposited most of my lunch into a nearby snow drift.

'Vomiting is a waste of protein,' said Vice-Consul Pryce, a short man, partial to sarcasm and chocolate peanuts. 'In the spirit of practicality, you may want to bag it for later.'

'No thanks.'

'Mixed into a goulash you'd never know,' he said with all seriousness.

'Look, thanks for the advice, but I'm not going to eat my own vomit.'

'That's because you've not been hungry enough. When you are, you'll eat carrion, lichen, cardboard, someone else's vomit, *anything*. Ever heard of Toccata, Chief Consul Sector Twelve?'

Almost everyone had heard of Toccata. She was rumoured to have a policy of rarely taking wrongdoers alive and Deputy Consuls died under her command at eight times the national average. There was

19. Not to be confused with Spring pantry, which is what everyone eats until the growing season begins.

also a rumour she'd seen the Gronk — up in the fire valleys where the snow never settles and the air is full of sulphurous fumes, as though the devil herself had made landfall.

'I heard she ate a nightwalker in order to survive a particularly bleak Winter,' I said.

'Two, I heard,' said Pryce, 'and that she now has a taste for it.'

'C'mon,' I said, expecting a leg-pull.

But he seemed deadly serious.

'There are times when survival dictates extreme measures. Some say the Bard wrote Sir John Falstaff into so many of his plays for that express purpose — someone unseasonably portly for the Winter Players to feast upon if things got bad.'

'Really?' I asked.

'Who knows? But Winter Cutlets should always be a consideration, when the hunger pangs hit, pantry is empty and hibernation isn't an option. Oh, and speaking of Toccata, don't mention her to the Chief. They had a thing going a few years back. He's still a little raw over it.'

'What happened?'

'He fell in love.'

'Really? He doesn't look the kind.'

'Oh, he's the kind all right. But then she split on him and, well, as I say, he's still a little raw.'

Coincidentally, Toccata had recently called the office, looking to speak to Logan. I told Pryce about it and he raised an eyebrow.

'Personal?'

'Professional. Something weird going on in Sector Twelve.'

'So what's new? There's *always* something weird going on in Sector Twelve.'

There were few leads regarding who killed Klaar. A recent snow-fall had wiped all the tracks, but Logan sent a couple of Consuls to speak to the friendlies to find out which gang had the bigger grudge.

'What happens now?' I asked as Logan and I drove back to the Consulate.

'We wait,' said the Chief. 'Once the hunger sets in, someone will come pleading for food in exchange for information. Nothing like a good roast beef dinner with gravy and Yorkshire pud followed by trifle to get people talking. "Fill the tum, loosen the tongue", as we say.'

The next two days were dominated by heavy snowstorms so I practised blind driving with Logan using the H4S radar set in the Sno-Trac. It was a little tricky to begin with, but I'd done several hours on the simulator, so didn't make a complete pig's ear of it.

'Want some advice?' asked Logan as I swerved my way around Cardiff navigating only by the radar returns on the H4S screen.

'Is it about washing?'

'No,' he said, 'it's this: plans are all well and good in the Summer, but in the Winter it's wiser to simply have an objective.'

'I thought we were meant to make a plan and stick to it?'

'Events move fast,' he said, 'and you need on-the-hoof flexibility to ensure the plan doesn't get in the way of the goal.'

It actually seemed like quite good advice.

'Thank you,' I said.

'You're welcome,' he replied, 'and less starch on my shirts — it's like wearing cardboard.'

Toccata called again once we were back in the office and Logan spoke to her for almost an hour in the privacy of his office. From what I could understand, Toccata wanted Logan to come over to help on a case, but Consuls didn't go off-sector this close to the Winter — protocol, apparently. There was also, it seemed, something about a woman named Aurora, who a quick piece of research revealed was HiberTech's Head of Security in Sector Twelve. From what I overheard of Logan and Toccata's conversation, she was hated by both of them. I asked Vice-Consul Pryce about Aurora and he warned me to 'stay away from those three — nothing but trouble'.

The day after that we helped the MediTechs round up all the Edwards and Janes.

'I never like this part of the job,' said Logan. In fact, no one enjoyed it as far as I could see — except the MediTechs themselves, who were finally going to do in the Winter what they had been preparing for all Summer. The redeployed, their limited usefulness over and physiologically unable to hibernate, were due to be parted out as soon as the recipients were in full hibernation. If nightwalkers were the unintended consequence of Morphenox, the free menial workers and transplantation possibilities were the unintended consequences of the unintended consequence. Screening had been carried out all Summer, and each Edward or Jane had the names of their intended recipients cold-branded on their various parts. Leg, face, fingers, organs – there wasn't much that couldn't be replaced. Something to do with the hibernatory state being especially conducive to non-rejection.[20]

'Never enough, eh?' said one of the MediTechs, consulting a clipboard and the thirty or so individuals we had collected from their places of work. They stood there blankly, swaying gently from side to side until they were loaded into a mammoth-truck and carted away.

'Doesn't seem right somehow,' I said, probably too loudly. Consul Thomas heard me.

'You'll not complain once you lose something to frost and want it replaced,' she said, patting her arm, which I noted was a great deal paler than the rest of her, 'and you will, eventually. You're not part of the Winter until the Winter's taken a part of you.'

On the fourth day before Slumberdown the local police conducted the seasonal handover of Jurisdiction, a ceremony that included the mayor, the Chief of Police and a large symbolic snowflake made of gingerbread and marzipan. I wasn't there; someone had to answer the phones in the office and finish the ironing.

Two days after that, *Beryl Cook* nearly had a meltdown. And this is when Mrs Tiffen comes back into the story.

---

20. It was due to low white cell count, part of the blood-thinning physiology peculiar to hibernation. I didn't know that at the time.

Oliver Tiffen goes hot

'... HotPots were replaced every thirty years whether they needed it or not, always during the early Summer. Exclusion zones were implemented and the work carried out by a team chosen by lottery from the over-sixty age group. Given that the average life expectancy was sixty-four, the effect of long-term radiation poisoning would be minimal. High risk emergency shutdown had their own workforce: The High Octanes ...'

– from *Seventeen Winters*, by Winter Consul Lance Jones

We drove across the city at daybreak, the tracks of the Sno-Trac clean and sharp over a fresh fall of snow, the sky slate-grey. Only the thin trails of vapour rising from the numerous Dormitoria gave any clue that we were in a city of almost half a million people.

Despite it being two days before Winter officially began, most people had already hunkered down, and anyone who wasn't yet asleep would be going through their pre-hibernatory nesting rituals. Yoga and Gregorian chants were always popular, with yoyo, tango, humming, bezique and watercolouring going in and out of favour as the vagaries of fashion saw fit. But for most people it was a simple slowing of activity, purposefully avoiding anything exciting. This was a winding down, a relaxing of mind and spirit.

To assist initial descent and a free return in case of an accidental awakening, the networks ran looped repeats of *Bonanza* throughout the Winter. Residents with Random Waking Syndrome kept a TV switched on at the foot of their bed, sound turned down low, the picture dimmed.

'It's only dull by endless repetition,' Logan had explained earlier, while we discussed strategies to ease anomalous wakers back to sleep, 'and the close familiarity of the characters and situations make for an often transcendental drifting of the mind.'

No one quite knew why *Bonanza* had become the TV series of choice for the Winter, but the more it was watched, the more suited to easement it became. If the machinations of the Cartwright family didn't work, you could always watch reruns of *Crossroads* or resort to the default entry-level route to welcome catatonia: *Ulysses*, *Moby Dick* or *War and Peace*.

I halted the Sno-Trac outside the *Beryl Cook* Dormitorium, the largest of twenty-seven Kipshops[21] on the seafront at Penarth. I made sure the compressed air tank was in the green so I could effect a restart, then stopped the engine and climbed out of the rear door. The recent fall of snow had partially melted in the morning sun then refrozen, and the ground felt like Rice Krispies beneath our boots.

'We've got the control rods fully in and the core temperature is still wavering on the red,' said the porter in an oddly enthusiastic way, as though a reactor fire would be a welcome diversion from the Winter boredom. He beckoned us in to the small control room just behind the reception and we all stared at the core temperature dial, which was indeed wavering on the danger level.

The heat sources that kept Dormitoria at Low Ideal[22] throughout the Winter were now Uranium Reactor Piles rather than the some-times erratic and unreliable 'GlowPits' of layered peat, pitchblende, coal and hardwood. By contrast, the uranium/graphite 'HotPots' were efficient and generally maintenance free, but could sometimes – very rarely, it was often stressed by Albion Nuclear – be temperamental in a dramatically showy kind of way.

'I can't go into the Winter with a potential reactor overheat and auto-shutdown on my hands,' said the porter. 'Who's going to pay for the rehoming if the *Beryl* goes dark midwinter? Not me.'

I looked down at the floor with, I think, a sense of mild concern.

'Fully shielded when they converted the GlowPit to a HotPot,' said Logan, sensing my disquiet. 'Twelve inches of lead between us and the stack. Of all the reactor-equipped Kipshops in Cardiff, none

21. Flopshop, Kipshop, Sleepshack, Slumberhouse – all slang for the venerable Dormitoria.

22. Fourteen degrees Celsius.

has failed any higher than a Code Orange, and that was in the *Cary Grant*.'

'The control rods jammed,' said the porter, 'but failsafes prevailed,' he added, with an air of disappointment.

We'd called the Duty Officer at Albion Nuclear, who initially suggested that we should wait 'until it got really bad' before doing something. After more urgent pressing, he concurred between yawns that someone should go down and have a look and to get back to him 'if we thought it looked serious'.

Logan asked me to find the nearest technician on the High Octane list but the porter saved me a call.

'We have Oliver Tiffen on the tenth floor,' he said. 'Nice chap. I'll get him down.'

For emergency scrams,[23] visual inspections or other potentially fatal situations, there was a list of sprightly reactor-savvy octogenarians for whom a fatal dose of radioactivity would not radically shorten their lives. They were paid handsomely for their services and there was a medal in it somewhere if you were needed, but owing to reasonably robust safety precautions and the low wattage of the piles, most weren't.

Mr Tiffen appeared in ten minutes, incongruously dressed in tweeds and plus-fours, and surprisingly underage – he looked barely forty-five. True, you could be any age to volunteer, but no matter what, members of the High Octane Group had to be at half-hour readiness at all times. Oliver Tiffen stared at the gauges in the control room and grimaced as the core temperature rose a few more degrees.

'This looks like fun and games,' he said, donning gardening gloves, a pair of goggles and a crude telephone headset. He wore a respirator around his neck in an old bag with an oxygen bottle strapped to the front, and carried a Gladstone bag full of spanners that jangled as he walked.

'Problematical?' asked Logan as Tiffen stared at the service log, which looked old and mildewy and was covered in coffee stains.

'If I'm right, we've got under twenty minutes before an explosion

---

23. An emergency reactor core shutdown procedure, to prevent a potentially dangerous overheat, fire and explosion.

rips the building apart and scatters burning fissile material for about a thousand yards in every direction.'

'And if you're wrong?' asked Logan.

'Then it's a failure of instrumentation or my expertise,' he said with a grin. 'You'd all better get clear just in case. Porter? You can stand by to flood the core chamber if I can't shut down the reactor in time.'

'It's that bad?'

'It's that bad. Here,' he added, passing a sealed envelope[24] to Logan, 'take this in case everything goes balls-down, would you?'

He then told the porter to stand by, opened the core access door with a key he kept around his neck, and disappeared inside. The door slammed shut and we heard his footsteps hurrying down the spiral staircase, clanging on the steel treads as he went.

'You should both leave if you want to,' said the porter, his hand hovering over a large pull-down handle that was marked 'EMERGENCY CORE FLOOD'.

As a porter he had initially seemed ineffectual and flippant, but now it had come to crunch time, he would do as all porters do – never abandon their sleeping charges and go down with their Dormitorium, if required. I was learning that the Winter had a curious integrity all of its own.

'We'll hang around,' said Logan, confident, I think, that between the porter and Tiffen the issue could be resolved. He didn't ask me if I would stay, but then as his Novice, I was kind of part of him. After a few minutes we heard Oliver Tiffen's voice over the crackly loudspeaker, and he explained the problem, which was kind of technical, but involved a loss of water in the safety tank or something, and that everything was 'cooking up down here'. We then heard 'oh shit', a few more choice swear words and then, in a calm and measured tone: *'flood flood flood'*.

The porter didn't hesitate for an instant, and pulled the lever. There was a rumbling from somewhere deep below that sounded

24. Not unusual; prepared last words, usually. Sometimes a will, sometimes a poem, a confession, an insult – sometimes even blank.

like rushing wet cement, then silence. The temperature gauge dropped suddenly and all the other dials slowly fell to zero.

'Well,' said the porter, 'that's me out of a job.'

The *Beryl Cook* had two hundred residents, and everyone still awake lent a hand to move them out. The walking awake and the dozing were sent to emergency bedrooms in other Dormitoria, but anyone in the treacly abyss of the Hib was consigned to *Honeycomb* Sleepshacks still in their beds, as they wouldn't know the difference until they woke up. The mayor herself actually turned up with a retinue of large and very yawny bureaucrats, who were all eager to downplay the accident, probably because it meant returning to bed quicker and less paperwork.

'I think we should call this a Level Three "Serious Incident",' she said, 'rather than a Level Four: "An Accident with Local Consequences".' Don't you?'

'Didn't the accident kill Mr Tiffen?' asked Logan, knowing the difference.

'Technically-speaking he wasn't killed by the reactor – he drowned. This is really more to do with the coastguard.'

'It was under twenty tons of boron slurry,' Logan pointed out.

'Agreed,' replied the mayor. 'They'll dig him out in the Spring. His sacrifice will be remembered, and he will be honoured.'

And she then posed on the front steps for a lone photographer who had turned up with a disinterested-looking journalist who asked a series of lacklustre questions. It was two days before Slumberdown. No one shows much enthusiasm about anything in the last week before bedding down.

'Come with me,' said Logan once the mayor had departed, yawning, back to City Hall.

All Dormitoria were built to a standardised design, not refined much since initial adoption by Constantine in the fourth century. A circular building, usually capped by a steep conical roof, with twenty or more floors and a central thermal distribution shaft that ran up the centre. The stairs were either embedded in the stout and well-insulated walls, or, as here, wound their way in a spiral fashion up the central void.

Oliver Tiffen's room was on the eighth floor and Logan used his

Omnikey to gain access. The room was dimly lit, and of the standard pizza layout: a one-eighth slice of the circular floor, with the door at the truncated sharp end. The rest was divided into bathroom, bedroom and living area. Heat and light were valued commodities, but from opposite directions: heat from the central core that ran up through the building, light through triple-glazed slots in the outer wall.

We found Mrs Tiffen in the bedroom, surrounded by packing cases of food. She was well nourished, but utterly vacant − Oliver Tiffen had been harbouring his wife since she turned nightwalker. She clacked her teeth at us, then launched into a lively rendition of 'Help Yourself' on the bouzouki.

'Plays it well, doesn't she?' said Logan.

It wasn't unusual for nightwalkers to display skills dredged up from the tatters of their memory. Most knew a few words and could do a trick of some sort, even as mundane as finding their way to the shops or tuning a wireless. A very few, however, could do quite extraordinary things, like ice-skate and play Canasta. Mrs Tiffen was one of these, or, in the parlance of nightwalkers, 'Tricksy'. Rumour had it the more advanced redeployed − the Edwards and Janes, for instance − were based on these individuals. More upstairs to rewire, apparently.

'Your husband just drowned under twenty tons of boron slurry,' said Logan to Mrs Tiffen, 'but he fulfilled his duty without fuss or drama. If you could be proud of him, you would be.'

Mrs Tiffen didn't react and just continued to play the bouzouki.

'Why go to all this trouble keeping her?' I asked as we stared at the woman, who seemed healthy enough, if a little pale in her demeanour. 'And to volunteer yourself so young for High Octane and such a potentially gruesome death?'

In answer, Logan passed me the envelope Oliver Tiffen had given him before he went down into the HotPot chamber. The letter was not long.

Despite appearances to the contrary, my wife is not dead, and is still trapped deep inside herself. It would be too much to hope you will look after her, but I would be grateful if she were neither parted out, nor redeployed.

'It's a fairly common belief,' said Logan, retrieving the letter, 'but understandable given the strong emotions at stake.'

'Will you do as he suggests and retire her?' I asked.

'No,' said Logan, deep in thought, 'I'm going to take her to Sector Twelve to be redeployed. It's a good excuse to look in on Toccata and see what she wants.'

Logan told me to consult *Bradshaw's Railway Guide* and I found it was possible to get to Sector Twelve and out again before Network Winter shutdown.

'What do you want me to do while you're away?' I asked.

'You're coming too, Worthing. It will be good for your training.'

'It will?' I said somewhat doubtfully.

My reluctance was easily explained: Talgarth, the principal town of Sector Twelve, was the largest centre of population in an area otherwise noted for its emptiness, and high proportion of womads and Villains. Roads were impassable during the Winter and food resupply impossible. Not a place you'd want to get stranded. Not a place you'd actually want to *be*.[25]

The rehousing of the *Beryl Cook*'s residents was completed by the time we had to head off on the train, five hours later. HiberTech don't take all Tricksy nightwalkers, so I'd filled in the paperwork and faxed off the request, and had a reply within ten minutes: deliver her to Sector Twelve in all haste.

'May I ask a question?' I said as we sat waiting for the train at Cardiff Central. Mrs Tiffen was sitting next to us, playing the increasingly ironic 'Help Yourself'. Nightwalker transportation wasn't rocket science: just keep them well fed. They only get troublesome when they get hungry; and when they get *really* hungry, they get *really* troublesome.

'Go ahead.'

'What does Toccata want you to help her with, and who's Aurora?'

'That's two questions.'

'I'm thinking perhaps they're both part of the same one.'

25. In the Winter, I mean. In the Summer, it's gorgeous. Hiking, swimming, cycling, good food – and friendly people.

He looked at me and smiled.

'Very ... astute. Here it is: that call from Toccata was about a viral dream that's been sweeping around Sector Twelve. Ordinary, level-headed people are seemingly having a dream about a blue Buick, then going nuts. Psychotic episodes, trying to kill people, screaming about severed hands and oak trees, being buried alive, stuff like that. She wanted my opinion.'

'Buicks, severed hands, oak trees and being buried alive?'

'It's a *dream*, Charlie, it's not meant to make sense. Did you cover viral dreams when you were at the Academy?'

'We only covered dreams as part of Module 6A: "The Physiology of non-Morphenox slumber".[26]

No one thought there was any need to teach any more: a dream is just the subconscious mind attempting to form a narrative from a jumble of thoughts, facts and memories and did nothing but sap the resources that led us healthily to the Spring.

'And Aurora?'

'Head of Security at HiberTech. A shit of the highest order. She and Toccata don't get along. Actually, it's worse than that; they *loathe* one another. When it comes to HiberTech/Consul politics and Sector Twelve, there is just one rule: avoid.'

'Aurora,' I murmured, 'the goddess of the dawn.'

'The goddess of trouble,' said Logan, climbing to his feet as our train arrived at the station, 'but I'd said I'd help out.'

I took a compartment with the bouzouki-playing Mrs Tiffen, fed her a bar of nutty nougat and, thus sated, she began to play. 'Help Yourself' on the bouzouki once again. Logan was less tolerant of bouzouki than I, so went and sat in first class.

Mrs Tiffen and I were joined by a woman who turned out to be the Winter actor, and the train left the station. I didn't yet know it, but accompanied by a woman of *no* dreams, I was on the way to meet the woman *of* my dreams.

---

26. 'Gorge and hope', as it was known.

Merthyr

'… The root of traditional "Winter embrace" lay in shared body warmth for survival. So while a Summer hug is only ever a brief clench, in the Winter, bodies are held intimately together, the left hand behind the neck, the right on the lower back, heads to the left, right cheeks touching, breath sounding in each other's ear. Outside of the Winter context, it would be considered at best inappropriate, at worst, physical trespass …'

– *The Hiberculture of Man*, by Morris Desmond

The Winter thespian had listened intently as I told her how I'd gone from Assistant House Manager at St Granata's to Winter Consul Novice in an afternoon. I didn't name Jack Logan as my mentor, but she'd understood the discretion. I hadn't told her about Toccata's stories regarding viral dreams owing to operational security, nor Mother Fallopia's unkindness, this time out of misplaced loyalty, but I told her all about the *Beryl Cook* overheat and Oliver Tiffen's sacrifice, which seemed to strike a chord.

'A brave man,' she murmured. 'Anyone close to you ever tripped the Night Fandango?'

'There was Sister Oesterious at St Granata's,' I replied. 'She'd been taken off to be thumped and dumped in the local pit only they hadn't hit her hard enough and she turned up three days later covered in fish-heads, old cabbage leaves and soggy newspaper. Looking back it seems kind of darkly comical, her lumbering in through the front gates with everyone screaming. Mother Fallopia was made of sterner stuff and retired her properly with a rounders bat behind the bike sheds. Lucy Knapp had nightmares for a week, but in general I think everyone was okay about it. What about you? Know anyone who nightwalked?' She rubbed her temple thoughtfully.

'My husband, Geoffrey. We met when performing as the front and back halves of a pantomime horse, and bonded over the "equestrian gavotte". It's a tricky dance to synchronise, especially as I had done the decent thing and took the rear half.'

She laughed.

'Geoffrey said it suited me as I was a horse's arse. I had to marry him, of course, and we had seventeen years of unbridled joy. He was my Romeo and my Macbeth, my Rochester and my Desmond. But we still donned the panto horse outfit and performed the equestrian gavotte at parties, just for kicks and giggles.'

She paused, and the smile dropped from her face.

'At Springrise five seasons ago I thought he was just having a foggy morning, but his light through yonder window never broke. He did a post-mortem trick, too: Romeo, the balcony scene. Over and over again. I thought he was still in there, too. Not unusual to believe so, I'm told. I didn't keep him for five years, though – he ate my sister's Norfolk terrier the following Tuesday and that was it. I called the HiberTech hotline and they took him away.'

Better I'd be Dead in Sleep/than asleep and dead
wandering the Winter deep/Winter Cutlets as my bread.

'I'm sorry for your loss.'

'He was redeployed as a road sweeper and I saw him once, I think, in Lee-on-the-Solent. Well, I *thought* it was him. HiberTech have a Redeployment Centre there, so it could have been one of many, I suppose. He was parted out the next Winter. His legs are on a gardener in Stourbridge right now and his eyes are currently looking across the Sound of Mull, which he would have liked. I don't know about the rest of him . . .'

She lapsed into silence. Best not to dwell, no matter how hard that can be.

I turned to the train window and stared out at a landscape that, while constantly changing in detail, remained much the same in aspect: snow and ice, bleak and empty, cold and unwelcoming. *The Winter.* There was a very good reason most of us slept through it.

Mrs Tiffen stopped playing and dropped into the rigid state

peculiar to nightwalkers known as *Rigor torpis*. It was a welcome respite from the playing, and although she could play 'Help Yourself' quite well, it was motor memory only – there was nothing in or on her mind at all.

'That's a relief,' said the actor, and for the remainder of the journey she imparted to me some tips about the Winter: primarily to resist borrowing money from bondsmen,[27] shun all contact with anyone of 'low, questionable or financially-negotiable morals' and to avoid the drowsies.

'One moment you're transfixed by their large eyes and honeyed words and wondering if there is anywhere you'd rather be,' she told me, 'and the next you're paying off the Debt from the hock-house wondering how you could have been so stupid.'

'I'll be careful.'

The train slowed as we approached Merthyr, the disused pit-workings silhouetted against the afternoon sky, the streetlights already on. This was as far as we went on the local train; we'd need a transregional fitted with a snowplough to take us 'over the hump' to Sector Twelve.

The actor stood up to retrieve her bags from the rack while I smeared a finger-full of peanut butter on the roof of Mrs Tiffen's mouth to keep her occupied. The actor opened the door to the compartment and stepped down onto the recently gritted platform.

'Well, good luck with your first season,' she said. 'Keep your wits about you, and be prepared in case Hydra comes knocking. Whenever I took on a part, I always made sure I knew the lines of the next one up the ladder. I bagged my first Hamlet that way.'

The Hydra system wasn't just for actors, it was for all of us. She gave me a Winter hug.

'May the Spring embrace you.'

'And embrace you, too.'

'Who was that?' asked Logan, who joined Mrs Tiffen and me from where he'd been travelling in first class.

---

27. Cash is fairly worthless in the Winter, so bondsmen advance loans and negotiate debts and credits, all for a fee.

'I didn't get her name,' I said, 'a thespian readying herself for a Winter tour.'

'A noble servant of the Winter,' said Logan, 'like us. Now listen: we've got just over an hour before our connection and I have to go and see someone. I'll meet you in Mrs Nesbit's in about fifty minutes. Order me a bacon sandwich and a cup of tea to go.'

'Yes, sir.'

'Oh, and Worthing?'

'Yes?'

'Don't lose the Vacant.'

And he was gone, walking briskly towards the exit. I stood on the platform for a moment in the gently falling snow, the air heavy with the pleasing odour of coal-smoke. By rights, you shouldn't smell smoke two weeks after industrial shutdown, but most of the coalfields under Tredegar, Rhondda and in the Taff Valley north of Merthyr were now burning underground, the hills leaking smoke through fissures in the ground, the intense heat transforming trees into twisted relics of charcoal. The boffins had said it was only a matter of time before the gases managed to lock in some global heat, but every year it grew colder, the glaciers advanced some more, the growing season shortened. But for us, at least there was a positive: Wales derived much of its revenue from the CO_2 release tariffs, negotiated early on, when six times higher than they are now.

I couldn't find a guard so walked towards the only train in the station. The engine had not yet arrived, and behind the single coach were two flat-bed railcars being loaded by a freightmaster in a fork-lift. He had the exhausted demeanour of a long-time Winterer; dark-rimmed eyes and slack, pale skin. Overwintering accelerated ageing by a factor of at least one and a half. When you committed your professional life to a Wintering career, you gave part of your physical life, too.

The wooden crates were marked Ambrosia Creamed Rice, Wagon Wheels, Mini-rolls and Dream Topping. Like much else, sound nutritional sense was suspended during Winter. From a morale point of view, eating comfort food made Winters seem less like cold purgatory, and more like a kid's party. More relevantly, the cases also had

'*HiberTech Industries – Sector 12 – Winter Urgent*' stencilled on the side. I knew it was the right train, but in time-honoured tradition asked the freightmaster to confirm it anyway.

His name, I learned, was Moody.

'I'd like us to be off as soon as the engine arrives and is coupled,' he said, glancing nervously at the sky from where snow was falling in broad, languid spirals, 'but the stationmaster is a stickler for punctuality, so it'll leave when it's scheduled: in fifty-eight minutes' time. Returning or staying over?'

'*Definitely* returning,' I replied.

'Wise move. Sector Twelve's not for the faint-hearted.'

'Do I look faint-hearted?'

'When it comes to Sector Twelve, *everyone's* faint-hearted.'

There was no real answer to this, and knowing the dead woman was going to get hungry again pretty soon, I took her with me to the one watering hole still open: Mrs Nesbit's Traditional Tearooms. At the last count there were eight thousand outlets of the popular eatery across the Northern Fed, with four hundred and six open throughout the Winter.[28] The establishment had a cosy familiarity about it: the logo of the company, here emblazoned bright and proud on the window, was the eponymous and wholly invented character of Mrs Nesbit herself. She had a winning folksy smile, a swirl of grey hair tied up in a bun and was wearing an old-style blouse and red dress beneath a kitchen apron. For reasons of familiarity and convenience – both ruthlessly exploited by NesCorp – it was the default snack bar for almost everyone, irrespective of social class or cultural background.

I walked inside, the bouzouki across my shoulder, the dead woman shambling in front of me, still occupied with trying to lick the peanut butter from the roof of her mouth. Inside the tearooms the air was heavy with the smell of baking, cheap jam and chicory-laced coffee, and predictably, the rooms were not busy. There were only six customers in an establishment big enough for ten times that number.

'We don't serve the dead in here.'

The comment came from a woman who I guessed by her almost

---

28. By legal mandate direct from the Ministry of Sleep.

translucent pallor and *two* Gold Solstice stars was a long-time Winterer. Most Winter branches of Mrs Nesbit's were run by burned-out ex-Consuls who would keep the supply of tea and fresh scones uninterrupted until their decades-long sleep deficit finally caught up with them.

'I'm not asking you to serve her,' I retorted, 'I'm asking you to serve me … who will then serve her.'

'The answer's no. Her dead body in here over my dead body in here.'

'Linguistically that was quite … poetic,' I conceded. 'A *chiasmus*, I think?'

'Closer to *polyptoton*, my guess. Now why don't you take the abomination and piss off?'

'I'm a Winter Consul,' I said, flashing my badge.

'My sincere apologies,' said the proprietress. 'Piss off … *with all due respect.*'

She held me in about as much esteem as a nightwalker. Just as I was wondering if I could fit Mrs Tiffen into a left-luggage locker for an hour and whether that was ethical or not, a voice piped up.

'Is that bouzouki *tetrachordo* or *trichordo*?'

It was a man's voice, low and confident.

'I have no idea,' I said, still staring at the proprietress but jabbing a thumb in Mrs Tiffen's direction, 'it belongs to her.'

The proprietress grimaced.

'It's worse when they're Tricksy. Like they're pretending they're alive.'

'It's called *Nonsentient Vestigial Memory*,' I said, 'and they can't pretend to be anything. But yes, she plays the bouzouki. And quite well, if you're interested.'

As if in response, the dead woman's fingers felt across me for the instrument. As soon as I handed it to her she launched once again into 'Help Yourself'.

'Why not let them stay?' said the man who had asked the bouzouki question. 'The deadhead can play for us. Besides, service retired look after service active.'

It was one of those adages that was based more on hope than reality, but I liked the sound of it.

'Very well,' said the proprietress at length, 'you and the Vacant can stay. But if it starts freaking out my customers, it's history.'

I thought of insisting Mrs Tiffen was a 'she' and not an 'it', but decided instead to take my small victory with quiet grace and say nothing. I ordered two bacon sandwiches – one for me, one to go, two coffees, same – then sausages, Jaffa cakes and marshmallows for Mrs Tiffen.

'With apricot jam,' I added.

'On what?'

'On everything of hers and quite thick.'

The proprietress growled at me and lumbered off. I pushed Mrs Tiffen into a booth and shoved her across so I could sit, then gave her the sugar lumps to eat.

'Mind if I join you?'

It was my benefactor from the other side of the room.

'Please do,' I said, welcoming the company.

He was, I guessed, somewhere between his fourth and fifth decade. His hair was already fully white and he was dressed in the solidly tailored clothes of a career Winterer. He sported a lopsided jaw from a poorly-healed break and he had a balding patch on the side of his head – follicle frost damage, most likely. Most noticeably, he was at Spring weight. In any other context he'd appear almost obscenely underweight. He might once have been Consular staff, but I had a pretty good idea of what he was now.

'She plays it quite well, doesn't she?' he said.

'If you like to listen to a short instrumental of a Tom Jones hit from the sixties and nothing else,' I said, 'it could become tolerable, given time.'

'Does she play "Delilah"?'

'Everyone asks that. No. And thanks for just now.'

'Think nothing of it,' he said with a boyish smile. 'You taking her up to HiberTech to be redeployed?'

'Yes; do you know how they do it?'

'No idea. HiberTech guard their secrets aggressively. The name's Hugo Foulnap.'

'Charlie Worthing,' I said, taking the calling card he'd offered me. I'd guessed correct – he was a Footman. He'd do anything for anybody, so long as you paid his hourly rate. They were mercenaries, Dormeopaths, odd-job men, nannies and bounty hunters all rolled into one. They'd even play Scrabble with you if you paid their rate, but only to win. Like most Winterers, Footmen took pride in their work.

'First Winter?' he asked.

'Do I wear it that badly?'

'Yup,' he said, 'I can see the fatigue on you already.'

I could feel it too, a dull ache that gnawed in my joints, and the deep-seated sense of nausea that belongs only with consciously delaying hibernation.

The coffees arrived. The proprietress scowled at me, stared daggers at the dead woman, then departed again.

'I had this call last week,' said Foulnap, stirring his coffee, 'from a woman who was going to go deep in the family's traditional sleep-spot, up in the hills beyond Abergavenny. Family farm or something, near Cwmyoy. Anyway, she'd packed the car, but the duvet was sticking out and jammed the boot lid. You know what she did?'

'What did she do?'

'She set fire to the duvet.'

'Did that work?'

'Worked really well. By the time I arrived, the car was completely burned out. All her food, her bedding, Morphenox – all gone. I had to resource everything.'

'How did you resource her Morphenox?'

'Let's just say I know a girl who knows a guy who knows a person who knows a girl.'

I took a sip of the coffee. It tasted like last season's acorns seared with a paraffin blowtorch.

'This coffee's *terrible*,' I said.

'Welcome to the Winter.'

We chatted some more. He told me an amusing story about how hibernating mammoths near Treherbert had been false-dawned[29] by

---

29.   False dawn: waking earlier than usual, generally due to increased warmth. Waking a sleeper can be achieved quite easily by warming them, although it can take four to five days. Ten ccs of Kenorbarbydol works faster – but with far greater risk.

the encroaching underground fires, and how they had been herded out through the snow and up and over the mountain to Hirwauna in a Hannibalesque adventure that had been the subject of a best-selling book and was soon to be a musical, using the puppeteers from *Warphant*.

'Actually, the mammoths sort of did it on their own,' said Foulnap, 'nose to tail, like some great big shaggy-haired pachydermical charm bracelet.'

We chatted politics as the clock wound round to our departure time. I asked Foulnap where the restrooms were and after he'd told me, suggested I left Mrs Tiffen with him.

I thanked him, left the tearooms and walked down the platform to the toilets. Once I'd had a pee, I washed my hands and then soaked my face in cold water and stared in the mirror. My eyes were bloodshot and seemed sunken into my head, my pallor grey. My ears had started ringing, my fingers and hands felt oddly large and I'd had several hot sweats. I'd been told to expect any or all of these symptoms as indications of Sleep Deprivation Narcosis, but as with altitude sickness, there was no good indication of who would get it, who would not, and to what degree of severity. But the thing I feared most was hallucinations. Had them once during a bad fever, and imagined myself playing pass-the-parcel – but no matter how much paper I tore off, the parcel never got any smaller.

Glad to have a few moments free of the relentless plucking of the bouzouki, I wandered absently onto the station concourse. It was a large, airy chamber with a glass ceiling now covered in snow, the light soft and directionless, the interior dim. The ticket office was still open but unmanned, and Welsh Tourist Office posters covered the walls.

I heard a shout from somewhere outside and I frowned. It sounded a lot like 'Lobster', but there was only one person who might be saying things like that, and they shouldn't be anywhere but safely in Mrs Nesbit's.

Mrs Tiffen.

With a sudden sense of foreboding I ran as fast as I could to the front entrance and pushed the heavy door open, the sharp air outside hitting me like a wall of ice. The light was failing and the wind was blowing the snow into rotating eddies among the buildings. There was no one to be seen, but I noted fresh tracks in the snow running out from the cab rank.

'The taxi before you,' I said to the driver of the remaining cab, an old man with a face so full of soft pendulous folds I don't think he'd seen the Summer, ever, 'who was in it?'

He stared at the Consul's badge I was showing him.

'I didn't see the man but the woman looked kind of …'

'…dead?'

'Yeah.'

After asking him to find out where the cab had gone and then to stand by to take me there, I ran back towards Mrs Nesbit's, almost slipping and falling as I trod the snow onto the marble floor. The bouzouki was still lying on the table with our half-finished plates.

I felt a nasty, hollow, sinking feeling. I'd liked Foulnap and, foolishly, *trusted him*. Footmen move with the prevailing cashflow, and nightwalkers can be monetarised in a number of ways. Given the dead woman's relative youth, parting her out on the underground transplant market could be a possibility, but add her potential fertility and there was another cash possibility: he was going to farm her. I looked up as the proprietress approached.

'Lose your date?' she asked in a mocking tone.

'Where will he have taken her?'

She furrowed her brow and stared at me, unsure quite what I was suggesting.

'Wait – you're going to try and get her back?'

'Yes.'

'How, exactly?'

It was a very good question. Taking on a seasoned Footman would be at best extremely foolhardy, and at worst suicidal – and in the current time frame and with my level of expertise, well on the other side of impossible.

'I'm not sure.'

She stared at me for a moment, her anger mellowing to an attitude, I think, of motherly concern. She suddenly reminded me of Sister Zygotia.

'What made you become a Consul?' she asked in a quiet voice.

'I needed a job that would grant me Morphenox.'

'Makes no sense,' she said. 'To avoid the risks of a no-drug Winter you take on *every* risk the Winter can throw at you?'

'Now you mention it,' I said, 'it does seem kind of dumb. But at least I'm away from St Granata's.'

Luckily, Chief Logan chose that moment to walk in the door.

'Hello, Fran,' he said, moving forward to greet her with the traditional Winter embrace, then making some reference to 'sprightly times' they'd spent together during some Winter I-don't-know-when in Sector something-or-other. Fran, it appeared, had been part of the established Winter crew on Logan's first placement. Consuling was a small, close-knit family, tighter than the military, they say. They chatted for a while – reminded each other of the time they were charged by a frost-deranged glyptodon – but it was only a matter of time before he noticed me.

'Remember my bacon sandwich, Worthing?' he asked, then, annoyingly and predictably: 'Where's Mrs Tiffen?'

'I ... remembered the bacon sandwich,' I said a bit stupidly, 'and the tea.'

'Good of you. And Mrs Tiffen?'

'She was ... *stolen*. I think she's going to be farmed.'

Logan gave me a pained expression.

'You bloody idiot, Worthing. Who took her?'

I explained as quickly as I could what had happened.

'Terrific,' said the Chief once I'd finished. 'You should cross off "babysitting nightwalkers" from the short list of things you can do. Pull your finger out, Worthing, or you'll be mucking out breedstock for the Winter. Fancy that?'

'No, sir,' I said. Looking after the Winter breedstock was a job usually reserved only for convicts and people who were, well, *hated*.

'But,' I added, 'we have to get her back, right?'

'No, we do not. Hold fast and think for a moment. We lose a nightwalker and HiberTech are mildly pissed off they lost a Tricksy walker, but really, who's hurting here?'

'Mrs Tiffen?'

'Mrs Tiffen died five years ago. What you lost was something she used to walk around in. She's gone, it's done, you screwed up, move on. Let's get on the train.'

I backed away.

'No.'

I said it in the manner of a petulant child, and regretted it instantly. Logan stared at me with a quiet, unblinking gaze.

'What do you reckon, Fran?' he said. 'Gross insubordination or the idealism of youth?'

'Idealism of youth,' she said. 'In the Summer it's perfectly harmless albeit mildly tedious – but in the Winter it's a killer on a par with hypothermia and the measles.'

Logan moved closer and lowered his voice.

'Listen up, Novice. Drop the high ethical stance or get out before you do something you can't live with. And let me tell you, it's inevitable, once the cold and the fear and the hunger get a grip. Something will go wrong, you'll try and make the best of two bad calls, and *bing*: the Winter has you in its pocket, and you're tundra. High ideals, my friend, are a luxury ill afforded.'

I stared at him and he took a deep breath.

'Yes, okay, we *try* and break up farming cells, and no, we don't like it. But the end product is a whole series of happy parents and up to a dozen children. And when it's all over, she'll be parted out at the end of their life. Agreed, bootleg parts – but *someone* benefits. We're Consuls, Worthing. We strive to ensure the most favourable outcome is enjoyed by the majority.'

'But the law—'

'During the Winter, we *are* the law. I'll say it again because you must have missed it: however unpleasant and barring injured pride, this is a favourable outcome. Now, we're going to Sector Twelve, I'll speak to Toccata and see what she has to say about this viral dream bullshit, then we come out on the last train and I try so very hard to forget this, and you try ever so hard not to screw up again. Is there any part of that you don't understand?'

I stared at the bouzouki, a crushed, empty feeling in the pit of my stomach. Failure has a taste all of its own – a sort of hot, sticky doughiness. We could tell HiberTech she died on the journey. They'd not even question it. Nightwalkers die all the time. I was right to make the point, but I wasn't going to flush my career down the pan for her.

But then a voice rang out, clear and bright, and everything changed.

Meet Aurora

'... The trading of Favours and Debts is essential currency as cash can mean little to nothing in the lawless world of the deep Winter. To add complexity, Debts and Favours can be traded, subdivided, sold on or even used as collateral on a loan. It is a risky investment – all Debts are nullified when the debtee dies. And if they are Consuls, they die often ...'

– A Guide to Winternomics – Consul Pamphlet 9a

'That was the shittiest piece of mentoring I've ever heard,' said a voice from across the room. It was a woman sitting with some workers in HiberTech uniforms, also waiting for the train. She had silver-streaked black hair tied up in a loose ponytail and a pale complexion that was almost creamy. Her battered combat fatigues displayed the shoulder stripe of the 4th Arid Legion, her twin Bambis were rigged for a cross-draw and around her neck was the dark burgundy pashmina worn by those who had served in the Ottoman campaign. Most notable about her, however, was her left eye, which looked blankly off and up – but her right eye stared at us all with a curiously unnerving intensity. She was knitting what appeared to be a bobble hat.

Logan stared back at her, momentarily shocked.

'Well, well, well,' he said at last, 'if *you're* here, Aurora, then who's guarding the gates of hell right now?'

'That's hardly original,' said Knitting Woman, getting up and walking closer. 'How's non-married life suiting you?'

Logan's face fell. I was assuming this was the Aurora who was the head of HiberTech Security – the one who didn't get along with Toccata, or seemingly with Logan either.

'You had no right to do what you did, Aurora.'

'Cry me a river, Logan. You and Toccata? It would never have

61

worked out and we all knew it. I was doing you both a favour.'

'Jealous, were you? Jealous that someone might have preferred Toccata over you?'

Fran and everyone else had muttered excuses about 'laundry' or an 'important call' and rapidly vacated the tearooms.

'Jealous?' she said. 'Of what you have to offer? A second-rate Consul and a third-rate vaudeville act peddling fourth-rate advice to a fifth-rate Novice?'

The Chief stared at her for a moment. There was something odd about the exchange, but I couldn't put my finger on it. Logan was holding back, thinking, pulling his punches. Until now, I didn't know that Logan and Toccata were to be married. This added a new dimension to everything.

'What do you actually want, Aurora?' asked Logan. 'Must be something pretty big to have you crawling out from under your rock.'

'I wanted to know what you're doing heading into Sector Twelve. Considering past events, it's something of a rash move.'

'I *was* delivering a nightwalker,' he said, 'I thought my fax made that clear.'

'You could have sent anyone to do that. There's nothing going on in Sector Twelve, Logan, just a deluded Chief Consul trying to rekindle some long-dead embers from a doomed love affair.'

'Why are you so concerned about Toccata all of a sudden?'

Aurora thought about this for a moment.

'Because despite everything, she's like a sister to me, and sisters hold together, even with our disagreements.'

They stared at each other for a moment.

'In any event,' she said, 'HiberTech need Tricksy nightwalkers for Project Lazarus. *Particularly* like the one your thicko Novice has lost — you need to go and get her back.'

'You want her, *you* get her back.'

'Because you can't?'

'She's dead, I don't like you, you didn't say please, I can't be arsed, it's cold outside — take your pick. You have no jurisdiction over me during the Winter.'

He was right over jurisdiction, but it didn't much matter. Mrs Tiffen *was* his responsibility, and since Aurora could make serious trouble for him, he would have to go and look for her. Logan glared at me, then at Aurora, then had another thought and gave a soft smile that I felt uneasy about.

'Okay,' he said, 'this is a terrific opportunity for a Graduation Assignment. Worthing here is tasked to find your precious dead woman. Once that's been achieved — or not — and if Charlie is still living, we will both travel to Sector Twelve. Whilst there, I *will* meet up with Toccata — without your meddling.'

'This is bollocks,' said Aurora, taking a step closer, 'and to relegate important work to the level of training exercise is grossly irresponsible.'

'It's not Slumberdown for another thirty-two hours,' I ventured, 'and I've not spent a single minute in the Winter. I'm not sure I'm ready—'

'You're ready when I say you are,' snapped Logan, 'besides, you lost her, you can get her back. This is now *your* operation. Win and you get to be a Deputy Winter Consul, fail and you're minding breedstock. So, what's your first move, Bright-eyes?'

It was like being back at St Granata's, being given some impossible task to perform — such as getting on the Great Hall's roof without a ladder, or making a soufflé with cauliflower instead of eggs, or trying to stop the Ford girls from squabbling.

I took a deep breath.

'I ... need to follow a lead I've established.'

He pressed a finger hard into my sternum.

'*Wrong.*'

'It is—?'

I was interrupted by two muted blasts from the train whistle. It was five minutes before the last train to Sector Twelve.

'*Exactly,*' said Logan. 'You need to delay the train.'

'How do I do that?'

'Your head on the rails?'

'Seriously?'

'I don't know. But put it this way: if you *don't* delay the train, I will punch you five times hard in the head.'

'Once would probably be enough as a punishment.'

'You don't need to be punished, you need motivating. And *not* getting punched five times is a terrific motivator. Take my word for it.'

'I'll be making an official complaint about this,' said Aurora.

'Yes, why don't you?' said Logan, and picking up his jacket, he made for the door. 'Don't fail me, Worthing.'

'I'll try not to,' I said, wondering how I could do anything *but* fail – and surely, this was actually his intention. Aurora stared at me with her one eye for a moment, then sat down at the counter next to me.

'Don't fail *any* of us,' she said in a kindly tone, while placing her warm hand on mine. 'HiberTech and I will be grateful if you succeed, and the gratitude of either would be in itself a valuable commodity. Oh, and listen, I didn't mean it when I called you "thicko" and "fifth rate". It was only theatre. Kind of in the moment – and it pissed off that ballbag Logan. Good luck.'

'Oh – right,' I said. 'Thanks.'

I grabbed my bag and the bouzouki and ran to Platform Three, where clouds of vapour were billowing from the locomotive as the driver vented excess steam into the chill air. I found the freightmaster in the second carriage, fast asleep.

Moody's eyes flickered inside his closed lids while he murmured: 'Mrs Nesbit, *please*, leave me alone.' It was a little unnerving: asleep in public was okay, asleep and *dreaming* in public was not really socially acceptable. I like to think of myself as fairly broad-minded, but even I felt a little uncomfortable.

'Hey,' I said, shaking his shoulder. His eyes opened wide and he suddenly looked terrified.

'*You don't want to leave the rocks!*' he yelled, grasping me by the arm so hard I almost yelped with pain.

'What rocks?'

'Leave the rocks and the hands will get you,' he said in something of a panic, his eyes swivelling to the left and right faster than I thought possible. 'You don't want to be buried alive and ... I am Don Hector!'

'Everything's fine,' I said, 'and believe me, you're not Don Hector.'

'How do you know?'

'You look nothing like him – and he died two years ago.'

'He only died in the real world,' said Moody, 'not in *here*.'

He touched his temple with his fingertip.

'Eh?'

'Damn,' he said, suddenly recovering his composure. 'I'm sorry. Fatigue. We've had some losses recently, and, well, I'm running treble shifts.'

'What was that about being buried alive?'

'Nothing. Blue Buick.'

'What?'

'What do you mean: "what"?'

'You said blue Buick.'

'I did? What if I did?' he replied defensively. 'Who are you anyway, to cast aspersions on my sleeping habits?'

Logan had mentioned blue Buicks when he told me about the viral dream. If Moody was organising freight this late in the season, he would certainly have come from Sector Twelve.

'Anyway,' he said, clapping his hands together, 'ready to go?'

'No,' I replied, making a mental note to report all this to Logan, 'I have to repo a nightwalker and I need you to hold this train for me.'

Moody stared at me with a half-smile. Punctuality was the guiding principle to which RailTecs pledged their lives. Often, quite literally.

'Oh yes,' he said, 'and how would I do that?'

He knew how to delay the train; he didn't need to ask. All we were really talking about was the price.

'How about a Favour?'

When you urgently needed something from somebody in the Winter, the only true currency was influence. A Favour was simply general assistance – a no-quibble cash advance, parking ticket quashed, hundredweight of pasta when you were skint and a few pounds too light, that kind of thing. But even so, Moody wasn't impressed.

'With all due respect, Deputy Consul,' he said, 'a Favour from you wouldn't buy me a pork scratching in Sector Twelve.'

I thought about being punched in the head five times.

'A ... *Debt*, then.'

The freightmaster raised his eyebrows. A Debt was bigger than a Favour by a factor of fifty. For a day or two you could have a Consul pretty much in your pocket.

'You must want that Vacant pretty badly,' he said.

'A lot depends upon it.'

'Okay, then,' he said with a short snorty giggle, his demeanour changed, 'you've got yourself a deal. I'll recheck the loading; probably take me an hour.'

I thanked him, ran off to the station exit and found the taxi driver waiting for me. Comically, he had vapour rising from his bald head. Mrs Tiffen had been taken to the *John Edward Jones* Dormitorium, about ten minutes' drive away.

'That'll be fifty euros,' said the taxi driver when I asked him to take me there.

'I'll pay when we get back.'

He turned around to look at me.

'You're a Novice, trying to repo a Tricksy walker from a Footman in a Dormitorium out in the Scorch?'

'Yes?'

'You'll pay in advance.'

I sighed, handed him a fifty, and we set off.

The John Edward Jones

'... Consolidated Power & Light looked after its workers well. They were the only Utilities company still offering double puddings from August to Slumberdown, and workers flocked to their recruitment offices. Forget pensions, cash bonuses or Tog-28 duvets; jam roly-poly and custard was the fringe benefit of choice ...'

– *CP&L Corporate History*

The smell of smoke grew stronger as we drove north out of town, and we soon entered a landscape of fire-consumed desolation. We passed carcasses of terraced houses and pit workings blackened by decades of fire, then a burned-out bandstand and abandoned cars, their bodywork rusted to a wafer. I noticed that the snow, which had blown into drifts eight foot deep in town, had gradually thinned out as we drove until there was no snow or ice at all, and the trees seemed not devoid of leaves by virtue of the Winter, but by *incineration*.

'We're in the fire valleys, aren't we?' I asked, a mild tremor in my voice.

'We call it the Scorch up here.'

After five minutes of the charcoal-toned landscape, we stopped outside a Dormitorium, the only one still occupied in a clutch of seven, the rest burned out and abandoned. The *John Edward Jones* was higher than the others – at least forty storeys – and looked to be typically K-14: a mixed-sleep-ability Flopshop, a place where one could hibernate or nap on a budget, with staff on hand to rouse any Winterer who had slipped unthinkingly too deep into the abyss. It would have been cheap, too, out of town, and in the Scorch. I picked up the bouzouki, climbed out of the cab and was immediately struck by the warmth in the air. In Cardiff and Merthyr it had been about ten below, but here the temperature was somewhere around Low Ideal. The smoke was heavier than in Merthyr, and drifted across the road, the fumes occasionally punctuated by acrid whiffs of sulphur. As I looked around, a dead tree on the ridge-line suddenly burst into flames.

Muted chatter greeted me from the Winterlounge as I walked in. Although I couldn't see the sleepers, I knew they were close. There is something about a Dormitorium that gives them away. The faintest smell of rotten eggs, a taste, a sound – a *presence*.

The lobby was lit sparingly with low-wattage bulbs, but made warm and welcoming by the orange glow from the fireplace. The portress was behind the reception desk and looked up at me with a quizzical expression as I approached. She had luxurious auburn hair, a nose with an interesting kink and was wearing spectacles.

'Food, flop, laundry, booze, drowsy, blackjack, cage-fighting or poker?'[30] she asked, reeling off my options.

'None,' I said. 'I'm looking for a Footman. Fiftyish, medium height, shabby combats. Came in here with a dead woman.'

'What, like in a body bag or something?'

'A nightwalker.'

'That would make more sense,' she said, 'not a lot, but some. Let me guess: you want her back?'

I sighed. No one in the Winter seemed the least intimidated by a Winter Consul, nor rated my chances. Perhaps it wasn't the uniform, but the resolve of the character inside it.

'Yes, I want her back. Which room did you say?'

'I didn't. Want some advice?'

'Does it involve leaving right now?'

'It does.'

'Then no thanks.'

As I pondered my next move, a man moved from the Winterlounge to the elevators, and within the soft caress of fresh-moved air I detected a faint whiff of carbolic soap. The smell of cleanliness stuck to medical professionals as yeast to a baker. If Foulnap wanted to farm Mrs Tiffen it would require extensive funding and logistical

30. The fire valleys, owing to a legal quirk, were not subject to gambling laws twenty days either side of the Winter.

support – so he'd need a medic at the outset to confirm viability. All I had to do was to follow the medic all the way to Foulnap.

'Listen,' I said to the portress, 'if I'm not down in thirty minutes, call Logan at the Mrs Nesbit's station branch and tell him he needs a new Novice.'

'Shall I just call him now?'

I gave her a glare that was totally wasted. She said 'Okey-dokey', then returned to her magazine.

I picked up the bouzouki and followed the medic into the elevator, smiled, apologised and double-clicked the button I'd seen he'd already pressed – the twenty-first floor. The doors closed and I felt my heart start to thump. I could see the man was wearing scrubs underneath his suit and he looked at me suspiciously, then at the bouzouki, which was probably the best disguise one could have. Winter Consuls don't carry musical instruments. And even if they did, it would never be a bouzouki. A viola, maybe. Or a tuba.

'I had an aunt who played the guitar,' said the medic.

'It's not a guitar,' I said in a calm voice, surprising myself.

He sighed deeply.

'She wasn't my aunt. Winterplayer?'

I thought quickly.

'I'm accompanying a … pantomime horse act.'

'Which end do you play?'

'I'm the arse. Our equestrian gavotte is to die for.'

'I'll keep an eye out for it.'

The lift doors opened on the twenty-first floor. I trod the worn carpet behind the man in the scrubs until he stopped at a bedroom where I wished him sound napping, then continued to where the circular corridor would place me out of sight. I waited until I heard the latch click shut, then doubled back to the door to listen. There seemed to be a discussion going on inside, and to a mixture of relief and dismay, I heard Foulnap's voice clearly.

I took the Bambi from my holster, noted my hand was shaking, re-placed it and retraced my steps to the elevator lobby, where I paced back and forth, pondering whether high ideals actually *were* a luxury – something to aim for, rather than to try and attain on my first

Winter. I could walk away now, tell Logan I couldn't find her, and that would be it. I could start my career properly, alive and having learned an important lesson.

I pressed my forehead against the cold doors of the elevator. Sister Zygotia had been a harsh critic and guardian – and, yes, a terror with a scrubbing brush at bath time – but had always maintained that one followed the course of honesty and righteousness, *no matter what*. If I walked away now it wouldn't be the start of my career, it would be the end.

I paused to gather my thoughts, drew my Bambi again, and then, with a hard knot of fear and nausea in the pit of my stomach, walked back down the corridor. I stopped outside Foulnap's room, and with shaking hand unlocked the door with my Omnikey and let it swing open.

Foulnap was on the phone. The medic I'd followed was to one side, and looked startled when he saw me. Sitting on a chair was a third man of Nordic appearance who had a fresh bite mark on his cheek. When he saw me, Foulnap ignored the Bambi I was pointing at him and simply told the person on the other end of the line that 'There was a f—ing moron trying to piss in his pocket' and he'd call them back.

'By all that's pointlessly brave, Worthing, is that you?'

He seemed more impressed than worried.

'You can do this,' I said, voice quavering.

'I can do this?' echoed Foulnap in a relaxed manner. 'Then what are you here for?'

'I was talking to *myself*,' I said with a croak. 'What I meant was that you *can't* do this.'

I could see my hands tremble and felt a cold sweat crawl up my back. Foulnap was right. I was a f—ing moron. I should have just walked away.

'That's much clearer. So: why can't I do this?'

'Because—'

Whump

I'd not been paying attention. Foulnap had drawn and triggered his Bambi in less time than it took me to realise that he could. I barely had time to register the shock wave rippling in the air before I was lifted from the ground and thrown backwards into a chair that had been placed next to the door, reducing it to matchwood. I fell to the floor stunned, my head spinning from where it had thumped into the wall just next to the light switch.

'Lobster,' said Mrs Tiffen from the bathroom.

My vision returned to reveal Foulnap standing over me with a look of annoyance. He relieved me of my weapon, then shook his head sadly.

'That's the thing about good advice,' he said. 'It's really a lot better to heed it.'

Foulnap's colleague, the one with the bite mark on his cheek, rose and pulled a weapon of his own from a holdall. Only it wasn't a hand weapon, it was the twenty-KiloNewton Thumper, normally used for riot control and punching pressure-holes in snowstorms. Deputy Consul Klaar had been repeatedly pummelled with something like this outside Nightgrowls. She'd liquefied internally under the shock waves and by the time we found her she'd leaked out, pooled in the footwell and frozen solid. They'd taken her to the morgue with the floor mats still attached.

Foulnap helped me sit up and I touched my mouth where it was bleeding.

'Believe it or not, I was as green as you when I started out,' he said in a gentle voice, pulling my lower eyelid down to peer at the whites of my eyes, a simple way to check if there was any lasting shock damage, 'full of dazzlingly good intentions but as stupid as the Winter is long.'

He stared at me for a moment, then pushed the slide release pin on my Bambi, twisted the vortex chamber and drew the Venturi tube backwards. In an instant the weapon was in five pieces. He poured the components into my pocket with a metallic rattle, then dropped the power cell in last as if to punctuate the gesture.

'I tell you what I'm going to do,' he said. 'You're completely unimportant and a very, very small fish, so I'm going to throw you back.

It's win-win: you don't have to die, and I don't have to kill you. Do we have a deal? It goes without saying that you'll not speak of this.'

I stared up at him. I could feel the taste of blood in my mouth, and my head ached badly. But through the lens of abject failure, my next course of action was suddenly brought into a sharp and pain-fully illogical focus. If I couldn't leave with Mrs Tiffen, *I wasn't going to leave at all*. My career ended right here, in the fire valleys north of Merthyr, defending someone who wasn't able to care that I was trying to save her from a fate that she could never be troubled about. Perhaps that was what being a Winter Consul was all about. Defending the inalienable rights of the unaware.

'There's no deal,' I said, my voice cracking, my mouth dry with fear. 'Mrs Tiffen comes with me. And yes, it goes without saying we'll forget this ever happened.'

Foulnap stared at me in disbelief and I exhaled and opened my mouth. Shock damage can be lessened if airways are open. But that didn't happen.

'What the hell's going on here?' came a voice from behind me, at the door.

It was Logan. I suddenly felt unassailably relieved – so much so that I actually felt tears well up in my eyes. I was safe.

Only I wasn't. Not at all. Not even a tiny bit.

'It's not my fault, Jack,' said Foulnap. 'I thought you said your new Novice would be a pushover?'

'I may have underestimated Worthing's sense of intestinal fortitude,' conceded Logan, staring at me with a sense of respect, I think. 'This is all my fault; I never should have let Charlie even *attempt* to search for Mrs Tiffen.'

I closed my eyes and felt a tremor of fear. Logan had a different tone to his voice. I realised now why I'd taken it this far; I somehow knew Foulnap didn't have murder in him. But Logan did. He would have called ahead to Foulnap to pluck Mrs Tiffen from my grasp on our way through to give him some deniability. He and Foulnap would be in the farming scam together. It would all have gone according to plan, too – except for me.

'Maybe we can trust the Novice,' said the man with the Thumper, who seemed to have changed his tune. 'I didn't sign up to all this in order to start killing Consuls.'

'I'm with Lopez on this one,' said Foulnap, giving a name to the third man in the room.

'We can't risk any of us being discovered,' said Logan. 'Besides, Aurora's in town.'

Lopez and Foulnap exchanged nervous looks.

'She is?' said Foulnap. 'How did she get wind of us?'

'We don't know that she did. I'll deal with Worthing, you deal with Mrs Tiffen. Get up, Charlie.'

I climbed unsteadily to my feet and he gestured for me to leave the room.

'You should have listened to me earlier,' he said as we padded around the circular corridor, 'and just let it all go.'

We stopped outside the elevators and Logan pressed the call button.

'Can I ask a favour?'

'What?'

'Will you tell Sister Zygotia where my body is?'

'You're being overdramatic, Worth—'

Bing.

The bell sounded and the elevator doors opened to reveal Aurora, who looked about as surprised as I'd seen anyone for a while, and her hands instantly went to draw her Bambis. Logan had the advantage and swung his weapon in her direction. He had a clear shot, could have thumped her dead there and then – *but he paused.*

What happened next seemed to occur with treacly slowness: I dropped to the floor as the twin pressure waves[31] that erupted from Aurora's weapons plucked at my clothes like a rush of wind before impacting on Logan's chest; I heard every atom of air expelled from his lungs with a crack, then saw him blown at incredible speed into the wall opposite with a sound like a log falling on wet leaves.

There was a momentary pause. Logan was still upright, partially

31. Seasoned practitioners of pulse weapons used two in unison to more accurately and dangerously focus the vortex rings. In the hands of the unskilled, however, death and serious injury were never far away.

embedded in the lath-and-plaster, a look of bitter resignation etched into his features, the whites of his dead eyes livid red with burst capillaries. Aurora dropped the used power cells from the butts of her Bambis and quickly reloaded; the smell of hot electrolyte filled the air and mixed with the coal-smoke to create a sickly-sweet aroma.

'Shit,' I said, defaulting to pointing out the bleeding obvious with my sudden change of fortunes, 'you just killed Jack Logan.'

'Shit,' she said, as surprised as I was, 'so I have. Toccata will be *seriously* pissed off.'

She took a step closer to where Logan was embedded, shrugged and said:

'Well, can't be helped.'

'What can't be helped?' I asked as I climbed to my feet. 'Logan dead or Toccata being pissed off?'

'Both. Where was he taking you?'

'I think he was going to kill me.'

'Then you owe me a life-debt. Lead the way to the Tricksy night-walker, Bucko, we've a train to catch. And hey, here's the plan: you do the talking and I'll stand there and look menacing. Yes?'

I was, I think, stunned. In shock. I'd not seen anyone die before. Few did. Because the old, the weak and the diseased were winnowed out by Winter's sympathetic hand, the only deaths I'd been aware of in the Summer were accidents, which probably explained the almost ridiculous levels of public curiosity surrounding traffic fatalities. Two weeks after I'd taken up residence in the *Melody Black*, someone was hit by a removals van outside. You could barely move for onlookers.

'Okay,' I said.

Fortified by Aurora's fearlessness, I led the way back around the corridor. As soon as we stepped into the room the guy with the Thumper thought he'd have a go, but one of Aurora's Bambis took his arm off at the elbow. She didn't pause for a moment and stepped forward to hold the second weapon a foot from Foulnap's face.

'Okay, okay,' he said, his voice unbowed but with the reality of the situation sharply in focus, 'what do you want?'

'Mrs Tiffen,' I said.

'You're making a serious mistake, Worthing, Aurora is not looking after your best interests.'

'And you are?'

'It's *really* complicated.'

'You seem familiar,' said Aurora to Foulnap. 'Do I know you?'

'Nope,' said Foulnap, 'just a Footman trying to turn a profit.'

'Do it another way. House painting, for instance, or plumbing, or invent a game like Jenga or Cluedo or something.'

Foulnap moved to the bathroom as the medic went to Lopez's aid, and a moment or two later Mrs Tiffen was in the room, as blank as ever. I gave her the bouzouki, which was still lying on the floor, and she instantly began to play 'Help Yourself' as we headed towards the elevators.

The train was still standing at the platform when the cab deposited us outside the station, and I could see Moody tightening the ratchet straps on the flatbed while, near by, a clearly agitated stationmaster consulted a large pocket watch.

We'd made it with seconds to spare.

Over the hump

—

'... The Winter is a necessarily harsh gardener. It weeds out the weak
and the elderly, the sick and the physically compromised. Inroads have
been made towards "Proactive Winter Support" to increase survivability
of those with high intellect but low constitution, but for large numbers
of the population it is both impractical and expensive. Only the strong
and the wealthy should ever see the Spring ...'

– James Sleepwell's speech defending denial of Morphenox rights to all

The train was soon wending its way north towards Sector Twelve,
the smoke so thick from the fire valleys it seeped into the carriage
like malevolent fog and made us all cough. Our discomfort was
short-lived, however, as once past the limits of the Welsh coalfields
the smoke cleared and we were once more steaming across a softly
undulating landscape that was mostly frozen reservoirs, quarries and
stunted oaks, all liberally draped with snow.

The pleasing view was the last thing on my mind. I was seated
at one end of the carriage in a state of numbness. My fingers felt
large and puffy and my chest so heavy and tight that I had to
unbutton my jacket and loosen my shirt. I was having trouble swallowing and my heart didn't seem to want to settle. Mrs Tiffen, oddly
enough, was now playing 'Delilah'. Seemed sort of apt, really. Not
the lyrics themselves, but listening to Tom Jones while steaming up
the valleys, even if on a bouzouki. After about ten minutes of trying
to calm down and achieving it only to a limited degree, I set to
work reassembling my Bambi, and had just finished when I heard a
voice.

'Mind if I join you?'

It was Aurora, and she sat without waiting for an answer.

'I'd be dead without you,' I said, 'thank you.'

'Oh, my pleasure,' she said, as if she'd done nothing more than given me a Mars Bar or an unwanted ticket to the zoo. 'Mind you,' she added, 'I'm worried that Toccata will throw a tantrum and do something weird. I think she really liked Logan, despite the fact that he was an arrogant twat.'

Oddly, I was unsure how I felt about all of this. The fallout would be dramatic, of course – you don't kill one of the country's leading Chief Consuls without someone asking questions – and although I'd liked and respected Logan, his association with a farming racket was, well, reprehensible – and he was about to execute me, so I couldn't feel *totally* sorry he was dead. But I didn't feel happy about it, either.

'I'm not sure I'm really cut out for all this,' I said.

She looked at me and smiled.

'There are no heroes in the Winter, just lucky survivors. Besides, you passed your Graduation Assignment. You're now a fully-fledged Winter Consul.'

The achievement seemed empty.

'My mentor almost killed me and, without you, he would have. My input to Mrs Tiffen was minimal, at best. I hardly think that counts as a pass.'

'The objective was achieved,' she said with a smile, 'and that's pretty much all that matters, especially in the Winter. What did Logan want to see Toccata about?'

'Something about blue Buicks and viral dreams.'

'What a load of balls,' said Aurora. 'There's no such thing as a viral dream.'

'But—'

'Why,' she said, 'do you have any evidence that there *is* a viral dream?'

I told her that Moody had muttered something about blue Buicks and Mrs Nesbit and the hands out to get him.

'Moody the RailTec?'

I nodded.

'And,' I said, thinking of my training, 'according to regulation SX-70 of the Continuity of Command directives, I will need to carry on Logan's investigation – or at least, make some enquiries.'

'About viral dreams? With Toccata?'

'I guess so.'

She patted my hand.

'Here's some advice. Dump off Bouzouki Girl at Hibertech and get on the last train home. The Sector Twelve Winter Consuls are a bunch of vipers, *especially* Toccata. You don't want to be mixed up with them.'

I'd heard this from several sources.

'Is it true Toccata ate two nightwalkers to survive the Winter?'

'Kept them alive until needed, I heard, and now has a taste for it. Anything else you remember about the two perps who were going to farm Bouzouki Girl?'

'There were three suspects, not two.'

She stared at me with her single eye for a moment while the other moved around, seemingly of its own accord.

'To the left, was she?'

'He. A MediTech.'

'That would explain it,' she said, pointing to her useless eye, 'I don't see things too well on my left.'

She showed me a sketch on her notepad. It was, predictably, of half a face − Foulnap's.

'The man who took the nightwalker. This him?'

I nodded, and she placed the pad in her breast pocket.

'Logan paused,' I said after a moment's thought, 'like he didn't want to kill you. Why was that?'

'I've no idea,' said Aurora, 'but it was to your clear advantage that he did, and his clear disadvantage that he didn't. Remember what I said: avoid the Winter Consuls in Sector Twelve − especially Toccata.'

She bade me goodbye, and wandered off down the carriage, leaving me to my thoughts. After half an hour or so the train stopped at Torpantu high station.

There was no movement of passengers or freight while the RailTecs set the brakes for the descent, and we were soon on our way again, first through a mile-long tunnel that cut the summit off the mountain, then past a weathered sign welcoming us to Sector Twelve and from there down a long incline at a measured pace. It had stopped snowing on this side of the ridge, and in the twilight I could just make out the shape of the mountains rising all around, their peaks draped in a soft blanket of snow. On the tighter bends the red glow of the locomotive five carriages ahead was clearly visible, and occasionally the train shuddered as the snowplough scythed its way through a drift while sparks from the funnel drifted past the windows like fireflies.

I fed the dead woman half a dozen custard creams and she mercifully dropped off into Torpor, a welcome relief. I got up to stretch my legs and walked to the end of the carriage, where I found Moody. He was staring out of the window, deep in thought, and looked up when I stopped next to him.

'I need to give you this,' I said, handing him a piece of paper outlining the nature of the Debt I'd promised: who it was to, the date and my signature.

'Tidy,' he said, placing it in his top pocket. 'Join me?'

I sat in a position from where I would be able to see if Mrs Tiffen went walkies or tried to chew the seats.

'How did you get the Vacant back?' asked Moody.

'Just good old-fashioned grit, I guess.'

'No, seriously,' said Moody, who'd figured me out well, 'how did you get her back?'

'Aurora stepped in and saved the day.'

'That figures,' said Moody. 'It also means you owe her. It's not a good habit to get into during the Winter, owing people stuff.'

'I owe *you*,' I said.

'True,' he said, 'and even that's not to your best advantage. You heading back home once you've dropped off your nightwalker?'

'Once I've spoken to Toccata about viral dreams.'

Moody jumped visibly and looked around the carriage. He leaned closer and lowered his voice.

'I can tell you something about viral dreams,' he said, 'but later, privately. I'll be in the Wincarnis. Easy to find – on the main square. Watch out for HiberTech, too. All that "Saviour of Humankind" stuff is utter tosh – HiberTech are in it only for the cash. Don Hector was always generally true to his ideals, but the others soon took his dream and turned it into a nightmare. And Project Lazarus will just make the whole thing worse.'

'What is Project Lazarus?'

'I'll tell what little I know at the Wincarnis later. But be careful in Sector Twelve: there's something contrary about it.'

'Contrary?'

'Unusual. Spooky. Y'know all those weird Winter legends and fables you hear about when you're a kid? The Wintervolk?'

I knew exactly what he meant, and I'd been fascinated by them for years, not just by their oddness, but by their variety: from the Thermalovaurs that fed off your heat, to the Winter Sirens who called you from your bed with the promise of song and dance and dreamy bundles but left you dead of exhaustion and spent of all moisture. Of the Tonttu or little people, who crept into your room at night to steal your teeth, and cash, and toes. Also the Chancer, who could walk though walls and fed off your fat as you slumbered, leaving you an empty bag of bones, and the Gizmo that crept into your ear and laid eggs that hatched into worms that fed off your dreams.

They were all great fun, but if there was one particular favourite of mine, it was the Gronk. Feeding off the shame of the unworthy while folding linen and humming Rodgers and Hammerstein hits had a certain inspiring randomness about it.

'Yes,' I said, 'I've heard of the Wintervolk.'

He leaned forward, touched me on the knee and lowered his voice to a whisper.

'*They come true in the Twelve.* They're here, they're real. Mid–Wales is the cradle of fable – forged in the dreaming minds of the sleepers.'

'O-kay,' I said. His narcosis was clearly well beyond just blue Buicks, severed hands and being buried alive.

'I'm serious,' he said. 'Porter Lloyd at the *Siddons* Dormitorium. Heard of him?'

'No.'

'He's met the Gronk. Or at least, came close enough to touch.'

'Go on.'

Moody cleared his throat.

'There once was a Winterstockman named Ichabod Block who managed a farm outside Rhayder, near to where the ice-sheet turns from ice to meltwater, and there's no habitation for miles around. It was said that Ichabod was a man of simple needs; that he was taciturn, and dissatisfied with his lot; that he had a wife named Maria and a daughter named Gretl. But they departed one afternoon to no one knows where a couple of years before and this made him moody, and introspective, and few would want to speak with him, or bear him in company.'

'We had someone like that at the Pool,' I said, thinking of Sister Contractia.[32]

'One Winter,' continued Moody, 'Ichabod contacted an acquaintance of his named Lloyd to whom he was owed a life-debt of several years' standing, and told him that he was being "vexed most troublesome" by Wintervolk. Lloyd had been a porter for a decade, so of the Winter's horrors, there was little to frighten him. He considered Wintervolk simply old washermen's tales, the unchallenged pub-chat of the hard-of-thinking.

'"How do you know it's Wintervolk?" asked Lloyd when they met.

'"Last week the hiburnal elks had their antlers trimmed and six of the eighty-nine cow-mammoths had their coats brushed. And inside the house," continued Ichabod, "the raisins were all picked out of the muesli, Gretl's *The King and I* album was stolen and I found all the books on my shelves reordered."

'"Alphabetically?" asked Lloyd.

'"No – by merit."

'"Ah".'

None but the Wintervolk would be so eccentrically daring.

The plan was simple: Porter Lloyd was to stand guard outside Ichabod's barn from sunset to sunrise, seated upon a leather armchair.

'Ichabod wanted to use him as Volkbait?' I asked.

---

32. Sister Contractia lived in the shed where the motor-mower belonged, and kept herself to herself. The policy of Socialised Childcare does not automatically attract those who like children.

'He did that,' replied Moody, 'for porters are by long tradition eunuchs, and the Wintervolk are known to favour those who are physically lesser. Ichabod, however, was hiding ten yards away and upwind, behind several bales of hay, Thumper at the ready, eager to despatch whatever made an appearance. Porter Lloyd was to stay awake, ready to raise the alarm.'

I noticed that several of the other passengers in the train had stopped talking and were leaning in, listening to the story.

'But sleep was impossible,' continued Moody. 'Porter Lloyd sat there wide awake, ears straining in the inky blackness, the only light the faint glimmer from a sky bright with the stars of a Winter night. Not a sound punctuated the darkness. Not a rustle, nor even a broken twig, nor even the grunt of a spooked mammoth. Lloyd pulled his parka up around him, and thought of his life, his failings, his aspirations, and the fact that he couldn't get the tune of "The Lonely Goatherd"[33] out of his head.'

Moody stopped speaking for a moment, took a sip from his hip thermos, then continued.

'As the grey dawn pushed the night behind it and the world once more stirred to wakefulness, Lloyd suddenly jerked awake. He had slept for the past two hours and had been woken by a cry from Ichabod. Two words, quite clear, with no meaning he could discern. He yawned and stretched and called out. But of answer, there came none, and upon investigation he found Ichabod's Thumper, the safety off but undischarged – and all his clothes, neatly folded on the ground, and still inside one another like Russian dolls. His socks were lining his shoes, his braces still buttoned up outside his shirt, a small pile of teeth fillings next to his watch.'

'He'd gone?' said one of the other passengers.

'Vanished. Lloyd called the Consuls but they gave up after three days, having found nothing but his hat wedged high in an oak two miles away. They concluded that he had suffered a night terror, lost his mind and fled. A new stockman was brought in to replace Ichabod, his disappearance a mystery.'

---

33. Track 1, Side 2, *The Sound of Music* film soundtrack LP.

'What were the two words he spoke?' I asked, already knowing the answer.

'He said: "Oh Gronk", with a – a sort of a sigh of tired realisation.'

There was silence in the railway carriage, the air heavy with a sense of dread and wonder. The Gronk was a recent addition to the range of Wintervolk, and I'd not heard about her first appearance. I glanced out of the window. We had reached the bottom of the incline, and were steaming along the shores of a frozen reservoir that boasted a stone dam and Gothic straining tower. I turned back to Moody. I knew the story wasn't over.

'There's more, isn't there?' I asked, and Moody nodded.

'The replacement Winterstockman noticed that the taste of the water turned sour over the coming weeks so he made his way up the vertical ladder and through a loft hatch that was barely two foot square. They found Ichabod in the cold water tank, complete except for a missing little finger.'

Moody paused for dramatic effect.

'The Consuls concluded suicide, and that Ichabod might have had an "inexplicable desire to cement Wintervolk legend". But Porter Lloyd had more than doubts. When searching for Ichabod he noted that the house was tidy, the washing done, the beds made up, *South Pacific*[34] playing on the gramophone. There was even a Lancashire hotpot on the stove, a note on the lid in a small, spidery hand.'

'What did it say?' asked one of the other passengers.

'It said: *"Not enough oregano"*.'

'He could have folded the clothes and cleaned and cooked himself,' said another passenger, peering around the seat back, 'and put on the record. Like the Consuls said, to perpetuate the legend.'

'It's *possible*,' said Moody, 'but Ichabod wasn't a tidy man – and more a Rice/Lloyd Webber sort of person.'

I had only a single question.

'Was Ichabod unworthy?'

Moody looked at all of us in turn.

34. Original Broadway cast recording, obviously. Ichabod's wife and daughter had been big fans.

'He wasn't the only one they found in the water tank. There were the bones of his wife and ten-year-old daughter who he'd previously maintained had walked out on him eight years before.'

Moody concluded his story, his small audience murmured appreciatively, and as tradition dictates, gave him food as a tip. Within a minute he had half a Mars Bar, eight wine gums, a small bar of nougat and a Murray Mint.

'We'll meet later in the Wincarnis,' he said, leaning back to have a nap, 'and I'll tell you all about the blue Buick – and HiberTech.'

I returned to my seat, where Mrs Tiffen was still safely in Torpor. We stopped briefly at Talybont to drop off a power worker, and whilst at the halt the RailTecs reset the brakes and pretty soon we were off again, but now more easily, the line clear, and with good speed.

We crossed a river cocooned in ice and snow, then passed through an abandoned junction, the platforms and station buildings covered in snow and ice. The train travelled on for another half-hour until with a gentle hiss and a muted squeal of the brakes we drew to a halt.

My outward journey was over.

Talgarth and HiberTech

'... The HiberTech facility's location in Mid–Wales proved fortuitous once the production of Morphenox required increased security. With the Snowdonian ice sheet beginning only thirty miles away in the north, and a population of Villains in the area to put off travellers, security was never usually a problem ...'

– *HiberTech: A Short History*, by Ronald Fudge

I roused Mrs Tiffen from her Torporific state with a lump of marzipan under her nose, fed her two slices of Fruity Malt Loaf and a Walker's Shortbread Finger, then guided her out the carriage door. The air was sharper than in Cardiff; our feet trod the snow with more of a squeak than a crunch. It was by now quite dark, and the town was illuminated not by electric light, but gas: the flickering orange light from the lamp-heads added a sense of ethereal gloom to the town, as though it were caught in a time warp.

The signboard on the platform announced the station as Talgarth, the small town that played host to the HiberTech complex. I told the stationmaster I was dropping my charge and would be returning on the same train, and she replied that I had at least two hours, so plenty of time.

While Moody supervised the unloading, I took Mrs Tiffen towards the station exit, where Aurora had already been met by a man who was tall, thin, and had a complexion like that of a freshly oiled rugby ball. I was put in mind of an ancient corpse that had been preserved in a peat bog.

'Deputy Worthing,'[35] said Aurora as Mrs Tiffen and I approached, 'allow me to introduce the Deputy Head of HiberTech Security,

---

35.   It was the first time I'd been given the honorific 'Deputy' rather than 'Novice'. I still wasn't sure about it.

Agent Lionel Hooke. He looks after stuff when I'm not around. *Highly* trustworthy. Was a captain in the army until he joined us.'

'You were ... Captain Hooke?'

'Yes,' he said, one eyelid twitching, 'and if you make any comments about crocodiles, alarm clocks or missing a hand, I will pluck out one of your eyeballs and make you swallow it.'

'I was thinking of no such thing,' I replied somewhat untruthfully, as every single one of those things had gone through my head.

'Hooke was joking about the eyeball,' said Aurora, before turning to the Deputy Head and asking in a more quizzical tone: 'You *were* joking?'

'Of course,' said Hooke after a pause, 'my little absurdity. To break the ice, you understand.'

And he gave me a smile that looked as though it had come from a hastily-read handbook on cultivating personal charm. Even more worrying, he moved in to give me a Winter embrace. He smelled of chewing tobacco, battery acid and recently dead horse. He also took the opportunity to whisper in my ear.

'Step out of line and I'll destroy you.'

'Good to meet you, too,' I stammered, realising that the introduction was simply so he knew who I was, not the other way round.

'Want a lift?' asked Aurora. I said I needed the exercise, so she wished me well, then departed with Agent Hooke in a four-wheel-drive command car that looked as though it was the unfortunate union of a truck and a family saloon.

Mrs Tiffen and I threaded our way through the empty town, following the signs towards the HiberTech facility. I noticed that fixed safety lines were very much in evidence – a 6mm steel cable running through eyelets bolted to walls and lamp-posts. Although we had provision for these in Cardiff and Swansea, they were used only in emergencies. Here, they looked not just used, but used a *lot*. If visibility dropped to zero, the fixed line would ensure you'd not get lost – so long as you clipped on with a lanyard.

I approached HiberTech with, I think, trepidation. It was hard to downplay the importance of Morphenox. Living through the Winter was now expected rather than a welcome bonus. Skill retention, lowered food consumption and the redeployment and transplant benefits were already reaping dividends in our post-gorge economic environment. The naturally slumbering Southern Alliance, once the equals of the Northern Fed, were now lagging behind in every single societal and fiscal measure you cared to mention. Any which way you looked at it, Morphenox was a winner – so long as you could earn the right to its use. If you could, all well and good. And if you couldn't, well, heck: at least you had something to which you could aspire.

The HiberTech facility was dark and quiet with no sign of anyone about. If it hadn't been for the parade of gas lights illuminating the road up and out of the town, one might have thought it long abandoned. The sixty-acre complex, I knew, was surrounded on all sides by intentionally open and featureless countryside, and four watchtowers on the corners of the twenty-metre-high wall gave the lookouts a good view in all directions. The large double doors were of banded steel construction, with narrow loopholes to either side. There was a telephone bolted to one side of the entrance, and I picked up the handset, shook off the snow, pressed the 'call' button and introduced myself.

'Deputy Consul Worthing, C, BDA26355F,' I said, 'delivering a nightwalker. Tiffen, L, HAB21417F.'

'Hmm,' came the voice, 'we were expecting Logan, J, JHK889521M.'

I told him that Logan had died and that under Continuity of Command Protocol SX-70 I was continuing his duties. There were more questions after this and eventually, seemingly satisfied, a guard unlocked the outer door and let us in. After the surrender of my Bambi we entered a large and expensively decorated reception lobby, with a domed ceiling, a grand staircase behind and several double-width corridors heading off into the complex. Facing the desk was a large stained-glass window of considerable opulence that told the story of HiberTech Industries, and on the wall was a large HiberTech logo that dwarfed the twin portraits of Gwendolyn XXXVIII and Don Hector. Also of note were two golf carts parked up with a nightwalker in each, staring blankly at the floor. This was surprising;

driving a golf cart was well beyond the skill level of any redeployed that I'd seen. Incongruously, they had been given name badges. Some wag had named them Chas and Dave.

'Welcome to HiberTech,' said the security guard in a cheery manner. His name, I noted from his badge, was Josh. He wore a black uniform with the HiberTech logo stitched on the top pocket, and behind him there were framed certificates of the 'HiberTech Reception Desk Employee of the Week', which were all him. Either he was the only one, or he was the only one any good at it.

'Always happy to have visitors,' he continued. 'I'm something of a visitor myself, being from Canada. You should visit. We have one hundred and forty-eight mountain ranges, but somehow we're mostly known for our trees. Most of the country is trees, actually.'

'I'd like to go,' I said, 'but isn't it all a little, well, frozen?'

'Only in a glaciated permanent snow ice-field and tundra-y sort of way. Oh, and let's get any confusion sorted out: lacrosse, our true national game, is *intentionally violent*, whereas hockey is *incidentally violent*, and unless you've got time to spare, don't ask me about counterfeit maple syrup. Goodness, is that a bouzouki?'

'It is,' I said, and Mrs Tiffen dutifully began to play 'Delilah'. Josh handed me back my documents.

'Can't be too careful,' he said. 'Infiltrators from RealSleep are never far away. Ever met one?'

'No,' I said, 'or at least, not that I know of: what do they look like?'

'They look like everyone else. That's the whole problem.'

He stared at me for a moment, with his right eyebrow arched just higher than his left.

'You look as though you've recently taken some bad karma.'

'You could say that.'

'I simply abhor *Weltschmerz*. What can I do to cheer you up?'

I thought about Logan.

'How are you at erasing poor life-changing decisions in a time-travelly sort of way?'

'I can't do anything about that, but perhaps I can ameliorate the pain it causes. Stop off on the way out and I'll fix you one of my creations.'

'Creations?'

'Trust me.'

Josh scribbled me out a visitor's pass, then had me sign a form on a clipboard as I looked about curiously. There were a few people moving around the corridors, but they walked in an unhurried manner, and no one was talking. Although busy, the facility was eerily silent.

'Is it usually this quiet?' I asked.

'Management think that idle chitter-chatter distracts the mind from creative thought,' he said, while selecting the best lemon out of a dozen he had below the counter and fetching a food mixer from a cupboard. 'Do you play Scrabble?'

'I once laid "Bezique" on the triple for two hundred and twenty-eight points.'

I'd stopped playing soon after. You'd have to, really. Every rack I'd pulled from then on was loaded with crushing disappointment.

'Wow,' said Josh, 'you will *so* take the pants off us. We meet in the Wincarnis most mornings, between ten and midday. Join us.'

I told him I was leaving on the next train.

'That's a shame,' he said. 'Well, another time. You can wait in that room over there, and holler if you need anything. Don't forget to stop by on the way out.'

The waiting room was painted in light hospital green, and contained only unbreakable chairs and faded posters on the wall. The largest was published by OffPop and depicted the twelfth Mrs Nesbit, looking winsome and mumsy and proclaiming that there were 'cash bonuses for baby production beyond lawful allocation'. More welcoming were a couple of Welsh Tourist Board posters. One was advertising the local area with the now-universal slogan 'Visit Wales – Not *Always* Raining' and the second of Rhosilli beach, the wreck of the *Argentinian Queen* stranded high on the shore, with the inviting and unassailably true slogan:

There will always be the Gower

There was also the smell of hospitals about the place, a mix of paint, bleach and fresh laundry. I fed Mrs Tiffen two gherkins and a packet of stringy cheese and she began playing 'Delilah' again, but more quietly, as though the gravity of the surroundings called for it.

About ten minutes later a woman walked around the corner, deeply absorbed in a report. She had short hair and small, pointed features. Very like Lucy Knapp, which was hardly surprising, as it *was* Lucy Knapp.

'Lucy—?'

'Hey, Charlie,' she said with a grin, 'heard you were heading our way.'

I got up and gave her a hug.

'What are you doing here?' I asked.

'I'm on placement to the Advanced Redeployment Unit as part of the HiberTech Fast Track Management Scheme. Amazing work they're doing.' She looked around. 'Where's Chief Consul Logan?'

'He died. Well, sort of killed, actually – by Aurora.'

'Really? Why?'

'He was going to kill me.'

'Why would anyone want to kill you?'

'It's a long story, and not one I'm proud of.'

'Tell me when you're ready. Is that her trick?' she asked, pointing to Mrs Tiffen, who was still playing 'Delilah'.

'Pretty much.'

'Impressive. Your Bouzouki Girl will be useful R&D; Project Lazarus involves the *enhanced* redeployment of nightwalkers to serve the community in far better ways than they do already.'

'So there *is* a Project Lazarus,' I said. 'What about Morphenox-B?'

'I can neither confirm nor deny,' she said with a smile, 'and just in case you missed it, the paperwork you signed at reception was a Non-Disclosure Agreement. If you whisper a word about anything you see in here, then Mr Hooke – did you meet Mr Hooke?'

I nodded.

'...is tasked to enforce compliance, and I've a feeling that's not something anyone might cherish. There's a story going round that he once took on a starving Arctic badger – and won.'

'That's not *so* impressive.'

Arctic badgers were notoriously bad tempered, but still no larger than a medium-sized dog. I'd not like to tackle one, but suitably armed, I'd probably be okay, give or take a missing finger or eye.

'When he was four,' said Lucy. 'He's womad stock; Oldivician, I think. Part of his midwinter freezerthon.'[36]

'Okay, that is *very* impressive.'

'So the story goes. C'mon, let's get you both over to "B" Wing.'

She beckoned me out of the waiting room and clapped her hands twice. Both golf-cart drivers looked up with the languid heavy-headed motion typical of a nightwalker, and she pointed at the one who'd been named Dave, who drove slowly up to us and stopped. He then simply sat there, waiting, staring at the wall above and to the right of us.

Lucy gestured for me to get myself and Mrs Tiffen on board, then sat herself.

'We're trying to extend the redeployed nightwalker skill set beyond sorting spuds and opening doors,' she said, 'but it's all very much in the Beta-testing stage at the moment – which is why we don't let them off-facility. It's company policy to always have a jam sandwich and a box of almond slices when you're in a golf cart with them. Despite their skills, they do still get a little bitey when hungry.'

Lucy told the driver where we were headed and we were off with a screech of tyres. There followed a singularly hair-raising trip of narrowly missed obstacles and recklessly negotiated blind corners with only the beeping of the warning siren to assist any pedestrians out of our path. Dave seemed to have only a cursory interest in his task, and throughout much of the journey stared at my arm as a dog might stare at a bone.

Lucy told me I would be meeting The Notable Goodnight, so to mind my manners.

'Really?'

'Yes, really.'

My surprise was easily explained: The Notable Charlotte Goodnight was the only surviving member of 'The HiberTech Five', the close-

36. 'Womads' or 'Winter nomads' often left their children out in the Winter to separate the weak from the strong.

knit team that had been with Don Hector during the development of Morphenox. Goodnight had been a sixteen-year-old chemistry prodigy when she joined the team, and had personally perfected Juvenox for the under-twelves. When Don Hector died, she was the logical choice to lead the company.

'What did Mother Fallopia say when you told her you were leaving?' asked Lucy as we hurtled along.

'She said that I was an ungrateful little shit, I'd be dead less than a week into the Winter, and if I had a known grave, she'd come and dance on it.'

'She said that?'

'Words to that effect.'

'You still did the right thing.'

We drove through a self-opening door which led into another long corridor, but this one open to the elements on one side. I'd seen aerial pictures of the facility and knew it was constructed much like a college around a quadrangle, but here the quad was a twelve-acre area of trees, shrubs and even a stream that, were it not frozen solid, would have risen in one corner, tumbled through rocks and gullies and cascaded down a waterfall before it vanished with a gurgle at the opposite corner.

'The entire facility was originally designed as a four-thousand-bed sanatorium for those suffering Hibernatory Narcosis,' said Lucy, following my gaze, 'but it was handed over to Don Hector and his team as his research bore more and more fruit. By the time they had developed a workable version of Morphenox, the whole site had been given over to hibernatory research: how more citizens might hope to survive it, how we might need less of it, and how to better handle the mental and physical issues surrounding early rising.'

'It's very impressive,' I said.

'It should be,' replied Lucy. 'HiberTech's mission statement is to forever rid humans of the debilitating social and economic effects of hibernation.'

'It's a bold promise.'

'HiberTech always think big. We're here.'

The golf cart screeched to a halt outside a door marked 'Project Lazarus'.

'Have-a-nice-day-enjoy-your-stay-at-HiberTech,' said Dave, repeating the words as though he'd learned them phonetically.

Lucy unlocked the door by way of a keypad and after several rights and lefts and another pair of swing doors, we found ourselves in a circular room with desks, chairs and filing cabinets. Radiating out from this circular chamber were eight corridors, and off these were secure cells, perhaps twenty or so to each corridor. I could hear noises – murmurings and bangings – along with the distinctively unpleasant odour of unwashed nightwalker. A little way down the corridor a male nurse with a rubber apron was hosing down a cell, the soiled water running into a central drain.

I stood there, looking around, one hand on Mrs Tiffen's elbow. To my right was a door with a glass panel, and, curiosity getting the better of me, I moved closer and peered in. A nightwalker dressed in a pale green jumpsuit was strapped to what looked like a barber's chair. Directly above him was a curious copper device the shape of a traffic cone but six times larger, the pointy end about an inch from the subject's forehead. Behind the operating table a pair of technicians were working on several large machines that were covered in gauges, buttons, dials and four large screens. The technicians were saying something, but it was muffled by the thick glass set into the door.

'You know what curiosity did to the cat?'

I turned. It was The Notable Goodnight.

She was older than she looked in the publicity pictures, but to my guess on the cusp of her seventh decade. A well-exercised mid-season weight, she had unblinking blue eyes and was dressed in a starched white uniform that seemed to exude no-nonsense efficiency. She stared at me with thinly disguised disdain.

'Oh,' I said, embarrassed at being caught snooping, 'sorry.'

'Well, do you?' she asked.

'Do I what?'

'Do you know what curiosity did to the cat?'

'It killed it, I guess.'

'I'm sorry, I can't hear you.'

'Killed it,' I said in a louder voice.

'Exactly. The meaning is quite clear, of course—'

She stopped, thought for a moment, then turned to Lucy.

'Lucy, dear, why *did* curiosity kill the cat?'

Lucy had been reading Mrs Tiffen's file but looked up abruptly as her name was spoken.

'Oh – er, the context of the saying remains obscure, ma'am, but the *idiomatic* meaning is quite clear.'

'*Exactly*,' said Goodnight, 'couldn't have put it better myself. An idiom. Our work here is unpalatable but necessary for the greater good. In idiomatic terms ... Lucy?'

'You can't make an omelette without breaking eggs?'

'Close enough.'

'Isn't that ... *proverbial* rather than idiomatic?' I asked.

They both stared at me for a moment.

'Lost interest and moving on,' said Goodnight. 'Where's Chief Logan?'

'Aurora killed him.'

'For kicks and giggles?'

'*Does* she kill people for kicks and giggles?'

'You don't get to ask questions, Consul. Does Toccata know Logan is dead?'

'I'm guessing probably not *yet*,' said Lucy.

'Who's going to tell her?' I asked.

'Not me,' said Lucy.

'Nor me,' said The Notable Goodnight, still staring at me. 'What's the deal with your head?'

I was taken aback by her directness, and put out a hand to touch the right side of my face, which bowed inwards and had a left-handed twist to it, which caused my right eye to sit lower than my left by about the width of an eyeball-and-a-half. To me and my friends and the sisters it was just me and unworthy of comment – indeed, not even noticed – but from the general public's reactions I could gauge the societal view was somewhere between intriguing and what the physiotypical term 'unsightly'.

'It's a congenital skull deformity,' I said.

'Oh,' she said dismissively, making me think her interest was entirely from a medical curiosity point of view. 'Not calcitic, then?'

'No, ma'am.'

'Bad luck on you,' she said. 'We've been working on reducing and even reversing the effects of calcium migration.'

'I don't see this as bad luck,' I said.

'Do you know what?' she said. 'I'm really not interested.'

And without warning she stuck an open safety pin into Mrs Tiffen's forearm. A spot of crimson welled up. I was the only one that flinched; the dead woman didn't even blink.

'The sight of blood upset you, Consul?' asked Goodnight. 'Misplaced empathy will get you killed.'

'With the greatest respect, ma'am, I thought that was curiosity.'

'Maybe that's what killed the cat,' said Goodnight after a moment's thought. 'Curiosity ... about empathy.'

She looked at Lucy, hoping for semantic assistance, but Lucy just shrugged.

'Okay, then,' said The Notable Goodnight, passing me her clipboard. 'Sign on the dotted line.'

'Do you get many?' I asked, taking the clipboard. 'Vacants that do really good tricks, I mean?'

The Notable Goodnight looked at me suspiciously.

'We don't give out stats,' said Lucy.

'Long-time company policy,' said The Notable Goodnight as I signed the custody form. 'RealSleep like to use our own stats to hang us, so we don't release them – facts can really confuse people. But in answer to your question, we had a Tricksy once named Dorothy who could translate anything you said into Morse code. We renamed her "Dot the dash". We redeployed her as a switchboard operator and in tests she could work seven-day, sixteen-hour shifts with only one break for toilet and dinner of thirty minutes. Now *that's* productivity for you – don't you agree?'

In truth, I found it all a little creepy.

'Yes,' I said, 'remarkable.'

'Remarkable?' she echoed disdainfully. 'Beetles, trapeze artists,

Rodin, hydrofoils and anything by Brunel are remarkable. What we do here is *beyond* remarkable.'

'Inspiring?' I suggested.

'Unprecedented,' said Goodnight, then took the clipboard, signed her name below mine, and my responsibility for Mrs Tiffen was over.

'Here's your bounty,' said Lucy, passing me a five-hundred-euro voucher redeemable at Mrs Nesbit's.

'Sorry,' she said, 'I know it's usually cash, but HiberTech have got some sort of promotion going.'

'Oh, yes,' said Goodnight, turning back to us, 'were there any changes?'

'Changes in what?'

'In *her*,' snapped Goodnight, pointing towards the dead woman. 'Changes in behaviour. Her playing, her demeanour. Got worse, got better, more fractious, less fractious, what?'

'She used to only play "Help Yourself" but now she only plays "Delilah". Is that normal?'

'It's not unusual. And we're done. HiberTech thanks you.'

And so saying, Goodnight took the dead woman by the arm and steered her off down one of the corridors towards the cells. Tellingly and chillingly, *without* the bouzouki. At the same time, Lucy led me back towards the exit, and once aboard the golf cart, we were off again in as reckless a manner as before. We tore along the edge of the quad, the gardens within so wild and tall and overgrown that it was difficult to see the facility on the other side.

'Used to be carefully manicured when Don Hector first arrived here,' said Lucy, following my gaze, 'miles of gravel paths among a variety of trees and manicured borders, it's said. A restful place for patients to wander. There's a waterfall known as the Witches' Pool, hothouses – even a grotto, a bandstand and a temple to Morpheus. All overgrown now.'

We passed back into the warmth through the double doors, the tyres squealing on the polished linoleum flooring.

'Don't you find all that redeployed stuff a little creepy?' I asked.

'It's challenging,' she confessed, 'but the possibility of actually having a usable workforce with a potential eight-and-a-half-million work-hours of productivity shouldn't be sniffed at. Imagine having the redeployed skilled enough to work in factories – the price of goods would fall dramatically.'

'And Morphenox-B?' I asked.

'For roll-out next Summer, and for everyone. It'll be a game changer – but you didn't hear that from me.'

She smiled, raised her eyebrows and commanded the golf-cart driver to stop.

He stopped obediently, and Lucy climbed out at the pharmaceutical manufacturing department.

'Are you heading straight back?' she asked. 'From what I've heard, you really don't want to get mixed up with the Consuls in Sector Twelve.'

'Straight home once I've seen someone.'

I climbed out of the cart so we could hug.

'May the Spring embrace you,' I said.

'And embrace you, too. See you next Fat Thursday. I'll save you a burger.'

I climbed back on board, Lucy shouted 'Reception' to the driver, and we lurched off once more. Pretty soon Lucy's form was lost from sight behind a corner and we carried on in the direction of reception in as dangerous a fashion as before.

My mind, however, was no longer worrying about death or fatal injury from golf-cart accidents, but Project Lazarus. Statistics about nightwalkers were always patchy but from what Lucy and The Notable Goodnight were saying, nightwalkers could be entering a new phase of usefulness. More annoyingly, my decision to take on an insanely dangerous overwintering gig simply to guarantee Morphenox rights might be rendered pointless if they were giving it away to all and sundry.

My thought trail petered out as we had quite suddenly slowed to a halt. I looked across at the driver. He was leaning forward and motionless, staring at the floor ahead. I put out a hand to touch him but as I did so he suddenly turned and fixed me with a confused stare.

'Will you tell her I'm sorry?' he said in a clear, lucid tone.

I was taken aback — it was as though he had suddenly forgotten he was a nightwalker.

'Tell who?'

'It was a huge mistake,' he added with a look of bewilderment, as though he didn't know what he was saying or quite why he was saying it, 'and not a week goes by without me thinking about her.'

A frown crossed his brow as though he were attempting to pick up a lost thread. He looked confused, then lost, and his lower lip began to tremble. And then tears — of *frustration*, I think — welled up in his eyes and rolled down his cheeks.

I laid a hand on his shoulder.

'Dave?' I said. 'Are you okay?'

But he said nothing and we were off again with a squeal of tyres. A minute or two later and we were back at reception.

'Thank-you-for-travelling-with-HiberTech,' said Dave mechanically, 'have-a-pleasant-onward-journey.'

I walked over to the reception desk to return my visitor's badge.

'Charlie!' said Josh. 'Check out what I've made for you to lift your spirits, so to speak. I call it the "Full Spectrum Swizzle" and it features blackberry, mint, cola and lemon syrups. I've juiced seven lemons and an entire watermelon to make it using a new, efficient and incredibly unsafe technique that I'm calling hand-in-a-blender. If you find a hard chewy bit, it might be the tip of my little finger.'

'Really?'

'Yes. In the forefront of culinary innovation,' he added cheerfully, 'there are always casualties.'

He held up a bandaged finger as if to demonstrate the fact, and I stared at the drink.

'You could have sieved it to get the finger out,' I said.

'Then you'd lose all the fruity bits. It's only the tip, mind, hardly anything at all.'

I tasted the drink, which was a cross between a smoothie and a mint latte. It was actually very good, and I told him so.

'Glad,' he said, 'very glad.'

I drank the rest, picked out the tip of the finger before I swallowed it and found that it was indeed quite small, and laid the empty glass on the counter.

'Thank you,' I said. 'I should report that my driver said that he wanted to apologise to a woman he once knew.'

'Are you sure?' he asked.

'Yes.'

'*Quite* sure?'

'Yes.'

'Didn't imagine it?'

'No.'

'Well,' he said, face falling, 'how about that? I'll make a note.'

He opened Dave's trip ledger and made a note. Only it wasn't a note, it was a black cross. Once this was done, he hastily shut the book and drew in a deep breath.

'An artefact from a previous life,' he muttered, 'a lost memory bubbling to the surface. But a memory without a functioning mind to give it relevance and context is no more than random words on a scrap of paper. Wouldn't you agree? It's really important to agree, you know.'

He looked at me with a pained expression on his face.

'I agree.'

'*Excellent,*' he said with a palpable sense of relief. 'You can retrieve your weapon on the way out. Drop in again to see us real soon, and don't forget about the Scrabble. Wincarnis, most mornings.'

I thanked him and made my way to the exit. I looked behind me and noticed that he was removing his picture from the 'Employee of the Week' panel. I was only really happy once I was safely out of the complex.

The Wincarnis

'… Professional Winterers were not well disposed towards those who peddled quack Dormeopathy: the self-appointed Nightshamans, Morpheists, Dreamdancers or homeodormeopaths. Citizens often thanked the spirits for delivering them from the Winter, when in reality they should have been thanking us: the porters, the techies, the quartermasters, the Consuls …'

– *Handbook of Winterology*, 9th edition, Hodder & Stoughton

There was still plenty of time until my train departed, so I headed into town to meet Moody, as we'd arranged. I took a right at a shuttered apothecary's, then crossed a bridge upon which an inept driver had wedged an articulated lorry which was now frozen into the bridge by a concretion of snow and ice. Beyond this was a main square of modest proportions, empty aside from two parked cars, a post box, a phone box and a bronze statue on a sandstone plinth.

Ahead of me and overlooking the square was the Winter Consulate, a domed granite-faced bunker that appeared to have been designed by someone whose architectural taste lay chiefly in harbour breakwaters. The style was termed *Ultra-Permanence*, and reflected the fashion for public buildings that could withstand the damage of glaciers, earthquakes and even a marble-sized meteorite. It reflected the mood of the Northern Fed: here to stay.

To my right there was a newly refurbished flour mill, closed, and a public convenience beneath a town hall, also closed. Opposite me there there was a wool shop – *open*, curiously enough, and then a Co-op and Ottoman takeaway – again, closed. There were a few people around but no one seem to be dawdling. Mostly heads-down against the cold, faces hidden in hooded parkas.

The Wincarnis Hotel was to my immediate left, the name of the establishment relating to a brightly coloured enamel sign advertising *Wincarnis Restorative Tonics* high above the door. The Edwardian lady depicted on the panel peered out at the world with a cheery grin, oblivious to the ice and snow, the enamelled colours appearing inordinately bright in the dullness of the gas lamps.

I stepped inside the lobby and walked across to the reception desk, where there was a girl probably no older than sixteen sitting behind the counter. She wore a gingham dress under two buttoned cardigans, and her straight brown hair was cut neatly into a pudding bowl. She was poring over a stack of open books, and writing in a small neat hand in a child's exercise book.

'Welcome to the Wincarnis,' she said in a cheery voice. 'Haven't seen you here before.'

'Passing through,' I said. 'I was to meet Moody. He here?'

'Nope, probably off somewhere muttering about Buicks and suchlike. What did you want to talk to him about?'

'Buicks and suchlike.'

'Figures,' she said.

She had what looked like schoolwork spread across the counter in front of her.

'Homework?' I asked.

'It's actually my doctoral thesis,' she said with a mildly offended air. *'Evidential confirmation of previously considered legendary or nebulous forms within the Winterstate.'*

'What does that mean?'

'It means I'm trying to prove the existence of Wintervolk.'

She might as well be attempting to prove unicorns or capture fairies in traps.

'That'll be tricky, don't you think?' I asked.

'It's borderline impossible.'

'Because they don't exist?'

'Oh, they exist all right – it's gathering evidence that's hard. But I wagered a local bondsman they existed, and Jim Treacle, well, he does like a wager.'

'What was the wager?' I asked, expecting a dozen Topics or something.

'Fifty grand.'

'Fifty grand?' It would take me twenty years to save up that sort of money. 'Why so much?'

'Long story. What do you make of this?'

She opened her satchel and took out a small box and then, with the utmost care, opened it to reveal a tiny hat, less than five centimetres across.

'Behold,' she said, 'the headgear of a Tonttu, one of the Winter little people.'

I stared at it for a moment. The stitching was undoubtedly fine, but the material was less like leather and more like … *plastic.*

'I think it's from a Barbie,' I said, 'one of her Western outfits.'

'Yes, I think so too,' she said with a sigh. 'The maker's name is stamped on the inside. Look.'

She showed me, then repacked the hat and placed it back in her bag.

'It's important to collect evidence,' she said, 'even if disproved. That's how science works. Being proved wrong and then advancing. If I'm proved wrong a lot, I must be making headway, right?'

'Works for me,' I said, 'but the Wintervolk are just stories, right? To frighten children into good behaviour and the sleep-shy into bedding down?'

'I'm taking a broader approach to the traditional definition of "existence" or even "proof",' she said, 'but I may have more luck here than anywhere else: the Gronk, Thermalovaur and Gizmo are pretty much only ever connected to Mid-Wales, and of those, the Gronk is pretty much brand new – the first mention of it was only twenty years ago, over near Rhayder.'

'Ichabod and the cold water tank?'

'That's the one.'

I told her that Moody had said the area was known as the cradle of fable.

'With good reason,' she replied, 'and I think the Gronk is due to return – to feed on the shame of the unworthy.'

'Rich pickings here, I take it?'

She rolled her eyes.

'She'll be *totally* spoiled for choice in the Twelve. Bondsmen and part-time Consul Jim Treacle Bondsman is my choice if the Big G comes to call, but on the Burden of Guilt stakes, he probably doesn't even come close to some of the oddballs kicking around. There's Jonesy, who lost sixty soldiers under her command, Toccata who is barely herself half the time, Fodder is *definitely* hiding something and most of the porters here have suffered fatal losses, probably through boredom or incompetence. But my money's on the Twelve's very own one-man obnoxs-a-thon, Deputy Hooke. I'm Laura Strowger, by the way.'

'Charlie Worthing,' I said.

We shook hands rather than Winter embraced; you don't with kids unless they're family.

'Well,' I said, 'good luck on your hunt for the Gronk.'

She thanked me and returned to her work, and I walked through to the Mrs Nesbit's café, a good-sized room of plain rustic decor: oak beams, half-panelled walls, antique copper pans and with two large windows that looked out on to the square. There was a drowsy and a potential client sitting in a cosy alcove near the crackling log fire, discussing Impressionist painters, the usual precursor to assisted slumber. From there she might move on to literature, poetry, the lute, and – failing all that – more intimate means. Few needed to. Given the traditionally high level of drowsying skill, most clients were unconscious somewhere between Dylan Thomas and Longfellow with a few lasting as far as W. H. Auden. Lutes rarely even came out of their cases.

The drowsy's eyes had the vacant, deeply-fatigued look of a winsomniac; someone who hadn't been to the nourishing abyss of slumber for years. She looked oddly familiar, and appeared to be in her sixth decade – and that was unusual, because serial overwinterers rarely made it past their fourth. Stupidly, I raised my hand and waved in recognition, and she, expressionless, did the same.

The remaining occupants of the lounge were winsomniacs, perhaps a dozen or so. They were sprawling rather than sitting, and oozed a sense of unexcited apathy. A pair were playing chess using lightweight pieces, several were reading books, but most were simply dozing, eyes and mouth partially open, saliva dribbling down their cheeks.

They languidly swivelled their eyes towards me as I walked in, then just as languidly swivelled them back and carried on with what they were doing, which was the quiet side of almost nothing.

'Welcome to Mrs Nesbit's,' said the winsomniac closest to me. He was dressed in long hessian robes, open sandals and wore dried Spring flowers entwined in his beard. He had green-rimmed spectacles and a kindly, pious face wrinkled into folds by sleepless Winters and the elements.

'Hullo,' I said, breaking the one rule of engaging with the sleep-shy: don't.

He introduced himself as Shamanic Bob.

'Deputy Consul Charlie Worthing,' I said.

'Passing through?'

'Yes; here to meet with Moody.'

'You'll get more sense from lichen. What's with your head?'

Unlike talking to The Notable Goodnight, where I needed to be polite, this was an answer I could have fun with.

'It's the final stages of an excruciatingly painful and incurable genital wasting disease. Luckily, it's only spread by skin contact. Sorry, I should have said that before I shook your hand. Remiss of me – apologies.'

Shamanic Bob smiled.

'Fair enough,' he said. 'I think I deserved that.'

'Yes, I think you did.'

He stood up, moved forward and drew me into the Winter embrace. The last time I'd been hugged by a shaman was about a decade before, and little had changed. He smelled of dry hessian, mould and biltong. He was also bony. *Really* bony. Like a sack of pickaxe handles. After we'd stood there for so long that I thought he'd fallen asleep, we parted.

'Do you want a coffee?' he said. 'We stock Nesbit Budget Grind. What it lacks in taste it makes up for in adaptability. Mixed into a paste it makes a very resilient tile grout.'

'That's very kind, thank you.'

'The machine's up there, and while you're about it, make one for me. Anyone else?'

There was weak assent from the entire room. Enthusiasm was a dirty word to winsomniacs. I walked across to the bar and made a large cafetière of coffee, then placed it on a central table. The winsomniacs made weak and ineffectual attempts to help themselves, so I handed them around. The sleep-shy were like that. Always getting other people to do stuff for them.

'On the house,' said Shamanic Bob as I handed him a coffee, then took one myself. It tasted like coal-tar soap mixed with charcoal and rust.

'Are you a follower of *The Book of Morpheus,* Worthing?' he asked.

'I'll be honest,' I said, 'I've nothing against anyone who believes, but I think it's a dangerous nonsense.'

'An unbeliever is but an opportunity,' said Bob with an unrealistic level of optimism, 'and a man surrounded by an abundance of opportunity is a rich man indeed. What brings you to Sector Twelve, Deputy? Are you here to … *dream?*'

I realised who they were, then. They were the polar opposite to those of us on Morphenox: using illegally-obtained dream enhancers, they shunned the featureless blackness that was the Morphenox hibernation experience, and rode out the Winter on a chemically-induced froth of energy-sapping subconscious escapism. And, given the rules surrounding Winter Asylum, they could do it for free, with legally mandated food and shelter.

Parasites, basically – of the worst sort.

'Oh,' I said, without much subtlety, 'you're *dreamers.*'

'Correct,' said Shamanic Bob with a faint smile, 'but don't be thinking we're victims of our lifestyle, we're here by choice. And believe you me,' he added in a lower voice, 'this is the place to score some D-Reem. One hundred per cent pure, uncut. We have a contact in HiberTech; we swap it kilo-for-the-gram with Tunnock's Teacakes.'

D-Reem was an *escalator,* a dream enhancer. Slang made it all cool and groovy, when actually it was all just monumentally dumb.

'Do you dream, Deputy?' he asked.

It was an easy assumption I was on Morphenox. I didn't dream. Or at least, nothing serious. Just the odd scrap during nightly nap.

'I've not dreamed since I was in single digits,' I said. 'I'm okay with that.'

'If you've not dreamed, you've never truly slept. Dreams are the place where you can be yourself; do anything, be anything. The mind set free – Morphenox muffles the mind and smothers the imagination.'

'I'll take your word for it.'

'You should ride the dream train,' continued Shamanic Bob with a smile, 'pop an escalator and see what you're missing. It's the dark and dirty cousin of Morphenox, but there couldn't be one without the other. It's night and day, my friend, hope and despair, Eldon and Manning, darkness and light. We're the flipside of sound slumbering, the crusty night-seepage you scrape off and sweep under the mattress.'

'I'm not sure I understand,' I said, at the same time doubting my implied presumption that there *was* something to understand.

'Do you know your Don Hector history?' he asked with what passes for enthusiasm amongst his calling. 'What the good doctor was doing for twenty years *before* he introduced Morphenox to the grateful masses?'

Come to think of it, I didn't. The story was that he spent two decades perfecting the drug; I'd not heard how he actually did it.

'Morphenox was a fluke,' said Shamanic Bob when I didn't answer, 'discovered wholly by chance.'

I was going to ask him to expand upon that when Moody turned up. Unfortunately, not in a manner I'd hoped or expected. We were interrupted by a shout and I looked out of the café window, where I could see a naked Moody running towards where we sat, his coarse wintercoat standing hard up against the cold. He was wielding an axe and yelling *'Blue Buick!'* at the top of his voice, and without pausing for a second swung the axe with all his might against the plate-glass window of Mrs Nesbit's – a pointless gesture given that it would be certified to withstand torrential rain, gale-borne debris and an enraged mammoth. He scratched the toughened glass, but that was about it.

'This isn't a great advert for dreaming,' said Shamanic Bob. 'Moody has been riding the arse end of the reality slope for quite a few days now.'

'I hope the Gronk lays eggs in your brain, Mrs Nesbit!' he yelled, raising the axe to swing it again. 'And they bury you alive!'

Just then a man strode unhurriedly around the corner. It was Agent Hooke, all tall and gangly and with a face like leather. He was cradling a Thumper, but not the old-fashioned one of Lopez's back at the *John Edward Jones*, it was the Mk VII – twice as powerful and available in matt black or nickel.

'HiberTech Security,' announced Hooke, standing thirty or so feet from the clearly confused RailTec. 'Drop or you get dropped.'

Moody turned to face him with a look of shock. It didn't appear that he was fully awake, let alone able to follow simple instructions.

'*Blue Buick!*' he yelled, then turned to face me, and there was a flash of recognition.

'You'll visit the blue Buick and Mrs Nesbit will harangue you, too,' he shouted, 'tell her nothing and whatever you do, *don't leave the rocks or the hands will get you!*'

And he raised the axe, turned, and charged at Hooke.

Whump

My ears popped as a doughnut-shaped pressure wave erupted from the front of Hooke's weapon and caught Moody full in the chest. I saw the pattern of a Tudor rose blossom on his chest hair before the secondary shock wave lifted him off his feet and propelled him backwards across the square into the unyielding stone of the town hall. There was a wettish thud and he fell into a lifeless heap on the ground; the compacted snow melted into water by the momentary pressure change to reveal cobbles and half an iron inspection cover. In a split second the pressure had normalised and the water instantly refroze as gin-clear ice, locking Moody's body to the ground. In the Winter, warmth is only ever a transitory commodity.

Hooke broke open the weapon, ejected the spent cell and replaced it with another from his pocket.

A movement caught my eye. It was Aurora running around the corner, weapon at the ready. She threw up her hands when she saw what had happened.

'You bloody idiot!' she yelled when she saw Moody's body. 'What happened to good old-fashioned proportionality?'

'I was well within my rights, Aurora,' said Hooke in an unrepentant tone. 'Moody was endangering my life and that of others. The law permits me to use reasonable force in such circumstances.'

He said it in the same sort of tone you might use to describe your favourite brand of butter.

'We *need* our infrastructure support staff,' said Aurora in an exasperated tone, 'even the deranged ones. Who's going to bring the rail network out of mothballs to meet the Springrise schedule? You?'

There followed an argument in which claims and counterclaims were issued, insults traded, demotions hinted. But ultimately, with little to no headway.

Within a few minutes other security agents had arrived, presumably alerted by the Thumper's pressure signature, which would have every barograph spiking within a mile. It was only then that Aurora spotted me in the window and walked over.

'Deputy Worthing,' she said as she walked into the café, Hooke by her side, 'how's the viral dreams investigation going?'

'One of your agents just killed my star witness.'

'It was self-defence,' said Hooke. 'You saw him run at me with an axe.'

'Did he?' asked Aurora.

'Yes,' I said, 'I suppose so.'

'I see you've met our resident parasites,' said Hooke, who had been looking around the café. 'Good evening, Shamanic Bob.'

'Good evening,' said Bob with a defiant smile. 'Come to wish us all a slow death?'

'You read me like a book,' said Hooke. 'Spooky. But let's face facts: you are the most loathsome of spongers.'

'That's *Mr* Loathsome Sponger to you,' said Shamanic Bob, his defiance not wavering in light of Hooke's insults, 'and I know my rights. You're private security, not Winter Consulate. You have no jurisdiction over me.'

But ever cautious, presumably on account of his dreaming habit, he decided to leave anyway.

'We'll talk again,' said Shamanic Bob to me, although it was unlikely. My train was due out soon. But despite what little I knew of HiberTech, I was intrigued by what he'd said about Morphenox being a fluke.

'Liars and schemers all,' said Hooke. 'Did you lend him any money?'

'No,' I said, 'but you should probably know they're scoring D-Reem from somebody in HiberTech.'

'It troubles us not one jot,' said Hooke. 'One less sleep-shy is one less mouth to feed.'

'I'm really sorry you weren't able to talk to Moody,' said Aurora, trying to move the conversation on and nodding towards where the security agents outside were using a heat gun to free Moody from the ice. They weren't very good at it; I could smell the singed hair from within the café. 'Mr Hooke was employed for his ruthless adherence to HiberTech's well-being, so subtlety isn't really his long suit. Do you accept my apology?'

'Yes, I guess.'

'Good. I have a few questions for you. Is that okay?'

'Sure.'

She pulled a photograph out of her breast pocket and laid it on the counter. The picture depicted a man in his forties, fairly nondescript, thinning hair, holding an iguana.

'Know this person?' she asked.

'Never seen him.'

'This is Hugo Foulnap. The *only* Hugo Foulnap. An accountant, he nightwalked twelve years ago and was parted out the same Winter. The Hugo Foulnap in the hotel room wasn't Hugo Foulnap at all.'

'Ah,' I said, unsure where she was going with this or what she wanted me to do. 'Why is he holding an iguana?'

'I don't think it's relevant. What do you think they were going to do with Mrs Tiffen?'

'She was going to be farmed.'

'Foulnap actually said that?'

'Not specifically, but it was fairly obvious.'

'Did he mention Kiki?'

'No.'

'Did Foulnap say anything that suggested he was with the Campaign for Real Sleep?'

'Nothing I can think of,' I said, but then added without really thinking, 'If you suspected he was with the Campaign, why didn't you arrest him?'

I knew it was impertinent the moment I'd said it, but it wasn't Aurora who reacted, it was Hooke.

'You've got some lip on you. Any more of that and I'll rearrange your face – although from the look of you, someone has already tried.'

He smirked at a joke that he thought was both funny and original, something in which he was entirely wrong on both counts.

'Then maybe you could *arrange* it for me and help us all out,' I said, having weathered far worse insults over the years. The interaction with Gary Findlay had been the turning point. He'd made fun of my looks for years but me biting off his ear was dubbed 'wholly disproportionate'. Mother Fallopia was bound by full disclosure policy after the event, and once I had 'Biter' on my record even the more sympathetic adopters hurried on past.

'I don't get it,' said Aurora, 'is there something unusual about Worthing's face?'

It suddenly struck me that she only saw the left-hand side of things – witness her curious half-sketch and not seeing the MediTech – so she might not see the wonky side of my head at all.

'I have a congenital skull deformity,' I said.

'Oh,' she replied, leaning over to try and see, and I think failing, 'then that makes Mr Hooke's comments entirely uncalled for – you're to apologise.'

'I apologise unreservedly, ma'am,' he said in a bland monotone.

'Not to *me*, you clot,' said Aurora, nodding her head in my direction.

'Oh,' he muttered, then turned to me and gave a fulsome if strained apology, adding that if I so wished I could make fun of the fact that he had lost his left testicle in a 'freak accident involving a revolving door' with no risk of retaliation either now or in the future.

I declined, and he took a step back.

'Sorry about that,' said Aurora. 'Hooke is particularly suited to thinking up imaginatively terrifying interrogation techniques, and sometimes forgets himself. Okay,' she added, picking up the photo, 'we're done. You have the thanks of HiberTech Industries for the safe delivery of the cabbage – and if you see any of the people from that hotel room I'd like you to contact HiberTech Security *immediately*. Yes?'

I told her I most assuredly would, but privately I was thinking that all I wanted to do was to speak to Chief Toccata, get home and then have nothing to do with Sector Twelve ever again. Aurora offered me her hand to shake and then pulled me into the Deep Winter embrace, her breathing husky and close to my ear. I could feel the flat of her thighs against mine, the hardness of the Bambi across her chest.

'Good luck, Charlie,' she said, her breath smelling of coffee, banana milk and Mintolas, 'I have the strongest feeling you're going to be a really good Consul.'

She released me and I turned and headed towards the exit. I checked my watch. My train was due to depart in forty-eight minutes.

Consulate and Fodder

'... The Fraternity-Community-Fertility social policy was borderline
obsolete now that Winters were becoming increasingly survivable. But
the Pool's redistribution, child-matching and charitable policies were
firmly entrenched. It wasn't so bad if you were cute, but any pooler
who'd spent even ten minutes as "remaindered" would have the whole
petting zoo banned in a heartbeat ...'

– A Critique of Socialised Childcare, by Keith Pankhurst

'I need to see Toccata,' I said to Laura once I was back at the entrance
lobby of the *Wincarnis*. 'That's the Consulate facing us, yes?'

'I'll come with you,' she said, so we pulled on our parkas and
overboots. 'I do filing over there for eight hours a week. Without it
I'd be just another one of the sleep-shy. I like to pay my way.'

'What's the deal with Hooke?' I asked as we stepped outside.

'Best avoided. He used to work in Military Intelligence but was
forced to resign due to his unbridled enthusiasm for "psychologically
invasive interrogation techniques". He's basically a nasty bully who's
been given some authority – never a winning combination. Or,' she
added, 'a totally winning combination. It's a question of perspective.'

'And Aurora?'

'She runs hot and cold, same as Toccata. When it comes to
HiberTech Security, the safe default position is to avoid all and
everything in as aggressive a fashion as possible.'

We walked past the statue that was positioned in the town square,
moved up some steps until we were at the Consulate's main door,
and Laura punched some numbers in on the keypad. We entered
the primary shock-gate, walked down a short corridor, then went
through the secondary shock-gate and into the main chamber. The
offices were identical in layout to the offices back in Cardiff – the
same as everywhere, in fact. The only difference was that the room

was partitioned about a quarter of the way in by a long counter that was piled with files, reports, SkillZero procedure manuals, fliers for state-registered winsomniacs and a large tear-off desk calendar that indicated there was one day until Slumberdown.

Behind the counter was an open-plan office with a half-dozen desks, all of them stacked high with unfiled and forgotten paperwork, paper cups, old newspapers and general bric-a-brac. There were the usual half-dozen or so super-sensitive barographs across one wall, and across another was a plethora of missing persons posters. Some new, some old, some ancient.

'Anyone over two seasons missing is logged as "Likely Carrion" and declared dead,' said Laura, 'but we keep the posters up as it helps to have human faces around, irrespective of who they were or their current status.'

We stared at them for a moment.

'We call it the "Wall of Lost Souls",' she added, then said, as I heard footsteps approaching: 'Ah, Fodder.'

I turned to find a powerfully-built man who was about two foot taller than me, probably weighed twice as much again and looked as though he could comfortably eat me for breakfast. He had crew-cut hair, half a left ear and eyes so dark his sockets seemed empty. His nose looked as though it had been broken at some point, healed unset, then broken, then healed again, then broken, then healed again. He carried a Thumper upon which was drawn a smiley face and the words *'Have a Nice Day'*, and sewn into the shock-vest was a D-ring. I'd not seen one before, but knew what it meant: once it was pulled, a pulse charge would detonate instantaneously. He'd be Consuling to the end – and if things got truly bad, he'd take as many Villains with him as he could. He was, in spirit rather than current profession, very much a soldier.

'Fodder, this is Charlie Worthing,' said Laura, 'Deputy Consul.'

I nodded respectfully and he stared at me without blinking.

'I've not seen any transfer paperwork,' he said after what seemed like an age.

I told him that I was delivering a nightwalker, but on account of Continuity Protocol SX-70 was representing Chief Logan on an investigation.

Laura and Fodder looked at one another, and I think I might have seen a glimmer of nervousness on Fodder's otherwise impassive features.

'Chief Logan is dead? How did that happen?'

'Aurora thumped him backwards into a wall when he was about to execute me. He'd been farming nightwalkers,' I added quickly by way of explanation, 'and couldn't trust me not to blab.'

There was silence for a few moments.

'Toccata will *not* be pleased,' said Fodder, 'not pleased at all – and I'm sure as shit I'm not going to be the one that tells her.'

'Nor me,' said Laura. 'Jonesy can do it – she can run the fastest.'

'Is Toccata around?' I asked. 'I could tell her.'

'Clearly, you don't know Toccata, and no, she's off-duty.'

'It's probably important enough to interrupt her break,' I persisted.

'It doesn't work that way. And besides, if she thinks you were *in any way* to blame for Logan's death, well, I don't much care for your chances.'

'C'mon,' I said, having always thought the stories about Toccata were overblown, as was almost everything in the Winter, 'she can't be *that* volatile.'

'She punched me in the eye so hard she detached my retina,' he said, 'and all I did was place the preposition at the end of the sentence.'

'That's grounds for an investigation, certainly a reprimand, maybe even charges,' I said, 'against Toccata,' I added, in case he misunderstood me. But Fodder shook his head.

'You don't understand. She's harsh, but she'll back up her team one hundred per cent. Besides, I'd already been warned three times.'

'He had, you know,' said Laura. 'She's very big on spelling, too. Often holds a surprise bee to try and catch us out. I got "Algonquin" wrong and she wouldn't speak to me for two weeks.'

'What did you want to know about anyway?' asked Fodder.

'Viral dreams. Something about a blue Buick.'

Fodder stared at me for a moment.

'Jonesy and I investigated this a couple of weeks back,' he said, 'but decided on no further action. There was this woman named

Suzy Watson. Pleasant girl. Single, late twenties. She slept during the late Summer like Moody and Roscoe and awoke two weeks ago. Only this time she was different. Withdrawn, and haunted by a … haunted by a …'

'…headless horseman?'

'No.'

'Nightmaiden, Gronk, bondsmen, what?'

'A dream,' said Fodder.

'Oh.'

I'd never given dreams much consideration before, not having had one since I went on Juvenox aged eight. What was there to know, beyond that which was obvious? An anachronistic and outmoded pursuit that signified little and did nothing except sap one's carefully accrued weight during hibernation.

'She wasn't on Morphenox?' I asked.

'No; they're all Beta Ceiling payscale in Railway Infrastructure Support – they don't qualify.'

'I didn't know that.'

'It's contentious,' said Fodder. 'Anyway, she wakes up feeling off-kilter, complaining about this dream, and then instead of improving, she gets *worse*. She has the dream again, night after night, and before long it takes her over. She becomes withdrawn and suspicious, then starts to have waking hallucinations. Pretty soon it's all she talks about and eventually, she goes into Mrs Nesbit's and attacks random customers with a machete. She kills one guy and hospitalises two more. Someone calls us as it's a sleep-related incident, and Toccata tells her to drop the machete. She doesn't, so she thumps her.'

'Dead?'

'When Consul Toccata thumps, she thumps to kill.'

'Is it true she eats nightwalkers just for fun?' I asked.

'It's rumoured,' said Laura, 'and that she garnishes them with mint jelly to make them more appetising.'

'After Suzy Watson, there was Roscoe Smalls,' continued Fodder, 'who babbled on about blue Buicks and boulders and Mrs Nesbit – then took the Cold Way Out. We found him huddled under the statue of Gwendolyn VII[37] outside the museum, frozen solid. He's still there. Then Moody got it. He had it worst of all.'

'Hooke whacked him dead just now,' I said. 'He was yelling about Mrs Nesbit and blue Buicks. What did all that mean?'

'Not sure,' said Fodder, 'but to us it looked like a mixed bag of Sleepstate Paranoia, Hibernational Narcosis and Waking Night Terrors – probably fed by an escalating conversational feedback loop.'

'Panicky Sub-betas are nothing new,' said Laura. 'One Winter it's about heating, the next it's about vermin, then dreams, then spiders, then someone thinks they've heard a nightmaiden or that the Gronk's after them. That's the problem with natural sleepers. They spook real easy, and once one of them has seen or heard something weird, they all have to. But common sense prevails: you can't catch dreams.'

I'd studied this phenomenon in the Academy. Panic could spread during the Winter like wildfire, especially amongst the Sub-beta payscalers, who were notorious chatterers. Feedback loops, echo chambers, circular reinforcement. All could play a part in escalating the utterly imaginary to the level of reality, sometimes with fatal consequences.

'They all had a dream of such fearsome reality that it flooded from their subconscious and invaded their waking hours,' said Fodder. 'The dream grew, it took them over. *It devoured them.*'

'I'm not being impudent or anything, but why was this deemed worthy of "no further action"?'

'Yes, agreed, weird,' said Fodder, taking no offence at my questioning, 'but it wasn't unprecedented. In fact, when it comes to weird stuff, viral dreams hardly make the Sector Twelve top ten.'

'Where's Toccata on the list?'

'Five or six. Shrimp, will you run Deputy Worthing off a copy of the report?'

Laura nodded and trotted off, a bounce in her step.

'Thanks for telling me all that,' I said, conscious that Consulates

---

37. Despite the universal adoption of surnames, the Welsh royal family still use the matronymic system. The Crown Princess is always Gwendolyn, which makes naming every ruler since 1183 really easy.

were under no obligation to share information. 'Did Toccata think there was anything in viral dreams?'

'She said she thought they were narcosis-induced night terrors, as did we.'

'So why do you think Toccata contacted Logan about it?'

Fodder shrugged.

'You'd have to ask her – which I don't recommend. She might have wanted to intrigue Logan to get him out here, or just to piss off Aurora. The pair of them have a complicated relationship. Do you like marshmallows?'

'Yes.'

'Here,' he said, and offered me one from a bag.

Laura returned with the report, which wasn't large, and marked, as Fodder had said, 'No Further Action'. It wouldn't be much of an epitaph for Moody, I thought.

I thanked them both and was buzzed out of the shock-gates to make my way back to the railway station. It had started to snow once more, but lazily – large flakes spinning slowly down out of the darkness.

The thawed and refrozen area where Moody had met his end was now covered by a light smattering of snow, and already someone had partially mended the crack on the window of Mrs Nesbit's with some silicon filler. I hurried on past, my time in Sector Twelve mercifully almost at an end. The Winter was wilder than I'd thought, and everything I had learned from the Consuls in Cardiff and the Academy had been pretty much overturned. There were the rules we were taught, and there were the rules we did our job by. The two were related, but as distant cousins rather than siblings. I needed to be back as a Novice, in Cardiff, doing laundry and photocopying. Away from HiberTech, RealSleep, Sector Twelve, Aurora, night-terrors and dreamers.

But that wasn't going to happen. There was another shock in store when I reached the station. The platform was empty. The Cardiff train had gone.

Marooned

'... The Campaign for Real Sleep or "RealSleep" were a bunch of dangerous disruptionists, hell bent on upsetting the delicate balance of the nation's hibernatory habits – or an unjustly-banned hibernatory rights group. It depends on your point of view. Not that it mattered. Support of a financial, material or spiritual nature was punishable by life imprisonment ...'

– *To Die, Perchance to Sleep? – the Rise and Fall of RealSleep,*
by Sophie Trotter

I tried to dispel my panic with denial.

'The Merthyr train,' I said to the stationmaster when I found her in a tiny office that smelled of coal-smoke, old socks and baking, 'just gone for coal and water or something, yes?'

She looked at me, then at an oversized pocket watch she carried in her undersized pocket.

'I let it go fifteen minutes early,' she said in a curt manner. 'They were in a hurry to get back through the Torpantu.'

'You said I had two hours.'

'I misspoke. But you can always take the next train. It's at Springrise plus two, 11.31, all stops to Merthyr, light refreshments available, off peak, Super Saver not valid – but no bicycles.'

'I can't wait sixteen weeks. I need to be back home *now*.'

'Perhaps you should have thought of that before you delayed the train in Cardiff. There's a moral in this story, my friend. Piss around with our timetables, and we'll piss around with yours. Enjoy your stay in the Douzey. You'll like it here. No wait, hang on, my mistake – you won't. If luckless circumstance, Villains, Toccata, cold or Wintervolk don't get you, the poor food almost certainly will.'

And she smiled.

I couldn't think of anything to say, so instead told her where to go and what to do with herself when she got there – a futile comment and she and I both knew it – then walked outside the station and stood in the gently falling snow, clenching and unclenching my fists as I tried to make sense of what had just happened. I wanted to find something to kick, but there was little around that wouldn't have been hard and unyielding and ultimately painful, so I just stood there, seething quietly, the snow gathering silently on the shoulders of my greatcoat, like great big crystallised tears.

I stood in a marinade of my own self-pity for ten minutes or so until the chill made me shiver, and more practical matters took precedence: survival. I moved to the top of the station footbridge to get a better sense of the local geography. The town was not located specifically around the town square as I had first supposed, but strung out in a line that began at HiberTech on the hill behind me, then stretched along a main road that headed off to the north-west, where forty or so Dormitoria rose in ranks on the opposite slope of the shallow valley, two or three miles distant. The only lights showing were the lanterns over the porters' lodges, and the gas lamps that illuminated the connecting roadway. There was almost no sound, and it already felt like midwinter, even though it was still officially Autumn for another twenty-nine hours.

'Worthing?' came a voice below me. 'What the hell are you still doing here?'

Below me was Aurora. She was alone, and buttoned up against the cold. It was, I confess, a relief to see her.

'They let the train go early,' I said.

'Why?'

'I'll come down.'

I walked down from the footbridge to where she was waiting for me.

'I'd upset the stationmaster when I delayed the train in Cardiff,' I explained. 'Sort of payback.'

'That's annoying,' she said, 'but not unexpected. What are you going to do?'

'I don't know. I was going to go back to the Consulate and see if they could get me out.'

'Probably not the wisest of moves, especially as you'll have to justify your actions to Toccata at some point. I know it was me that pulled the trigger, but you got into this situation because you insisted on retrieving Bouzouki Girl. While a brave act, it could be seen as reckless, and, well, you *did* disobey orders and a Chief Consul ended up dead.'

It didn't sound good when she said it like that.

'One who was involved in illegal activity.'

'I wish things were that simple,' she said, 'but when Toccata's involved, logic becomes somewhat … *mutable.*'

She stared at me for a moment.

'Look,' she said, 'this *is* kind of my fault, so I'll wangle you a Sno-Trac and you can drive yourself to Hereford; the Winter network Railplane[38] goes from there. The road is flagged all the way, so pretty easy to navigate. But don't go in the dark as Villains have been active recently – I'll find you a bed for a night. Sound okay?'

'Yes,' I said, 'sounds very okay. Thank you.'

She gave me a smile that was really very charming.

'Okay, then. Now, if you don't mind swapping anonymity for squalor, there's space in the *Sarah Siddons*, where you can crash for a couple of days in case the weather's no good tomorrow. It's a Beta Pay Ceiling Dormitorium so you'll be slumming it with natural sleepers, but it's warm and dry and vermin-free, which is more than can be said for the *Howell Harris*. They had rats in there a couple of years back, and three residents were eaten. It was kind of funny, actually, given the inflated rates they charge. What do you say?'

'What you suggest,' I said, glad that I at least had a plan of sorts – and, more importantly, shelter.

Aurora said the walk would do us good, so we started off down the road towards the gaggle of Dormitoria at the other end of town, our voices muffled, our breath showing white in the sharp air. The low rooftops of the surrounding houses were smooth-capped with snow that looked as though it had been sculpted from polystyrene

38. An overhead-gantry propeller-driven monorail that can sail above the drifts. Covers only major routes during the Winter.

foam, and a noise limit sign close by read 55 decibels,[39] a level of hush that would be unworkable in Cardiff. We only started making arrests above 62dB[40] these days, and even a momentary spike beyond 75dB[41] was hardly regarded as criminal.

'I'm really sorry about Mr Hooke being such an arse,' she said. 'He wasn't my choice, but sometimes you have to work with what you're given.'

We both turned as we heard a noise behind us. It was the drowsy I'd seen earlier in the Wincarnis, shuffling through the snow. She was swathed in large and expensive badger-furs that would have looked a lot better – and fresher – when they were on the badger.

'Good evening. Zsazsa,' said Aurora, 'have you met Deputy Worthing?'

'No,' she said, 'delighted.'

She gave me a welcoming smile instead of an embrace, then turned back to Aurora.

'Tell Mr Hooke from me that I don't do non-sleepy-fun-freebies, and if he persists on asking me to recite *Ozymandias* pro bono, I'll punch him in the eye.'

'I'll tell him,' she said.

'Good of you,' said Zsazsa, and she shuffled off into the gathering gloom, stumbled on a hidden kerbstone, swore, then moved on.

'Why does Zsazsa look so familiar?' I asked once she was out of earshot.

'She was the third Mrs Nesbit, the one between Gina Lollobrigida and Brenda Klaxon.'

She wasn't the Mrs Nesbit I knew when I was a kid, obviously, but knowing all the old Nesbits was like knowing every actor who ever played Jane Bond, especially the solitary male one, something that was quite controversial at the time.[42]

'How on earth did she end up here?' I asked.

---

39. 55db: normal speaking level.
40. 62db: restaurant conversation.
41. 75db: vacuum cleaner in front room on 'full'.
42. Who was surprisingly good, as it turned out, if a little oversensitive.

'Four ill-advised marriages and some truly appalling financial advice.'

The actress playing the folksy homespun icon of the food giant in all the TV ads was periodically regenerated to great fanfare and publicity. Former Mrs Nesbits usually went on to a career in celebrity endorsements, book deals and then either panto or politics – sometimes both – which made it all the more unusual that Zsazsa LeChat, to give her her full name, had ended up eking out a living as a drowsy in the fringe sectors.

'The fixed line will save your life in a blizzard,' said Aurora as we walked on, indicating the cable that was running through eyelets bolted to a succession of white-painted posts by the side of the road. 'All the arrows point to the main square, so if you get lost the default option is to go back there and start again.'

'Useful to know,' I said.

We passed a yard selling trailers with an ancient BP sign outside and there chanced across a man leaning against a lamp-post. He was wrapped up against the cold in a Woncho, a poncho made of heavy Welsh blanket, and was smoking a long corncob pipe that was a good three decades out of fashion, and six refills past replacement.

'Walking to the other end of town?' he asked.

Aurora said we were, and the stranger said he'd join us, as there was 'safety in numbers'.

He introduced himself as Jim Treacle, bondsman and part-time Consul. He was a youngish man with dark hair, and delicate features. He coughed twice, smiled, and then clasped my outstretched hand to pull me into the Winter embrace. He smelled of mouldy string, liquorice and ink.

'Welcome to the Douzey,' said Treacle with a weak laugh, 'where leaving is the best part of visiting, and staying is the worst part of anything.'

He coughed again, a deep, rattly death-knell of a cough. I'd heard it from winsomniacs, but never for very long.

'Have you been overwintering long, Mr Treacle?' I asked as we walked on.

'Twelve years,' he said, 'but only in this godforsaken hole for four.

I'd underwritten some bad Debts and took a bribe – it was a tiny one, actually, blown all out of proportion – and, well, it was here or prison. I chose prison, obviously, but the judge overruled me. Said prison wasn't harsh enough.'

'This is more harsh than prison?'

'The food's better, I grant you, but it's the fringe unbenefits that make this place so hideous. I've experienced almost every terror in the last four years. A run-in with Lucky Ned's gang, near-starvation, frost-bite, irate debtors, Toccata in a rage, and a massed nightwalker attack.'

'That's only frightening in a languid sort of way, you big baby,' put in Aurora. 'They don't move so fast, and if they're well fed, not dangerous at all.'

'It's the look they give you,' he said, with a shiver, 'full of vacant malevolence.'

'I heard you have a wager going with Laura,' I said.

'Yes indeed,' he replied with an unpleasant smirk, 'on the existence of the Gronk.'

'The wager is as good as won,' said Aurora. 'There is no Gronk; the Wintervolk are merely myths – stories for children and idiots.'

'I think *something* weird is going on,' I said, as I'd heard a few Gronk stories over the years. 'Six years ago on the line just south of the Torpantu, a four-man maintenance crew were taken on a moon-less night without a button or a zip being undone. No one saw hide nor hair of them again. Their underclothes, shirts, belts and fleeces were still *inside* their overalls – and folded.'

'The clothes in my bureau are folded,' said Treacle. 'It doesn't mean the Gronk lives in the utilities.'

They'd been taken, the story went, because they were *unworthy*. All four had been found guilty of physical trespass and were free-working until prison at Springrise.

'I heard,' I said, 'the Gronk *teases* the shame from you, and then, right at the moment when you realise the crushing enormity of your actions and how nothing could ever be right again, she draws out your soul. They say that when you expire your shame and guilt are expunged and the burden of your sins is removed. You go to your maker forgiven, and pure.'

'What a load of old tosh,' said Treacle.

'I concur,' said Aurora with a laugh. 'You shouldn't waste your thoughts on spooks and ghoulies, Charlie.'

I suddenly felt slightly foolish, but there was no TV at the Pool, and stories had made up a fair proportion of our entertainment.

'You must give the legend *some* credence, Mr Treacle,' I said, 'or why stop at fifty thousand for your wager? Why not a million?'

'Because any wager has to be able to be met by both sides.'

Aurora and I exchanged glances. Laura didn't look like she had anything *near* that sort of cash.

'Jim,' said Aurora, suddenly intrigued, 'what actually *was* her side of the bet?'

'Her secondborn in the fullness of womanhood.'

There was a sudden shocked silence.

'For God's sake, Jim,' said Aurora, 'she's only *sixteen*. That makes you less of a bondsman and something closer to a trafficker, doesn't it?'

'I forgive you your gross impudence,' replied Treacle in an even tone, 'but she instigated the wager. *Pleaded* with me to take it. It's all perfectly legal. You'd not bat an eyelid if she brokered her reproductive futures through Wackford's for some upfront cash.'

This was quite possibly true and we trudged on in silence, the still air illuminated by the warm orange glow of the gas lamps. We passed the Talgarth Pleasure Gardens and boating lake, the beds and borders invisible beneath the drifts. Beyond the wrought-iron gates I could see the statue of Gwendolyn VII and a fountain which had frozen solid while still running, so was now simply a misshapen chrysanthemum of ice.

'See the lump in the snow under the statue?' said Aurora. 'Roscoe Smalls. Took the Cold Way Out over that viral dream nonsense. Did you learn anything new from Fodder?'

'Not much.'

'I liked Roscoe,' said Jim Treacle, 'and Suzy too, although Moody could be, well, *moody*. Luckily, none of them were insured, so no loss to the company.'

Jim Treacle didn't just offer loans, it seemed.

Behind the statue of Gwendolyn VII and the freeze-paused fountain was a large building of dark, rain-streaked stone. The entranceway
was framed by four massive Doric columns stretching down from a
triangular tympanum, and above and behind this was a copper-
sheathed dome, dark green with verdigris. The building was dark
and silent, already locked in the icy grip of Winter.

'That's the regional museum,' said Aurora. 'It's very good. There's
Bob Beamish's running shoes, the gown Sylvia Syms wore for the
1959 Academy Awards, lots of Don Hector memorabilia, and the
remains of the first bicycle to go twice the speed of horse. Lots of
stamps, too, including the "Anglesey" 2d Lloyd-George Mauve.[43] It's
the only one in the world. You can see the funfair just beyond.'

She was right. Just visible in the gathering gloom was a helter-
skelter, a parachute drop and a roller coaster, the heavy wooden
lattice covered by a thick blanket of snow.

We moved on and immediately on our right, once past a frozen
stream, was the first of the Dormitoria. It was set back from the road
and difficult to see in any detail other than that it was circular, made
of stone and had a steeply pitched conical slate roof. It must have been
about sixteen storeys – diminutive by modern standards – and the only
sign of life was a single porter's oil lamp outside the main entrance.

'The *Geraldus Cambrensis*,' said Aurora. 'Built in 1236, it's the oldest
continuously-occupied Dormitorium in Wales. Worth a visit to the
area on its own.'

We continued up the hill.

'Do you get much mischief out here in the Winter?' I asked.

'Skirmishes with Villains are the most dramatic,' said Jim Treacle.
'Lucky Ned operates in the area but prefers quiet thievery rather
than frontal assault – there's a truce, apparently, brokered by Toccata.
They've been doing some kidnapping, but not from the Sector, as
per the terms of the truce.'

---

43. The 2d Lloyd-George was only valuable because it carries an Anglesey cancellation, one of only three so stamped during the Beaumaris Post Office's
contractual one day in 1921 and delivered three letters before being abandoned
due to ice sheet encroachment.

'For ransom or domestic service?' I asked, recalling Dai Powell's experience.

'Domestic service. Cooking and cleaning and housework and so forth. We also have pseudo-hibernatory sneak thieves,' continued Treacle, 'never less than two stowaways and Snuffling and Puffling is not unknown. There's a serial roomsneaker who's been dubbed "The Llanigon Puddler" and usually a motley collection of winsomniacs and nightwalkers, but other than that, not much.'

'It's the boredom and the weather that get to you here,' added Aurora, 'especially when the temperature plunges, the snowfalls are thicker than soup and the wind chucks up drifts the size of mammoths. Even in a Sno-Trac it can take an age to get around, and a blizzard can strand you for weeks. Been in a white-out? Scary stuff. You a brave person?'

'I don't know.'

'You'll find out soon enough.'

We walked on another hundred yards in silence.

'This is me,' said Treacle as we reached a crossroads next to a large and slightly dilapidated billboard advertising 'Ashbrook Garage – All makes of cars repaired, Land Rovers a speciality'. Treacle handed me his card. There wasn't a phone number, just the time he'd be in the Wincarnis.

'In case you need some ready cash. If you're in a jam, call Treacle. I buy indulgences, too – Favours, Debts and so forth – so repayment doesn't have to be like for like.'

I said that I'd be leaving almost straight away, but I'd bear that in mind.

He grinned and then headed towards a Dormitorium that was signposted *Howell Harris*.

'Watch out for him,' said Aurora once he was out of earshot. 'A bondsman's only motivating factor is cash. But he does take bribes, which makes him usefully compliant.'

We set off again, took a left at the advertising hoarding, walked past a petrol station, also closed and shuttered, and then took a right into what I think had once been the parkland of a stately home. We walked along a slight incline, past Summer residences, the shutters up. We were now on the other side of the valley from HiberTech, and although the facility was visible as a collection of sparkling lights, it was impossible to make out the shape in the darkness. As I was pondering this, an owl fell from the sky to the road beside us and twitched its wings feebly in the snow. Of the seven bird species on the Albion Peninsula that were hiburnal, owls weren't one of them.

We walked further into the sleep district, where around us the Dormitoria rose out of the ground like a forest of giant toadstools. Each was larger than the *Cambrensis*, but all the traditional shape: circular, minimal windows, steep conical roof.

As we moved past the sunward towers and to the cheaper north-side buildings beyond, I noticed the quality of the Dormitoria become steadily worse. Six structures were no more than rubble to the third floor and two or three were merely empty concrete circles on the ground, the capped HotPot deep below still just active enough to keep the slab above from freezing. But just as I was beginning to think that Aurora would be putting me up in something no better than a Winterstock shed, she stopped and nodded towards a large Dormitorium that had loomed out of the snow-swirled gloom in front of us.

'Welcome,' she said, 'to the *Sarah Siddons*.'

The Sarah Siddons

'... The profession of nightwatchman from which the porter had evolved was by long tradition filled by eunuchs. Although no longer mandatory, the Worshipful Guild of Nightwatchmen clung doggedly to the practice, and still enjoyed popular support: sixteen weeks pacing corridors was a job that most thought better to entrust to someone who had unequivocally committed themselves to the calling ...'

– *Handbook of Winterology*, 6th edition, Hodder & Stoughton

The *Siddons* was at least thirty storeys high and unusually broad, a sure sign of a once-desirable residence. The façade had been rendered and then scored to emulate Portland stone, with a decorative doorway that represented yawning night-satyrs and snow-nymphs. It was impressive but shabby, and not assisted by the location: light industrial units had been built on the cheaper land this far from the centre of town, and the area looked run down and depressed.

'Yes, I know,' said Aurora, 'a bit of a dump. When built, it enjoyed full sun and wasn't obscured at all, but more modern dorms have been built in front of it over the years.'

Once we'd hung up our outclothes and swapped our snow boots for slippers, I looked around. Someone had made an attempt to reinvigorate the scruffy interior, but it hadn't really worked. Mismatched carpet and threadbare modernist furniture only made the once-impressive lobby look cheap and neglected, and the numerous coats of clumsily-applied paint stole the subtlety from the plasterwork. I sniffed the air. As in the *John Edward Jones* back in Merthyr, there was the subtle yet unmistakable odour of slumber in the air – gummy sweat and the eggy whiff of hibernation mixed with semi-stale air breathed out past unbrushed teeth.

The porter was waiting to receive us. He was impeccably dressed, quite bald and wore small, gold-framed spectacles upon a face that seemed as close to a sphere as a human head is ever likely to get. I was suddenly put in mind of Bunsen Honeydew[44] from the Muppets, and chuckled. He stared at me and narrowed his eyes.

'You were just thinking of Bunsen Honeydew, weren't you?'

'No.'

He raised an eyebrow.

'Yes – okay, a bit. Sorry.'

'Deputy Worthing,' said Aurora, 'may I present Porter Lloyd?'

I must have looked surprised for he sighed and said: 'Yes, *that* Porter Lloyd. Worst thing I ever did, being Volkbait for Ichabod.'

'Because it was frightening?'

'No, the endless repetition of the story. I've had the words to "Lonely Goatherd" running around in my head for two decades, and while sometimes annoying, on the plus side it does put a jaunty step in my stride when I'm feeling down.'

Aurora yodelled the chorus and gave us both a grin.

'There's always one,' said the Porter good-humouredly, and walked around to embrace me. He smelled of lemon soap, Hoover bags and mothballs and was a head shorter than me.

'Welcome to the Douzey,' he said. 'It's not as bad as people say. I was sorry to hear about Moody. Who pulled the trigger?'

'Mr Hooke,' said Aurora, 'and in self-defence, before you ask.'

'News travels fast,' I said.

'There are seventy-six porters in the Sector,' said Lloyd as he returned to his place behind the reception desk, 'and none of us venture out in the Winter. Having a permanently open line on the telephone network helps. Pick up the receiver and just talk. There's usually someone listening, and if there isn't, there soon will be. If all else fails, you can always talk to yourself or listen to the static. To be honest, listening to static can be more relaxing than listening to many of the others – especially Mr Rubucon over at the *George Melly*. What can I help you with?'

'A place to stay for one to three days,' said Aurora, 'billed to HiberTech.'

---

44. He works in Muppet Labs, if it's slipped your mind. His assistant is Beaker.

'You've come to the right place,' said Lloyd happily. 'We've only had nine illegal bedroom incursions since 1990: three snaffles, one Dormicide and five incidents of Trespass – three visual, one tactile and an unspeakable. We're not proud of that, obviously, but it's the lowest rate of hiburnal outrage in the Sector. You'll also be pleased to know that no resident has been eaten in their sleep here for almost thirty-seven years.'

The lights flickered for a moment, went out, then came back on again.

'Hydro Twelve has been on the fritz recently,' said Lloyd by way of explanation. 'What sort of room had you in mind? Cell, Basic, Featured, Deluxe or Super-Deluxe?'

'Do you dream?' asked Aurora quite suddenly, while fixing me with a quizzical expression. It wasn't usually the sort of question you asked, but she was the head of HiberTech Security.

'Not since I was eight.'

She looked at me for a moment.

'Suzy Watson was recently gathered into the night,' said Aurora, 'why not hers? The positive energy of a young sleeper will drive the bad dreaming from the room.'

'O-kay,' said the porter.

'Why did you ask if I'd dreamed?'

'No reason. Worthing here will also need to hire your Sno-Trac,' she said to Lloyd. 'We'll get it back to you as soon as we can. And this next bit's delicate: we're hoping to keep Worthing's presence as something not to be broadcast any wider than between ourselves. Worthing here was partially to blame for Jack Logan's death and you know what Toccata's like.'

'Well,' I said, 'I wasn't *really*—'

'I heard about Logan on the Open Network, too,' interrupted Lloyd, 'a great loss. Might be wiser keeping quiet. Do you need anything else?'

I thought for a moment.

'I'd like to fax my office back in Cardiff, tell them I'm delayed.'

'Leave that to me,' said Aurora. 'I'll say you'll be back in three days, five at the outset. I have to report about Jack Logan anyway –

and absolve you of any wrongdoing. Least I can do. Get a good night's sleep – the first few days in the Winter can be tough.'

I thanked her and she wished me well, gave us both a cheery wave, and was gone.

Once the front door had clicked shut, Lloyd had me sign for the Sno-Trac keys.

'It's in the basement,' he said. 'Do you want to take it now?'

'Aurora didn't think travelling at night wise,' I said.

'True,' said Lloyd, suddenly looking a little uncomfortable, 'but, well, things in Sector Twelve have a way of getting complicated very quickly. You might think the risk of a night journey less than a stay in Sector Twelve.'

'You think I should get out?'

He looked to left and right and lowered his voice.

'Entirely a matter for you.'

I considered it seriously, until I looked outside. The wind was getting up and visibility, while not yet zero, could make driving very tricky – and I had no desire to be stuck in a Sno-Trac somewhere between nowhere and nowhere.

'I'll see how it looks in the morning.'

'Very well.'

Lloyd picked my room key off the board and we walked towards the lift. As we crossed the semi-circular lobby under the watchful eye of the ever-present portraits of Gwendolyn XXXVIII and Don Hector, I peered into the dark, wood-panelled Winterlounge, and could see a half-dozen individuals scattered around either reading, playing board games or talking quietly. All of them boasted the beautifully corpulent curves of healthy Autumn weight, and were languid in movement and manner.

'That's a lot of yawners,'[45] I said to Lloyd. 'What's keeping them up?'

'This viral dream stuff has spooked the residents, and none of them want to go to sleep in case they dream the Buick dream and then go the way of Watson, Smalls and Moody. Mind you, this bunch are fighting a losing battle anyway.'

---

45. Someone 'on the cusp of heading off down into the Hib'.

As if to punctuate his statement, the most healthily bloated of the sleep-ready residents yawned. When you get to that size and the ambient cools to fifteen degrees Celsius or below, it takes a Herculean[46] effort to stave off the slumber.

The paternoster lift started up as soon as we stepped in and slowly hauled us upwards with a gurgling of water from the auto-ballast. There were no doors on the elevator and the view of the corridors as we drifted upwards was dull, but uniform. Offerings to Morpheus were at the foot of most doors, along with fair dreaming candles freshly lit. There were a lot of them, too – the corridors were alive with hundreds of little lights, flickering in the faint breeze that occasionally wafted through the building.

There was nothing like this in the *Melody Black* back in Cardiff, but that was Alpha payscale and Morphenox – without pharmaceutical means to mitigate the fat-burning ferocity of the Dreamstate, the residents of the *Siddons* had retained their superstitious beliefs. Those of us on Morphenox no longer needed a deity to enter our dreams and watch over us, for the drug had rendered the god redundant. Veneration had moved from the spiritual to the pharmaceutical – and if what Lucy had suggested was true, all of this might be gone by next Winter.

'Tell me,' I said as Lloyd and I passed the third floor at a speed that was probably only marginally faster than taking the stairs, 'do the yawners in the Winterlounge *really* think they're going to catch the viral dream?'

'They do – and I kind of agree with them.'

'Why?'

'Because I've dreamt scraps of the dream too. Hands, an oak tree, scratched boulders, the blue Buick. But this is what's weird: when I compared my dream with Moody and Smalls, there were *other* similarities, details we'd never discussed that were the same. *Something* is going on.'

'Why didn't you go nuts the way of Moody, Roscoe and Suzy?' I asked. 'Any ideas?'

46. As in the sixth labour of Hercules: 'Remain awake as the Winter takes your comrades under its wing'.

'No idea at all. But as I say, I only got scraps. I have this feeling that I dream more than I remember, and that I never left the rocks. If you do dream, you'd be advised to do the same.'

'But I don't dream.'

'I know that, but if you do. This is our floor.'

We stepped off the lift, which carried on for a couple of seconds before the delicate balance system sensed it was no longer under load, and stopped.

'Okay, then,' he said, clapping his hands together, 'in an emergency I'm in 801, below you, one floor down. Oh, and since HiberTech are footing the bill, will you make good use of room service?'

I said I would. He wished me goodnight and stepped onto the 'down' side of the paternoster, which gurgled for a moment, then sank with him out of sight.

Room 901 was halfway around the corridor on the southern side of the building, opposite the stairs. Pictures of a young woman had been laid at the bottom of the door along with condolence cards. I'd taken over a dead person's room or bed or even shoes or best friend before – we all have – but this time it felt odd, and I shivered.

Room 901

'… The *Sarah Siddons* was thirty-three storeys high, eighty yards overall diameter, floor to ceiling three yards, eight rooms to a floor. The central hollow core where the rising heat would be ducted was exactly five yards wide, including stairs. Built in 1906, it is very typical of many Dormitoria of the period …'

– *The Dormitoria of Mid-Wales*, Strand Publishing

I pushed the door open against a small pile of mail. Most were *cartes de bon hiber* from people who did not yet know Suzy Watson was dead, and the rest were bills and fliers. I placed them on a chair, then looked around. The room was of the standard 'pizza slice' layout, and while the fittings and fixtures, carpets and wallpaper were not *exactly* ancient, they were certainly past their best. I went into the kitchen area. The fridge was empty except for some milk that had gone beyond yoghurt and was now entering a state unknown to science, and a few shrivelled somethings that defied easy identification. There was a picture of Don Hector on the wall and next to the television was a phonograph with a large collection of cylinders. I looked through them. They were a mixture of old favourites – *Dark Side of the Moon*, *Rumours*, *Ziggy Stardust* – mixed with jazz and a little Puccini.

The apartment would have been utterly unremarkable, in fact, but for one thing: dominating the bedroom wall was a painting of Clytemnestra, depicting her just after she had murdered her husband. The portrait was spectacular not only by virtue of subject, but also for its *size*, occupying the wall from floor to ceiling and in a large ornate gilt frame that had been trimmed at the bottom to allow it to fit. Clytemnestra was topless and wore a curious half-smile upon her features, her chin raised with a sense of good-natured sociopathy.

History does not relate exactly *when* during the Winter Clytemnestra had murdered Agamemnon, and it was a subject of much conjecture. If committed at Springrise it might have been an impulsive act; dismissed as *mal à le dormir*, the fog of sleep. The more generous artistic renditions had her looking skinny and confused. In contrast, this painting had her depicted with the easy confidence of life-affirming weightiness. The artist was here suggesting it was an act of premeditation; that she had stayed up, murdered Agamemnon soon after he'd slipped under, then descended into the Hib with her slowly decaying husband by her side. It changed the interpretation of her character, and her motivations – little wonder there was much academic debate.

'Who's the topless bunny with the blade?'

I jumped with fright and spun round.

Standing in the middle of the room was a woman wearing paint-streaked dungarees and a large and very baggy man's shirt. Her raven-black hair was knotted high in an untidy bun that was secured with a pencil, and she was drying some paintbrushes with a rag. She was looking, not at me, but at the painting of Clytemnestra.

'I've got a better question,' I said. 'What are you doing in my apartment?'

She turned to look at me and I was suddenly struck by her dark and brooding good looks. She had piercing violet eyes, a faintly Ottoman appearance and high, expressive eyebrows. She was about ten years older than me, and was, without any question, an extraordinary-looking woman. But her appeal was more than simple beauty; there was a bearing, a spirit, a *strength*.

'The door was open and I was intrigued,' she said, 'and anyway, it's not your apartment,' she said. 'It's Suzy's.'

'Oh, yes,' I said somewhat awkwardly, 'right.'

It was not a winning response, but I was transfixed not just by her looks, but by her *manner*, a heady mix of allure and confidence. I knew then that I would never see a more striking individual as long as I lived.

'Still awake?' I asked.

'I like to stay up,' she said. 'I live four doors down. Never came in here, though. So: who's the bunny?'

'It's Clytemnestra,' I said, walking closer.

'Ah,' she said, suddenly understanding, 'the premeditated viewpoint.'

We both stared at the painting for a moment.

'And,' I added, trying to sound intelligent, 'a cautionary lesson in co-hibernating.'

'We never hibernated together, my husband and I,' she replied absently, 'not after watching Zeffirelli's *Winter Crossed Lovers*.'

She was referring to the scene where Romeo wakes to find Juliet next to him, expecting his bride but instead finding little but taut skin stretched across her bones, and the dark stain of putrefaction upon the bedsheets. I saw the film when I was nine, and that image never leaves you. Years later, Baz Luhrmann played the scene entirely on DiCaprio's face. He didn't need to show us Juliet's remains; Zeffirelli had already planted the horror in our minds.

'Did it work out for her?' asked the dark-haired woman. 'Clytemnestra murdering her husband, I mean?'

'She and her lover got to rule Mycenae for seven years.'

She nodded approvingly, still staring at the painting, but I was more interested in her. The nape of her neck, her unpierced ears, and her jet-black hair that seemed to have a soft luxuriance about it. She turned and caught me looking at her, so I looked away, then realised that was too obvious so looked back – and felt myself fall into her gaze, as one might fall into the charms of an exceptional painting.

'You're a Winter Consul,' she announced.

'Does it show?'

'You wear it heavily, like a cloak. Are you sure it's what you want to be?'

'I'm ... not sure.'

'I always think it's best to be sure of at least one thing in life.'

'And what are you sure of?' I asked, trying to maintain a credible conversation.

'That I'm no longer sure of *anything*,' she replied, with a sudden air of melancholy. She tipped her head on one side, paused for thought, then offered to paint my portrait for five hundred euros, unframed. I had neither the time nor the funds to be painted, but very much liked the idea of more time in her company, especially if it involved her staring at me intently, for whatever reason.

'You could find a better subject,' I murmured, indicating my face. I'd come to terms with my looks soon after biting off Gary Findlay's ear. All the frustration I'd ever had was discharged in that one violent event. Gary lost an ear, but I gained clarity and became the curator of my own appearance.

'Are you Pool or kinborne?' she asked.

'Pool.'

'My husband was Pool.'

And then, quite unexpectedly, she placed a soft hand on the twisted side of my head. The only person to have touched me there was Sister Zygotia and Lucy, once, when she was drunk. My eye twitched and I felt a shiver of fear run up the side of my body. She had no right to be so forward, but the intimacy, even without affection, was curiously thrilling in a way that was difficult to explain. But I was deluding myself: she was older, Alpha, and completely outside and above the profile of a potential partner. I was being unutterably foolish, and put the thoughts to the back of my head.

'I might find a better subject, yes,' she said, gently pushing my head into profile with an index finger on the tip of my nose, 'but not one of such ... *inspiring intrigue.*'

It was the finest compliment my appearance had ever received,[47] and I blinked rapidly to hide the dampness that had risen to my eyes.

'Then I accept.'

'Come on, then.'

I caught a whiff of her scent as she turned on a heel and walked past me, a delicate mix of oil paints, fresh laundry and musk. We walked around the circular inner corridor to the room on the opposite side of the building and she beckoned me inside. Every inch of wall space was covered with canvases and anything not hung was stacked against the walls.

There was one painting that dominated: an impressionistic rendering of Rhosilli beach on the Gower Peninsula, fully six

47. It still is.

foot wide and three foot high. In the background was the beached wreck of the liner the *Argentinian Queen*, rusting away to inevitable collapse, the blue paint just visible beneath the encroaching rust. There were wispy mare's tails in the sky, the headland merely a jagged profile in the distant haze. In the foreground, on the large and otherwise empty beach, was an orange-and-red parasol of spectacular size and splendour. Hidden beneath it were two bathers, partially obscured and sitting on a blue-and-white striped towel.

It was a remarkable painting, and I told her so.

'It's tolerable,' she said with little emotion. 'I call it: *There will always be the Gower.*'

'I visited many times,' I said, mesmerised by the painting, 'when the wreck was about this intact.'

'Collapsed into the sea now,' she said, 'the inevitable action of wind and tide. Did you ever stop off at Mumbles Pier for cockles, bacon and laver bread on toast?'

'How could one not?'

There was a paint-spattered easel set up in the middle of the room, on which sat an unfinished portrait of a male nude facing the viewer. There was something special about the picture – a certain raw and very seasonal energy in a taut, well-filled physique. It wasn't a coy rendering of a nude, either – every detail of his body had been meticulously represented. Every hair, every muscle. There was no part of him she hadn't found worthy of meticulous attention – *except his face.* There were no features at all. The painting was all physicality, and no identity, except the shape of the jaw. It looked somehow familiar, as though I'd seen it before, and recently.

'Friend of yours?' I asked.

'He was my husband.'

'You'll paint his face in last?'

'The portrait's finished,' she replied. 'He vanished one evening just before beginning an overwinter.'

'What happened to him?' I asked, and she flashed me an angry look.

I was, I admit, surprised by her reaction. People vanish all the time so it's not considered an inappropriate subject. They found Billy DeFroid's remains scattered across a car park come the thaw, and Sister Placentia was happy to tell anyone who asked – even down to which bits they never found.

'I have my suspicions,' she said, suddenly calming down, 'and although I don't *know* he's dead, it's been too long to assume anything other than the worst.'

She paused for thought and stared at the painting again.

'Although his features begin to fade in my memory, his body I'll remember always. The way it felt under my fingertips, the weight of it upon mine. He vanished the Spring before we were planning for a family. I'd bulked up especially for the confinement.'

'O-kay,' I said, embarrassed by her candour, 'I'm sorry for your losses.'

She stared at the painting thoughtfully.

'He liked the snow but not the Winter,' she said in a quiet voice, 'valued the climb greater than the view from the summit. He didn't smile much, but when he did, the world smiled with him, and we bundled as though it were the first time, and would be the last.'

'I've never known someone like that,' I said. 'All my friends are just, well, *ordinary*.'

'Don't underestimate mediocrity,' she said. 'Lasting happiness, I've found, only really favours the unadventurous. Take a seat.'

She directed me towards a high-back chair and picked up a Polaroid camera. She pulled it open, put a new flashbulb in the holder, cocked the shutter and pointed it at me, then focused.

'Look down,' she said, half hidden behind the camera, 'just your eyes.'

I did as she asked.

'Have you ever bundled?'

'Yes.'

'On your own doesn't count.'

'Then no.'

'Imagine it now,' she said, 'with that special one. Not the one in your mind, but the one in your heart. The one to whom your physical thoughts turn when you can feel the heat rising in your body, the yearning for intimacy. And when those thoughts have filled your mind, look up.'

I thought about pretty much everyone I'd ever fancied over the years but rejected them all, then found myself thinking about the painter, there in front of me with her dark hair, dark manner and dark strangeness. I thought of her and me closely entwined in a tight knot of passion, and looked up.

The flash went off, then there was a crinkly noise as the spent flashbulb cooled. She flicked the release, pulled out the paper tab, tore it off and discarded it, then looked at her watch.

'I'll be gone from the Sector in a couple of days,' I said, handing her my card. 'You can reach me here.'

She took the card, waited another ten seconds then opened the door on the back of the Polaroid and peeled the print from the negative. She looked at it, nodded approval then set the picture upon her work desk to dry.

'Have you rights to Morphenox?' she asked.

'Yes.'

'But you won't need it, what with staying up?'

'No, I guess not.'

'I've been neglecting my bulking up this season,' she confessed, 'and need something to see me through the Hib. Give me your dose and I'll knock two hundred euros off the painting.'

Now I came to think of it, she was looking a little light. Transferring my Morphenox to her was illegal, of course, but I *did* have a dosage on me and, wanting to do what I could to maximise her chances of survival, I agreed.

'Only on condition you don't pay me. No money off the painting – nothing. I'll be in enough trouble as it is if I'm rumbled.'

She understood the reasoning, thanked me, then moved to one of her larger canvases, which depicted Gwendolyn IX on horseback, leading the troops. She never did such a thing in reality, but over-dramatic portraits of the great woman were bread-and-butter for the jobbing artist – that, *memento mori*, still–lifes of flowers in a jar[48] and prize cow-mammoths. She picked up a palette, dabbed her brush in some paint and then moved it absently around on the canvas. It was like I suddenly wasn't there.

'Well, okay,' I said, 'I'll be off, then.'

She said nothing and I moved away, but she spoke again when I reached the door.

'The wise money says not to leave the rocks.'

'What rocks?'

'The ones under the oak,' she said without looking up, 'near the blue Buick.'

'You've had the dream?'

'I've had scraps.'

'I'll be fine,' I said, 'I don't have dreams.'

'Everyone needs dreams,' she said simply. 'If you don't have them, they can't come true.'

I wanted to ask her more but she'd returned to her painting and begun to hum. The conversation was over, and I returned to my room.

With the fatigue now almost overpowering, I elected to turn in. I fully wound the phonograph, selected an ultra-long play of the *Preludio Sinfonica*, slipped it on the player and pressed *Start & Repeat*. This done, I placed my Bambi under the pillow, undressed, climbed into bed and pulled up the blankets to stare at the ceiling, hands behind my head, the calming strains of music wafting in from the next room.

The situation was not what I had intended. I was in a strange town in a fringe sector, about to hit the sack in the apartment of a woman who had suffered a fatal attack of Hibernational Narcosis mixed with night terrors. I'd lost my mentor and a much-respected Consul to boot, partly as a result of my own intransigence. Mind you, if Logan hadn't paused when the lift doors had opened, then Aurora would be dead instead of him – but then probably me as well.

Conscious that I should only be night–napping and not tumbling

---

48. Always a firm favourite, no idea why.

down the slope to deep hibernation, I set my Taser-clock[49] for an early rise the following morning and attached the electrode to my earlobe, then switched off the light. In the faint gloom I could just make out the shape of Clytemnestra: happy that she'd just murdered her husband. I thought of the artist, and what she asked me to think of when she took the picture, then my thoughts jumbled as grateful slumber bore down upon me. Thoughts of Aurora, the dead woman with the bouzouki, the Hugo Foulnap-who-wasn't, Porter Lloyd, Jack Logan and finally Moody telling me that I would visit the blue Buick, and to not leave the rocks.

But I knew it would all be okay. I wasn't going to dream.

But I did, of course.

49. It was a travelling version named the 'LazeeTazee'. I'd brought it for the train journey, just in case.

Trip to the Gower

'... Among Early Risers, the wake failure rate hovered around thirty per cent, even amongst those who had been doing it for decades. About a third would simply pull off the Taser, roll over, grunt, and not stir until their contingency was burned away and hunger brought them floundering back to the surface. Early rising wasn't for the weak-hearted ...'

    – *Winter Physiology for the Consul Service*, by Dr Rosie Patella

Flashes of light, incoherence, a shout, then darkness. But an *unusual* form of darkness. Not darkness as in nothing being there, or hibernatory darkness, thick, unyielding and timeless, but darkness as a heavy velvet curtain. I could hear and smell what was behind the curtain, but it had not yet lifted. There were whisperings of words unrecognised, then the rustle of trees and the sweet scent of a childhood Summer: freshly-turned hay, hot mud while dibbling with a stick in drying puddles, harvest, meadows.

Then, the darkness turned ... *glossy*. A cascade of disjointed images. Jack Logan embedded in the wall, partially plastered over. Moody, Mrs Tiffen, the Siddons and Porter Lloyd humming 'The Lonely Goatherd'. And then, with a sudden short blast of static, I was sitting on Rhosilli beach beneath the shade of an orange-and-red parasol of spectacular size and splendour. Dominating the view was the wreck of the *Argentinian Queen*, the passenger liner now rusted and half-collapsed with gaping holes in her hull, nibbled by decades of surf.

I looked around and saw that I was not alone: sitting on the beach towel next to me was the artist I'd seen back in the *Siddons*. She was wearing a perfectly-fitting one-piece swimsuit the colour of Spring-fresh leaves and her large and inquisitive eyes were staring intently into mine, her jet-black hair moving in a breeze that carried with it the scent-memories of Summer holidays: sun lotion, ice cream and drying seaweed. Her name I now knew was Birgitta, and she gave me a captivating smile, then pushed some loose hair behind her ear. I could sense the intoxicating feeling of indivisible oneness, something that I had yet to feel in life – to know someone loves you, and to know you love them back equally; that you belong only with each other; that you *are* each other.

'I love you, Charlie.'

'I love you, Birgitta.'

The breakers boomed and a little girl chased a beach ball towards shore's edge with a gurgle of laughter.

And then, I knew: for the first time since childhood, I was *dreaming*. I'd remembered them as being vague and hazy, but this dream felt more real than reality itself – I could feel the gritty texture in the sand, see the foam flecking on the waves, smell the salt in the sea air.

I looked down and noticed that I too was dressed for the beach; a one-piece swimsuit in black with contrasting white pumps. They weren't my shoes, they weren't my feet. It wasn't even my body. Different, taut and excitingly different. It felt like Birgitta's missing husband's body.

I corrected myself. I wasn't *like* Birgitta's missing husband. I *was* Birgitta's missing husband. In love with her, and loved by her. Together, as one.

'Is this really me?' I asked, somewhat stupidly.

Birgitta blinked at me with a look of mild amusement.

'You're Charlie now, *my* Charlie,' she said with a giggle. 'Try not to think about the facility and HiberTech Security. Just today and tomorrow, forty-eight hours. You and me. What Dreams May Come.'

'What Dreams May Come,' I replied, looking around. 'Where is this place?'

She laughed again. She didn't need to tell me; I already knew. We were on the Gower Peninsula. I'd been there many times as a child; the view of Worm's Head and the rusting passenger liner was stuck to the inside of my head like glue.

She looked at me again and smiled.

'No matter what, there will always be the Gower.'

We both laughed at the comment, which was cheesy and utterly true, all in one.

'I love you, Charlie.'

'I love you, Birgitta.'

The waves boomed and the seagulls cackled, a beach ball bounced past and the same child with the same gurgle of laughter chased after it. I knew then *exactly* where and when I was. I had found the high point in Birgitta and Charles' relationship, the precise moment when everything was beautiful and wonderful and pristine and *right*, before the shadows drew on and the Winter closed in. The holidays I'd spent there had been high points for me, too, small oases of joy in an otherwise dismal, Pool-trapped existence.

'Happy snap?' said a photographer holding a Polaroid. 'Proper tidy you'll look and as reasonably priced as—'

— I was suddenly awake, drenched in sweat, my heart thumping so rapidly in my chest that I felt it might burst. I sat up and flicked the light switch but there was nothing; the only glow was from the emergency lights, which had automatically switched on. Hydro Twelve, recently on the fritz, looked as though it had failed.

Something in the room struck me as odd and out of place, but it took me a moment or two to figure out what it was: *Clytemnestra was missing*. I froze, not wanting to make a single noise, lest she knew where I was. The ornate frame was still there, the background still there – painted curtains, painted marble steps, even the drops of painted blood on the painted floor. But of Queen Clytemnestra, there was nothing. It looked as though she had simply stepped out of the frame.

I pulled my Bambi from under the pillow, then the flashlight from the bedside table, and padded softly to the living room, which was also empty. I checked the bathroom then anywhere narrow where she might have concealed herself, such as behind the wardrobe or under the kitchen units, but without any success. I went to the door, which was still locked, and for a brief moment was confused, until I noticed there was a slender gap under the door, and I figured she'd probably got out that way.

I opened the door to a corridor still illuminated by the flickering fair dreaming candles, but this too was empty, so I trod noiselessly to the stairway that spiralled up the heat-well in the centre of the building, then stopped as I heard the soft tread of shoes against the stone. I tried to remember if Clytemnestra had been wearing sandals but could not, so waited until the footsteps were opposite my floor, and then stepped out, flashlight in hand.

It was Charles, as Birgitta had painted him. Completely naked but with no features. Oddly, he was carrying a mug of hot chocolate. He jumped, and spilt some on the steps.

'Why are you out of your painting?' I asked.

'Out of my what?' asked Charles, which was impossible because he had no mouth. But then I realised it wasn't Charles at all but Porter Lloyd and with all the features traditionally associated with a face. He wasn't naked, either. I lowered the Bambi.

'Sorry,' I said, 'I thought you were a thin layer of oil paint.'

'A thin layer of *what*? Actually, it doesn't matter. Can I help you?'

'I was looking for Clytemnestra. Sort of queenly, tall, topless, fine wintercoat – oh, and carrying a bloody dagger.'

Lloyd smiled.

'No, I haven't seen her about.'

'You're sure?'

'I *think* I would have remembered that.'

'She might be difficult to see,' I persisted, 'because if you viewed her edge on, she'd only be the thickness of a sheet of paper and wouldn't be that obvious.'

'I see,' said Lloyd, with a look of understanding – and about time too, to be honest. 'Now don't take this the wrong way,' he said, 'but you may have a touch of narcosis.'

This was ridiculous, and I told him so.

'Hear me out,' he said. 'Historical topless figures don't peel themselves out of paintings, and you wandering naked about the *Siddons* in the small hours doesn't seem very sensible, wouldn't you agree?'

'I'm not naked,' I said, shivering.

'If you're not naked,' he said slowly, 'then how is it that I can see your doo-dads and your hoo-hah?'

'You can't.'

'They're as clear as the nose on my face.'

'That's a *terrible* use of an idiom.'

'Agreed – but take a look for yourself.'

I looked down, and now that he mentioned it, I *was* naked – except for a single sock, one of Suzy's, maroon in colour. I shivered again as the lights flickered back on, power returning, and the reality of the situation began to dawn.

'Sod it,' I said, 'I'm narced, aren't I?'

Lloyd nodded kindly. Hearing about narcosis is one thing, experiencing it quite another. Lloyd took my hand and led me back upstairs to my room, the full stupidity of my actions now becoming abundantly clear. Clytemnestra was exactly where she'd been all along, happily ensconced in the gilt frame, her immovable expression of murderous intent unchanged. My clothes, which I could have sworn I'd put on, were lying where I'd left them on the back of the chair.

'I think I was dreaming,' I said with a sigh.

'Of blue Buicks and oak trees and hands and stuff?'

'Actually, no.'

'Then probably part of the narcosis. Have this hot chocolate; I'll make another for myself.'

I told him I would be fine, but he insisted because I hadn't yet put anything on room service. I agreed, and he wished me goodnight and departed.

Once I'd drunk the hot chocolate I settled back into bed, feeling unutterably foolish. Narcosis is something that you think will never happen to you, but when it does, it's kind of scary – but only after the event. When it's happening, it's the best reality in town, with the possible exception of the dream in the Gower with Birgitta. I wanted to get back there if possible, so lay back, closed my eyes again and was soon fast asleep.

Dream, wake, repeat

'... The provenance of the Louvre Mona Lisa was finally established in the Spring of 1983, when margin notes written contemporaneously by Agostino Vespucci declared that "a fine painting of Lisa del Giocondo as she prepares to slumber is currently being [painted] by Leonardo". Given that the Louvre Mona Lisa has her depicted as undeniably thin, the true da Vinci is now thought to be the Fat Lisa currently on display in Isleworth ...'

– Art and the Sleeping Artist, by Sir Troy Bongg

There was dreamless sleep, at first, and darkness. But not *quite* as I remembered the darkness, as simply shapeless, timeless ebony, but darkness as in an unlit hall – full of memories, and places, and peoples and things – the marker-stones of my life's experience. Then a chasm, like a rent of linen, but both visual and aural, and in a second I was back: Birgitta, on the beach, blue-and-white towel, the bathing suit of fresh-leaf green and that orange-and-red parasol of spectacular size and splendour. The day was the same, the beach was the same, the *Argentinian Queen* was the same. I too was the same – not Charlie Worthing, but another, different, Charlie: Birgitta's Charlie, sitting with her on the striped towel, wearing a black bathing suit and white pumps.

She looked at me and smiled, and I felt myself smile back. The dream was, as far as I could see, identical in every detail. The gulls cackled from on high, and the scent of the tide drifted in on the breeze. She gave me her captivating smile, and pushed the hair once more behind her ear. I was Charles, and she was Birgitta, and this was their perfect moment.

'I love you, Charlie.'

'I love you, Birgitta.'

The breakers boomed and then the child, with a gurgle of laughter, chased a beach ball toward shore's edge. Again.

'Is this really me?' I asked, repeating myself before I'd realised it. Birgitta blinked at me and smiled.

'You're Charlie now, *my* Charlie,' she said with a giggle. 'Try not to think about the facility and HiberTech Security. Just today and tomorrow, forty-eight hours. You and me. What Dreams May Come.'

'What Dreams May Come,' I replied.

Knowing that I might wake soon, I looked around, eager to soak in the fine detail.

Behind us was a path leading back up to the car park, where there would be a café of whitewashed clapboard that sold the best pistachio ice cream in the nation. We were close to where Birgitta's mother lived, and would be staying in the room above the car house with its double brass bed, boxwood panelling and lace curtains. We'd leave early on Sunday and stop at Mumbles Pier to eat cockles and laver bread, while 'Groove Me' played on a wireless close by. I knew all these things without knowing how I knew, and odder still, I couldn't just remember backwards, I could remember *forwards*. The beach was only a memory of better times, many years before. Following this, Birgitta and I had travelled separately to Sector Twelve. She'd painted and I'd worked at HiberTech as an orderly in the Sleep Sciences Division, Project Lazarus. We'd met rarely but passionately, and then we'd been parted, this time for good.

'Happy snap?' said a photographer who was plying his trade up and down the beach. 'Proper tidy you'll look and as reasonably priced as anywhere you'll find.'

This was as far as I'd got in the dream the first time round and I expected to be awoken again, but I wasn't. We agreed and he took the Polaroid, handed it to us and told us he would be back to pick up payment if it came out 'to our proper satisfaction'. We watched the picture emerge, cementing the moment in time. It was the first time I got to see what I looked like. Birgitta's Charles was ridiculously handsome, with fine features and dark curly hair that half obscured his eyes. Despite this, he looked somehow lost, hopeless and ultimately doomed—

— I was sitting at the base of an ancient oak, looking up. The spread of the tree went almost to the periphery of my vision, and the light of a fresh Summer's morning filtered through the leaves. I blinked several times and sat up. The beach dream had abruptly cut out. Not with a fade or a segue but a *tear*. I was now in another place, another dream – one that I realised very quickly that Watson, Smalls, Moody, Birgitta and Lloyd had all visited before me.

I was sitting atop a rough stack of boulders that had been piled against the tree in a haphazard manner. The stones were large and of a bluish sandstone, smooth and flat and now an artificial island around the trunk. All about me the deep blue sky was punctuated by puffy clouds, and the surrounding grass stretched away in every direction to the horizon.

This felt, like the Birgitta dream that immediately preceded it, utterly real. Every detail was there about me – the texture in the bark, the veins in the leaves, the yellow bursts of lichen upon the rocks. The only evidence I had that this wasn't real was that *I knew it wasn't*. Nothing else. If that was so, then I could understand how Moody and Watson might have confused the two.

I looked at my hands. They still weren't mine. But they weren't Charles' either.

They were old. A good seven decades, wrinkled, covered with liver spots and trembling. I felt weak, too, and the left side of my body had a sort of fuzzy dullness to it. Oddly, or perhaps not so oddly given his presence in all our lives, I was now dreaming I was Don Hector. His oldness, his dignity, his manner. But I wasn't wholly him, I was partly him. Me, dreaming I was him, or him, dreaming he was me – I could only be sure I *wasn't* Don Hector as he'd died two years before.

I laughed out loud. Not simply at the bold invention of my mind, but the *clarity*. If this was what dreaming was like, then I had missed a phenomenon of considerable entertainment and distraction. Sure, the extra energy spent in their subconscious creation would require additional pounds at Slumberdown, but from what I could see, it would be worth it. This was a new, exciting reality.

This was escape.

I inhaled deeply and the sweet scent of Summer filled my lungs, the subtle odour of warm grass and meadowsweet. I looked around to see if Clytemnestra wasn't also somewhere about, hanging over me with her dagger, and was relieved to find that she wasn't. But something else *was*, something that had been predicted along with the oak and the boulders.

The blue Buick.

The car was from the more reserved and elegant era of American automotive design, before the dominance of fins and chrome. It wasn't new, and far from pristine. Rust speckled the chrome bumpers, poorly repaired crash damage had wrinkled the offside front wing and the driver's window was jammed half down and discoloured milky-white. Next to the Buick a picnic was laid out on a red blanket, a bottle of wine in a cooler, a folding chair. Beyond the car, about a half-mile away, I could see, sitting quite by itself on the unceasing carpet of green a Morpheleum, a temple to the god Morpheus. Old, abandoned, but looking incongruous, yet somehow safe.

I could make an intelligent guess as to how these two dream scenarios had been created in my mind. First of a woman whom I'd met and liked and mixed with her paintings and my holidays in the Gower, and secondly, the dream I had been told about, mixed with the inescapable omniscience of Don Hector and HiberTech. I already had the broad parameters; my mind had filled in the rest like so much builder's plaster. It was quite a feat – no wonder dreams burned energy.

I was about to step from the boulders when I stopped. Birgitta, Moody and Porter Lloyd had all warned me: *stay on the rocks.*

Intrigued, I stepped down to one of the lower stones and prodded the soil with an inquisitive toe. Almost immediately a hand shot out of the ground and closed around my ankle with a vice-like grip. I cried out in horror, swayed and almost fell off the rocks, then recovered and pulled back as hard as I could, my fingernails splitting and cracking where I grasped the stone. And then, after we had tussled for a few seconds the hand abruptly let go and swiftly sank from view while I retreated to the highest point of the rock-pile. Notwithstanding the fact that I knew that none of this was real, I sat shaking, breathing in short gasps. I then noticed that there were *more* hands – dozens if not hundreds – and watched with an increasing sense of horror as they moved slowly around the tree, as attackers might circle a hopeless last defence. Occasionally they would halt to fuss with a tussock of grass, sniff the air and occasionally squabble before carrying on with their patrol. I knew now what Moody had meant when he spoke in horrified tones of *the hands*.

No, wait, back up a moment. Upon reflection, *I couldn't have known* what Moody had been frightened of. He'd only made mention of 'hands out to get him'. I must have simply invented the scenario to fit in with the trees and the rocks. The outline was the same, the dream was different.

And then, quite suddenly, a woman's sharp voice from behind me cut into my trail of thought, and that was strange, because there'd been no one there when I last looked.

'We know of a remote farm in Lincolnshire,' came the woman's voice in a slow, persuasive tone, 'where Mrs Buckley lives. Every July, peas grow there.'

I turned. There was a woman standing next to the Buick, and she was staring at me with a folksy smile, had grey hair tied up in a bun and was wearing a white blouse and a red dress around which was tied a kitchen apron. It was Mrs Nesbit, as she appeared in the endless corporate logos, film and TV commercials – but not the *current* Mrs Nesbit actress: this was a much younger Zsazsa LeChat, from eight Mrs Nesbits ago. She looked as though she was unaware of her surroundings, and there was a sense of shimmering *otherness* about her – as though she were not part of the dream, but somehow trespassing within it.

I'd added a younger Zsazsa to the dream, too.

'Hello,' I said.

There was a short blast of static and she spoke again. But although the voice appeared to be coming from Mrs Nesbit, the words didn't match the movements of her mouth. She was the one from where the voice was emerging, but she wasn't the one speaking. It *was* Mrs Nesbit, and it *wasn't*, just as I was both myself and Don Hector, all at the same time.

'Deputy Worthing?' she said, and her voice seemed to sear a hole into my mind like a red–hot needle. I felt myself lift out of the

Dreamstate as the pain brought me perilously close to waking, and for a moment I could see the faint outline of Clytemnestra, the open door to the living room and the bedside clock before I fell back into the Dreamstate.

'Steady, Charlie, we need you asleep. Now: who do you think you are?'

'I think I'm ... Don Hector.'

'Presumptuous of you, wouldn't you say? Describe the Buick.'

'It's blue, the colour of the sky,' I said, 'it's not new and has various damaged parts, a bit of rust, an AA badge on the grille, off kilter.'

Mrs Nesbit smiled again. She was looking at me, but her eyes were unseeing. What I was witnessing, she could not. She seemed more brightly coloured than the surroundings, and had a thin sparkly aura that ran all around her.

'Tell me about your childhood.'

'Pool from birth,' I said, 'insurance write-off. I wasn't adopted on account of my noggin and biting off Gary Findlay's ear.'

'Not *you* – the other you. I want to know about Don Hector.'

'Nothing,' I said, 'I'm only dreaming I'm him.'

But there *was* something, as there was when I was Birgitta's husband. Vague, nebulous, but there, crouching in the back of my mind like a perching osprey: on a kid's trike when I was very young, going as fast as I could on the carpeted corridor of a large country house, trying to escape something – grief, I think.

'I was on a trike,' I said. 'It's a week past Springrise, and I can recall a sense of maternal absence. I can feel the loss.'

And I could, an angry lump of emptiness that wouldn't leave my chest. The same sort of lump I felt at the Pool when prospective parents passed unblinking on their hurried way to the other kids, the ones not made distinctly and beautifully unique by a touch of asymmetry.

'Good – you're in. Now listen carefully. Is there a cylinder anywhere close by?'

'What sort of cylinder?'

'A wax cylinder.'

'With music on it? There's lots in the apartment.'

'No; in the dream. *We need the cylinder* – and you need to find it. Explore the recesses of Don Hector's mind.'

I looked around. The only thing in sight other than the oak tree and the picnic and the car was the Morpheleum, sitting on the horizon.

'There's a temple to Morpheus. About half a mile away.'

'Good. Try and get there. Using the Buick offers the best chance, we've learned.'

'You've tried it?'

'In a manner of speaking.'

I looked at the empty space between myself and the car. It was barely ten paces away, but as I watched, a hand surfaced momentarily between myself and the Buick, then sank out of sight.

'I can't,' I said.

'The hands?'

'Yes, the hands. They'll get me.'

'They'll *always* get you, Charlie. Trying to drive to the temple, not being able to. Anything to stop you finding the cylinder, stop you reaching the Morpheleum. But the cylinder *is* in there somewhere. The temple is a good start. The clock is running – I suggest you start driving, and fast.'

I elected to do as she said, but then noticed with a feeling of dread that the hands were not simply severed hands, but small hand-like *creatures*, the wrist domed over with skin like a healed stump, and not looking like part of a human at all. I put my own hand in my pocket, pulled out a rabbit's-foot key ring and made a dash for the Buick.

I couldn't run as fast as I wanted. I was weak, and my feet felt draggy. Within a few paces I could sense the hands grasp the hem of my trousers, and from here they started to climb my legs, making me heavier, impeding my progress. I made it to the car and tried to get in but the weight and volume of the hands made it impossible to move, let alone drive. I kicked and pushed and tore at the hands but even if I dislodged one, two more would stream out of the earth to take their place. I heaved myself into the driver's seat and slipped the key into the ignition. The oil and generator lights flicked on and the car's engine burst into life. Without a foot to work the clutch, I simply pushed the gear lever into first. The gearbox clunked, the car lurched and the engine stalled. I shouted as a wave of hands erupted from the soil, flowed into the car in a flood and covered my face and then dragged me outside. I had a fleeting glimpse of the shimmery Mrs Nesbit before I was pulled beneath the ground, the taste of soil in my mouth, the earth above me pressing heavily on my chest and a sense of enveloping darkness. I tried to yell but my mouth was full of dry soil and—

— a voice. But not Mrs Nesbit's.

'What are you still doing here?'

'I'm sorry?'

'I'll rephrase that: what in all that's cold and dead and putrid are you still doing here?'

Jonesy

'… Skill erosion due to hibernational mortality could be disastrous to complex manufacturing, infrastructure and management systems, so almost every job was devised with SkillZero protocols in mind. Anyone who achieved an 82% pass or higher in General Skills could run anything from a fast food joint to a Graphite Reactor …'

– *Handbook of Winterology*, 6th edition, Hodder & Stoughton

I didn't recognise the voice, but figured it was a Deputy sent by Chief Logan to make sure I didn't lapse into full hibernation, always a risk with first-time Winterers. I was grateful to be back in Cardiff. Spending my first assignment in Sector something-or-rather at the *Sarah Whatsit* Dormitorium hadn't sounded like a huge barrel of fun, although I couldn't as yet remember how I'd managed to get back.

On the Railplane, I expect.

'You with me, Worthing?'

'I'm with you,' I croaked, my throat dry, my vocal cords stiff with disuse.

'Truly?'

'No.'

I felt myself groan. My head felt like mud, my eyes were gummed tight shut and I really only had one thought in my head: that I desperately, urgently, painfully wanted to go back to sleep.

'There was a striped towel,' I said, as memories started to return, firing randomly around inside my mind like lottery balls, 'and a beach ball. A child, a girl, laughing. A woman in a swimsuit, a wrecked liner – the *Argentinian Queen*.'

'It's called Arousal Confusion,' came the woman's voice from the darkness. 'You won't know shit for a couple of minutes and you'll talk utter bollocks.'

'She took a Polaroid,' I said, 'and the orange-and-red parasol was of spectacular size and splendour.'

'As I said,' remarked the voice, 'utter bollocks. Your mind has been dormant, and your memory is still remapping. Until it does, you'll be all over the shop. Can you remember your name?'

I lay for a few minutes in the blackness, my eyes still gummed shut, and waited for my thoughts to gather.

'Charlie Worthing,' I said as soon as the fact popped into my head, 'BDA26355F. I'll be twenty-three on the ninth after Springrise and I'm resident at room five-oh-six at the *Melody Black*, Cardiff.'

'Better, but still nonsense,' said the voice, 'but to go back to my initial enquiry: you told Laura and Fodder you were leaving on the last train. So: what are you still doing here?'

I had to think *really* hard. There had been talk about taking a Sno-Trac somewhere. Nope, it had gone again.

'Okay,' came the voice, 'I think it's time to draw back the curtains.'

She placed something damp in my palm and I gently massaged the hard sleep-crust that had sealed my eyes tight shut. I pulled at my top eyelid, the crust broke with an almost-audible *snik*, and in an instant my vision returned – garish and distorted to begin with, but as my long-dormant cortex kicked into life, the world pulled itself into some semblance of order.

I saw Clytemnestra first, exactly the same as I'd seen her last. But with Clytemnestra came the unwelcome news that I had not returned to Cardiff.

'The *Sarah Siddons*,' I sighed, 'Sector Twelve.'

'It grows on you like mildew and needy cousins,' said a woman who was sitting on a chair next to the bed. 'We call it "The Twelve" or more usually "The Douzey". You may get to enjoy it. It's not likely, but you might.'

She had mousy-brown hair cut short, was dressed in the off-white Winter combat fatigues usually favoured by Consuls, Footmen and the military, and was looking at me with a bemused smile. She was either a very healthy forty or a horribly unhealthy twenty, had faintly Southern features and above her name badge wore a pair of silver storks. She carried a pair of Bambis on her hips and, like Fodder, had a D-ring sewn into her shock-vest.

'Hello,' I said, blinking away the gumminess from my vision.

'I'm Vice-Consul Bronwen Jones,' she said. 'Everyone calls me Jonesy. Bit obvious for a nickname and I'm not dead keen on it. I wanted something more along the lines of "IceMaiden" or "BlackWidow" or "FrostCrumpet" but you don't get to choose these things.'

'FrostCrumpet?'

'That was always a third choice,' she admitted, 'not my favourite either.'

'I used to be called "Wonky",' I said, hoping to ingratiate myself with the thinnest of shared experiences, 'I'm hoping that doesn't stick.'

'It will now.'

She offered me her left hand for me to shake. Her right was mostly missing, and what remained had healed raggedly: Winter patch-me-ups always ended up looking worse.

A kettle started whistling somewhere and Jonesy got up and vanished into the next room while I stretched, my muscles quivering with the effort and instantly tightening into a crampy spasm. I tried several times to get up with varying levels of success, and could stand unaided by the time Jonesy reappeared with two mugs. It was hot chocolate, sweet and thick, and as I drank I felt my core temperature rise. The clouds in my head began to part more rapidly, and with this, unwelcome memories returned. Aurora had thumped Logan so hard he'd been embedded into a wall, I'd been marooned in Sector Twelve and was spending a few nights in the *Sarah Siddons* before I was to drive myself out. I also had an uncomfortable feeling that I might have dreamed myself back into the Gower from a memorable holiday when I was a kid, mixed up with several paintings and the artist whom I'd inexplicably named Birgitta, which was kind of odd as the only Birgitta I'd known was a bitey spaniel with smelly ears once owned by Sister Placentia.

All of this was worrying. Not the dream itself, which was

undeniably enjoyable yet random nonsense, but the very *act* of dreaming. Only Sub-beta payscalers actually *dreamt*. If it got out that I was a dreamer, I would be finished socially and, worse, I'd have taken on the risks of the Winter Consul Service for nothing. Until I figured out what was what, no one could know.

I stretched my muscles and felt them cramp again almost instantly.

'Take it easy to begin with,' said Jonesy as she opened the shutters, 'slow wins prizes.'

A grey light flooded the apartment. I sat up in bed, pushed back the bedclothes and had my third big shock of the morning.

I was thin. *Really* thin.

Jonesy raised an eyebrow.

'Sailing a bit close to the wind?' she asked, staring at my scrawny body. 'It's a brave or foolhardy person who heads into their first Winter without contingency. Don't let Toccata find out. She takes reckless disregard of the BMI seriously. Actually,' she added after a moment's thought, 'she kind of takes *everything* seriously. Even taking seriously she takes seriously.'

For the moment, Toccata's opinion didn't really matter. It would later – big time – but not right now. I had only one question.

'What day is it?'

'Slumberdown plus twenty-seven.'

'*What?*'

'Plus twenty-seven. You've been out four weeks.'

It took a moment or two for me to digest this fact. I looked at my alarm clock, which had stopped not long after I'd gone to sleep. Without it, I'd inadvertently tumbled down the slope into hibernation. It was embarrassing. Falling asleep on your first overwintering gig was strictly for amateurs.

'So,' said Jonesy, 'let's start again: what are you doing here?'

I explained about as quickly and truthfully as I could. That Aurora had saved me from Logan; that I'd spoken to Laura and Fodder in the Consulate; that I'd been marooned; had met up again with Aurora; was going to drive myself out; was allocated this room.

'The next thing I know, you're waking me up.'

'Oversleep, did you?' she said with a smile. 'That's not a good start.'

'No,' I agreed, '*not* a good start at all. But why wake me now,' I added, 'why not four weeks ago?'

'Your office in Cardiff,' she said, 'they called several times asking where you were as they need confirmation of Aurora's account of what happened to Logan. We'd told them you'd departed on the last train, but when they insisted we look further four weeks later, that dope Treacle said he'd walked with you and Aurora in this direction. We did a sweep of the Domitoria, and there you were. You were lucky.'

She was right. If I'd only been carrying two weeks' contingency instead of four I'd likely be dead right now.

'Now,' said Jonesy, 'you need to explain everything to Toccata. She's busy until one o'clock. Do you want breakfast?'

I nodded. She told me to keep stretching and then went back into the kitchen area. I moved to the end of the bed, grasped the bedstead and heaved myself to my feet. I paused, took a few steps, stumbled, regained my balance then walked unsteadily to the bathroom, where I relieved myself of something that smelled of overripe silage, looked like yacht varnish and felt as though it were burning a new way out.

This done, I stepped into the shower to wash the gammy nightcrust from my wintercoat, and while I did so, I thought about the painter. Oddly, the dream had not been a faint jumble of broken images softened into broad ambiguity by the fog of sleep, but as strong and as real as anything that actually *had* happened: the trip up here, Logan's death, Foulnap – even the flailing nightwalker on the operating table at HiberTech and the shiny wetness of the cobbles where Hooke had whacked Moody.

Once I'd soaped and scrubbed twice I ran a number-two clipper through my felted hair and dumped the tangled mass in the bin. I stopped frequently to stretch the gnawing stiffness from my limbs, and once I'd combed all over to remove the lice eggs, eight nightworms and a half-dozen hook-daddies, I stood under the gloriously hot water[50] and tried to push down a sense of rising panic and failure.

---

50. Another huge advantage of nuclear heating: abundant hot water.

After ten minutes and with no positive thoughts about my current predicament, I stepped out, gazed at my scrawny body in the mirror, then clipped my nails short, felt my teeth for any telltale signs of decay or looseness, and slipped on a pair of Suzy's jogging trousers and a T-shirt. I then went to the window to peer at the Winter, something I'd never witnessed before.

The landscape was utterly without colour. A grey overcast stretched to the mountains, the town and country draped in white, the hard edges of the buildings rounded and softened by the heaps of accreted snow. There was barely any movement; the only sign of life was half a dozen dog-head buzzards wheeling tightly over some waste ground behind the *Siddons*.

'They'll be circling the landfill,' said Jonesy, who had arrived by my side. 'We dumped a couple of winsomniacs up there a few days ago; things aren't freezing as quickly so the scent carries.'

'The thaw?' I asked.

'No, just the end of a milder spell. There's worse weather on the way – a pretty big one in a couple of days: fifty below freezing, they say. The porters will be pulling the rods in preparation. We'll want to be inside when it hits. Breakfast is ready.'

We sat down at the table. There was everything: bacon, beans, two kippers, buttered toast, mushrooms, sausage and sauté potatoes. Despite the joyous bounty of the spread, everything was either long-life, tinned or dry-packed. Nothing is fresh in the Winter, they say – except the wind.

We tucked in; Jonesy had made almost the same size for herself.

'This is nice,' she said.

She looked at me and smiled, then patted my hand in an oddly affectionate manner, and left hers resting on mine. It was her tattered hand, all livid scar tissue and string-sized stitch marks. I didn't move my hand away through not wanting to offend, so waited until she moved her hand to pass me the salt, and then elected to keep my hands off the table in future.

'It's sort of like being long-partnered,' she added.

'I'm sorry?'

'Sort of like being long-partnered,' she repeated, 'sitting here together, enjoying our retirement and sharing a sense of past histories together, a warm and cosy sense of familiarity.'

The alarm bells started ringing.

'I'm ... not sure I follow you. Retirement sounds nice, but hardly realistic.'

'That's the whole idea. Since Consuls rarely die of old age, I thought we could have our fond dotage *now*, while we still can. We could meet up after work, and just kind of sit together in companionable silence. You might darn a sock and make comments from time to time while I read, and you could say "Yes, dear", or "That's interesting" when I say something intelligent you don't understand. We could even play Cluedo, but only if I can be Miss Scarlett and not the murderers.'

'That's not *quite* how Cluedo works,' I said, and she frowned, so I gave her a quick run-down on the rules while we ate.

'You seem very expert,' she said, which was hardly a word I'd use – Cluedo isn't that complex.

'Sister Zygotia used to play it with us at the Pool,' I said.

Not many people talked about the Pool. But now that we were, Jonesy was curious.

'Were you there long?'

'Last one out.'

'What was it like?'

Pools, like meals, terriers and promises, all varied in quality – there were Pools barely suitable for livestock and there was the highly desirable Wackford & Co. with branches in Paris, London and New York.

'Any institution has room for improvement,' I said, 'but on the whole I think it was okay – I just stayed there too long. Look,' I added, 'I don't want to appear ungrateful or anything, but I'd be a lot happier just heading off home, straight back to Cardiff.'

'No can do, Wonky. Toccata wants to see you, so that's what's going to happen. Pass the ketchup.'

'There isn't any.'

'Yes,' she said with a mournful expression, 'we watered it down and told the winsomniacs it was tomato soup.'

We fell silent for a moment, but Jonesy, I realised, was never quiet for long. She liked to chatter in order, I think, to fill the dead air, and the Winter was full of dead air. I learned that she was a first-generation settled Guestworker, an outsider of mixed-hemisphere parents. Her mother had been an Argentinian maid who had fallen in love and slept over. Scandalous at the time, but little thought of today.

'I joined the Service after several tours in the Ottoman,' she said, then fell silent for a moment. 'Lost some people out there under my command,' she said, 'lost some *good* people.'

'Is that why you're in Sector Twelve?' I asked.

'It's all about payback, I think,' she said, as if not fully sure herself. 'Could have retired, but working under Toccata is never dull. Besides, I may actually do some good. It's not risk-free, but honourable conduct rarely is.'

Once breakfast was done, Jonesy said she had some errands to run and she'd meet me at midday to go and see Toccata.

'You could make up some really good "Do you remember whens",' she said, 'reminiscences of our early life together, y'know?'

'Yes, I suppose I could.'

'Try now.'

'I'm not good at off-the-cuff invent—'

'Did you like your breakfast? The one I made for you?'

'Yes.'

'Then let's hear the story of how we met.'

She stared at me in a dangerous fashion. The breezy, chatty Jonesy was really only one part of her — the saner part.

'Okay, then,' I said, trying to think of something original and failing, 'we were — um — cast as ... the front and back halves of a pantomime horse.'

'Trippy,' said Jonesy, more intrigued than I'd hoped, 'and why would that have happened?'

'Part of a ... Winter talent show?'

'Good.'

'We don't get along at first—'

'Why is that?'

'Because you insisted I was the back half?'

'Totally plausible. Carry on.'

'But because the show must go on and the "equestrian gavotte" requires synchronised footsteps, we sort of forget our differences, practise together in private and then emerge victorious ... and in love.'

'Brilliant,' she said, beaming all over.

'Really? I thought it sounded *particularly* corny.'

'The best relationships always begin like a bad rom-com in my experience. I'll find a tartan travel rug and a picnic set for the Sno-Trac,' she added, now quite enthused by the whole idea. 'You're washing up breakfast, but you can argue with me about it if you want — sort of like "I did it last time".'

'You made breakfast,' I said, 'it would only be fair.'

'Well, okay,' she said, mildly disappointed.

Jonesy got up, pulled on her coat and opened the front door.

'I've left a basket of food on the kitchen counter. I'll meet you outside at midday.'

She then wished me a pleasant day, told me to not force my first shit out as I'd *definitely* regret it, and that there was a package outside in the corridor.

'Thank you,' I said to her retreating form as she moved along the curved corridor, and she waved a hand without looking back.

The parcel was large and flat and wrapped in brown paper and string. I brought it inside, cut the string with my pocket knife to find it was a painting, a portrait, of me. I rested the painting on the bookcase, then stepped back.

It was the picture I had commissioned from the painter. But it wasn't wholly original. It was the same painting I had seen in her studio four weeks before, the one of her faceless husband. But it was no longer her husband and no longer naked. It was *me*, with my features and a black one-piece swimsuit painted over. She'd even added white pumps over his previously naked feet, and a blue-and-white striped towel for me to sit on.

There was something very disturbing about the painting. It wasn't because she had recycled a canvas of her obviously-missed husband for a stranger she barely knew, but this: she'd painted me on the

Gower, as in my dream, and, more bizarrely, it looked for all the world as though she had painted me from her viewpoint, there on the beach. In the dream she had said she loved me, and this was a painting of me, hearing her say it. Which sort of defied logic: it should have been the other way round. Reality, *then* dream. I stared at the painting for a good ten minutes, trying to figure it out, but getting nowhere. In any event, I thought the likeness was good. I now owed her five hundred euros, which on reflection was money I could ill afford, but at least it would give me an opportunity to talk to her again.

I walked around the room several times, managed two press-ups and sat for a while on the bed feeling fatigued and itchy, then fetched the portrait of me and placed it next to Clytemnestra, in order to soften her psychopathic glare. I then went and made myself some tea, had another shower, and stared out of the window.

After an hour of this I grew bored and restless so decided to go and see Porter Lloyd. I pulled on my uniform, threw my bag around my shoulder and departed, but stopped at the painter's door as I walked around the corridor. I scribbled a note of thanks and my address so she could invoice me come Springrise, and was going to pop it through the letterbox when I stopped. The name under the bell was Birgitta, and I felt a sudden pang of confusion. I hadn't known her name. She'd not told me. *I'd heard it in the dream.* I took a deep breath, supposed that I must have seen it without registering it, and, still confused, walked downstairs.

Starving in the basement

――――

'... The 1815 "Victoire" calendar was the one followed by all members
of the Northern Fed, and listed the 118 days of Winter as a single month
centred around the Winter solstice. The remaining 252 days were grouped
into an efficient nine months of 28 days each, with a leap year every
nineteen to make up for orbital discrepancy ...'

– *The History of Celestial Timekeeping*, by Brian Gnomon

'I'm so, so sorry,' said Porter Lloyd when I found him at reception,
'I had no idea you were still up there.'

'I hadn't taken the Sno-Trac,' I said, 'so you *must* have known I
was still here.'

'I don't like to go in the basement much,' he said, 'so wouldn't
know if it was here or not. How late for work were you?'

'Four weeks,' I said, 'probably some kind of record.'

He gave a short laugh, and I joined in, feeling stupid. I then asked
about the night I thought Clytemnestra had peeled herself out of
the painting.

'That was the first night,' said Lloyd, 'I didn't see you after that.
I can only apologise again. I work with the information I'm given.'

I looked out of the window at the weather, which was overcast but
clear. I suddenly had a daring thought: I didn't have to hang around
to see Toccata at all. Technically I didn't take orders from her – I was
based out of Cardiff.

'I think I'd better be leaving,' I said. 'Sno-Trac in the basement,
you say?'

'Indeed,' he said, 'I'll take you.'

Lloyd took a long dog-catcher's stick and a press photographer's
flashgun from under the desk, the kind that accepts flashbulbs the
size of ping-pong balls. We crossed the lobby and passed through a
small door, then took the stairwell into the bowels of the Dormitorium.

166

It was noticeably warmer when we reached the second sub-basement as we were closer to the HotPot, and the copper heat-exchanger pipes made odd gurgling noises as valves automatically opened and closed. The iron stair rail, I noted, was warm to the touch.

'Quite hot down here,' I said.

'Cold snap on its way,' explained Lloyd, 'the rods are out in anticipation.'

'Expecting trouble?' I asked, indicating the flashgun and dog-catcher's pole he was carrying.

'The *Sarah Siddons* is only at sixty per cent occupancy,' he confessed, 'so I take on "basement lodgers" for a fee.'

'*Basement* lodgers?'

'Nightwalkers from the Dormitoria this end of town. Other Porters find them and park them with me until HiberTech or the Consuls get involved. I've got six, all told. Unusually high, I know. Morphenox isn't totally without faults, is it?'

He was making comment on the fact that only those on the drug ever walked. For every three thousand or so who felt the Spring sunshine on their faces, one would be a nightwalker, and no one considered those odds anything less than acceptable.

'I've been feeding them a turnip and three Weetabix a day, so − fingers crossed − they haven't yet resorted to eating one another.'

I hadn't thought for one moment I was going to have to run the gauntlet of potentially cannibalistic nightwalkers, and told him so.

'Don't worry,' he said, 'even a child could outrun them. Just make sure you've no chocolate or Oxo cubes in your pockets. They can smell them a mile off; drives them nuts.'

We arrived at a steel door which had six names chalked upon it, along with the dates they were locked in. Lloyd dug a flashbulb from his jacket pocket and pushed it into the reflector bowl.

'I trigger it manually,' he explained. 'The bright light scrambles the remnants of their brain long enough to get away if needed.'

He rapped his knuckles against the last name on the door.

'Watch out for Eddie Tangiers. Big guy, strong as an ox − I lured him in here only a week ago. Used a trail of fruit gums, if you're interested. Not *quite* as effective as marshmallows, but less bulky to carry – and more economic.'

'Good tip. Thanks. How will I know him?'

'Oh, you'll know him: kind of big, kind of dead, kind of needs to be avoided. Good luck. The Sno-Trac will be on your left, fifty yards in.'

After pausing to listen at the door, Lloyd pulled back the spring-loaded door bolt, opened the door and then fired the flashgun. There was a bright flash in which happily a nightwalker was *not* revealed, and a waft of warm air greeted us from the semi-gloom, and with it the smell of decomposition. Lloyd hurriedly ejected the spent bulb and pushed in another from his pocket.

'One or two are definitely greeners,' he said, wrinkling his nose. 'Maybe I didn't feed them enough Weetabix. '

I stepped in and snapped on my flashlight. A meagre light filtered down the light-wells by which I could see the general layout of the basement: doughnut-shaped around the central core, with sturdy brick vaulting to support the building above. Serried ranks of cars, motorbikes, trucks, haywains and agricultural equipment, most covered by dustsheets, were parked in two rows with access along the inside radius. I paused for a moment, but Lloyd didn't; I heard the door clang shut and his footsteps retreated rapidly back up the stairs.

I found the Sno-Trac with ease, but it wouldn't be going anywhere. Someone had left the compressed air tank open and the air had leaked out – there was nothing to start the engine. I paused for thought and then decided to exit by way of the ramp and then have a scout around outside whilst I figured out my options.

I trod silently along the rows of vehicles. Not because I didn't want the deadheads to know I was here, I just wanted to hear them first. About a third of the way around the basement and with the exit just visible on the far side, I came across the first nightwalker but it was now little but bones, picked clean.

'One down, five to go,' I murmured to myself and moved on, shivering within a cold sweat despite the warmth, a pulse thumping in my neck. The second and third nightwalkers I found close by, nothing more than a jumbled heap of bare bones and gristle, wedged between two cars. It wasn't unusual to find them grouped together. Nightwalkers, when resting between feeding, usually gathered around a point of focus. A skylight, a heater duct, or something that made a soothing noise, like a wireless tuned to static, a water wheel, wind chimes, a caged bird. It suddenly struck me that there were none of these in the basement. Only cars covered in sheets, brick walls, vaulted ceilings and electricity cables carried on rusty trunking.

An uneasy feeling welled up inside me. The car they had gathered around was larger than the others. Larger and smoother and—

I grasped the sheet and drew it off.

It was the blue Buick.

I stared at it with a sense of growing confusion. It was the same car I'd dreamed about. But it wasn't just the same make, colour and model – it was *exactly the same car* – missing hubcaps, AA sign askew, rusty bumpers, front damage, driver's window jammed half down. I shivered and rubbed my temples, looked away, then back, then touched it. The car was real. I'd dreamed about something I'd never seen.

I ran my fingertips across the bonnet, feeling hot and panicky. There were no hands, no Mrs Nesbit, no oak, no boulders, just the car. I trod silently to the driver's side and opened the door. There was a musty, long-stored smell inside, like the bottom of an infrequently aired closet. There was little to be found except a tin of Mrs Nesbit travel sweets and several unpaid parking tickets, but in the door pocket I found the vehicle documents. The name on the registration papers was Don Hector, which added to my consternation. I checked behind the sun visor and the keys fell into the footwell.

There was a rabbit's-foot key ring attached. I'd dreamed that, too.

I took a couple of startled steps back and experienced a hot, uncomfortable feeling as the dream returned, aggressively invading my consciousness. I could see the dappled light of an oak tree's spreading boughs appear on the concrete floor as quite suddenly the Buick before me transformed into the Buick in the dream, while around me on the concrete floor were the hands, alive, writhing like small skin-covered spiders.

'*The hands!*' I gasped with a shudder of revulsion, then realised that I was sounding like Moody. On an impulse I called out. Not to Sister Zygotia or Lucy or Jonesy or Aurora, but to *Birgitta*. I didn't expect this to have any effect, but it did: all of a sudden the field and trees and hands had vanished and I was back in the stuffy closeness of the garage.

I waited a few moments to get my breath back and for my heart to stop thumping.

It's Hibernatory Narcosis, idiot.

The most dangerous side effects of anomalous inter-Winter rousing were never physiological, but *psychological*: narcosis in its mildest form was a sense of tingling or numbness, which then ran the gamut from feeling drowsy, to feeling drunk, to hallucinations where scraps of momentarily unsuppressed dreams caused reality ambiguity that could result in paranoia, dissociative behaviour and, in extreme cases, violence to oneself and others.

But it wasn't all bad: on the plus side, I knew that thinking of Birgitta could bale me out of any hallucinations. It was a handy trick. I'd use it again. But on the down side, I was experiencing a similar narcosis to that of Watson, Smalls and Moody. And aside from the whole Birgitta dream, which they never mentioned, *I was seeing things they had been seeing*. Perhaps not in precisely the same way, but close enough – and it hadn't done them any good.

I peered around the empty car park. It was gloomy and cheerless, with only the occasional drop of water splashing on the ground to punctuate the silence. My flashlight had dropped from my grasp and rolled under the car, where it was illuminating the left rear tyre. It was out of reach so I lay upon the concrete to squeeze under the Buick. I stretched out and touched the flashlight with my fingertips but it rolled away and the light fell upon another nightwalker, dead under the car. It was a woman with dark, matted hair.

I crawled under farther, grabbed the flashlight and was about to wriggle out when I felt a vice-like grip tighten around my upper arm. I jumped in fright and swung the flashlight around. I had been wrong: the nightwalker under the car was far from dead. Her teeth were yellow, her clothes filthy and her fingernails rough and broken. She gazed at me with a disconcerting absence of humanity and in the way an expectant hungry child might stare at an ice cream. Lloyd's fears had been well founded: three Weetabix and a turnip a day had *not* been enough. I was also, I noted, in no immediate danger of being bitten. One of her dungaree straps had snagged around the car's jacking point.

I was about to back out when she produced a low whispery growl, somewhere deep in her ragged throat. I stopped, but not because she'd spoken. Nightwalkers often knew a few words; it was so commonplace it wasn't seen as a trick worth noting. No, the reason I stopped was because the short sentence was chillingly familiar.

'Charlie,' she said, 'I ... love you.'

I stared into the violet eyes with a mixture of horror, surprise and loss – and I knew exactly who it was.

'Birgitta?'

She didn't respond, and I poked her cheek with my flashlight to make sure I wasn't hallucinating. It *was* her: thinner than when I'd seen her last, and considerably less full of life. I put out my hand to touch her but she snapped at my fingers and grasped my forearm so tightly I could feel her fingernails puncture the skin.

'Charlie,' she said again, 'I ... love you.'

'No,' I said, as the full relevance of her words struck home, 'no, no, not possible.'

It had happened again: first her name, then the car, then the rabbit's-foot key ring, then her saying she loved Charlie as she had in the dream. It wasn't meant to work that way. It couldn't work that way.

Reality, *then* dream. Cause, *then* effect.

She snapped her teeth at me again. I had some Cadbury's Fruit & Nut on me, which she ate without preamble, along with my last shortbread finger and half a Wagon Wheel I was keeping for emergencies.

'Is this why you're under the Buick?' I asked. 'Drawn to it by the dream?'

The questioning was pointless, as Birgitta was now well beyond the capacity for intelligent conversation. But oddly, beneath the grime and matted hair, dirt and cobwebs, her eyes were precisely as I remembered them – violet, and of extraordinary clarity and brightness.

As I was pondering her looks, the paradox of her acting out my dream, the almost unthinkable reality that it was I who had supplied her with the Morphenox and that she would now have to be retired, I heard a shuffling noise close by. I flicked the flashlight around and could see two chunky male legs from mid-shin down, presumably Eddie Tangiers, the newcomer Lloyd had warned me about. I made to roll out the opposite side but noticed there was a nightwalker this side, too – a female, wearing bunny slippers.

As I watched, a bony set of fingers clasped the bottom edge of the car's rear mudguard and an expressionless face peered in at me upside down. She was somewhere in her twenties, had a pale complexion, was missing an eye and wore a tiara stuck in her rumpled blond hair. I was concerned to be surrounded and outnumbered by three people who regarded me only as today's one major food group, but there were two things in my favour: first that they were slow, and second, that they were very, very stupid.

'I guess the marriage is off,' I said, noting that Glitzy Tiara had an engagement ring around a grimy finger. She reached an arm towards me. I pulled back, avoided Birgitta and looked to the other side of the car, where Eddie Tangiers was now attempting to grab my ankle with a muscular arm. This was more problematical. He looked weighty, strong, and had no functioning part of his brain to feel pain, mercy or reason. A thump from my Bambi would send him sprawling but the shock wave might rupture a fuel tank or, much worse, bounce off a tyre and render *me* unconscious, something that could potentially ruin my day.

Tangiers caught hold of my ankle and began to pull. I grabbed the Buick's rear axle to steady myself and kicked his hand, but all I managed to do was to bark my shin against the base of a suspension arm. I pulled the Bambi from my holster while Birgitta clung tightly to my forearm, teeth snapping. I fumbled with the safety and—

Whump

The air was suddenly full of loose dust, and I was momentarily blinded. Initially, I thought that I had accidentally discharged the

Bambi, but I hadn't; it was still cold. Irrespective, Tangiers had let go of my leg and was now lying in a heap on the bonnet of the car opposite, his mind momentarily scrambled by the concussion. I blinked and looked out. Another pair of feet had appeared by the side of the car but they were moving not with the slow shuffle of a nightwalker, but with full motor control. A Winterer. The thump had come from them.

'Helloooo!' came a chirpy woman's voice. 'Are we having heaps of fun down there?'

'I've been in happier predicaments,' I said in as confident a manner as I could, 'and look, I know this sounds kinda daft, but I'm a Deputy Consul and I've got this under control.'

'Under control? Hah!' came the voice, then, more quietly: 'Wait a moment – is that Charlie?'

I said that it was.

'It's Aurora. Would you give me a hand with this fella? He's at least a hundred and twenty kilos, and every single one of them wants me for lunch.'

The situation called for teamwork.

'There's another one with a tiara off to your left.'

Whump

The thump was directed away from me this time, and only a small amount of dirt fell from beneath the car. Beyond the front of the Buick I could see Glitzy Tiara being deposited in front of the Austin Maxi opposite, an untidy tangle of badly grazed arms and legs. I rolled out from under the car and stood up. Aurora looked pretty much the same: unseeing left eye, a shabby Winter chic look but with the addition of a panga[51] in a scabbard on her back.

'Thanks for that,' she said cheerily. 'So, why did you come back?'

'Come back? I never left.'

'So what have you been doing for the past four weeks?'

I sighed.

51. It's like a machete but with more heft.

'I ... fell asleep.'

She hid a smile.

'You're kidding?'

'No. Spark out. My alarm clock failed.'

'You're a twit, Worthing, but listen, it does happen. Jack Logan was renowned for it when a Novice. Overslept and missed a stake-out by a week.' She paused for a moment. 'Whatever happened to Jack Logan?'

I stared at her. She was asking me in a *where are they now?* sort of way.

'You ... killed him?'

'So I did,' she said, snapping her fingers, 'what a to-do. Toccata wasn't happy, I can tell you. I am *so* glad I wasn't the one who had to tell her.'

I think I wanted to move the conversation on.

'No one knew where I was until Jonesy came looking. Weren't you going to fax my office explaining how I was getting back?'

Aurora thought for a moment.

'I told Agent Hooke to do it. Did it not get there?'

'It seems not.'

'I'll ask him about it. Shit,' she said, poking my frame with an inquisitive finger, 'there's almost nothing left of you at all.'

I told her I'd be on all-day breakfasts for a week, but in the literal meaning of the phrase, and she said she'd do what she could to gain me extra rations. After that we got on with more pressing matters: the male nightwalker was now getting to his feet in an uncertain manner. Deadheads don't stun as easily or for as long as those with full mental capacity. Less upstairs to scramble, Logan had said. But with the two of us it didn't take much to bind his wrists, and once this was done, Aurora tied him to the bumper of a nearby VW Beetle, where he tugged constantly to try and get away, like a dog eager to worry a squirrel.

'Have you met Eddie Tangiers?' asked Aurora, in the same way you might introduce someone at a cocktail party.

'Well, no,' I said, faintly embarrassed, for Tangiers was not just well built, handsome and physically very Alpha, but was entirely naked – and displaying a tumescence of considerable size and rigidity.

'Tangiers was a Tier One sire,' she said, 'and was in the Twelve plying his trade when he became stranded. When Eddie was alive, he had pretty much only one thing on his mind – now it's *all* he'll ever have on his mind. If you have some phials and liquid nitrogen on you, we could make a packet – this guy is sitting on a fortune.'

I must have looked shocked for she pulled a face.

'It's a *joke*, Worthing. You need them out here like you need food and warmth. His only use now will be for quoits practice or as a hatstand. Step to your left.'

While we had been talking, Glitzy Tiara had picked herself up and was shambling towards us, her pinched face streaked with dirt, her shoulder dislocated by the fall. Aurora stepped forward and popped her shoulder back in with a technique that was as expert as it was nonchalant, then tied her up a safe distance from Tangiers.

'Job done,' said Aurora with a grin. 'Snickers?'

'Thank you.'

Aurora produced several chocolate bars from an inside pocket, gave one to me and then fed two each to the nightwalkers, wrapper and all.

'Glitzy Tiara wants to talk,' I said, for the female nightwalker was mouthing words in between bites of chocolate.

'You're right,' agreed Aurora. 'Shall we find out what?'

She produced a water bottle from her bag and poured a little down the nightwalker's throat. Glitzy Tiara coughed, then swallowed, and with her throat now wet I could tell she had a raspy Carmarthen accent. She must have been talking since the moment her higher brain functions evaporated, for her voice box was ragged and worn.

'Tinned passata, grated mozzarella … bread flour,' she said. 'Peppers all colours, anchovies.'

'Sounds like pizza night,' said Aurora. 'Want some more Snickers? It was a sponsorship deal. I've got hundreds of them in the truck.'

'Go on, then.'

She handed me a pack of five.

'I guess I owe you my thanks again,' I said.

'No,' she said, 'it's partly my fault you're still here. I should have done a follow-up.'

'A Romanesco cauliflower,' murmured Glitzy Tiara, 'and some oolong tea.'

'Doesn't sound like she'll be heading for the local JollyMart, does she?' said Aurora. 'Is that one anything to do with you?'

Aurora pointed to where we could see Birgitta's feet emerging from under the Buick. They were moving in a helpless sort of manner.

'Yes,' I said, 'she tried to bite me when I wasn't looking.'

'Does she do tricks?'

'She eats dead people.'

'Hardly a trick, is it?' Aurora remarked, squatting down and looking under the car.

'No,' I conceded, 'more like a survival instinct.'

'Hang on,' said Aurora, 'I think this is Birgitta.'

'Manderlay,' I said without thinking. I hadn't heard or read the name anywhere; I just knew it. It was also confusing but somehow not surprising that I knew she had served in the Ottoman, that her favourite colour was yellow ochre, she liked dogs, William Thackeray and walking in the Peak District, and her birthday was the first 9th after Springrise, same as me.

'It's a shame,' said Aurora, staring at the shambling ruin that had once been Birgitta.

It was something considerably more than a shame.

'Wait a minute,' she said, 'I'm sure Birgitta was Beta payscale. Someone must have sold her their Morphenox. Someone ... who might not have needed it this Winter.'

She looked pointedly at me as she said it, and I hoped the heat in my cheeks didn't show.

'Don't sweat it,' she said, 'I won't tell a soul, although if you *hadn't* sold it to her, she'd not be a deadhead.'

I really didn't want or need this pointing out.

'I didn't sell her my Morphenox,' I said, truthfully enough.

'Oh? Well, it doesn't matter one way or the other, really.'

She pulled out her Bambi and pointed it at Birgitta. Non-Tricksy nightwalkers were often summarily retired when found.

'No!' I said, a little too hastily. 'I mean, I'll take care of it. It's something I should get used to.'

'Fair enough,' said Aurora, reholstering the Bambi.

'Why are you here in the basement?' I asked, eager to change the subject. 'If you don't mind me asking.'

She nodded towards the Vacants.

'Gathering up some nightwalkers for HiberTech. Project Lazarus always needs Tricksy subjects, so I came to have a look. The breeder will probably get farmed, but Glitzy Tiara they'll take. I'll get them over there smartish, too, before Toccata intervenes. She has old-fashioned ideas about what we do in the facility, and just retires them all and then claims standard bounty by presenting the left thumb to Vermin Control.'

Aurora made to move off, but then stared at the large blue automobile for a moment.

'Wait a moment. This is a blue Buick, isn't it?'

I nodded.

'The one that Watson and Moody were babbling about?'

'And several others, too, yes.'

She paused, looked at the car, then at the remains of the nightwalkers, then at the rabbit's-foot key ring I was still holding in my hand.

'What's your interest in this car, Worthing?'

I had to think. I knew almost no one in Sector Twelve. Birgitta regarded me as you might an ambulatory dinner, Jonesy and Fodder were loyal to Toccata and Lloyd was a porter, whose first priority was the continued smooth running of the Dormitorium. Laura had her head filled with myths and fables and Treacle was little more than a jailbird and a baby-peddler. I needed a friend. Aurora had saved my life – twice – and on that basis alone was about as good a friend as I was ever likely to get.

'It's complicated,' I said with a sigh, realising that I'd have to tell Aurora things I could never tell anyone, 'because although I've never set foot in this car park, I've seen the blue Buick and the rabbit's-foot key ring before.'

She raised the eyebrow over her non-seeing eye.

'In my … *dreams.*'

My shoulders slumped as a sweep of memories came back, but

this time it was textures only – the leaves, the splays of lichen on the rocks, the granular appearance of the soil, the rust on the Buick bumpers, the crackled paint on the car body. I thought of Birgitta on the beach to clear it out, and with the gurgling laugh of the child with the beach ball, the flashback evaporated.

'I so need a Dormeopath,' I said in a useless sort of voice.

Aurora told me that back in her civvy days she used to be a Sleepy-D, and that she wasn't doing anything for the next hour.

'We could have a coffee at the Wincarnis,' she said.

I glanced at my watch. Jonesy wasn't expecting to meet me until midday.

'Do we have time for me to retrieve Birgitta?'

'All the time you want.'

I crawled underneath the car and looked into Birgitta's violet eyes, hoping for some sort of recognition, but she simply stared at me blankly.

'I love you, Charlie,' she whispered.

'I love you, too,' I whispered back, my heart thumping. I knew I meant it, too – and not when I'd been her husband, but for myself, now. Yes, it was dumb, illogical and, admittedly, a little creepy, but who wouldn't? She was smart, driven, talented, and, as a bonus, exceptionally pleasing to the eye. Everything, in fact, except being alive – and that she didn't love me back, and couldn't and wouldn't, not ever.

'Kiki needs the cylinder,' she said, kind of mirroring Mrs Nesbit's demand for the cylinder in my dream. I fed her two Snickers then helped her out from under the car. Once out, she stood there, rocking on the balls of her feet, eyes scanning randomly around the basement until she found me, then locked hard on to my eyes. For a brief moment I thought she was there – but then her eyes wandered off again, and the moment was gone.

'So,' I said once we'd attached dog leads to the nightwalkers and headed for the exit ramp, 'the panga in a scabbard on your back. Is that actually practical?'

'Not really,' said Aurora, demonstrating how, if heavily dressed, it was almost impossible to reach in a hurry, 'but it's very in at the moment. Oh, word of advice: don't use a panga on nightwalkers. It's *really* messy.'

Glitzy Tiara mumbled about multi-pack toilet roll and the wisdom of 'Buy One Get One Free' deals while Eddie Tangiers attempted, while we walked, to bundle with each vehicle we passed and, once, a concrete building support. It might have been funny if it wasn't kind of sad.

'I've got some plasters and iodine in the truck,' said Aurora, for Tangiers' activities were not damage-free.

'Yes,' I said, 'that's gotta hurt.'

The Wincarnis

'… In the main square of every town there would be a large block of stone, inset with a bronze ring. Capital offenders would be stripped, shackled to the ring, then abandoned. Below the survival threshold of minus ten, the offender would last between two and six hours. Fear, drowsiness, torpor, death …'

– *Law and Order on the Winterlands*, by Idris Roberts

Aurora's transport was an ex-military command car painted in light sand camouflage, the wheels to the height of my chest. She pushed the fresh snow off the windshield while I tied the nightwalkers' leads to the back of the truck. We climbed aboard, the vehicle started with a hiss of compressed air, and as we drove towards the centre of town at a slow walking pace, I tried to make sense of what had just happened. There was no rational explanation as to how Birgitta could say the very same thing in life that I'd dreamed about the previous night. It didn't make sense. It *couldn't* make sense. Logic would demand that you dream about things that you'd already witnessed – dreams follow reality, not the other way round.

'How are you on HotPots?' asked Aurora as we took a right at the billboard.

'Nothing beyond General Skills training.'

'The *Cambrensis*' HotPot had an unexplained overheat a week ago,' she explained, gesturing towards the Dormitorium as we drove past.

'Luckily, the fuel rods dropped into the pond when it cooked up and shut itself down. Toccata ordered the *Cambrensis* abandoned. One of the rehoused residents was Carmen Miranda.'

'What, with the fruit hat and everything?' I asked.

'The very same.'

'But Carmen Miranda must be – *ancient*.'

'She credits the Samba for her longevity,' said Aurora, 'but I think it's more likely a statistical quirk of the ageing process.'

'Wow,' I said, surprised that she should be still alive, and, odder still, living out here. 'What's she doing now?'

'Not much,' said Aurora. 'When they opened her door they discovered that she'd walked. Joesy had to retire her.'

The tyres crunched on the rutted, refrozen snow as we passed the railway station and then finally reached the main square, where Aurora parked her vehicle, the three Vacants still tied to the back.

The town square appeared larger in full daylight, and unchanged these past four weeks aside from more snow and ice. We'd parked next to the bronze statue, and I could see now that it was a preacher, set on a sandstone plinth. He was holding a prayer book and in mid-oration, his features obscured by a concretion of snow that had turned to ice, thawed then refrozen, so the figure appeared to be both melting and weeping. Below the statue a man sat huddled in a foetal position, his blue-white arms clasped around his knees.

'Who's that?' I asked.

'Howell Harris,' said Aurora, 'a preacher who lived near here. There's a Dormitorium named after him. Died last century some time. Should be a statue of Don Hector, really – or Gwendolyn the – what are we up to now?

'Thirty-eighth, I think. Not the statue – the frozen guy.'

'Oh,' said Aurora, 'him. That's Jedediah Bloom, Sector Footman.'

'What did he do?' I said, looking closer.

'We caught him trying to smuggle drugs out of HiberTech, and that's a mandatory Frigicution – even if it was only to supply the winsomniacs.'

I stared at Bloom, thinking it was a bit harsh, even so.

'I was off-duty at the time,' said Aurora, probably thinking the same as I, 'and Hooke was acting Head of Security. He has very many fine qualities but the notion of proportionality is not one of them.'

I kneeled down and stared at the cadaver with an odd sense of morbid curiosity. Bloom was frozen quite solid. His pallid blue-grey skin was flecked with snow, and every single follicle of his winterdown was standing hard out in a last-ditch effort to forestall the inevitable. He was covered with a dusting of snowflakes, which made him look fluffy, and his milky eyes were wide open and staring off into the middle distance, his expression placid. Near the end you start to feel warm, hallucinate, and then lose all fear.

'He looks like he died only last night,' I said.

'He did,' said Aurora, 'as fresh as frozen peas.'

I hastily stood up, the recentness of his death somehow making the event seem more shocking. Bloom was the grim reality of Frigicution.

'That's the thing about the Winter,' said Aurora, 'it takes the lawless the same as it takes the diseased and the underweight and the elderly. Society's spring cleaner, hoovering up the substandard before they become a burden.'

Aurora walked toward the Wincarnis, and I followed. Above the door, the Edwardian woman on the Restorative Tonics sign was still grinning out at the Winter, her cheery smile and bright enamelled colours undiminished by season or cold.

Shamanic Bob looked up from the reception desk from where he had appeared to be dozing.

'Back to ride the night train to Dreamville?' he asked me.

'No,' I said.

'How are you and your odious bunch of sleep-shy?' asked Aurora. 'Thinned out much?'

'I'll pass on your good wishes,' said Shamanic Bob sarcastically.

We walked into the bar. At one table were a foursome playing Scrabble but they remained oblivious to our arrival. I recognised the receptionist named Josh from HiberTech, but not the others. The only other customers in the room were the drowsy named Zsazsa, who was more intriguing now her younger self had starred in my dream, and a dozen dozing dreamers, who paid us no attention at all.

'There are now fifty-four winsomniacs in the Sector,' said Aurora, sitting down and taking off her gloves, 'and there's been no wastage for almost five days. I left a note suggesting to Toccata that we tell them there's a good selection of videos at the *Captain Mayberry*. The trek would have at least a thirty per cent attrition rate, perhaps as high as forty if we timed it during an ice storm.'

'Is that legal?' I asked.

'The trick is to try and get them to do potentially fatal things voluntarily with a full understanding of the risks. We call it ethical reduction.'[52]

'Unless there *isn't* a good stock of videos in the *Mayberry*,' I said.

'And therein lies the problem,' replied Aurora. 'The selection isn't terrific. Mostly *Police Academy* comedies, endless *Die Hard* sequels and boxed sets of *Emmerdale* and *Dynasty*. Hey, Shambob. Two coffees.'

There was a grunt from Shamanic Bob and he moved with almost snail-like speed towards the coffee machine.

Aurora brought out her knitting. It wasn't a bobble hat this time, it was a sock with an Argyle pattern. We'd sat near the window so we could keep an eye on the nightwalkers. Since you couldn't actually own another human being, possession – and the bounty thereof – was based nominally on custody and proximity. But on reflection, I doubted, given Aurora's standing, that anyone would try and steal them.

'So,' she said, 'let me be your Dormeopath. Tell me as much or as little as you want.'

I paused to gather my thoughts, and told her how the blue Buick dream had been circulating around the *Sarah Siddons*. How I hadn't thought much about it; how I thought it was simply a Sub-beta dream panic.

'That's our view and that of the Consuls,' said Aurora, 'although we didn't know there actually *was* a blue Buick parked up in the garage. What sort of dreams were you having?'

'Not dreams as I imagined them to be,' I began. 'Half-remembered artefacts, disjointed and vague – but strong, vivid and full of detail. I know this sounds silly, but I dreamed I was Don Hector, with his feelings and his memories.'

'Go on.'

I recounted everything in as much detail as I could, but purposefully omitted the Birgitta dream because it seemed strangely private,

---

52. 'Proactive thinnage' was another euphemism, as was 'assisted winnowing'.

and an odd amalgam of my own childhood holiday memory and Birgitta's painting. I only told Aurora about the blue Buick, thinking I would apply any advice across to the other dream.

'Why am I dreaming about rocks, cars and disembodied hands?' I asked.

'Search me,' she said, 'and on the face of it this is all batshit crazy, but this is my take: the parts of the dream you were told about are easy to explain, simple auto-suggestion. They mentioned it, you dreamt it. You saw stuff, knew about Zsazsa, it was included. The rest of the dream was you just filling in the gaps.'

'I agree,' I said, 'but what about the rabbit's-foot key ring and the car being precisely the same? I dreamt those and *later* I'm finding they have a basis in reality.'

'I'm going out on a limb here, but all I can suggest is that the recall of your dream is still in a state of delayed suggestion. Memory remains plastic after waking, and it's possible everything you *think* was in the dream might not actually have been in the dream at all.'

'You mean,' I said slowly, 'the details of my dream have been joggled in retrospectively? The rabbit's foot and the detail on the Buick *weren't* in the dream?'

'The mind needs to remap on waking,' she said, 'and reinforce the millions of neural pathways. Slumber is pretty well understood from a physiological point of view; it's how personality and memory recover from the doldrums of synaptic tick-over that is hibernation's greatest mystery. So what I'm thinking is that it's possible for more recent memories to fill the place of absent, older ones. A fair description would be a severe case of déjà vu. Not just a feeling that something has happened before, but a *certainty* that it has – and in that certainty, doubt, confusion, fear, paranoia.'

'So even dreaming myself as Don Hector might not have happened? I only created that in my head when I knew the car was his?'

'I hadn't thought of that, but yes, it's a plausible explanation.'

'Ah,' I said, mulling it over.

ShamBob entered the lounge and put down a large plate of chips in front of Zsazsa, then moved towards us with two coffees.

It was real coffee and I inhaled the mellow fragrance gratefully.

'It wasn't all déjà vu,' I said, still with questions. 'The blue Buick, for one. What was that doing in the garage?'

Aurora had to consider this carefully.

'The car could have been there for years. Suzy Watson might have chanced upon the Buick and she constructs a nightmare around it during her Dreamstate. She tells everyone including Moody, they relate the dream to you – bingo.'

'But that precise model?'

'You only heard it was blue and a Buick from Suzy,' said Aurora, 'the reality was—'

'—added when I actually saw it. Okay, I get it now.'

I thought of Birgitta. If this were true, the plasticity of the dream would have created the scenario with her, too. Her second name would have been chalked up on the basement door, and the vision in the leaf-green swimsuit could have been created when I imagined her equivalent look in the painting she did of me. Even telling me she loved Charlie might only have happened for the first time under the car, and it would be directed at her husband, not me.

I lapsed into silence.

'Hard to accept, I know,' she said, 'but narcosis is like that. This is intriguing, so tell me if you have any other dreams. But here's a tip: if you value your career, *tell no one else about the dream.*'

'I haven't, and don't intend to.'

She smiled, opened her hands and stretched them towards me. I placed mine between them and she clasped them tightly, the shorthand of the Winter embrace. It was firm, trusting and, unlike the full embrace, actually felt warm. As we clasped, I noted that a functioning eye wasn't all she'd lost. She was missing her ring finger – from both hands.

The alarm on her watch buzzed at her plaintively.

'That's me out of here,' she said, stifling a yawn while her unseeing eye blinked rapidly, 'and one other thing: you'll be seeing Toccata pretty soon and she and I have something of a … strained relationship. It'll be better for us both if this meeting remained private. As far as you're concerned, I rescued you from the nightwalkers in the car park, and we parted company outside the *Siddons* – yes?'

This didn't sound good, and Aurora sensed my reticence.

'I need an oath on this, Charlie. I saved your butt twice, remember.'

'Okay,' I said, 'oath.'

'Good. Now, I don't want to seem underhand or insulting but Toccata's a poisonous, untrustworthy, self-serving little reptile – with a severe personality disorder and a disquieting capacity for cannibalism.'

'That sounds underhand, insulting – and slanderous.'

'It's fair comment. I'll leave Birgitta for you to deal with. There's a pit behind the *Siddons* where you can thump her and dump her. It's normal to sprinkle on some lime for when the thaw sets in. Here's another tip: get her to walk there herself. It'll save you a lot of heavy lifting. Oh, and don't forget her thumb to claim the bounty.'

I tried to swallow, but found I couldn't.

'Right,' I croaked, 'good tip, thank you.'

'No problem. By the way, did you see Hugo Foulnap again?'

'No, but then I've been asleep.'

'Of course. Well, keep an eye out and if you see him, talk to me first. Oh, and give Toccata a message from me: "Queen's knight takes bishop, hope you are devoured by slime in your sleep". Got it?'

'Queen's knight takes bishop … and the other stuff. Yes, got it.'

She smiled, and quite without warning leaned forward, placed a soft hand around my neck and kissed me full on the mouth. I was taken aback, but before I could say or do anything she was up and out of the door. I looked around the lounge to see if anyone had observed us and saw ShamBob cleaning some coffee cups in an indiscreet manner.

I touched my lips where Aurora had kissed me. It hadn't been a misplaced peck; she had parted her lips slightly upon contact and I'd tasted her warm mouth on mine. She smelled of clean laundry, Aveda conditioner and Ludlow scent, and her shirt had been only loosely buttoned. When she leaned forward I had seen the top of her left breast, and clearly visible amidst the soft down of her winter-coat, there was a birthmark the shape of Guernsey.

Shamanic Bob walked over and sat down opposite me.

'What are you doing back so soon?'

'I've not been away.'

'Undercover?' he said in a conspiratorial tone.

'Under the *covers*,' I said, 'over at the *Siddons*. I overslept.'

'I shouldn't spread that around,' he said with a smile, 'but the first Winter up can sure be a dog. So tell me about Aurora: have you known her long?'

Gossip is thin on the ground during Slumbertime. To souls bored by the tedium of the Winter it can become a commodity of value, fourth only to protein, warmth and loyalty. But it struck me that an association with Aurora might actually help me, given that most people seemed to be frightened of her.

'Four weeks,' I said, truthfully enough.

'O-kay,' said ShamBob slowly, 'and what – if I might be so bold – does Chief Toccata say about it?'

'Is that relevant?' I asked.

ShamBob's mouth actually dropped open. I wasn't sure why but he was either shocked, or impressed, or outraged, or a mixture of all three.

I was going to leave, but then I remembered about the last time we'd met. He'd said something about Morphenox being a fluke, and I asked him what he meant by that.

He smiled. Winsomniacs liked conspiracy theories almost as much as they liked undersleeping on someone else's dollar.

'Morphenox was originally plain old "F-652",' he began, 'developed as a powerful Dreamblocker, devised so there could be a non-dreaming control group during trials of a cancelled project named *Dreamspace*, where Don Hector was trying to make us dream not less, but better. But then someone noticed the dreamless group were losing significantly less weight during hibernation, and that was the turning point: up until that point, no one realised just how much energy dreams were burning. Block them and go to sleep lighter. It's that simple.'

This took a moment to sink in.

'You're kidding?'

'I'm not.'

'A revolution in Hibernetics,' I said slowly, 'wealth, power, influence and the current geopolitical landscape, based on the unexpected results of a control group?'

He grinned.

187

'Quite something, eh? Trouble is, they can never seem to manufacture enough of it to go around. If I was a cynical man, I'd think there was a degree of social control regarding its limited distribution.'

Maisie Rogers had said the same thing. The lines were fairly clear – along wealth and class, mostly. The global hibernating village, equal in sleep, equal in dignity, was a myth.

'And,' he continued, 'any news of an improved Morphenox with full distribution benefits should be met with caution. HiberTech cares more for dosh than dozing.'

'We're not having this conversation,' I said. 'Tell me about Project Dreamspace. What do you mean: "wanting to make us dream not less, but better"?'

But I might have been talking to myself. Shamanic Bob, exhausted by the efforts of conversation, had fallen fast asleep on the table and was snoring loudly.

The Consulate

'... "Lucky" Ned Farnesworth and his gang were the poster children
of Villains everywhere. So reviled, in fact, that the thump-target dummies
at the Academy were shaped like Ned himself. Farnesworth had been
a stockbroker, mammoth farmer, stamp dealer and professional gambler.
Highly intelligent but utterly ruthless, he commanded huge loyalty
among his followers – and fear from the Consul Service ...'

– 'Winter Villains' Top Trump card circa 1994

The three nightwalkers tethered to the back of the command vehicle
were rocking gently back and forth as a precursor to Torpor, but
Aurora herself was nowhere to be seen. I released Birgitta and fed
her two flapjacks.

'I love you, Charlie,' she said.

'Don't,' I replied in a quiet voice, 'it really doesn't help.'

'Kiki needs the cylinder,' she added.

'And neither does that. Which Kiki? RealSleep's Kiki or another
one?'

She didn't answer, and we walked back to the *Siddons* in relative
silence, my mind coming to terms with the fact that my dream had
been moulded retrospectively. I tried to see if there were elements
in the Birgitta dream that might refute this hypothesis, but there was
nothing. Everything that had occurred in the dream was my narcosis-
befuddled mind filling in my memory cracks like so much builder's
plaster. I trudged quietly through the snow-packed streets holding
Birgitta's hand, something that, while purely one-sided, did feel oddly
comforting.

Jonesy was already waiting for me outside the *Siddons,* next to a
red-and-white Consulate Sno-Trac, the engine almost completely
silenced, the only sound the faint rattle of the rain-trap on top of

the exhaust stack. It was parked next to a telephone box that was half buried in a snowdrift, and Jonesy was reading an ancient copy of *Wonder Woman & the Wintervolk Kid*, and chuckling occasionally. Next to her was a tartan travel rug folded neatly atop a picnic set. She was taking the 'long-partnered' game seriously.

'Caught one already?' she asked as soon as she saw us. 'Quick work. Goodness, isn't that Birgitta?'

'Legally-speaking, it's just something she used to walk around in.'

'We sang together in the choir,' said Jonesy. 'Did a very passable Pirate Queen in last year's *Pirates of Penzance*. Nice enough girl, if a little prickly. She turned down a five-figure two-child deal from a team scouting for Wackford & Co.'

'She'd have had very beautiful children.'

'Hence the five-figure deal. She could have bought herself out of the Douzey on the Wackford deal and moved to somewhere less lugubrious – no one figured out why she didn't.'

I think I knew the reason. She told me she'd married, but the whole thing seemed secretive. Possibly a *union de l'amour* – committed personally to one another, but not recognised in law.

'Does Baggy do any tricks?' she asked.

'She used to be into cannibalism and now she's into Snickers, mumbling and shortbread.'

'More of a reason for immediate retirement than a trick, wouldn't you say?'

'I suppose, yes.'

Jonesy looked at her watch.

'Toccata isn't back yet, but we need to be ready to move when she is. Do you want me to retire her for you?'

I looked across at Birgitta, who seemed utterly unconcerned by everything. I weighed the matter carefully. Disposing of Birgitta – even if she herself was long gone – just didn't feel right. And not just because I had liked her, but for the simple fact that I was, in some small way, responsible for her current status. I had given her the Morphenox, after all.

'It's *possible* she might do tricks,' I said with some reticence, 'perhaps we should—'

'Did you ever wonder how I did this?' asked Jonesy, holding up the withered remnant. She had only a finger and thumb remaining on her right hand.

I hadn't given it a second thought. Consuls often left body parts littered around the Winter, and indeed, anyone who hadn't lost a bit of themselves by their fifth season were clearly risk-averse. But if Jonesy mentioned it, it was probably for a reason.

'It had crossed my mind,' I replied obligingly.

'I was jumped by nightwalkers,' she said in a matter-of-fact way, 'gone hive-mind over in Builth Wells. Rare but not unheard of. They took chunks out of any exposed flesh. I'd be nightwalker shit if it wasn't for Toccata wading in. I'll do any of them now. I've even,' she added, with an excited gleam in her eye, 'whacked a celebrity nightwalker. Guess which one.'

'Was it Carmen Miranda?'

'Oh,' she said, disappointed that her dubious claim to fame had been scooped, 'you heard about that.'

She nodded towards Birgitta.

'But anyway: I don't mind retiring them. In fact, I'm trying to set a new Regional Retiring Record. I've got sixty-one so far. So let me do it. Please?'

I thanked her but said that I should be the one to do it.

I returned a half-hour later. Jonesy was already in the Sno-Trac listening to a weather report on the shortwave, and I opened the rear door and picked my way through the cabin to join her. A Sno-Trac would usually take eight people plus driver, but this one was configured for freight. It was practical but not fast and, most importantly, had an efficient heater and a modern H4S radar set.

But it wasn't the TechSpecs of the Sno-Trac that were forefront in my mind.

I'd wrapped Birgitta's left thumb in a pocket handkerchief and I laid it on the coaming. It had been probably the least pleasant moment of my life so far, and I could still feel myself shaking. But I had done what had to be done.

'You all right, Wonky?' asked Jonesy, sensing my agitation.

'No, not really – and I'd be a whole lot happier if you didn't call me Wonky.'

'We're way beyond that now.'

She indicated Birgitta's thumb.

'First one?'

I nodded.

'The first is always the hardest, but believe me, the feelings of nausea will pass. Toccata's returned and you're driving.'

The ride to the Winter Consulate would have been simple, but Jonesy insisted we went around the one-way system, which took an extra fifteen minutes at the excruciatingly slow 55 dB sound limit. She pointed out the theatre as we rumbled past.

'André Preview drops in two weeks from now and a week after that there'll be something from the Wolfitt Players. Last season we had the Reduced Shakespeare Company doing "Highlights of the Mostly Complete History of Condensing Stuff (abridged)".'

'Any good?'

'Quick – even for them. Listen, have you thought up any more good reminiscences for us to talk about?'

'I … haven't really given it much thought.'

'I'm working on a really good one about going to the Hotbox in Swindon like *years* ago and listening to the last performance of Holroyd Wilson. We kissed for the first time outside, but I was horribly drunk and then vomited on your feet.'

'I still have those shoes,' I said.

'You *kept* them?' said Jonesy. 'You're one sick sentimental puppy, Wonky.'

'It wasn't sentiment,' I said, 'it was economics. They were expensive. What does Toccata want to say to me?'

'She'll want to know about Logan, I imagine, then she needs to decide what to do with you. It's possible you'll join us. We're short-handed as we lost two Deputies recently; one to an ice storm and the other to stupidity – it was my ex-partner, Cotton. Found Dead in Sleep.'

'I'm sorry to hear that.'

'Tried to kip *au Jeffries* in an outhouse under skins and branches.

Quite lovely but not too bright. We bundled once or twice, but only recreationally, of course.'

'Of course,' I said, now used to open talk about such matters. 'So with those two missing, how many Consuls do you have?'

She counted them out on her fingers.

'There's the Chief, me, Fodder — we served together in the Ottoman. Despite a gruff exterior he's quite the sweetheart. We've never bundled, but it's a possibility what with Cotton dead. I always think it best to bundle with only one co-Winterer at a time, don't you?'

'That might be considered sound advice, yes.'

'Also on the list is Danny Pockets, a freelancer from Swansea who was called in to assist with Pantry Defence. He's on a Daily Rate, which isn't really fair on the rest of us. Laura Strowger helps out but is civilian, so doesn't count, really, and the last is the bondsman Jim Treacle, who is a hopeless twerp without a shred of charm, winterskills or decency. He thinks I'm going to marry him.'

'Will you?'

'I'd sooner marry Agent Hooke, but it's complicated: my mum borrowed lavishly from Treacle to bag a rich widower from Sector Fifteen. That didn't work out, so Treacle transferred the loan to my hand in marriage. Not sure how *that* happened. Anyway, we're trying to spin out the Hard No for as long as possible, otherwise it's a loan default and he can take my mum's house. If you can get Treacle to write off the Debt and head elsewhere, there's five hundred euros in it for you. Park anywhere.'

I pulled in and checked the compressed air reservoir was full before shutting down.

'A tip about Chief Consul Toccata,' said Jonesy. 'Honesty is the *only* policy and don't speak unless spoken to. She's not so bad; just runs hot and cold. But don't fret. If she respects you as a person, everything will be fine.'

'Can I ask a question?'

'Sure.'

'Is it true Toccata eats nightwalkers garnished with mint?'

'Absolutely not.'

'That's a relief.'

'No, I heard she *feeds* them peppermint for several weeks before-hand – to make them more flavoursome.'

'She keeps them alive until needed?'

'Needs must in the Winter, Wonky. Believe me, if you were starving you'd eat your dead mother's partly-decomposed foot. What do you think the Consular staff ate in Sector Eight North during the Winter of '76? Snow?'

I said nothing.

'C'mon,' she added, smiling to try and dilute some of the less palatable truths about the Winter, 'and if I were you, don't mention eating nightwalkers to Toccata. It's a touchy subject.'

Aurora's four-wheel drive was still parked outside the Consulate, unchanged from when I'd seen it last. Eddie Tangiers and Glitzy Tiara were still tied to the back and had dropped into unmoving *Rigor torpis* as a defence against the cold.

'Well, well,' said Jonesy, 'two more for the Sector Twelve retirement plan.'

'They're Aurora's,' I said, probably a mite too defensively. 'She was planning to take them up to HiberTech.'

'Must have run out of time. Treacle will be on the front desk. I'll catch you up.'

She patted me on the shoulder and climbed into Aurora's four-wheel drive.

I was buzzed in through the shock-gates, where little had changed. On the counter was a tear-off calendar telling me there were ninety-one days until Springrise, and at the rear I could see Laura, doing some filing. She looked at me curiously and gave a cheery wave, which I returned. Beyond the desks was a frosted-glass partition to an inner office with a half-glazed door, upon which were painted the words:

Ms A. Toccata Chief Winter Consul Sector 12

Through the frosted glass I could see Toccata as a shadowy figure who appeared to be having an animated conversation on the telephone. I say 'conversation', but it really seemed to be a one-sided rant. The glass was soundproofed so her voice was muffled and indistinct, but it seemed she was yelling about the incompetence of the other party, and sporadically peppering her speech with a colourful array of expletives. I felt myself tense. I wasn't going to enjoy this.

Standing behind the counter and speaking on the telephone in more measured tones was Jim Treacle. He looked fatter than when I'd last seen him; only bondsmen could afford to gain weight in the Winter. He looked up, smiled and placed a finger in the air to indicate he'd not be long.

'We've currently got fifty-four extra winsomniacs, which is way in excess of our official allocation,' he said on the phone, 'so if we don't get at least two hundred person-days of food by the end of the week, then the Chief Consul will come over and explain her displeasure to you in person with a steel spike.' There was a pause. 'Yes, those were her *precise* words and I think she will almost certainly make good on her threat. Good day, sir.'

He put the phone down, coughed his deep racking cough and then turned to face me.

'So, Worthing,' he said with a grin, 'Jonesy said you overslept big time.'

'I had an alarm clock issue.'

'Sure you did.'

He leaned forward.

'Did Jonesy mention me at all?'

'No,' I lied, 'I don't think so.'

'I'm up to be married to her with a siring-in rider, but I think she's getting cold feet. What do you think?'

Jonesy didn't tell me Treacle had contracted for genetic rights within the marriage. It was kind of a big deal and controversial. Women needed more genetic options than partner choice alone might provide, and there was talk about enshrining that right in law. I lowered my voice too.

'It's a big decision.'

'I know; there was this Deputy with whom she was bundling, but now Cotton's dead I'm hoping she'll retire from recreational oopla and transfer her permanent affections to me.'

'That's … one of many uniquely plausible scenarios,' I said.

'I agree,' said Treacle, 'but you're here and you're young and even though a bit squiffy looking, no offence—'

'Little taken.'

'—I'm still worried your most attractive feature might bump you up her list.'

'And what *is* my most attractive feature?' I asked, curious to know.

'You're not me. Promise me you'll turn her down if she makes a play? And just so we're clear, "making a play" is defined as anything beyond typical co-worker stuff: dinner, walking hand in hand through the snow, playing Cluedo or inventing past histories. *Especially* inventing past histories. You agree?'

'O-kay.'

'Good. Toccata will be out as soon as she's finished ranting. The coffee is over there. If you have any easy questions, just holler.'

Treacle moved off to deal with some paperwork and I went to pour myself what Treacle had generously described as coffee. I sniffed it gingerly. It smelled of rotting mushrooms mixed in with lamp oil, and tasted about the same.

'I don't drink coffee yet,' came a voice behind me, 'and from what I've smelled and seen, I probably won't start.'

It was Laura Strowger, who had wandered over to say hello. She'd heard that I'd overslept and been forgotten, and her attitude was sympathetic, rather than mocking, which made a change. I hoped Toccata would be the same.

'Has the Gronk made an appearance?' I asked.

'Not so far,' she said, 'but we still have ninety-one days to go. I've been laying out unfolded clothes at strategic places around the locality and will be watching them closely. What do you make of this?'

She dug a Polaroid from her shoulder bag and showed it to me. All I could see was a lump in the snow next to a gas lamp. I stared at the photo for a moment.

'Did it move much?'

'Hardly at all,' she replied, delighted that I was showing any interest. 'Frostgoblins are known to wait for long hours in one place before they pounce.'

'Pounce to do *what*, exactly?'

'Nobody knows,' she said, eyes wide open, 'hence my research.'

I handed back the photo.

'It's a fire hydrant, isn't it?'

'Yes,' she said, staring at the Polaroid in a crestfallen manner, 'almost certainly. Treacle agreed that photographic evidence would be allowable,' she went on. 'Do you have a camera?'

I said that I didn't, so she fetched me a Consul-issue Kodak Instamatic fitted with a fresh flashcube, and two spares in a box. A crude device, but without batteries of any sort, they were more reliable in subzero than anything else on the market.

'Take as many snaps as you want and then get the camera back to me; but wind it on with care; the cold makes the film brittle.'

'Can the Gronk *be* photographed?' I asked, shoving the camera in my bag.

'I've no idea,' she replied. 'I'm beginning to think that Wintervolk might be something akin to an escalating night terror that gives physicality to the fears within the mind. It makes it a much harder sell to Treacle. Firstly whether an existential fear has the equivalency of a tangible one, and if it does and can kill you, does that count as proven existence?'

'Are you *sure* you're only sixteen?' I asked. 'You seem kind of ... *smart*.'

'That was *really* patronising,' she said, 'but I forgive you. I have a genetic disorder of the hypothalamus that prevents me hibernating. I sleep about eight hours in the twenty-four all year round. While my peers have been unproductively pumping out the zeds, I've been adding to my knowledge base and maturity. My mental age is closer to twenty-two. It doesn't make me a sage, but I'm certainly not a teenager.'

'Is this a rare condition? I've never heard of it.'

'It's rare,' she sighed, 'hence the wager.'

'I know this is none of my business,' I said, 'but why agree to wager your firstborn on something as nebulous as the Gronk? It seems almost insanely reckless, if you don't mind me saying.'

She stared at me for a moment.

'It's not for my firstborn,' she said slowly, 'it's for my *secondborn*.'

'How does that make it any better?'

'Here's how: when I was two my parents sold the option on my firstborn to Partwood Associates to pay off their gambling debts. The option was resold several times before being packaged with other subprime child options and eventually on to Jim Treacle as part of a collateralised child obligation. My genetic sleep disorder means I possess a genome in which HiberTech have a great deal of interest. I've chosen not to license my genetic rights, and my unborn should have that right, too. I don't want them to go to HiberTech to be some kind of – I don't know – lab rat.'

'How much is the firstborn child option worth?'

'Treacle has told HiberTech he wants two million euros at my eighteenth.'

'You'll get half. That's the deal.'

'It's not about the money, and they can't force me to have children – but I think I want to, and if I do, well, I want them to be born unencumbered by legalities.'

'Okay, but you've got a buy-back clause. Legally, there's *always* a buy-back clause.'

'*Precisely*, but it was pegged at fifty thousand by the courts and I barely have a grand.'

'So if you lose the wager,' I said slowly, 'you lose the genetic rights to two children, Treacle and you make a fortune – but HiberTech obtain legal access to a couple of kids with a potentially valuable genome?'

'Pretty much. But if I *win* the wager,' she added, 'I get no money but retain my children's rights.'

'You're very brave.'

'Nope,' she said sadly, 'I'm just a girl who's all out of options – and who had rubbish parents.'

'It could have been worse,' I said, 'they could have harvested and then sold all your eggs the day after your sixteenth birthday to pay for a, I don't know – a new roof, kitchen extension and a minibus.'

'I guess. But this is the only wager Treacle would take. The Gronk is out there. I just have to get some evidence. Keep that camera handy, won't you?'

She jumped down from the counter where she'd been sitting, gave me a cheery smile and returned to her work. She was technically a winsomniac, but was earning her tuck. There was a world of difference between the deserving and undeserving awake.

My attention wandered back to the wall that was covered with the pictures of the missing. A sea of faces, all absent. Most ages, every gender, no pattern. As I scanned the posters a particular set of eyes caught my attention, sunk deep in the overlapping mass of lost souls. They were the same eyes I'd seen staring back at me from the Polaroid in my dream, the one that had been taken of me and Birgitta by the photographer on the Gower. Charles. *Birgitta's* Charles. I reached out and plucked the picture from the board.

The missing man used to work at HiberTech as an orderly, and his name, I read, was Charles Webster. He went missing three years before, just after starting a Winter season – pretty much as Birgitta had described her missing husband.

And that wasn't possible.

I couldn't have recognised him because I didn't know what he looked like. *Reality first, then dream.* I felt myself grow woozy again, and oak-dappled sunlight began to filter through to the office floor. I steadied myself against a table and took long, slow breaths. Treacle hadn't noticed my attack of the narcs, Laura was busy filing and Toccata was still ranting behind the glass partition. I calmed myself, and repeated *Birgitta Birgitta Birgitta Birgitta* to quell the sense of rising panic. It worked, and now calmer, I ran over the likely scenario: I'd clothed my dream with Charles Webster's name and face retrospectively. That he had the same first name as mine was coincidence, nothing more.

'What you got there?'

I jumped, but it was only Treacle.

'Some guy named Webster,' I mumbled, passing him the flyer, 'went missing three years ago.'

Treacle stared at the picture and nodded.

'First season I was here. We never found him. Actually,' he added, 'we never looked. HiberTech staff are HiberTech problems. Why the interest?'

I had to think quickly.

'We were at the same Pool, though ten years apart. I think he was popular with the sisterhood and they'd always wanted to know what happened to him.'

'Ah,' said Treacle, 'keep it if you want.'

'Thank you,' I said, and folded up the flyer and put it in my pocket.

'Hullo, Treacle,' said Jonesy, entering through the shock-gate and sitting down to pull off her boots. 'Enter these in the Vermin Control book and tally up my record, will you?'

She tossed an evidence bag containing two freshly severed thumbs on the desk.

'Will do,' said Treacle cheerily. 'That must be sixty-two, yes?'

'Sixty-three.'

There was another explosive level of muffled swearing from behind the frosted glass.

Treacle and Jonesy smiled as though this sort of thing happened all the time, and we heard the phone slammed down, then a crash as something was either kicked or thrown across the room.

'She's a bit ... *sweary*,' I said.

'You should hear her when she really gets pissed off.'

I had a thought and pulled Birgitta's severed thumb out of my pocket. It was still wrapped in a handkerchief, the blood now caked dark brown. I felt a sense of nausea rise up within me, and handed it to Jonesy.

'Here,' I said, 'do you want to add this to your score?'

'Oh, you *darling*!' she said, eagerly accepting the prize and carefully placing it on the counter next to the other two. She beamed at me and went off to her desk. Treacle glared at me as though I'd just given her flowers, chocolates, a TOG-28 coat *and* a card.

'I thought you said I'd have no problems from you?' he said, once she was out of earshot.

'It was only a thumb,' I whispered back.

'That's how it started with Cotton,' said Treacle in a grumbly sort of voice, 'first a thumb, then a gift, sort-of-real coffee in the Wincarnis. Next thing you know you've been bumped up to number one on her bundling list. If you are, will you describe what it's like for three hundred euros?'

'No.'

'Cotton did,' he said in a whiny sort of voice.

'I'm not Cotton.'

Jonesy didn't see or hear this exchange; she was busy pecking out a report on a typewriter that more closely resembled an antiquated pipe organ. Treacle held up Birgitta's thumb.

'Whose thumb is this anyway?'

'Birgitta,' I said, 'from the *Siddons*.'

'Baggy went walkies?' he murmured. 'That's a shame – she was quite delightful in a perpetually pissed-off sort of way. Amazing eyes, and a terrific painter. We dated once.'

'Really?' I said, not meaning it to sound quite so incredulous. Treacle sighed.

'If you must know,' he said, 'I bought a date with her at a charity auction in aid of the Sector Twelve Pool. She didn't find any of my jokes or anecdotes remotely interesting, then threatened to bite me on the face if I tried to kiss her when we said goodnight. She didn't elaborate, but I figured a second date was out of the question.'

'Very astute of you.'

He held up the two thumbs and stared at them.

'The large thumb was from a travelling sire named Eddie Tangiers,' I said, 'the smaller from a female, also *Siddons*, mid-twenties, freshly married.'

'I'll call Lloyd,' he muttered, 'he'll know.'

He wrote down 'Tangiers' and 'Manderlay' and 'Newlywed *Siddons*' on a slip of paper and went off to confirm them.

'What do you think?' asked Jonesy, who had finished her report and was hunting in vain for a stapler.

'What do I think about what?'

'About Treacle.'

'Owning Laura's child options makes him something of a heel.'

'To a bondsman, that's good business — and legal. They'll both be millionaires when Laura hits eighteen; I can see her point, though. I meant *aside* from that.'

'He's very keen on you.'

'I know,' she said, looking all crestfallen. 'Do you think I should just kill him and make it look like a Gronk attack? It would help Laura out, too.'

'You could pay back the dowry,' I suggested.

'Yeah, right — and who would I borrow the cash from? Treacle himself?'

'No, you could—'

I didn't get to finish my sentence as the door to Toccata's office had opened. I turned, expecting to see Winter Consul Toccata. But it wasn't — it was Aurora. I opened my mouth to greet her but then stopped. Although she looked the same, her demeanour seemed utterly different. Aurora had been relaxed and friendly, whereas this woman seemed sharp, driven, and utterly without humour. She strode forward with a purposeful swagger and a clearly aggressive sense of purpose. The only other differences I could see were in her clothes, which were now Consular uniform, and her eyes. Unlike Aurora's, her *right* was gazing absently off and looking blank, and her *left* fixed me with a steely glare.

But they weren't twins. Aurora and Toccata were the same person.

Toccata

'... The barograph recorded atmospheric pressure as a trace of ink on a 12hr strip of paper and was not only useful for gauging the weather, but could detect a pulse weapon's discharge at a kilometre, less in a snowstorm. A skilled reader could often tell not just the weapon's power and vortex gradient from the bump or spike profile, but the range, too ...'

— *Handbook of Winterology*, 1st edition, Hodder & Stoughton

'Well, well,' said Toccata, 'the forgotten sleeper of the *Sarah Siddons*. Charlie Worthing, isn't it?'

Confused by the sudden turn of events, I blurted out the first thing that came into my head.

'You know I am.'

Toccata's eye flashed dangerously.

'I never ask questions I already know the answer to. Waste of my time, waste of yours. So, again: are you ...'

Her voice trailed off. She narrowed her eye and looked at Treacle and Jonesy in turn.

'Oh, I get it,' she said, 'a bunch of comedians. You didn't tell Worthing Aurora and I we looked vaguely similar, did you?'

'Since Jonesy found Worthing,' said Treacle, pointing an accusatory finger at her and demonstrating in the clearest manner why Jonesy wanted nothing to do with him. 'She could have done so. In fact, I thought she had. Which is why I didn't.'

'I wanted to see the shocked look on Worthing's face,' said Jonesy after giving Treacle a withering look. 'The Winters are long and we have to make our own entertainment.'

'Make it some other way,' growled Toccata, 'whittling or ice sculpture or something.'

She turned back to me.

'But you *are* Charlie Worthing, I take it?'

'I am, ma'am.'

'Charlie prefers to be called Wonky,' said Jonesy.

'I doubt that *so* very much,' said Toccata, 'but Wonky it is. You were there when Jack Logan was … murdered?'

She almost chose the word 'died' but then pulled back and substituted 'murder' instead. It was not hard to see either how she felt about it, nor who ultimately was to blame.

'Yes, I was.'

'He was one of the best,' she said. 'How did she get the drop on him?'

I knew now why he'd paused: he couldn't kill Aurora because he'd be killing Toccata, too. Odd, I thought, that he could countenance farming a nightwalker – but would rather be dead than kill someone he was once in love with.

'He could easily have thumped Aurora,' I said in a quiet voice, 'but he paused. And in that moment, she had him.'

'Paused?' said Toccata. 'Why would he do that?'

I looked at Jonesy for help but she just stared back at me.

'I don't know,' I said.

'I've read Aurora's misspelled and poorly worded report,' said Toccata after staring at me for a few seconds. 'It claims you were about to be executed and that Aurora thumped Logan "in order to save the life of a Novice Consul". Why was he going to kill you? What had you done?'

'I hadn't *done* anything,' I said, 'but I'd given him the impression that I would have reported about how he and Foulnap were going to farm Mrs Tiffen.'

'You knew that for a fact? Did he actually *say* he was going to kill you?'

I thought hard.

'On reflection,' I said slowly, 'perhaps they didn't want me dead.'

'Explain yourself.'

I took a deep breath.

'The conversation began with Lopez saying: "Maybe we can trust the Novice, I didn't sign up to all this in order to start killing Consuls".

Then Foulnap said that he was with Lopez on this, and Logan said: "We can't risk any of us being discovered, besides, Aurora's in town".'

Jonesy and Toccata looked at one another.

'Go on.'

'Then Foulnap asked: "How did she get wind of us?" and Logan said: "We don't know that she did. I'll deal with Worthing, you deal with Mrs Tiffen". He then gestured for me to leave the room and we did, and he then said: "You should have listened to me earlier and just let it all go". And I then asked him if he could tell Sister Zygotia where she could find my body, and he told me not to be overdramatic. And that's when the elevator doors opened to reveal Aurora. He was dead five seconds later.'

I finished my account and fell silent. Toccata peered at me carefully, but when she next spoke it wasn't about Logan.

'Was that word for word?'

'Pretty much.'

'You must have a very good memory, Worthing.'

'Second prize in the Swansea Town Memory Bee. Six hundred and forty-eight random words memorised after only two readings.'

'Did Logan know about this?'

'I think it's why he employed me.'

Toccata and Jonesy looked at one another again. There was something going on, something I wasn't aware of. Mind you, I could have guessed that from all the way back in Cardiff.

'So,' she said, 'why didn't you just keep your mouth shut as Logan asked?'

'Because I'd sworn to uphold the law.'

'No, you hadn't: you'd sworn to uphold the sanctity of the sleep-state and ensure the most favourable outcome is enjoyed by the majority.'

'Isn't that the same thing?'

'Not the same thing at all. What if Logan was on to something bigger? Something so big and so righteous and so important that your death would have simply been side-issue collateral, a necessary yet barely regrettable loss on the road to the most favourable outcome?'

'Was he?'

'It's hypothetical, Worthing. Work with me on this.'

'Then yes,' I said, 'I could have done what he'd asked. Let Foulnap take Mrs Tiffen, gone on as if nothing had happened. But I didn't. I did what I felt was right.'

'The road to Spring is littered with well-intentioned morons,' remarked Toccata, 'but I'm satisfied you were acting upon conscience.'

She stared at me again.

'You met her today, didn't you?'

'Yes, ma'am,' I said, relieved we were moving away from the subject of Logan's death, 'she stopped three nightwalkers from eating me. Oh, and she had a message: Queen's knight takes bishop.'

I decided to leave out the 'being eaten alive by slime' part of the message.

'Queen's knight takes bishop?' said Toccata with a sudden burst of bright-eye enthusiasm. 'An uncharacteristically dumb move, unless ... *unless* she's attempting the courageously risky yet certifiably insane Will Francis Queen & Double Rook Sacrifice. You'd better come in.'

She led me through to her office, which was beyond disordered. Papers and files were stacked almost to the roof and were so precariously balanced they looked as if they might collapse at any second, burying us all. She beckoned for Jonesy to join us, indicated for me to sit, then went to a chessboard set out in mid-game. She moved the knight and picked out the bishop. I noted she was playing black, and had to rotate the board several times so she could see all the pieces.

'It *is* the Will Francis,' she muttered under her breath, then moved her rook. Not to take Aurora's queen, which was horribly exposed, but to take a pawn and place Aurora's king in check. 'Which can,' she continued, 'be defeated by the Mays Single Pawn Do-or-Die Offensive.'

I looked at Jonesy, who shrugged.

'When you see the dopey cow again,' she said without looking up, 'queen's rook takes bishop's pawn two, check – and tell her from me that I hope she gets the mildew and her tits fall off.'

'Yes, ma'am,' I said, still confused. Not by the chess game itself, in which their play might be best described as 'eccentrically inspiring', but that they *could* play each other.

'Right,' said Toccata as she sat down behind her desk, 'to work.' She looked up and was about to say something, then stopped.

'Where have you gone, Worthing?'

'Here,' I said, sitting precisely where I had been all along.

She turned her head to place me well to the left of her.

'Of course you are. Jonesy? Explain.'

'Best move to the other side of the room, Worthing; the Chief can only see the left side of anything.'

I got up and moved as requested, noting that the left side of her desk was clean and orderly while the right was a cluttered mass of old coffee cups, items of dirty washing and forgotten filing. The tower of dusty paperwork was also to her right, where she probably had no idea it existed – along with a stuffed ground sloth that had seen better days. I should have guessed about this, what with Aurora not seeing the *left* side of anything. I should have foreseen what happened next, too.

'That's better,' said Toccata, studying me intently, 'now, what's the deal with your face?'

'It's a congenital bone deformity.'

'On *both* sides? That's a serious downer if ever I saw one.'

'No, it's just on the left.'

Her eyelid twitched for a moment. If she never saw the right of anything, her visual cortex would make up the shortfall by extrapolation. My left side became the yardstick of *both* sides. To her, I must have been an intriguing sight. Charlie double-wonky Worthing. But on the plus side, at least my eyes would be on the same level – just low on my face, about the same level as my nose. To her, I must have had a forehead the size of Vermont.

'What are you sniggering about, Worthing?'

'Nothing – I just had an amusing thought about Vermont.'

She glared at me with her single eye: powerful, unblinking, straight into my soul. It reminded of being given the eye by Mother Fallopia at the Pool. Even the most badly behaved kids would have their egos reduced to something resembling guacamole by its power.

'On reflection,' I added quickly, 'you're right – serious downer.'

Aurora Toccata, the Chief Consul of Sector Twelve and also the head of HiberTech Security, was a Halfer. It was less popular these days owing to better recruitment levels and decreased mortality, but some committed Winterers had trained themselves to sleep hemispherically – one side of the brain at a time. It enabled them to be more fully on top of problems, use less pantry and essentially offer the Consular Service two workers for the price of one. Most Halfers exhibited mildly separate personalities, but they at least shared a consciousness and a memory. Unusually, *uniquely*, even – it seemed that Toccata and Aurora had no idea what the other was up to at all.

'So, Wonky Worthing,' said Toccata, 'you are henceforth inducted into the Consulate Service here in Sector Twelve. Pledge your allegiance and accept the deputisation.'

'Do I have a choice?'

'None at all.'

'Then I accept,' I said.

'Wise of you. Now we've established that I'm your Chief, fill me in on how you got to the Douzey.'

I repeated what I'd told Jonesy – that after Logan died I'd delivered Mrs Tiffen to The Notable Goodnight at HiberTech, and since Toccata wasn't about I spoke to Fodder about viral dreams, then was stranded by a stationmaster. Aurora found me a room and suggested I get out on a Sno-Trac.

'Next thing I know Jonesy is waking me up,' I concluded.

I didn't think I'd mention anything about the dreams, nor about talking to Aurora in the Wincarnis. It wasn't a good start, lying to one's boss. But I needed to be cautious.

'Hugo Foulnap?' she echoed. 'Seen him since?'

'No – but Aurora thinks he might not be a Footman at all, but somehow involved with the Campaign for Real Sleep.'

She gazed at me for a moment.

'A wild accusation, if ever I heard one. She wouldn't know a real fact if it jumped up and bit her on the arse. I have an idea why Logan brought you here, but what's confusing me is that Aurora wants you here too.'

'I'm sorry?'

'Why do you think she marooned you here?'

'She didn't maroon me,' I said, 'the stationmaster did.'

'The lines were down from Slumberdown minus two to plus eight,' said Toccata. 'The only way the stationmaster could know if you delayed the train in Cardiff was if Aurora told her. Turn up soon after you missed your train, did she? As if by magic?'

'Well, yes,' I said.

'Did she suggest you shouldn't tell us you were here?'

I nodded.

'Exactly. So: why is she interested in you remaining in Sector Twelve?'

I didn't know quite what to think. Aurora had told me Toccata would be difficult – and unlikely to tell the truth. But now it looked as though Aurora *herself* might have been manipulative.

'I don't know,' I said again.

Toccata looked at me for almost a minute without saying anything.

'Where did you meet Aurora today?'

'The basement of the *Siddons*.'

'Met her by accident there too, did you?'

'Why, yes…' I stopped. It might not have been an accident there, either. She'd have known I might go to get the Sno-Trac, and it would have been child's play to empty the air reservoir so I couldn't start the engine. 'No, I was …'

I was about to say 'trying to get a Sno-Trac out of here' but thought perhaps not.

'Yes or no? What were you doing?'

'We were both in the basement of the *Siddons*. I was … on an errand for Porter Lloyd and Aurora was looking for Tricksy walkers to take to HiberTech.'

Toccata grunted and looked at Jonesy.

'We missed some?'

'Six,' said Jonesy with a shrug, 'Lloyd sent a memo but it was mislaid. Three survived, Wonky retired Baggy and the other two I dealt with.'

'I don't like what HiberTech do with them,' said Toccata. 'Pull them apart, stick them back together, hope for the best, use them as mindless drones. It's not dignified, even for a deadhead. What else happened? Leave out nothing.'

I considered my oath carefully. Aurora had *specifically* told me not to tell anyone. I wasn't sure, but was an oath made to one of them binding on both? Probably not. But since my oath to Aurora began the moment we tied our walkers to her truck outside the *Siddons*, anything before this was knowledge I could share.

'She gave me some advice about early rising,' I said, feeling uncomfortable under Toccata's baleful monogaze, 'eat lots, keep warm, watch out for walkers, avoid Jim Treacle and the drowsies, that kind of stuff – then we parted outside the *Siddons*.'

'That's it?'

'That's it.'

She stared at me in silence for a few moments.

'I dislike many things, but do you know what I dislike most of all?'

'No, ma'am.'

'Gaps. I *loathe* gaps. Gaps in doors, gaps in windows, gaps in bathroom tiles, long gaps between sequels to books. But you know which gaps I hate the most?'

'No, ma'am.'

'Gaps in my knowledge. You left the *Siddons* at 10.30 in Aurora's command car and met up with Jonesy at midday.'

She tapped her head.

'I don't like secrets and I don't like Aurora. I was going to get married, start a family. Aurora stuck her oar in and Logan hightailed it out of the Sector. That wasn't enough for her and next thing I know she's killed him – protecting your useless bony arse. So when a Deputy who has newly arrived in more-than-fishy circumstances has a time gap of ninety minutes, I get *seriously* pissed off. So let's start again: what did you two talk about?'

'We didn't.'

'So you said nothing at all over a cosy coffee and sandwich in the Wincarnis?'

My heart sank. The denials meant nothing. She knew – through ShamBob, most likely, or anyone from the Scrabble club. I was a fool to think that there could be any secrets in Sector Twelve. Our meeting had probably already been around the Open Telephone Network. Twice.

'Just … stuff,' I stammered, 'gossip, advice.'

'Oh, wait,' she said, 'so you *did* speak to her. Just a second ago you said you didn't. You're a lying little bedshit, Worthing. Do you know the penalty for lying to a Sector Chief?'

I'd grown hot and sweaty by now. A prickly heat was dancing down my back and I could feel beads of sweat on my brow. I'd never had a grilling like this before. I could even see Jonesy beginning to look around, wishing herself out of the office.

'Dismissal,' I said.

'I'm sorry, I can't hear you.'

'*Dismissal.*'

'No, it's a punch in the eye, *then* dismissal. Strictly speaking it's dismissal only, the punch in the eye I added strictly for my own pleasure. Now, let's start again. What did you talk about?'

I stared at Toccata, then at Jonesy.

'You're going to have to tell her,' said Jonesy.

I sat there, feeling hot and wretched and with a pained expression on my face.

'Frozen Gronk's piss in a handbag,' said Toccata, 'did she oath you?'

'No,' I said, thinking quickly. During the sleepstate, loyalty was often all there was, and I certainly wasn't going to break a pledge to someone who had saved my pulse twice. But then, I had a thought. If Toccata saw me as wonky on both sides, Aurora must see me as pleasingly physiotypical. Maybe that was why she kissed me at the Wincarnis. *She'd found me attractive.* I had an idea. Daring, true, but an idea.

'I didn't know she was you—'

Toccata thumped her fists on the desk, then rose to her feet.

'*She's not me.* Never assume that she's anything even *like* me!'

'Sorry, I didn't know you and she ... didn't get along. If I had, we wouldn't have ...'

'Wouldn't have what?'

'Wouldn't have ... *bundled.*'

Jonesy coughed almost explosively into her coffee, spilling it all over the carpet, while Toccata merely laughed.

'We both know that never happened,' said Toccata. 'Aurora's never been fussy over the who and what, but she always goes for lookers. Believe me, you ain't one of them. I want the truth, or you'll be mopping toilets until Springrise. With no teeth and broken fingers,' she added, in case the option sounded in any way attractive.

I stared at her for a moment, then at Jonesy. Oddly, taunts over my appearance always gave me clarity, and renewed confidence.

'She likes the snow but not the Winter,' I said, recalling Birgitta's impassioned description of her husband, 'values the climb greater than the view from the summit. She doesn't smile much, but when she does the world smiles with her. She wears Ludlow scent,' I added in a quiet voice, 'and has a birthmark the shape of Guernsey right here.'

I touched my fingertip to my chest. There was silence in the room. Toccata glared at me dangerously.

'I realise it was a huge mistake,' I said, 'but an opportunity like that had never come my way before. I was ... *flattered.*'

Toccata stared at me, then at Jonesy, then back at me.

'I had no idea it would anger you. It won't happen again, I promise.'

'It had better not or your tongue's coming out – and not in the painless way.'

Toccata stared at me for a moment, trying to figure, I think, the best course of action. 'Okay,' she said, 'couple of things: when you see Foulnap again you come and see me and me *first* and – are you listening to this bit?'

'Yes.'

'I want to know what Aurora's up to. You're not telling me the whole story – I'm not sure you even know the whole story – but I need to know more. Why she's interested in you. And spoiler alert:

it's not your charm or your looks. She's a user, and you're either being used or are about to be.'

'You want me to *spy* on her?'

'Very astute of you. Oh, and double-cross me and you'll be carrion for the hiburnals come the morning. Welcome to the Douzey. What's our mission statement again?'

'That we are to uphold the sanctity of the sleepstate, and ensure the most favourable outcome is enjoyed by the majority.'

'Good. Might learn something over the Winter. Might have some fun; shit, you might even *survive*. But treat us like fools, follow a private agenda or undermine us in any way, and I'll be down on you like a ton of grade "A" glyptodon shit. Do you think I'm speaking metaphorically?'

'No, ma'am.'

'Good. Now piss off.'

I stood up, saluted, and walked out of her office. I was sodden with nervous sweat. I found the changing rooms, took off my jacket and leaned against the cold lockers, heart thumping.

HiberTech

'I should have told you they were the same person,' said Jonesy when she found me sitting in the staff rec room, head in hands, 'sorry about that.'

I looked up. She was trying to hide a smile and not doing it very well.

'To be honest,' she added, 'your face *was* pretty funny when you saw her. Like that time we were at Glastonbury together and Piano Keyes fell off the stage. Remember?'

'No.'

'It wasn't funny when he fell off the stage, or not funny your face, or no, you don't remember the time we were at Glastonbury?'

'Some, all, I don't know. Well, okay, *sort* of funny,' I added, giving her a half-smile to at least pretend I was being a good sport. But it wasn't funny right now. Far from it. And we were never at Glastonbury together, with or without Piano Keyes. She was making up nostalgia, and wasn't particularly good at it.

'Can I ask a question?' I said.

'Shoot.'

'How can Toccata be a Chief Consul with a split consciousness?'

'One could ask just as easily how Aurora can be the Head of HiberTech Security with the same problem. It's Winter Best Practice to deal with Aurora *or* Toccata, but not both. I guess you've figured the good eye switches depending on who's at home. Right is Aurora, left is Toccata.'

'I'll remember that.'

'It could save your life.'

I paused.

'Why does Toccata want me to spy on Aurora and HiberTech?'

'With those two, nothing is ever clear-cut. I heartily recommend you just say nothing and follow orders.'

'Yes,' I replied soberly, 'it's probably the most important thing I've learned from the Logan fiasco.'

'Now you're getting it. Oh, and some advice: if Aurora *does* want you to be her dumbundle, you should try to be more discreet.'

'I was hoping the term "bundlechum" would be more appropriate.'

'No,' she said after a moment's thought, 'I think "dumbundle" suits the circumstances better.' She pointed behind me. 'You've met Fodder?'

The colossus of Sector Twelve was standing behind us. He looked about the same as when I'd seen him last, just wearing warmer clothes and appearing even taller and more powerful.

'Hullo, Wonky,' he said.

'Can we please drop the whole Wonky thing?' I asked. 'It's not really doing much for me.'

'Jim Treacle would kill for a nickname,' said Fodder.

'He's been dropping hints we could call him "Sticky" for three seasons,' said Jonesy, 'but we won't give him the honour.'

'What have I done that honours *me* with a nickname?'

'You went back to get Mrs Tiffen.'

'True – but Logan died because of it.'

'It was the unforeseen outcome of courageous motivation and adherence to duty,' said Fodder in a quiet voice. 'Despite everything that happened afterwards, you have grit. You concur, Jonesy?'

'I do,' said Jonesy.

'Then accept the honour, Wonky. Cherish the accolade, never complain again.'

And he pulled me into a Winter embrace. He smelled of woodsmoke, musty clothes and spent thermalites, and held me for quite a long time, and far harder than was comfortable, and kissed me softly on the ear, twice.

'So, Wonky,' he said once he'd let me go, 'is that coffee any good?'

'It's the worst I've ever tasted.'

'Excellent – after twelve years of wintering I can't drink anything else. Pour me one, would you?'

So I did while he stared at me with his dark empty eyes.

'What's that worthless bag of shit's nickname again?' came Toccata's voice from the other side of the office.

'Wonky,' said Fodder and Jonesy in unison.

'Thanks for that,' I said in a quiet voice.

'Wonky?' shouted Toccata. 'Out the front in five.'

'What do you think she wants?' I asked, jumping to my feet.

'Don't know,' said Fodder. 'Perhaps she wants to have you for lunch.'

'Very funny.'

'You can drive,' said Toccata, climbing into the passenger seat of Aurora's four-wheel drive, now without the nightwalkers tied to the back.

'Isn't this Aurora's transport?' I asked, starting the vehicle anyway.

'Like I give a shit,' said Toccata. 'We're going up to HiberTech to see Aurora.'

'Okay,' I said, wondering how that was possible. 'For what reason?'

'Pantry resupply mainly, but also to find out why you were marooned. I want to see how they react to you, too. Keep your eyes and ears open and report back everything you hear. *Especially* any details about Project Lazarus. Let's see how good that memory of yours actually is.'

I reversed out of the parking lot and drove down into the town square, past Howell Harris and the lorry still stuck fast on the bridge. Toccata stared at me the whole time, then reached out a hand and tweaked my bony forearm.

'You're very skinny,' she said. 'Did you do any dreaming on your four-week sojourn to the dark side?'

'No, ma'am.'

'Good,' she said. 'The one thing I loathe more than winsomniacs is dreamers. Feet on the ground, head out of the clouds. Agree?'

'Yes, ma'am.'

'I don't like subordinates always agreeing,' she said. 'Sycophants have no place in my department. You're to speak your mind when the opportunity calls for it.'

'How will I know when that is?'

'I shall inform you. Park over there.'

We'd arrived at the HiberTech facility, which looked a little cheerier in the daylight, but not by much.

We were buzzed in as before and Josh was still at the receptionist desk, only with four more 'Employee of the Week' pictures behind him. The golf-cart driver, Dave, I noted, had been replaced by another rewired nightwalker, this time a woman. Her hair had been given the buzzcut usually associated with any nightwalker who had been redeployed, and she blinked occasionally while she stared at the floor, but was otherwise utterly vacant.

Josh nodded a nervous greeting to us both and Toccata said she wanted to see Aurora.

'What, now?'

'Yes, now.'

'I don't think she's in.'

'Why don't you check?'

'Okay.'

Toccata went and sat on one of the benches while Josh picked up the phone.

'Dave the driver deployed elsewhere?' I said to Josh.

'Simpler duties,' he replied, 'currently employed as a thermostat in F-Block. Recognise his replacement?'

It was only when Josh mentioned it I realised it was Mrs Tiffen. I took a step forward to greet her, but then stopped myself. She wouldn't know who I was, and from the look of her, she had lost the ability to play the bouzouki, too. I think I preferred her when she could, no matter how annoying that might have been. I turned back to Josh, who was looking at me with a concerned expression on his face.

'I don't like it here,' he said in a low voice. 'What's happening, what's going to happen. With Project Lazarus, I mean.'

'What do you mean?'

'Walls have ears,' he said nervously. 'But look, just supposing I knew someone who wanted to get in touch with RealSleep, would you be able to make contact?'

'No,' I said, wondering if this request was genuine, or part of a

HiberTech plot to check me out, 'and I'm not sure you should be asking.'

'Fair enough,' he said, 'but here's something: if you can get out of Sector Twelve in any way, shape or form, then do it.'

'That's not particularly original advice.'

'No,' said Josh with a sigh, 'and I wish I'd heeded it when I first heard it.'

He pointed a pencil at Toccata.

'You do know they're the same person?'

'I found out the hard way.'

'Has she threatened to pull out your tongue if you step out of line?'

'Yes, and not in the painless way.'

'As far as we know it's a bluff,' said Josh, 'but it's hard to say. Does that make you feel any better?'

'Not much.'

He made the call, then handed us our visitor badges and walked around to instruct one of the redeployed on the golf carts. Not Mrs Tiffen, though, the one with the badge denoting him as 'Chas'. Josh helped us on board, showed the redeployed the map, and we were off, just not quite as dangerously as before.

'The other redeployed golf-cart driver was Mrs Tiffen,' I said to Toccata, 'the woman I brought over here four weeks ago.'

'That's quick work,' she replied. 'Do you know how much money they make from the redeployed?'

'No.'

'Lots,' she said, not sounding as if she knew either, 'but they'll make a shitload more if Vacants can be made skilled, although the unions won't be happy. Peppermint?' She held out a small white bag. 'Take two. Shit, take the whole bag.'

I thought of what Jonesy had told me, about how Toccata fed nightwalkers peppermint to make them more palatable.

'No, thanks.'

'Go on,' she said, 'you look like you need feeding up.'

'Maybe later,' I said, but took the bag anyway.

We were driven down several corridors, took a left turn and

stopped outside two large double doors where Mr Hooke was waiting for us.

'I-will-wait-for-you-here,' said the golf-cart driver, and I looked at him, intending to say thank you, and found myself staring. His badge still described him as Chas, but he was, in fact, *Charles*, whose likeness decorated my dream – albeit retrospectively, agreed – and was also on the missing persons flier I had in my back pocket. He had a beard and cropped hair, but it was the same person. If he'd vanished in Sector Twelve, he hadn't gone very far, nor for that long.

'Well, well,' said Toccata as Mr Hooke approached us, 'the return of the living dead. Eaten any babies today?'

'Unfunny as usual,' said Hooke in an even tone, ignoring me entirely. 'Would you like to come in?'

He opened the door to their offices and we entered a wood-panelled room about the size of a gymnasium. The staff had their heads down and were either working or speaking on the telephone in low voices. One, near the back, was typing on a telex machine.

'I'd like to see Aurora,' said Toccata as we walked towards the side offices.

'That's not possible,' said Hooke.

'Every single time she does this,' said Toccata in an exasperated tone. 'She can't hide from me for ever.'

Actually, I thought, yes, she probably could.

'Whilst Aurora is otherwise engaged,' said Hooke, who looked as though he had been through this many, many times, 'I assume all her duties, and the position of Head of Security. So how can I help you?'

Toccata pointed at me.

'I want to know why Aurora took over responsibility for a marooned Deputy Consul, and having done so, left them to almost sleep themselves out over the past four weeks.'

Mr Hooke looked at me, then back at Toccata.

'I have no idea,' he said, staring at her without expression.

'Make a guess.'

He shrugged.

'I don't make guesses.'

'Give it a whirl. For me. Just this once.'

'Perhaps,' began Hooke, 'she felt she was in some way to blame for Worthing's marooning. Perhaps she was just caring for someone looking lost in the Winter. Perhaps she was just being kind.'

'Aurora has no understanding of the word. She's motivated only by what HiberTech ask of her.'

'We could argue over this all day, ma'am,' said Hooke, sounding like they probably did, quite a lot, 'but it seems to me a simple mistake. Deputy Worthing overslept. It happens. Why don't you just take it up with Aurora?'

'I try, but she's always avoiding me.'

'She says the same about you. Now, is there anything else I can help you with?'

'Pantry,' she said. 'You've got shitloads of it and I want some to feed to the sleep-shy.'

'If it were up to me, I'd drown them all and then compost their remains and use it to nourish the Winter beet,' said Hooke, 'but we live, apparently, in more enlightened times. Why don't you come into the office?'

He gestured us to a side office which I noted had Aurora's name painted on the door. He invited Toccata inside, but pointed at a seat outside the office for me.

I sat down, then heard Toccata's voice rise in volume as she started to question why HiberTech couldn't spare any food for the rest of the Sector, and Agent Hooke's voice coldly explaining that it wasn't up to private companies to deal with the shortcomings of government.

'Does this happen a lot?' I asked a youngish-looking worker sitting quite near me. He looked up abruptly, as though he had hoped I wasn't going to say anything.

'All the time. It's like a recurring gag in a sitcom, only it's not funny.'

'Sitcom,' I said, 'yes. Are there any toilets close by? I've been on the coffee since I woke up.'

He directed me to the second on the left down the corridor, and I thanked him and walked out of the room. I didn't want the loo; I wanted a closer look at our driver, who was still staring ahead blankly. I was right; it *was* Charles Webster. The picture on the missing person's flyer matched: he had a mole beneath his right eye.

'Hello, Charles,' I said. There was no reaction. I reminded myself that the connection between him and Birgitta was weak. All I had was Birgitta's admission – before she nightwalked – that her husband vanished. That was it. No name, no idea where he vanished to or even when. I had no confirmation they were the same person, aside from the dream, which was no confirmation at all.

'Birgitta says "hi",' I said, but there was no reaction. I tried again: 'There will always be the—'

'—*Gower,*' said Webster, or, at least, something that I thought sounded like 'Gower'. On reflection, it might have just been a mumble.

I heard voices from down the corridor and looked up as The Notable Goodnight attended by a gaggle of assistants walked around the corner, Lucy amongst them. I briefly heard something about deep memory reacquisition before they saw me and all stopped talking.

'Well,' said The Notable Goodnight, staring at me with an imperious eye, 'Charlie Worthing. What are you doing here?'

'Consul business, ma'am.'

'Indeed?'

'Yes; to do with extra food for the winsomniacs. We have fifty-four of them.'

'Have you tried starvation? Clears them out in a jiffy, I'm told.'

Lucy whispered something in her ear.

'I've been instructed to tell you that was a joke. Dark, but a joke. Funny, yes?'

'Yes,' I said, 'very.'

She grunted and they all moved on except for Lucy.

'Good to see you, Charlie,' she said as we tapped fists. 'Someone said you overslept. Is that true?'

I rolled up my sleeve and showed her my forearm, which more closely resembled a stick draped with furry skin.

'Wow,' she said, 'you lost all that in only four weeks?'

'Dreams,' I said, 'and they're kind of still with me.'

I told her about the retrospective nature of my dreams and she nodded knowingly.

'Narcosis can do weird things to the mind,' she said. 'How are you getting along with the Consuls?'

'Sort of okay.'

'I shouldn't really tell you this, but be *extremely* wary of Toccata. She's allowing her hatred of Aurora to cloud her judgement and invents all manner of conspiracies. HiberTech has been wanting to get rid of her for years, but it's kind of complicated when Aurora is so valuable. Toccata can be volatile, and we don't want any wrinkles when we roll out Project Lazarus. I can't say much, but there's talk of Morphenox-B being available to everyone.'

'That's good,' I said.

'It's *very* exciting. Be careful, Charlie. You know you can call me if you need anything. I'll always be a friend first and an employee of HiberTech second.'

And she gave me a hug, waved goodbye and hurried off down the corridor just as the door to the HiberTech offices opened and Toccata walked out.

'Wanker,' said Toccata, joining me in the golf cart. 'I'd poison him quite happily and dance on his grave given half a chance. A compliant toady, acquiescing to Aurora at every level.'

She told Charles to return us to reception, which he did, without word, complaint or delay.

'Have a nice Winter,' said Josh as he saw us off. 'May the Spring embrace you.'

'And embrace you, too.'

'That was interesting,' said Toccata once we had retrieved our weapons and were walking back to the command car outside.

'What was?'

'That they all seemed quite uninterested.'

'Uninterested in what?'

'In *you*. HiberTech regard every unusual face as someone who is a potential RealSleep member, ne'er-do-well or loser. They paid you no heed and even allowed you to wander off – where did you go?'

'The loo.'

'Right – which makes me suspicious that they've been told to leave you alone. Why is this?'

'I'm not sure being ignored is grounds for suspicion,' I said.

'You don't know them like I do. Speak to anyone about Project Lazarus?'

I told her I knew someone there – an old friend from the Pool, and she had said that it would be a game changer.

'In what way?'

'Universal availability of Morphenox-B, apparently. That's good, right?'

'So everyone says,' she said, 'and it will triple the number of nightwalkers to redeploy. Greater survivability, sure, but lots of cheap labour. I've always been suspicious of game changers,' she added. 'Sometimes the game doesn't need changing – or no one has a clear idea of which game will be changed, and for what and how much.'

'I don't understand.'

'No,' she said, 'neither do I.'

I thought for a moment, then said: 'Something odd happened.'

'What?'

'The Notable Goodnight wandered past.'

'And?'

'She knew my name. She met me once, four weeks ago. Is she good with names?'

'She barely knows mine,' said Toccata, 'why would she remember you? Make an impression?'

'Not in the least.'

'As I said,' murmured Toccata, 'something about you has interested HiberTech. It'll be an opportunistic exploitation, or my name's not Toccata.'

We climbed into the command car and drove slowly back down towards the town. I was in Sector Twelve only because of Aurora. First by letting the train go, then finding me an apartment on the ninth floor of the *Siddons*, then not checking back or telling anyone I was there. The meeting in the *Siddons* basement that morning might have been contrived, too, in order for her to come over all chummy and helpful.

'Permission to speak, ma'am?'

'Go on.'

'Why do *you* think HiberTech are interested in me?'

She stared at me with her one good eye for several seconds.

'I have no idea, Wonky. But believe me, it won't be anything trivial.'

Fodder

―――

'… Porters never went out during the Winter, mostly out of duty to their charges. Even in a dire emergency – fire, Villain or nightwalker incursion, HotPot overheat, starvation – no porter would abandon the building if there was a single sleeper left inside. A porter went down with their building …'

– *The Oldest Profession*, by Porter Fabrisio

I went and found Jonesy as soon as we got back.

'Let me guess,' she said, 'Aurora wasn't anywhere to be found?'

'Not hard to figure. Can I ask you something?'

'Shoot.'

I took Charles Webster's missing persons flier from my back pocket and showed it to her.

'So?'

'He's up at HiberTech, redeployed as one of their golf-cart drivers.'

'And?'

'He's a missing person, yet turns up at HiberTech?'

She looked at me, then at the flier, then led me towards the records office, which was situated at the far end of the Consulate.

'These are the Sector Twelve files,' she said as we walked in. 'Every person who ever arrived, every person who ever left. The ones who died, the ones who married, the ones who had children. Hibernation records, work records, special skills register, schools records, fertility reports, genetic screening, Dormitoria, car, dental and food records. The lot. Hang on a tick.'

She rummaged for a moment in a large and very battered grey filing cabinet, and then handed me Webster's file. His address was the *Cambrensis*, room 106, his job HiberTech 'Medical Orderly Grade II'. There was a copy of his birth certificate, several references from the *Thomas Carlyle* Dormitorium in Sector Fifty-eight North, a General

Skills certificate pass confirmation and letters of recommendation from his previous employments as a bus driver, aquarium maintenance engineer and insurance salesman. There was also a 'Partial Death' certificate – HiberTech had logged him as having been delivered to their Sleep Sciences Division twelve weeks after he went missing.

'He was signed across to The Notable Goodnight by Agent Hooke,' I said, reading a copy of the chain-of-possession document. 'Is that unusual?'

'Not really,' said Jonesy.

There was nothing about being married to Birgitta, but then I didn't really expect there to be. Beyond my dream, the only evidence they might be the same person was that they both vanished, and could have the same first name. That was it. I sighed. Webster was just a guy I'd picked to clothe the empty face in my dream, nothing more, nothing less. He might not even have said 'Gower' at all – just a mumble, an artefact briefly bubbling to the surface.

'Happy?' said Jonesy.

'It's just my mild narcosis,' I said, 'overactive imagination. Oh, and I think you should probably know if you're planning to bundle with Fodder: when we Winter embraced, he kissed me very gently on the ear.'

'Yeah, I heard he does that.'

I yawned, and then apologised.

'You're looking tired,' said Jonesy. 'It's best to take it easy the first couple of days. Come with me.'

I followed her out of records and into the office, where we found Fodder balancing a hunting knife on the tip of his finger.

'Hey, Fod,' said Jonesy, 'will you show Wonky around town before nightfall? You both live at the *Siddons*, so it makes sense to end up there.'

'Delighted,' said Fodder.

'You may want to keep an eye out for intruders,' added Treacle, who was at the front desk. 'We've had a couple of reports of a possible incursion of people or creatures unknown at the far end of town.'

★　★　★

I felt the cold wind slice into my exposed skin as we stepped outside. It had shifted around to the north and already flurries of snow were portending a heavier fall some time within the next forty-eight hours. Fodder, instead of taking one of the Sno-Tracs parked outside, strode off on foot.

'No transport?' I asked, following close behind.

'Where practical I walk,' he replied. 'Once cocooned in a Sno-Trac, the senses are numbed. Out on the fringes you need a feel for the air, the wind, the environs. The Three Vs can strike at a moment's notice.'

'The Three Vs?'

'Villains, Vacants and Volk. Hear that?'

We stopped. I listened intently but all I could hear was the faint whisper of ice crystals blowing across the drifts.

'No.'

'*Exactly*. There's nothing there. But one day there will be – and you want to sense it or them before you can see them – or they can see you.'

'I understand,' I said, 'you think there *are* Volk?'

'I've seen some weird stuff,' he said, 'but nothing that makes me think the Gronk exists – which is a shame. I'd like Laura to win her bet.'

We trudged on, the snow swirling around us, the visibility barely thirty feet, the daylight dull, soft and directionless. Fodder put on a knitted hat shaped like a penguin, which looked faintly ridiculous. He might or might not have known this, but I'm firmly convinced no one in their right mind would point it out.

'Treacle said something about an intruder report.'

'We get them from time to time, but if it had been a credible sighting Jonesy would have made more of a hoo-hah. Megafauna are too smart to be out, but Winter nomads have been known to move through. We leave them be, and even scavengers are not particularly disliked, so long as they don't enter buildings. Villains are something else entirely: no rules outside their own society and a strange mix of violent ruthlessness, decorum and an overdeveloped sense of entitlement. There's been an uneasy truce these past three years with Lucky Ned.'

'What were the terms?'

'Exclusion zones. We don't go on to their patch if they don't come on ours. It means admitting that there are areas that are no-go in Mid-Wales, but Toccata can work with that, she says.'

Fodder lapsed into silence and we joined the long straight road that led towards the gardens and the museum, the only sound the breath of our exertions and our feet as we tramped through the snow. I had a thought.

'You have the right to Morphenox but don't use it, do you?'

'Is it that obvious that I don't?'

'You live in the *Siddons*,' I said, 'a Sub-beta payscale Kipshop – but you're a Consul. I put two and two together.'

'It's an honest place to sleep. The soft rasp of natural snoring is comforting, like rain on a tin roof. Morphenox dulls the subconscious,' he added, 'and steals your dreams. I like to dream.'

'And do you?'

'Every night, always the same. The Ottomans used to hit us with their Gigawatt Highrollers. I'm in the forward OP in a six-by-six Bedford softside, reporting on incoming size and velocity. There's no moisture so the pulse rings are visible only as faint ripples in the hot air, a couple of hundred yards wide. I report on a stonker that's coming our way but it's faster and tighter than the rest, and by a thousand yards out it starts to cone. By the time it reaches me the torus has a spin so tight that implosive collapse is inevitable. No time to run – pointless anyway – and then my eardrums burst and I'm waking in the sand, alone, with the sun already overhead and the Bedford upside down two hundred yards away. I've lost my foot and most of my clothes and part of my skin is blasted off. Worst of all, I can feel the moisture leaching out of my body. My eyes crisp over, my tongue feels like leather, my skin blisters and then cracks, like mud on a dry lake bed.'

'You *want* to dream that?'

'It stops me dreaming about the really unpleasant stuff. Nightmares are catharsis; they purge the mind to make the day bearable.'

'Oh,' I said, not wanting to think what his other dreams might be. 'Do you dream of anything else? Like ... blue Buicks, for instance?'

He turned to look at me with a quizzical expression.

'We looked into what Moody and the others claimed,' said Fodder. 'Personally, I've dreamt nothing, but then I live on the eighteenth floor; it's the ninth floor of the *Siddons* that's full of bad dreaming.'

He was right, come to think of it: everyone who had dreamed of the blue Buick seemed to have come from the ninth.

We continued on the journey, Fodder pointing out places of interest. Which Dormitorium was which, why I should avoid the porter at the *Captain Mayberry*, where the electrical sub-station, phone exchanges and cold refuge points were situated. He imparted the knowledge without fanfare, and occasionally punctuated the observations with local lore: a serial sneak thief here, an incident with Lucky Ned's gang there – and shockingly, the harbouring undertaken by Olaf Yawnersson, who kept two Tricksy nightwalkers alive for almost three years.

'He did the honourable thing when we discovered them hidden in his basement,' said Fodder. 'But despite considerable investigation he left no evidence of his depraved acts. The Cold Way Out was probably the best thing for him.'

But most of all, Fodder told me to memorise the town precisely. 'Your aim,' he said, 'is to know Sector Twelve like the swirls on your own wintercoat, and be able to navigate the streets when a combination of blizzard, gale-strength winds and darkness reduces visibility to zero – *without* the fixed line.'

'Without?'

'It's the first thing Villains would cut. Rely on the line, and you'll be utterly lost without it.'

As if to demonstrate the wisdom of his statement, there was a sudden squall that reduced visibility to less than ten feet. I instinctively moved closer to Fodder, who, instead of clipping on to the line as Winter Best Practice dictated, simply extended his baton and used that to feel his way. He put out a hand for me to hold and I did so, his massive hand both warm and surprisingly soft.

To navigate through the town we used the gas lamps, each one a useful beacon to focus upon before pushing on to the next. They were burning even though it was still day, the light-valves fooled by the heavy overcast. There was a gas lamp by the ornate iron gates outside the museum, and the small tongue of flame flickered as gasps of cold air found their way into the lamp–head.

'It's very beautiful, isn't it?' said Fodder, pausing briefly to stare admiringly at the wavering light, the railings, the stonework and statue draped in snow.

'Sort of desolate,' I said, 'in a magnificent kind of way.'

'A beauty that both preserves and kills,' he murmured thoughtfully, then pointed towards the museum, which we could see only as a grey shape in the snowstorm.

'Danny Pockets is in there,' said Fodder. 'His specific job is to defend the building against intruders. Dull, but essential.'

'Communal Food Store?'

'Bingo. Winter pantry is under considerable strain due to the winsomniacs, and any theft would spell disaster. Let's go and have a look.'

The Museum

'... Winter pantry was always kept well hidden, and defended with extreme prejudice. Although adequate vegetables would still be clamped from the previous Summer and haunches of beef and lamb available in the cold stores, Spring Tuck was of a more convenient nature: coming out of the Hib, the last thing anyone wanted to do was wrestle their food from the cold ...'

— Handbook of Winterology, 1st edition, Hodder & Stoughton

We passed through the iron gates and walked around the statue of Gwendolyn VII, which looked considerably larger up close – about the size of a coach – then crossed the soft unbroken expanse of white in front of the museum. Fodder led us to the side entrance and tugged at the bell-pull.

'Who is it?' came a crackly man's voice from the intercom.

'Llewelyn the not-last-as-it-turned-out,' said Fodder, waving at the viewing lens above the door.

The lock clunked and Fodder looked around cautiously before pulling open the heavy steel door. We stepped inside and closed the outer door before ringing the bell to signal Pockets to open the inner. Once through the cork-lined doors and out of our coats and boots we padded up the corridor past glass cases, suits of armour, works of art and a stuffed sabre-tooth tiger that was, boasted the label, the fifth from extinction when it was hit by a bus near Boughrood.

We turned the corner to the central atrium. Sitting beneath the ornately painted dome and marble-inlaid foyer was a military-spec Airwitzer of considerable size and power. To one side of the weapon was a half-empty crate of military-spec thermalites, a couple of Golgothas and a desk with a red telephone and a clockwork barograph. But more pertinent to me was the figure sitting behind the cannon.

It was Hugo Foulnap. He was sitting in the triggerman's position, and staring at me with the look of someone who had just been reminded of an old and hugely disliked acquaintance. He was fresh in my mind from less than a day before, but to him we'd crossed swords four weeks ago. Hibernation has a contracting effect upon time.

He put a finger to his lips as soon as Fodder wasn't watching, and out of curiosity and a certain nervousness, I decided to play along.

'This here is Danny Pockets,' said Fodder, 'not usually part of the crew but on loan from Sector Eighteen.'

We both nodded a greeting and embraced in an awkward manner. Fodder didn't notice, or if he did, he made no sign of it.

Foulnap was pretty much the same as I'd seen him last, aside from a healed cut above his left eye that looked self-stitched, and longer hair, which he had tied back in a ponytail. He was dressed in a cumbersome Mk III shock-suit that looked – along with the Airwitzer – as though it should be displayed *in* the museum rather than defending it. I'd trained in the use of shock-suits and found them hot and restrictive. Most preferred to not wear one and just use the extra mobility to get out of trouble. Me, I'd prefer to not be in the trouble at all, shock-suit or no.

'You take Pantry Defence very seriously,' I said, nodding towards the vortex cannon. Anyone without suited protection was a trigger-pull away from resembling goulash.

'Sector Fifteen had their pantry stolen five Winters ago,' said Foulnap, 'and with thirty mouths to feed and the Winter the harshest for a century, the residents were forced to do things they'd rather not.'

'Winter Cutlets,' said Fodder in a matter-of-fact way. 'I'm going to figure out the duty roster. Why don't you two get acquainted?'

He vanished through a low doorway in the direction of *Rocks and Minerals*. There was a pause, and a desk lamp was switched on.

'I was wondering if we'd meet again,' Foulnap said. 'Have you told anyone about me?'

'I've only just seen you.'

'That's true. What happened to Bouzouki Girl?'

'I took her to HiberTech.'

'To be dismantled and redeployed? I hope you're pleased with yourself.'

'Better that than your plan.'

'Things are rarely how they appear,' he said. 'Because of you I lost a good friend and a respected mentor and colleague. You've got thirty seconds to convince me you're not a threat.'

He hooked his thumb into the ring of the pulse grenade strapped to his chest, then moved to flip up the visor on the shock-suit. He'd be hurt on detonation – a few broken ribs, bloodshot eyes, probably – but this close in, I'd be dead or left so I could barely feed myself. Most times it was better to not survive non-lethal. There was talk of rolling out high-velocity projectile weapons as a more humane alternative to the Concussive Vortex Cannon, but legislators and the public had little stomach for them.

'I knew you were somewhere in Sector Twelve,' I said, 'and I also knew Toccata knew it.'

He stared at me for a few seconds.

'How could you possibly know that?'

'Toccata asked me to tell her *when* I saw you but Aurora asked me to tell her *if* I saw you. The world of difference.'

'Yes,' he said, 'the world of difference.'

'I could have taken that information to Aurora, but I didn't. Enough to convince you I'm not working for HiberTech?'

He lowered his hand and I breathed a sigh of relief.

'For the moment,' he said, 'I'm going to have to trust you.'

'Aurora thinks you're with the Campaign for Real Sleep,' I said.

'What do you think?' he asked.

'Past events suggest I should just keep my lip firmly buttoned, and concentrate on surviving the Winter.'

'Sounds like a winning strategy to me.'

Fodder reappeared from the office and pinned the Pantry Duty roster on the wall. I was doing alternative afternoons, starting tomorrow. I was going to have to remember to bring a book.

'You two getting along?' asked Fodder.

'We have an understanding.'

'Then you can share the operation of the Airwitzer.'

Foulnap dutifully demonstrated how the weapon worked. It was like a Bambi, only much bigger, and the trigger wasn't instantaneous. He pointed towards a rack of Thumpers mounted on the wall.

'And once all these avenues are exhausted,' said Fodder, 'we pull the pin on the Golgotha and take them and the building with us.'

He patted the large rugby-ball-shaped grenade that was gaffer-taped to the Airwitzer.

'What do you think of the plan?' asked Fodder.

'What it lacks in finesse it makes up for in finality,' I said, and they both nodded. Pantry theft was a serious deal.

'Can I have a look around the museum?' I asked. 'To get an idea of layout?'

'Be my guest,' said Fodder. 'The ceramics and glassware sections are particularly fine, there's a Caravaggio on the second floor and three Turners – not to mention our Kyffin Williams collection. A few rare stamps, too, and the preserved trigger finger and hat brim of Ffion "Mad Dog" McJames.[53] We'll continue on in half an hour.'

I thanked them both then walked along the empty corridors, looking in through open doors at the dusty exhibits, assisted by the dim glow of the emergency lighting. There were Neolithic remains, the hull of a dugout canoe found in a local lake, and several artefacts from the First Ottoman Campaign. There also seemed to be a goodly amount of junk relating to the World's Fair which was held here in 1923, an entire wing devoted to Don Hector and HiberTech, and the finest collections of stamps in the region. I peered into the crystal case that held the world's only 2d Lloyd-George Mauve with the Anglesey cancellation, but it didn't look that impressive.

I walked up the ornate central staircase and paused on the landing, staring with a sense of disquiet at a glass case that contained a local murderer named Armstrong. He'd been freeze-dried over half a century before, placed on a chair for all to see, dressed in the clothes in which he'd been hanged. It was fortunate he'd been found guilty

53. Mid-Wales' most notorious Villain. Mad as a barrel of Arctic badgers and four times as dangerous.

in the Summer. In the Winter he'd have been Frigicuted and his remains taken by animals – there would have been nothing left to exhibit except a few teeth perhaps, and kidney stones if he'd had any.

There was a barely audible *thud*, not much more than if someone jumps heavily onto the floor above. My training at the Academy kicked in without me really having to think. When you hear a thump you don't pause, not even for a second. Non-lethal are always close-quarters weapons, and close-quarter fighting can develop at a frightening pace.

Villains

'... The Winter Nomads, known to all as "womads", were precisely as
their name suggests. Displaced during the Great Ottoman Diasporas of
the 14th and 15th centuries, they scratched a living in the far north and
are notoriously intolerant of outsiders. Utterly law-abiding, it is rumoured
that they do not hibernate at all, and suffer no ill-effects in spite of
it ...'

— *Handbook of Winterology*, 4th edition, Hodder & Stoughton

I ran downstairs to the central atrium, where Foulnap was at readiness on the Airwitzer and Fodder was staring intently at the softly
ticking barograph. The instrument was so delicate it could record
the ambient pressure change of a swiftly opened door, a passing truck
or even a sneeze at close quarters, and would record it all on a paper
strip several yards long. Looking over Fodder's shoulder I could see
the trace depicted the telltale signature of a weapon being deployed
close by. I picked up the red phone and pressed the button marked
Consulate. During incidents like this, teamwork was everything.

'Spike or bump?' asked Foulnap.

'Sharp rise, curved shoulder and slow out-gradient,' Fodder
returned, peering at the trace. 'Looks like a Masterblaster,[54] and within
two hundred yards.'

'Treacle, Consulate,' said Jim, answering the telephone.

'Worthing, at the museum,' I said. 'We've picked up a bump on
the trace, range two hundred yards, Fodder thinks it's a Masterblaster.'

'We're not picking anything up from here,' said Treacle. 'What do
you need?'

I looked at Fodder, who said we'd engage on our own, but to

---

54. An obsolete weapon a little bit more powerful but much lighter than a
Thumper, but prone to fatigue failure.

alert the Chief just in case. I repeated the message, hung up, and jotted down the time on the incident log.

We heard the shattering of glass from somewhere in the bowels of the building as the trace recorded another bump.

Fodder took command in an effortless 'we're all going to survive this' sort of way, and began to issue orders in a slow, methodical manner.

Panic is for fools.

'Wonky, you're with me,' he said, handing me a Schtumperschreck, the most formidable weapon in our arsenal that was still just possible to lift. 'Pockets, stay in the lobby and defend the pantry with your life. Let's go.'

My heart was thumping, but oddly not quite as heavily as when I went in to retrieve Mrs Tiffen. I figured Fodder had seen plenty of action, and losing a Deputy on their first day wouldn't reflect well on his judgement. We opened the first shock-gate, and once that was secure behind us and we'd donned boots and coats, Fodder spun the locking wheel, opened the outer door and stepped into the Winter. It was still snowing and just light enough to see, but the visibility was barely twenty feet. Fodder didn't pause for a moment and started to march as quickly as he could through the swirling snow, keeping tight to the exterior wall of the museum. I followed as close as I could and as fast as I could, but the Schtumper was heavy, and I wasn't as strong or as fit nor possessed of such a long stride, and quite soon Fodder was lost to view. All I could hear was the panting of my own breath, and all I could see were swirling flakes and the wall of the museum to my right. I didn't stop, though, and after about another half a minute of running almost semi-blind, I ran into the back of a static Fodder and bashed my lip against the butt of his Thumper so hard it brought tears to my eyes.

'Careful,' hissed Fodder. We were now at the back of the museum, outside an oak-banded rear entrance door, which had been thumped recently – the ice was clear like glass where the accreted snow had melted and then instantly refrozen.

'Not a hope of getting in here,' said Fodder. 'They were trying to draw us out.'

'And?'

'They succeeded.'

He kicked a couple of backpacks that had been left in the snow. 'Two of them, I'd say.'

Fodder examined their tracks in the snow and walked off with me close behind. I found it mildly disconcerting that he was moving *away* from any visual reference point, but as he said, you have to know the town like the swirls on your wintercoat. We moved along for perhaps five minutes, following the tracks that were almost obscured by the fresh falling snow, and within a hundred yards or so we came across the entrance to the Talgarth Jollity Funfair, which was not much more than a brick-built ticket office and turnstile. Fodder opened the door to the office and beckoned me inside. The room had only a counter, various posters advertising other local attractions – gliding, local flour mill, pony-trekking – and a desk with several chairs. The floor was dusty and strewn with fliers, blown from their shelves. Fodder stopped and crouched, as did I.

'Got a compass?'

I nodded.

'They'll return this way when they think we've gone,' he whispered. 'Stay here, and in precisely six minutes, go outside and fire the Schtumper to the east. That will give away your position, so you are then to retreat thirty paces towards the museum, and if anything comes out of the snowstorm that isn't me, let them get within knockout range and pop them. If they're armed, then full choke to kill.'

'It'll end the truce,' I said.

'If it's Lucky Ned,' said Fodder, 'then him being here is breaking the truce. Six minutes, yes?'

'Six minutes.'

He then stepped out of the door, hopped over the turnstile, looked around, and walked silently away into the gloom. I moved backwards to sit against the wall of the ticket office next to the door so I had a view of the outside, then stared at the radium glow of my watch hands as they crept round. I expected to hear the muffled *whump* of a Thumper or the harsher *whap* of a Bambi, but there was nothing. Not a single sound reached my ears as I lay crouched, the cold from the floor gradually creeping into my leg.

I thought of Mrs Tiffen, who had been redeployed, then Josh and how he wasn't happy with it. Then Lucy Knapp and her pride at working at HiberTech, and Aurora and what it might actually have been like – physically and psychologically – if I *had* bundled with her. I thought of Toccata and her aggressive manner, then about Laura's desire to see Wintervolk proven, the somewhat-unhinged Jonesy with her fictional nostalgia and Fodder with his much-needed nightmares, and then Birgitta. Finally, I thought about how I should have heeded everyone's advice and let Mrs Tiffen go. Logan would be alive right now and I'd be back in Cardiff, safely watching the Winter from indoors, and not crouched in an empty room during a blizzard, armed to the teeth and with orders to kill someone.

At the appointed time I stood up, stepped outside and checked which way was east. I lifted the weapon, leaned forward to counteract the kick, and pulled the trigger.

I knew that firing a vortex cannon into a snowstorm would be an impressive feat, and I wasn't disappointed. The localised temperature increase that accompanied the sudden pressure change melted the snow-flakes instantaneously, and there was suddenly clarity in the air – a momentary cone of perfect vision, rolling away from me in a languid manner. I could see the wooden lattice of the roller coaster and a brightly coloured hoarding advertising thrills and spills, then the helter-skelter beyond, and an ice-cream kiosk. The view did not last long. The melted snow turned back to ice as soon as the pressure equalised and the world reverted to nothing more than a swirling white mass.

I pushed the second thermalite into the battery chamber, then counted thirty paces back towards the museum, the track we'd made on the way out now only visible as smoothed-off dents in the undulating white carpet. I stood there, safety off, thumb on the choke button, wondering who or what would come through the snowstorm toward me. A good five minutes must have passed and I heard a thud, then another, but I wasn't expert enough to tell from which weapon they had originated.

All of a sudden I was aware of the squeak and crunch of some-thing moving in an untroubled fashion through the snow, less than thirty feet away to the left of me. They made no attempt to move

silently and seemed to be lumbering rather than walking, and at a
reasonable pace. I was put in mind of a large herbivore, which wasn't
possible – Megafauna would never be awake, and even if they were,
they would not be out in this. Only Villains, womads, Consuls and
idiots ventured out in a snowstorm in the Winter.

I swallowed down my fear and as the sound drew closer I decided
to tempt providence and hail whoever it was. But as soon as I opened
my mouth to speak the footfalls abruptly stopped and I heard a
shuffle in the snow as the figure turned to face me. I couldn't see
them, but I somehow knew that whoever it was could see me. Or
sense me, at any rate. I was also acutely aware that this wasn't Fodder.
I had put my hand in my bag to pull out the camera that Laura had
given me when a voice made me jump.

'I wonder if you wouldn't mind awfully dropping that weapon?'

I had been so fixated on the presence to my left that I had not
been paying attention, and a figure had crept up on me out of
the snow storm and was now holding a Bambi to my head. He
was dressed in the mismatched blend of clothes that was the
adopted uniform of the Winter Villain: much-mended ski salopettes
with a mammoth-wool tweed jacket under a down-filled puffa,
criss-crossed with belts of thermalites. He had large boots, again
mismatched, a sturdy tea cosy for a hat which was embroidered
'A gift from Whitby' and was missing his nose – frostbite, I figured.
There was also a scar the thickness of a little finger that ran from
his forehead to his chin by way of his left eye – which held a
cracked monocle.

'Well, take me to Mansion House ball and dance me the Dashing
White Sergeant,' he said in the cut-glass tones of the English upper
classes, 'I seem to have bagged myself a Novice.'

I'd never met a Villain before, so didn't quite know what to say –
and he was right, I *was* still a Novice, despite what anyone said.

'You speak English?' he asked, because I'd paused. 'The tongue of
a civilised race?'

'We don't speak it much out this way,' I replied, thinking carefully
as I hadn't used my English for a while and was a little rusty. 'I
thought we were at peace, you and we?'

'That Fodder of yours tore up the accord when he cracked m'boy on the nut,' he said. 'We are merely lost travellers, old stick, trying to make our way back to the warm embrace of home and hearth.'

All Villains were English, and descendants of the upper classes who had been pushed to the edges of the Albion Peninsula after the devastating Class Wars of the nineteenth century. They had preserved their culture down the years, defiant against their victors. Large houses, crab-apple marmalade and trout-kippers for breakfast, hunting, shooting, fishing, balls, society gatherings. But most importantly, they liked servants and aggressively maintained their banned titles. Almost every Villain in Mid-Wales was a duke or a lord or a baroness or some such.[55]

'Is your way home through the museum?' I asked.

He smiled.

'I'm not going to argue the toss, old stick,' he said, 'you should be grateful I'm going to spare your life. A few positions have opened up in the household and someone of your youth would be perfect to learn the complexities of domestic service. Did you know there are six different types of fork, each for a specific purpose?[56] How's your washing and ironing, by the way? We can start you off in the scullery.'

'Terrible – and my cleaning and cooking are not very good either.'

He grinned.

'Excellent – your training starts as soon as we get back. Ten years should make a fine servant of you; perhaps as a pastry chef. A lifetime in the service of others is a lifetime well served.'

It wasn't *quite* how I would have interpreted the saying. He took the Schtumper from me, then my Bambi. My eyes flicked from the Villain to the empty snowstorm behind, hoping for Fodder, and the Villain guessed my thoughts perfectly.

'Your large friend will have a shocker of a headache come the morning,' he said. 'The larger they are, the harder they fall.'

55. It was rumoured that the descendants of the exiled royal family, far from residing on a large farm in British Columbia, were actually living in a rambling fourteen-bedroomed mansionette near Lampeter.

56. There are actually eight. I counted them later.

He pushed his Bambi hard into my head and stepped closer. The scar on his face looked like an untidy weld, and the folds in his skin were ingrained with dirt. The gap where his nose had been was only semi-healed; I could see the pink of his sinuses inside – they moved when he breathed like the gills of a stranded fish.

'Well, mustn't dawdle,' he said. 'The devil makes work for idle hands. After you – I insist.'

I took a pace forward but there was a low moan, like the sound of wind when it howls around the guttering. We both stared towards where I'd heard the shuffling steps, and I heard the chortle of a bemused child. The hair rose on the back of my neck, and I could see that the Villain had heard it too.

'Friend of yours, Novice?'

'Not of mine,' I said, this time in my mother tongue, 'and not of yours, either.'

'Well, damn and blast,' whispered the Villain as he realised what it was, 'I need a Gronk like I need a forty-thousand-acre estate and death duties.'

If you live on the edge of the Winter, you know what's real and what isn't. He dropped the Schtumperschreck and drew his other Bambi so he was holding one in each hand. He didn't panic at all, just gritted his teeth and moved forward.

'Now listen here,' he said, his voice fading as he walked into the snowstorm, 'I'll show you how an Englishman faces de—'

When I woke up I was on my back in the snow with everything quiet, snowflakes melting on my eyelashes and running into my eyes. I climbed to my feet but couldn't see the Villain anywhere, so followed a trail that was less a set of footprints and more a *furrow* where someone had been dragged. I found one discharged Bambi after about thirty feet, then another, then the Villain's clothes. The salopettes, tea-cosy hat, and the puffa, tweed jacket, complete with stained dress-shirt, two T-shirts and a vest, all inside one another. I looked around to see where he might have gone from there, but there was nothing – I was surrounded by virgin snow with the words of 'So Long, Farewell' running around inside my head.

Truce busted

'Scavengers are the bottom feeders of the Winter, taking what they can, when they can, to survive. Differentiated from Villains by their general adherence to a limited code of Winter conduct and from womads by their permanent residence, usually converted oil tankers or cement lorries. They are reputed to be citizens who had to turn cannibalistic during the Winter, and now shun society due to shame.'

— *Handbook of Winterology*, 4th edition, Hodder & Stoughton

Jonesy and Toccata arrived twenty minutes later, having homed in on the pulser I had set the moment I found Fodder, just near the helter-skelter. He was covered by a thin layer of fresh snow and had a large purple bruise on the side of his face. In front of him was another Villain, also unconscious. Fodder came round first. He had a splitting headache, but was otherwise unhurt.

'Do you know him?' asked Toccata when they rolled the first Villain over to get a look at him. He had a cold-gnarled leathery complexion, but no-one recognised him.

'No,' said Jonesy while going through his pockets, 'but this was probably the reason they were trying to break in.'

She handed Toccata a small book she'd found entitled *Gibbons' Pocket Philatelist*. A bus ticket was marking the page devoted to the stamps printed during Lloyd-George's premiership.

'They were after a *stamp*,' said Toccata with a sigh. She slapped the Villain around the face. He groaned, blinked and sat up. One eye was milky and blind, the other bloodshot. He wasn't much older than me.

'You'd break our truce for a stamp?' she asked in English.

The young Villain looked at her, then the rest of us.

'It's the 2d Lloyd-George Mauve,' he said, 'with the Anglesey cancellation. The only one in the world. But in answer to your question: yes, I should jolly well say so. *Well* worth it. Clearly, you have a woefully poor grasp of the value and excitement of stamp collecting. Where's Father?'

'We don't know.'

'If you don't answer truthfully,' snorted the Villain, 'you might find me irked, and you wouldn't like me when I'm irked. Devilry may ensue. Now, again: where's Father?'

'Same answer as last time,' said Toccata. 'Heading home is my guess.'

'If you've harmed a hair on his head, Janus, there'll be retribution of the blood-spilling variety – and with no apologies for absence.'

'I've a better idea,' said Jonesy, 'why don't you just piss off home, you odious little maggot?'

The Villain got up, looked at us all in turn, told us he had 'never been so insulted in his life' and walked off into the gathering dusk.

'Did you get the other fella?' asked Fodder once the Villain was lost to view.

'He was got,' I said slowly, 'but I'm not sure by who.'

'Whom,' said Toccata, correcting me, 'not sure by *whom*. What did he mean when he called me "Janus"?'

We all shook our heads and mumbled that we had no idea.

Toccata's Sno-Trac had been parked next to the main entrance of the museum, and now that the snowstorm had abated, we could see the headlight cluster as eight circles of light shining through the gloom. The Villain's carefully folded clothes were still lying where they'd been found, and Toccata examined them with interest while the others stood silently by.

'He was going to kidnap me into domestic service,' I said, 'working up from the scullery to become a pastry chef. Then there was a giggle in the air and the Winter took him.'

'Took him?'

'I think so. I didn't see anything. I was unconscious.'

They all exchanged glances, their expressions making quite clear that they thought I was involved.

'What did the Villain look like?' asked Toccata, pulling a wallet from the pocket of his folded jacket.

'He had a scar across his eye,' I said, 'bad teeth, about fifty, weather-beaten, no nose, monocle.'

243

Toccata stood up and handed me a long-expired season ticket to
the Oval.

'Shit, Wonky,' she said, handing me the season ticket, 'you just
killed Lucky Ned.'

I looked at the ticket. It said 'Edward Nodds', but he was better
known amongst his people and law enforcement agencies as the Rt
Hon. Edward Warchester Stamford Noddington, 13th Earl of
Farnesworth. 'I didn't kill anyone.'

'*Somebody* did.'

'His family won't be happy,' said Jonesy.

'We shouldn't tell anyone that Wonky killed him,' said Fodder.

'I didn't kill him,' I said in an increasingly exasperated fashion,
'there was something there – something that could sense me through
the snow. Once Ned had gone I was suddenly hearing "So Long,
Farewell" running around my head. It's still there now.'

'"So Long, Farewell"?' asked Fodder.

'From *The Sound of Music*. The Gronk is very fond of Rodgers
and Hammerstein.'

'Are you suggesting the Gronk took him?'

'The Gronk's a myth,' said Jonesy, 'you're still narced.'

We all stood for a while in silence, staring at the folded clothes.

'The one thing we're sure of is this,' said Toccata. 'The Winter has
seen the end of a particularly unpleasant individual. But it means
the truce is busted and Lady Farnesworth won't be happy. With a
bit of luck, perhaps they'll accept he got lost. But Fodder's right: we
don't tell anyone that Wonky was the last person that saw him alive.'

She looked at us all in turn.

'And we're done. I'll want a full report on my desk by say, oh, I
don't know – suit yourself.'

Toccata trudged off back in the direction of the Sno-Trac; we
saw the lights swing around in the semi-dark, then vanish into the
greyness.

'So,' said Jonesy, 'now that the Chief's gone: what really happened?'

'Yes,' said Fodder, 'spill the beans, Wonk.'

'I don't know,' I said in a quiet voice.

'Is this something to do with Laura's wager?' asked Jonesy as we retraced our steps back towards the museum. 'I'd be overjoyed if Treacle lost the bet, but think very carefully before bearing false witness against a bondsman. Treacle has a seriously overstuffed Debt-bank, and every single one of those Favours could be used to make your life a misery.'

I told them again that I didn't know what had happened, but that wasn't strictly true. The child's laugh I'd heard was uncannily similar to the one I'd heard in my dream: the kid with the beach ball. Parts of my dream were trying to get out.

Fodder and I headed home to the *Siddons*, which we reached without any further drama. We found Lloyd at the reception desk, darning a sock that was a great deal of darn and very little sock. He nodded a greeting and Fodder looked at his watch.

'We're done, Wonk. If you're in the lobby at oh–nine–hundred tomorrow morning either myself or Jonesy will take you out on patrol.'

He tapped me on the chest.

'You may want to bulk up a little. The cold can really suck out the reserves.'

I thanked him, told him I'd stuff myself stupid with whatever food was to hand, and he walked off across the lobby towards the elevators.

'How are you getting on with the big fella?' asked Lloyd once Fodder had gone.

'Okay, I think. He kissed me on the ear when we were embracing.'

'I shouldn't read anything into it. He does that to everyone. Were there many nightwalkers alive in the basement this morning?'

'Three. I met up with Aurora down there. Did that happen wholly by chance?'

I was looking for a sign that he'd been rumbled. That he was somehow involved.

'Why would she plan that?' he asked, seemingly without the tell-tale sign I was looking for.

'I don't know.'

'If this is a Toccata/Aurora politics issue, there's one rule,' he said. 'Don't get caught in the middle. How did you get along with Toccata?'

'I think she hates me – and no one told me that she and Aurora were the same person.'

'I thought everyone knew,' he said. 'That would explain why you took the clinically insane decision to off-season with Aurora.'

'You heard about that?'

'No one's talking about much else on the Open Network. There's also a rumour going around that someone was killed in the Pleasure Gardens just now. Is that true?'

I took a deep breath and told Lloyd what had happened out in the snow, behind the museum, every detail. He'd lived the Winter for over thirty seasons, had been there when Ichabod was taken; I wanted to know what he thought.

'She's back,' he said once I'd finished. 'When they find the body he'll be missing his little finger. The Gronk does that. Sort of like a trophy. Did you hear a gurgle of child's laughter just before Lucky Ned was taken?'

I felt the hairs on the back of my neck rise again, and told him that, yes, I had.

He nodded sagely.

'The reason Wintervolk can't be sensed, hunted, cornered or killed is because they exist only as dreams that have survived beyond the vessel that gave them life. They swirl amongst us, flitting from host to host, then make landfall occasionally to wreak havoc, and once they have done so, depart, back into the collective subconscious.'

'That's quite far-fetched.'

'Maybe. Some say the entity that we know as the Gronk is actually the orphaned nightmare of Gretl, the daughter of Ichabod Block, the one he murdered in her sleep. *Gretl Block,* Gronk, get it?'

'That's pretty tenuous.'

'The Gronk first appeared twenty years ago, not long after Gretl died – and she was a huge fan of Rodgers and Hammerstein.'

'*Still* pretty tenuous.'

'Agreed,' said Lloyd, staring at the desk.

We'd been told to invoke the Rule of Least Astonishment[57] when assessing aberrant Winter phenomena, and this seemed a good time

---

57. Simply put: the easiest and most likely explanation, however mundane, is probably correct.

to do so, because everything *was* less astonishing than suggesting the Gronk took Lucky Ned. It could have been a nightwalker, Consul, winsomniac, sleepwalker – even someone in a modern Mk XXII shock-suit, the one with an H4S built in. And what better way to cover one's tracks than by making it *look* as if it was the Gronk? Lucky Ned might have engineered the whole thing to put the fear of Morpheus up us. Villains like to mess with your head.

I thanked Lloyd and walked towards the elevator with, I admit, a dull feeling in my stomach. But it wasn't just the hunger, the stresses of the day, meeting Toccata or even that I'd been there when the Gronk appeared and took Lucky Ned – no, there was something else, something that had been nagging at my conscience all afternoon, something that just wouldn't go away.

Birgitta.

Something rotten in the winter

'... The Dormitorium as a social hub lives long in the resident's psyche. A place of safe harbour, warmth and slumber, it is not hard to see why loyalty to a particular Kipshop can be so strong. Moving is rare; your Dormitorium name, number and floor family become part of what you are. Abandon them and you abandon part of yourself ...'

– *Handbook of Winterology*, 10th edition, Hodder & Stoughton

I took the paternoster to the ninth floor, unlocked the door to my apartment and chucked my jacket over the back of the sofa. I slid a cylinder at random onto the phonograph and pretty soon the restful melody of the *Suite Bergamesque* filled the air. I walked to the kitchen area and brewed myself a cup of tea, ate a bag of cashews and made a large peanut butter and jam sandwich. I then picked a packet of Jaffa cakes and three Club Oranges from the basket, placed the tuck in my pockets and quietly opened the door. Unsurprisingly, there was no one about but I removed my slippers anyway and padded in my socks around the corridor. I stopped outside Birgitta's room, paused to check the coast was clear, then unlocked the door and slipped inside.

The room was pretty much as I had seen it that morning: full of paintings, but with anything organic either chewed or eaten: all the spare food, most of the cardboard and even the candles, soap and the rubber off a spatula. Before Lloyd had released Birgitta into the basement she had consumed what little protein she could find – even the curtains looked chewed.

I moved cautiously through to the bedroom. Birgitta was sprawled awkwardly on the bed, quite still. I checked her pulse and found she was merely in Torpor. Emotionally and intellectually brain dead she might be, but the stewardship part of her hypothalamus was functioning perfectly.

The hard part had been getting her unseen up the stairs, the most unpleasant task the removal of her thumb. I turned up the heating then sat on the bed and waited. About twenty minutes later her eyelids flickered open.

'I love you, Charlie,' she said.

'I don't doubt it,' I said, 'but not this Charlie, *your* Charlie. I was beguiled by the hope that you meant me, but you didn't. It was another Charlie. It was a ... *nominative coincidence*.'

I fed her the sandwich and the chocolate and then gave her a pint of water to drink. I hadn't been able to bring myself to retire her that morning, so merely sidestepped the issue in order to keep all options open. Trouble is, my options hadn't increased since this morning, they'd narrowed. I'd thought Birgitta and I had a connection, but we hadn't. As Aurora had explained, I'd simply joggled her into my dream retrospectively. It was only a matter of time before she was discovered, and no amount of talking would get me off the hook. Harbouring was harbouring, no matter who did it, or the motivations. I would have to do now what I should have done that morning.

Jonesy was right: the first is always the hardest.

I held Birgitta's head gently in one arm, set my Bambi to the *test* setting and pressed the weapon against the back of her head, just where the spine connects to the skull. I paused, then felt uncommanded tears well up in my eyes. It was fortunate they did; I moved to wipe them away and Birgitta shifted to reveal the corner of a sketchbook under the blankets on her bed. I gently released her and pulled back the covers. She had been drawing, and recently: that morning, *after* I brought her back to her room.

'Kiki needs the cylinder,' she said.

On the first page of the notebook was a sketch of the blue Buick as I'd seen it down in the basement, the oak tree near by, the pile of stones heaped around the trunk. There were the remains of a picnic near the car, and in the distance, a Morpheleum. There was a figure, too, sitting on the stones: Don Hector, looking dejected, while around the stones were hundreds of hands sticking out of the ground, waiting to get him.

I shivered uncontrollably. It was the dream that I'd had, the dream that Birgitta must have had, too. Which can't work unless the dream *was* viral – or this too was obeying the retrospective memory theory. I turned over the pad to reveal another sketch, this time depicting a scene under an old car. Someone in the picture was trying to reach for a flashlight they'd dropped, the light revealing the profile of a face that was, in Birgitta's past words: 'of inspiring intrigue'. It was me. But it wasn't just me, it was the *recent memory* of me. This morning, when we'd met under the Buick. Birgitta had lost almost everything, but retained the complex eye-to-hand coordination of the artist she once had been.

'I fooled myself I'd met your husband,' I said in a quiet voice, 'over at HiberTech. Guy named Webster. Has a beard and drives a golf cart. One of the redeployed.'

She looked blankly about, but made no hint of either understanding what I had said, or of even being conscious of her surroundings. I handed her a pen several times, but the only time she grasped on to it, she let it drop almost immediately. She was drawing from memory – a human photocopier. A complex trick, but a trick none-theless. I felt a sense of hopelessness rise within me. Even if I could slip her past Toccata's policy of retiring all nightwalkers and somehow explain satisfactorily why she was still alive, HiberTech would just disassemble what remained of her mind and redeploy her as a menial worker, a mindless drone. I don't think she would have wanted that. No, I had to do what I should have done that morning.

I went into the kitchen to fetch her more water, but when I came back there was another picture on the pad: a man in a golf cart with a beard. Not from life, as the golf cart was different, as was the corridor. But that didn't matter right now. There was something more important going on.

She had processed what I'd said.

'Shit,' I said, 'you can understand me.'

I snapped my fingers in front of her face but she didn't so much as blink.

'There will always be the Gower,' she said in a quiet voice.

'Okay, then,' I said, sitting down next to her, 'my name is Charlie

Worthing, I'm a Novice Consul – well, Deputy now, I guess – and to everyone else you're simply a Tricksy nightwalker and as good as dead, but I know that you're not. Can you even begin to explain to me where you think you are right now?'

This time, I waited for her reply. She did nothing for fifteen minutes, then picked up the pen and rapidly drew another sketch. It was of the beach in the Gower, the wreck of the *Argentinian Queen*, an orange-and-red parasol of spectacular size and splendour. There was the little girl, too, running after a beach ball, and Birgitta was dressed as she was now, sketching. The pictures of the Buick dream and me and her under the car were all laid upon the sand. As soon as she'd finished she stopped and stared at the floor, exhausted by the activity. I stared for some time at the sketches, and at her.

She was alive in there, dreaming herself in the Gower. *Her mind was functioning.* I stared into Birgitta's eyes and tried to catch sight of her trapped inside, but there was nothing. She looked across my shoulder, at the corner of the room, the curtains, back again. She caught my gaze eventually and her bright violet eyes locked hard onto mine for a few seconds.

'Birgitta?' I said. 'Can you hear me?'

'I love you, Charlie.'

I sighed, trying to figure out what all this meant on a broader scale. The actor I met on the train might have been correct when she said her husband was still alive, and Mr Tiffen's complex subterfuge to protect his wife would make complete sense if he believed the same. There was Olaf Yawnersson, too, here in the Douzey, who had harboured a couple of nightwalkers for over three years, without evidence of any crime. Perhaps he too saw something that convinced him that his nightwalkers weren't truly dead. There had been other, anecdotal stories of family members being convinced of their cannibalistically brain-dead loved one's inner consciousness, but all had been denied by HiberTech and the nightwalkers were then either parted out, retired, used for experiments or redeployed. If what these people believed was true and HiberTech knew about it, then their actions would be nothing short of, well, *heinous*.

'Kiki needs the cylinder.'

'I'm sure she does,' I said, 'if I even knew what that meant.'

I fed Birgitta several more Jaffa cakes then sat her in the tub and scrubbed out the grime that had turned her tortoiseshell wintercoat into a matted mess. She sat impassively in the tub as I washed her as you might a dog or an infant, and didn't murmur as I clipped off her matted head-hair, then rubbed lice oil into her scalp and changed the bandage on her thumb. I then dressed her in clean clothes and tidied up, made sure there was plenty of paper and pens within easy reach and told her I would be back to give her breakfast.

Once I'd locked the door firmly behind me, I returned to my room, made a cup of Nesbit-brand cocoa, then took off my clothes and settled into bed. It wasn't late, but I was tired. I picked up my notebook with the intent to fill in my journal but then thought I had better not in case of prying eyes, so just laid back and gazed at Clytemnestra, who stared back at me with her unalterable pigment-based psychopathy.

I had survived my first full day in Sector Twelve but only just. I was suffering Hibernational Narcosis that presented as a déjà-vu memory reversion. This, enough as it was, was not the sum total of my problems: I had lied to Toccata about my relationship with Aurora, possible RealSleep activist Hugo Foulnap was masquerading as a Consul with Toccata's knowledge, and I'd discovered it was feasible nightwalkers weren't quite as dead as it seemed. Given that The Notable Goodnight had asked me if I'd seen any learned behaviour from Mrs Tiffen, they'd probably figured it out too. Quite how this fitted in with Project Lazarus I wasn't sure — if it did at all — but rolling out universal rights to Morphenox would increase the quantity of nightwalkers, and if they could be redeployed to do more than just simple tasks, this could be a potentially valuable workforce asset for HiberTech.

But all my problems seemed trivial in the light of the most important task facing me: keeping Birgitta alive, safe, warm, well fed and away from prying eyes. Perhaps if I got her to Springrise and took her to the press, all would be well. Then Morphenox and the nightwalker phenomenon could be scrutinised, questions could be asked, Birgitta studied. But that bred a bigger problem. Food. Ninety-one days of food. If I let Birgitta get hungry, she'd revert to cannibalism, and I'd be first on the menu. I tried to think of a credible scheme whereby I could access the well-guarded pantry and snaffle some food, but before long my trail of optimistic thought dried up. Her discovery was not a question of *if*, but when. And when she was discovered, that was me done for good. Prison, out of a job and worse, *far* worse, the lasting disapproval of Sister Zygotia. I'd end my days as a community Footman, wandering the Winter on a capped ten euros per hour, waiting for my luck to finally turn sour.

I needed escape, and when I found it two hours later, it was trebly welcome. It relieved my fatigue, removed me from my troubles, and returned me to Birgitta. Not to the living nightwalker Birgitta locked in her room, whom I would protect with my life and reputation, but the dream Birgitta lodged within my subconscious.

On the Gower.

Again.

Dream again

'... Study of glaciers revealed year on year advancement, but few politicians ever wanted to get behind the notion of climate change, and policy lagged accordingly. The inconvenient truth was that at current estimates and without a coherent strategy, everything North of the 42nd parallel would be ice sheet in two hundred years...'

— *Surviving Snowball Earth*, by Jeremy Wainscott

It felt as though a bar or block had lifted in my mind and that my dream cogs, long gummed with disuse, had finally found a way to move. I dreamed of the white-softened town, the snow pure and unsullied after a recent fall. I saw Jonesy dressed as the front half of a pantomime horse and surrounded by her collection of thumbs, all sixty-three of them, then Mother Fallopia glaring at me severely, standing over a sleeping Birgitta, amongst dozens of paintings of Charlie Webster *also* looking at me severely.

And then I was outside and could see Aurora moving amongst the drifts entirely naked, her body hair a light mousy colour, no more than an inch long except where it thinned to the naked strip of skin that ran along her spine in the shape of a poplar leaf, the *linea decalvare* so beloved of classical painters. She turned and was suddenly Toccata, sitting at a table with me on a large platter, basted in honey glaze and with an apple in my mouth.

But while these were all a little odd, they were just plain, standard dreams. I *knew* they were dreams and they were dismissed as such. I had been waiting, as though labouring through endless trailers and adverts at the cinema, knowing that finally, with a burst of sound and light, the main attraction would begin and I could settle down, and relax, and enjoy.

And it did — with a joyous blur of colour and light, away from the lower subconscious and into the exaggerated reality of the higher Dreamstate.

We were back in the Gower, the *Argentinian Queen* on the beach by the shoreline, the blue paintwork showing through the rust, cable stays loose and swinging in the breeze. Everything was precisely as it had been before, like watching a movie for the second or third time – predictably familiar and unwavering in the precision of its repetition. The sand, the sun, the large orange-and-red parasol of spectacular size and splendour, Birgitta in her one-piece swimsuit the colour of freshly unfurled leaves. She looked at me, pushed her hair behind her ear, smiled, and everything at that moment was perfect once more. All was Summertopia, and nothing could shake the sense of overwhelming bliss. The child ran past with the beach ball and the peal of laughter, and that was her cue. The same words, the identical inflection.

'I love you, Charlie.'

'I love you, Birgitta.'

And despite the disjointed Dreamstate I found myself in and the impossibility of the situation out in the real world, I did. Not for what I could see in front of me on this lazy weekend a decade in the past, but here and now, secure in the knowledge that I was loving her in a protective way, deep within the dreary midwinter of Sector Twelve and the shabbiness of the *Sarah Siddons*. Hiding her, looking after her needs, attempting to find a way forward into something that might resemble survival and justice.

I looked at my hands again and touched my symmetrical head, the rasp of stubble against my fingertips. I felt my nose: straight, aquiline, distinguished.

'I like being Charles,' I said.

'You're Charles now, *my* Charles,' said Birgitta with a delightful giggle. 'Try not to think about the facility and HiberTech Security. Just today and tomorrow, forty-eight hours. You and me. What Dreams May Come.'

It was the same line. Repeated word for word.

'What Dreams May Come,' I replied, then, by way of experiment, added: 'While Krugers with Lugers take potshots at hotshots.'

Birgitta frowned.

'What?'

'… is enough to make mammoths with a gram's worth of hammocks feel down with a clown from Manchester Town.'

I then did a cartwheel in the soft sand. I hadn't done one for a while and saw stars for a moment, but when I looked at Birgitta again she had an expression of such abject confusion that I felt quite concerned.

'You're Charles now, *my* Charles?' she said in an uncertain tone.

'I am for the moment.'

'You and me? What … Dreams May Come.'

I'd changed the dream. Not just lines, but *actions*. And I'd changed Birgitta's responses, too.

'What Dreams May Come,' I said.

'Happy snap?' said the photographer. 'Proper tidy you'll look and as—'

'—reasonably priced as they come?' I said. 'Was that what you were going to say?'

'Well, yes,' said the photographer, looking at Birgitta, who shrugged. I knew that I was now leading the dream, and not just being a passenger within it.

'We've not much time,' I said, feeling the shadow of the blue Buick dream fast approaching our beach idyll. 'I want to see more of you and me, away from the beach. When and where did we meet for the last time?'

The smile dropped from her face.

'You don't need me to tell you, Charlie, you already know.'

It was true, I did. It was in the *Cambrensis*, a week prior to Slumberdown, three years before. But just then, the little girl approached with the beach ball and the gurgle of laughter but she didn't pass by this time; she stopped and stared at me.

'Be careful, Charlie,' she said. 'If you look into someone else's dreams, all you ever find are nightmares.'

And she ran off with her beach ball.

I readied myself, then jumped to another dream, a dream-within-the-dream. I didn't know I was able to do this, but I could. Like finding you can play the piano when you're eighteen but somehow you always *knew* – astonishing and expected, all at the same time.

I was outside a dark, cheerless Dormitorium, dismal and forbidding in age-darkened stone. The dream, like the dream I'd just left, was hyper-realistic, distinguishable from reality only because I knew it wasn't. I'd seen this building before, out in the real world. It was the *Geraldus Cambrensis*.

I caught a glimpse of my reflection in the glazed panel of the door and saw Charlie Webster staring back at me. He looked harder, more weary, older, stressed. I pushed open the door, wondering where my subconscious was taking me.

The style of the interior was from the thirteenth century, when only the clergy and aristocracy used Dormitoria and slumber was inextricably linked with death, renewal and religion. A curved stair-case led up behind the lobby towards the central void, but modern sofas were positioned either side of the central desk, where the porter was doing some paperwork. Zsazsa was reading a copy of the *Ludlow Vogue* while sitting on one of the sofas, while on the other I could see Agent Hooke partially hidden behind a newspaper. There was a third figure in a phone booth to one side, which looked as though it was either Aurora or Toccata, but impossible to say which.

'Good evening,' said the porter.

'Good evening,' I replied. 'Any messages?'

The Consul Charlie part of me didn't know him, but the Birgitta's Charlie part of me did.

'Just one,' he replied, and handed me a note from my pigeonhole.

There will always be the Gower

It wasn't the porter's writing. It was Birgitta's, and meant only one thing: they were on to me, and I should get to the safe house without delay, stay quiet, await instructions.

I thanked the porter, turned, but instead of making my escape as Birgitta had suggested, I trotted up the stairs to the first floor. I heard the rustle of a newspaper being folded and footsteps on the stone floor below, but I did not quicken my pace. If I could hear Agent Hooke, he would be able to hear me.

The building was demonstrably ancient, gloomy and in a poor state of repair. Buckets had been scattered around to catch the leaks in the vaulted corridor, and large blooms of mould had erupted across the damp plaster. I moved on around the curved corridor, entered room 106 and cautiously locked the door behind me.

The room was not large, had an arched ceiling rendered in plaster and was panelled in pine linenfold, some of which had been repaired poorly, and in haste. There was a single sash window which opened on to a fire escape and, upon the wall, a clock set inside a multi-spiked star with its hands frozen at 10.55. There were no books, no personal ornaments, no pictures, no photographs. Webster seemed to me either a man without a past, or a man eager not to have one.

Without thinking, I reached into the leather satchel slung from my shoulder, and removed a round cardboard tube of the sort used to carry music or Dictaphone cylinders. It was the recording cylinder that I'd been told to get to Kiki. But I didn't know who Kiki was, nor how to get it there, nor where I'd got it. I was part Charles Webster, not all of him; I was only witnessing a small window into his life. I crossed to the fireplace and pushed the cylinder onto a handy ledge high up inside the chimney. This done, I took a match to the note the porter had given me and watched it burn to ash.

I was just beginning to wonder when Birgitta would turn up when – predictably enough, given this was my dream – there was a tap on the window, and I saw her wave at me from the fire escape outside. But she wasn't the Birgitta from the beach, it was a serious Birgitta, a late-season Birgitta, a bulked-up-make-baby-in-the-Spring Birgitta, a worried Birgitta – and not, I think, for herself.

'For God's sake, Charlie,' she said when I opened the window and helped her climb in, 'didn't the porter show you my note?'

But at least she was there, even if pissed off. Her dark hair was loosely bunched up in a ponytail, and beneath her parka she was dressed in paint-spattered dungarees.

'I did get your note,' I said, going along with the narrative, enjoying the frisson of danger. I'd seen the *Cambrensis* in the distance, knew where Webster had lived; I'd seen his address on file. I was filling in the gaps. This was a dream to be savoured, an experience to enjoy. The adventure was wholly in my head, and I was going to enjoy every moment.

'Then why didn't you go to the safe house?' she continued, her anger rooted more in concern than annoyance. 'Kiki would have arranged your evacuation.'

The dream was becoming more like a spy thriller by the second: Birgitta and I were not in the Douzey as economic migrants. We were engaged in infiltration work for the Campaign for Real Sleep. I was in deep cover at HiberTech, working my way up the unskilled labour chain to gain access to sensitive information.

'I'm just an orderly. I'll act dumb. They've got nothing.'

'Not this time. She was there, in the phone booth, when I walked in. She *knows*.'

I didn't know what I was meant to say right then, but it was okay; Birgitta spoke for me. And when she did, it was pretty much as expected.

'Kiki needs the cylinder.'

Of course. She would say that. I was still filling in the blanks with whatever was to hand. I'd said it before: a dream is just the subconscious mind attempting to form a narrative from a jumble of thoughts, facts and memories.

'It's safe,' I said, meaning the tube I'd just hidden up the chimney, 'and I'll come back for it, I promise – and get it to Kiki.'

She raised an eyebrow.

'I'm not leaving Sector Twelve until you do.'

There was a thump on the door. It was expected, but we jumped, even so.

'Webster?' came a voice that could have belonged to either Toccata or Aurora.

'Who's there?' I asked in an innocent, sing-song sort of way.

'Who do you think?' came the voice again. 'The Gronk? Open the sodding door.'

Birgitta and I looked at one another.

'They'll search the place,' I whispered, 'there must be nothing linking you and me. Here.'

I reached up and plucked a faded photo from where it was hidden beneath the star-shaped clock. It was the Polaroid of us both, a wafer of time from that perfect and now distant moment back on the Rhosilli. I handed it to Birgitta.

'You kept it?' she said. 'Seriously bad move. I'll destroy it.'

She shoved the Polaroid in her pocket and we stared at one another for a few moments. If the beach had been the high point, this was the low. It would be the last time we/they'd see one another, and I think we/they both knew it. Our final words came easily enough.

'I love you, Charlie.'

'I love you, Birgitta.'

We said the words tonelessly, without feeling, just as the night-walker Birgitta had been saying them to me out in the real world. She hadn't been saying them in a dull monotone, she was repeating them exactly as she'd last said them. Unhurried, an expression of fact, not an anthem of passion.

And then she was gone, back out of the window and away down the fire escape. The door wobbled as someone outside loosed off a Thumper, and the lock flew off with a loud report and embedded itself in the far wall. A second thump reduced the door to a cloud of wood splinters and—

— I was under the oak tree, sitting on the jumbled heap of scratched boulders, the air heavy with the scent of Summer, the sky an azure blue, the light filtering through the spreading boughs to scatter a dappled light upon the ground.

Like before, there was no transition, no warning, nothing. One moment I was in the *Cambrensis* about to get busted, the next I was under the oak. I sat up and looked around. I wasn't Webster any more, I was Don Hector. My skin hung slackly from my jowls, my limbs ached and my vision felt dim and constricted. The fuzziness was still there on my left-hand side, and deep inside my chest I could feel a rattle that I knew was not a passing infection, but a funeral march.

I climbed unsteadily to my feet and looked around. The blue

Buick was there, the Morpheleum was there on the horizon, the picnic was all laid out – and Mrs Nesbit was there, the wavy bluish aura crackling around her.

'We know of a remote farm in Lincolnshire where Mrs Buckley lives. Every July—'

She didn't get to finish. Her voice was abruptly cut out by the *other* voice, the hectoring Mrs Nesbit that didn't match the mouth of the shimmering vision. This time, I recognised it. The Notable Goodnight.

'Worthing?'

'Yes.'

'Are you there, under the oak, in the sun, the blue Buick and the picnic close by?'

'Yes,' I said, staring at where I could see a hand hiding behind a flower a few paces away.

'Where did you go just now? You were dreaming of something. Was it relevant to our search for the cylinder?'

'No,' I replied quickly, 'just some stuff from the Pool – a memorable game of indoor cricket when Billy DeFroid knocked the hand off the statue of St Morpheus, then mended it with chewing gum while sitting on the shoulders of Ed Dweezle.'

'That's very interesting,' said Mrs Nesbit.

'Is it?'

'No. It's probably the *least* interesting thing I've heard. There's only one dream I want to hear about, and that's the one that contains the cylinder. We need to know where it is. We need it back.'

I knew now what the cylinder was, at least physically: a *recording* cylinder, probably made of wax and with an audio soundtrack, and hidden up the chimney back at the *Cambrensis*.

'The one that Kiki is after?' I asked.

There was a pause.

'That's right, Worthing. The one that Kiki is after.'

'What's on the cylinder?' I asked.

'Nothing that concerns you. Just try and remember who Don Hector gave it to, or where it is now. It's important. Try and get to the Morpheleum. You may have better luck than the others.'

'Others?'

'I meant … the *other* time you tried.'

But I wasn't really listening. I knew Webster had been given the cylinder but I wanted to know where he got it. Close the circle, if you like. What was more, I *knew* that I had to get to the temple of Morpheus, the one I could see on the horizon. I climbed down from the boulders as fast as my limited mobility would allow, then limped off across the open ground towards the Buick, feeling in my pocket for the rabbit's-foot key ring. I kicked away a hand that had grabbed my trouser leg, then yanked open the car door and climbed in. There was little short-term gain; within a second the hands were swarming across the bonnet in an aggrieved manner, their skin squeaking on the glass as they tried to squeeze in through the slot at the top of the driver's jammed window. Their numbers were soon so great that they appeared less like hands and more like finger-sized maggots writhing in a tin.

I fumbled for the car keys, started the engine, slammed the car into gear and was off with a jerk. Fortuitously, most of the hands fell or slid off the car and the ones that were inside I simply tossed outside. Pretty soon I was quite alone, driving across the grassy landscape, the only sound the wheels as they rumbled across the turf.

The temple took less than a minute to reach, and I pulled up, stopped the engine and climbed out. The hands that had remained stuck to the car seemed to have been stunned into inactivity by the sudden change in events, and were now silently observing me while rocking on their knuckles.

I walked towards the Morpheleum, which had been realised perfectly within my dream – lichen blooms had erupted upon the age-softened carvings, cracks had opened up in the masonry and ivy had locked the building in a tight death-grip.

'Are you at the temple?' asked Mrs Nesbit, who was still there, standing right next to me, shimmering softly.

'I'm there.'

'The first to do so,' she said, 'you are doing well. But there is no respite until you find the cylinder. Only death frees you from this dream.'

'You're a bundle of laughs, Goodnight,' I said.

'I am Mrs Nesbit,' said Mrs Nesbit after a pause that was too long to mean anything other than that she wasn't. 'And if I *was* Goodnight – which I'm not – you should use the accolade "Notable". I think she's deserved it after a lifetime of selfless toil, don't you?'

'Yes, ma'am.'

'Find the cylinder. Explore the temple. Go.'

I tentatively reached out to touch the building and with an almost seamless transition moved to a different dream. I was still Don Hector but it wasn't high Summer any more, it was late Autumn, and a grey overcast portended of rain to come. I shivered, even though wearing an overcoat, and looked around. The blue Buick had gone but the Morpheleum remained, looking darker and more forbidding but identical and now in an overgrown wood with dead brambles, silver birch and saplings of ash, their branches bare, ready for the Winter. I knew where I was – in the overgrown gardens within the quadrangle back at HiberTech. This was the place where Don Hector went for peace and solitude. His and his alone.

But if I had thought I'd left Mrs Nesbit behind, I was mistaken. She was right there next to me in the Morpheleum. She wasn't attached to the landscape, she was attached to *me*.

'What's happening?' she said.

'They're not dead,' I said in a state of confusion, airing my views about nightwalkers before I'd even realised it. 'The catastrophic neural collapse brought on by Morphenox-induced Hibernational Hypoxia is not a collapse at all – it's a state of displaced consciousness below the threshold of detection.'

I didn't know what I was talking about; this was Don Hector speaking, not me.

'We know that,' said Mrs Nesbit, 'hence the need for the cylinder. Now, let's take this one step at a time. Are you still outside the temple to Morpheus?'

'Yes.'

'Go inside.'

I stepped forward and squeezed between the heavy bronze doors. The interior was the size of a badminton court and illuminated by narrow windows set deep into the thick masonry. There was a central aisle with two arcades running parallel on either side, separated from the main chamber by a series of arches that sat atop columns of a simple, unfussy design. I walked to the sanctuary at the rear, where a domed roof was centred above a dusty altar covered in offerings to ensure sound and safe sleeping. Mostly flowers and foodstuffs, they had rotted away many years before and were little more than desiccated scraps.

'Don't make us do anything you might regret,' said Mrs Nesbit, who was now in the temple and casting a bluish glow onto the stonework, 'because we can make our dreams into your nightmares.'

'Perhaps,' I said, 'you could make that your mission statement and company motto.'

'Bravely spoken,' said Mrs Nesbit, 'but we'll have the last laugh. You're almost out of dreamtime. We'll speak again.'

She vanished abruptly, and my ear twitched as I heard the scratch of a shoe against stone. Partially hidden in the shadows was a man dressed in a medical orderly's uniform of a collarless white jacket with a flap buttoned diagonally up the front. I recognised him immediately: Charles Webster, my confident and distinctly unwonky sleep-avatar.

I had *been* him only two minutes before, now I was looking *at* him.

'Don Hector?' he asked in a nervous voice.

'What do you want?' I asked.

'I'm a friend of Kiki.'

I beckoned him closer and gave him a plain cardboard tube, the same one that Webster would hide up the chimney, moments before being arrested. It was all backwards, but dreams, I learned, were rarely linear.

'Look after the cylinder as you would your life,' I said, 'and get it to Kiki. We'll not speak again.'

Webster understood the gravity of the situation and swiftly departed. Within a few minutes there were criss-crossing flashlights outside and The Notable Goodnight entered, followed by Hooke and several other people I presumed were HiberTech Security.

They were one step behind both of us. Right now, Webster was on his way to hide the cylinder.

'Where is it?' said Goodnight, striding towards me. 'What have you done with it? Who did you give it to?'

I gave her a smile, then the middle finger.

'All our work,' implored Goodnight, 'everything we stood for, everything we built. Please, Don Hector, do the right thing.'

I smiled. Don Hector didn't have to justify his/my actions to anyone.

'We'll squeeze it out of him,' said Agent Hooke. 'He might resist out here, but not in his dreaming mind. We've drawn worse secrets out of better people than him.'

'Blue Buick,' I said.

'What?' asked Goodnight.

'I said, "blue Buick". Because it's all you'll get from me. A picnic I once had, on my own, in a field overlooking the Wye where there's this glorious oak that has large stones piled up around the trunk. I used to sit and read, the car parked close by, some wine in a cooler, cheese. That's what's in my mind, and that's all I'm going to dream about. I'll be adding a few guardians of my own, too. Severed hands like hairless mole-rats, just in case you decide to go in, or send others in your place. You'll get nothing from me.'

'Take him,' said Goodnight, but I was already gone – back to the pile of boulders around the oak, the blue Buick parked close by, the picnic half eaten. I knew the dream was about to end as the carpet of rippling hands flooded towards me, across the ground, over the boulders. I didn't struggle as they ran up my body. I didn't care when their combined weight toppled me and I felt a tooth break as I hit the rock below me; didn't care as I felt myself being pulled through the gaps in the stones; didn't care as I felt myself once more suffocating beneath the soil, the damp earth pressing heavily on my chest. I didn't care because—

Dawn and the dead

'... Average temperatures across Wales are a balmy sixteen degrees, but with seasonal highs and lows of plus thirty-two and minus sixty-eight. The residents are well adapted to the climate, being generally impervious to hardship, more hirsute, and with a propensity to minimal weight loss during slumber ...'

— *Handbook of Winterology*, 4th edition, Hodder & Stoughton

My eyes flickered open, my temples throbbed, my mouth felt dry. For the briefest of moments I thought I was once again safely back in the *Melody Black*, but no. Clytemnestra was staring down at me with a look that was beginning to feel increasingly oppressive, and next to her, the portrait of me wearing Birgitta's husband's body seemed also to have changed – he was looking less like someone in love, and more like someone with severe wakestipation.

I stretched, downed the glass of water I'd left for myself, then swung my legs out and lowered my feet to the soothingly cold boards of the floor. Regardless of the weirdness, I'd enjoyed the dream. It looked as though I had created a narrative that had all the ingredients of a thriller: a good-looking young couple in love and working for a shadowy organisation, an agent in peril, a missing recording cylinder, an interrogation, loss, betrayal. And all with me centre stage. Perhaps this was subconsciously what I saw for myself, my dream-fuddled mind generating a sense of excitement and drama that so far had been absent from my utterly conventional life. If I had another life, I'd dedicate it to non-Morphenox slumber, with all the dreams that come – and the attendant dormelogical risks. Perhaps Shamanic Bob and his dreamers had something after all.

There was a knock at the door. I guessed it must be Aurora, and I was correct. Her left eye was staring off and up to the right, while the right fixed me with a keen sense of clarity. The abrasively offensive

Toccata part of her was gone; she was back to her more ebullient self. I actually felt quite relieved to see her.

'I was passing,' she said cheerily, 'and I wanted to check you were okay.'

I didn't know what to say, so said what I was thinking.

'I didn't realise you and Toccata were—'

Aurora glared at me with such a look of hurt, anger and confusion that I stopped mid-sentence.

'I was about to say,' I began again, 'that I was unaware you and Toccata were ... so *alike*.'

She stared at me for a while, her good eye unblinking while her unseeing left eye twisted in its socket in a disturbing manner.

'We are *not* alike,' she said finally, 'not even the slightest bit. Does *that woman* think we are?'

'Well, no,' I replied, truthfully enough.

'Exactly. And that's the way we're going to keep it. Understand?'

'Yes, ma'am.'

I filled the empty pause that followed by offering her coffee.

'You have some?' she asked. 'The real stuff, I mean?'

'Sadly not,' I replied with some regret. 'Nesbit Value Brand.'

She shrugged, told me it couldn't be helped and then walked in, quietly closing the door behind her. She took off her coat, dumped it on a nearby chair and jumped up to sit on the kitchen counter.

'What do they call this?' she said, tapping the work surface.

'A peninsula, I think.'

I was no expert on kitchen furniture and was still confused over Aurora and Toccata's insistence that they were two people.

'Free-standing, it would be an island.'

She nodded thoughtfully.

'I have one that connects from one side of the kitchen to the other,' she said. 'Would that be a kitchen isthmus?'

'I'd say a counter.'

'That's what I thought. Isthmus would be more logical, though, don't you think?'

'I suppose, yes. Milk?'

'You have some?'

'Only powdered,' I said, staring into the empty fridge.

'That'll do. Hey, listen: I heard you told the Chief we'd bundled.'

She said it as if it were possibly the funniest – and unlikeliest – thing she'd ever heard.

'I had to say *something*,' I replied. 'She knew we'd met in the Wincarnis when I said we hadn't, so I needed a good reason for lying.'

'Did she believe you? I mean, did she think that the whole you and I scenario was plausible?'

'I think so, yes.'

'Ah,' she said, deep in thought, 'that says a lot about how she views me. But you kept your oath to me?'

'I did. She had a message for you: Queen's rook takes bishop's pawn two – check.'

I didn't think I'd repeat the rest of the missive.

'*What?*' exclaimed Aurora, and she reached into the folds of her jacket to produce a travelling chess set. She opened it, placed it on the counter and moved the pieces.

'Damn and blast that woman to hell,' she said. '*Foiled*. I think I may have to concede.' She showed me the game. 'What do you think?'

'I'm not very good at chess.'

'Nor me, it appears,' she said, and snapped the set closed. She looked at me and raised an eyebrow. She could tell something was troubling me.

'What's up, Charlie?'

'Did you engineer the meeting with me in the basement yesterday morning?'

'What possible reason could I have for doing that?'

'I don't know. Also: the lines were down to Cardiff so the stationmaster must have heard from someone on the train that I'd delayed it. Was that you?'

'Is Toccata messing with your head?' she asked. 'Because she does that. Divide, cast doubt, dissemble. No, I didn't tell the stationmaster anything. And strictly off the record, I understand that Toccata and Logan's association went beyond intimacy – and into illegal activities.

Farming, the unlicensed sale of body parts. We think that was the true purpose of his visit; nothing to do with viral dreams. We don't trust Jonesy either. I'll tell you why: do you know what happened to nightwalkers Tangiers and Glitzy Tiara? I left them tied to the back of my truck, and now they've gone.'

'Jonesy retired them.'

'Yes, I heard. But if so, then where did she dump them? There's nothing in the night pit or the morgue. We checked. We're not sure where they've gone – or why.'

'Farming?' I asked, knowing that Foulnap was up here too – and that Toccata knew he was. Glitzy Tiara certainly looked of child-bearing age, and Tangiers, well, if they wanted to flog healthy offspring by post, they could farm him too.

'It's a strong possibility,' said Aurora, 'although we have no proof, as yet. Life in Sector Twelve is never what it seems, Charlie. Keep an eye out for me, would you?'

I told her I would, the kettle boiled and I poured the water onto the coffee granules.

'So,' she said in more friendly tone, 'is the retrospective memory theory helping with the narcosis?'

I explained that it was, bizarrely.

'I can feel a lot more relaxed knowing there's a twisted logic behind what's going on,' I added, 'but being narced and not knowing it is strange. The hectoring Mrs Nesbit no longer seems as fearful as she once did.'

'What did she want?'

'A wax cylinder – y'know, of the recording sort.'

'What's on it?'

'According to my seriously overdramatic imagination, something that could seriously damage HiberTech – and I think I dreamed where it was . . . That's what Mrs Nesbit wants. Only Mrs Nesbit doesn't sound like Mrs Nesbit – she sounds like The Notable Goodnight.'

'That sounds quite trippy.'

'The dream is like that. Complex, confusing and as real as real gets – sometimes, more so.'

She took the coffee I'd made for her, and I tasted mine. Musty walnuts.

'Okay, then,' said Aurora after she'd taken a sip, grimaced, then tipped the remainder down the sink, 'just remind yourself that dreams are nonsense, an overactive cortex attempting to connect the random meanderings of the mind. The cylinder seems to be highly central, though. Where did you say it was? In your dream, I mean?'

'If dreams are nonsense,' I said, 'how could it matter that I saw where it was hidden?'

Aurora stared at me for a moment.

'It doesn't matter at all. I was just thinking that talking it out might help.'

'They're just dreams,' I said, 'as you stated – nonsense and random meanderings.'

She stared at me, cocked her head on one side and narrowed her eye.

'Do you want to come and work for me at HiberTech?'

This was unexpected, and I asked in what capacity.

'General duties,' she said. 'You seem like a bright kid and it would be good to have you around. Standard WinterPay Level III, but a five-thousand-euro handshake, unlimited pudding and a weekly Cadbury's Fruit & Nut allocation. HiberTech Security have their own residential block inside the facility; very nice – faces the quad. The rooms are twice as big as these and you have your own rede-ployed valet. There's real coffee and sushi on Fridays. We don't like to slum it. Just resign when you see the Chief; I can have the paper-work completed in a jiffy – so long as you're not working for RealSleep or any of their affiliates?'

'No, of course not.'

'Is there anything embarrassing we might find in a background check? And we *will* do one, so no holding back.'

'I did six weeks' community service for Incitement to Deprive,' I said. 'Sleepy phone tennis that went wrong.'

'Small beer, Charlie.'

'... and bit off Gary Findlay's ear.'

'Biting off ears and stuff *totally* counts in your favour at HiberTech. You'll take the job?'

I thought about Birgitta and her need for food.

'Is the five grand in cash?'

'Yes, if you want it, sure.'

'I'm kind of settled here in the *Siddons*. Can I think about it?'

'Sure,' she said, surprised, I think, that I didn't leap at the offer, 'but don't shilly-shally. There are others in the frame.'

She looked at her watch, then at me again.

'That's me done here,' she said. 'Agent Hooke was covering for me last night, and I need to unravel any problems he's stirred up. His anger management issues actually have their *own* anger management issues.'

I waited for ten minutes after she'd left, then washed and dressed and made some sandwiches of whatever was left in the picnic basket. Taramasalata and toothpaste weren't my first choice for a snack, but Birgitta wouldn't complain and it was food, first and foremost.

I found Birgitta stuck fast in *Rigor torpis* when I let myself into her room. She was sitting cross-legged on the bed, mid-sketch, pen poised.

Her overnight drawing efforts numbered eight. Four of them were the interior of her room and another of her and her husband on the beach with the parasol but seen from behind them. There was one of the interior of the basement car park depicting her first encounter with the other nightwalkers, and two others were general scenes of the town: the main square in Summer with the Wincarnis in the background and another of the bridge over the river, water running freely, but still with an articulated lorry stuck fast – only a different one, not the lorry stuck there now. It must be a regular feature of the town.

I placed the pictures on top of the wardrobe with the others and then, once Birgitta had risen out of *torpis*, fed her the taramasalata and toothpaste sandwich, and when that wasn't quite enough, a large bowl of muesli.

Once I'd finished feeding her breakfast, I made sure she had access to pens and paper before leaving and locking the door behind me.

I had inventoried all my remaining food and figured I would probably run out tomorrow evening. I would be the first item on the menu when she got hungry, and if she couldn't eat me, she'd either starve or try to escape – and that would be one more whole heap of trouble to deal with.

I headed off towards the elevator but stopped at the door to the apartment next to mine, room 902. It would be unoccupied, turned upside-down if the occupants were dead but still in residence, and removed completely once the corpse was removed. This room, I knew, was vacant. And since most ninth-floorers seemed to have blue-Buicked in some form or another – Moody, Roscoe, Suzy Watson, Birgitta, Porter Lloyd – it seemed prudent to have a look inside. Unaccountably, I suddenly felt a nervous knot that sat low in my stomach. A portent, if you like. The same thing I'd felt when going to repo Mrs Tiffen.

My Omnikey turned easily in the lock and the door opened on well-oiled hinges. But it wasn't unoccupied, it was abandoned: the blinds were down, the mattress rolled up and tied with a cord. There was no furniture, blankets, food or carpets. The only thing in the room was a large steamer trunk pushed against our shared wall, the sort of thing roving hibernators used when travelling away to Longsleep. Unusually, the lock was pre-Omnilock, which dated the trunk from before 1931. Not illegal to own, as it was pre-legislation, but unlawful to lock and unlock – a legal peculiarity.

I walked into the bathroom and looked around but there was nothing here, either, just a single toilet roll and two empty coffee mugs. I was just about to leave when something caught my eye. Folded on the edge of the sink was a face flannel. I pressed a finger against the material, and instead of being hard and dry as I expected, it was soft, yielding and *damp*. The room had been visited recently.

The strip-lights in the bathroom flickered and the Charles I'd been in the dream remembered something new: I was in a lab somewhere, the smell of ozone in the air, blue light flickering from cathode tubes, myriads of flickering lights, the hum of machinery. To my left was a large inverted copper cone, similar to the one that I'd seen through the window of the lab at HiberTech, when Goodnight warned me about curiosity and what it did to the cat. I felt the sharp tip of the cone against my temple, a searing pain, and then the image was gone and I was once more alone in the bathroom.

I sighed, then washed my face in the basin using the flannel, and once I had, a thought struck me: just what, *precisely*, had Aurora been doing in the *Siddons* this morning? I didn't suppose it was solely to see me – and it also occurred to me that when we led the three nightwalkers out of the basement the previous morning there had been fresh snow on Aurora's command car, yet the morning had been clear and bright. She'd been at the *Siddons* at least part of the night on both occasions. And since she didn't sleep, she must have been here on business. HiberTech business.

Aurora was right: life in Sector Twelve is rarely what it seems.

A remote farm in Lincolnshire

'... Despite a conducive sleep environment, inadvertent Risers below a certain Body Mass Index would often not go back to sleep, which caused a headache for porters and placed an increased burden on pantry. There were no fines, but the negative feedback in SleepAdvisor could impact upon the following year's popularity – and rates. A visit by a drowsy could be an effective and economic alternative ...'

– *Handbook of Winterology*, 4th edition, Hodder & Stoughton

It was just getting light when I went downstairs. Reception was empty, and a glance at the lobby thermometer revealed that the building was three and a half degrees up on the previous evening. It was usual to add heat prior to a cold snap, but adding too much too early could trigger an awakening, a false dawn. Heat management was considered more an art than a science. I hoped Lloyd knew what he was doing.

I walked into the dining room. Of the thirty or so tables, only four had been laid, each in a separate corner of the room.

'Good morning,' said Lloyd, who had a waiter's apron tied around his waist. 'Kip tight?'

'Like a dormule. Tell me, Mr Lloyd, who is in room 902?'

A flicker of consternation crossed his features but it was soon gone.

'It's currently empty. We're not at full capacity, so much the pity.'

'Has it been used recently?'

'Not to my knowledge. But I have many duties, and nearly all of them take me away from the front desk.'

'May I ask you something you can't repeat?' I asked, suddenly having an idea.

'Of course,' he said.

'I need extra food over and above Daily Requirements to bulk myself up. Would you know someone who might be able to assist, but with no questions asked?'

The porter nodded his head slowly.

'Canned or powdered?'

'Canned. Fruit, rice pudding, beans – that sort of thing.'

'Risk and rarity quadruple the price tag,' he said after a pause. 'You're not the only person hungry. Forty euros a can, ten per cent discount for twenty or more.'

It was ten times the Summer price, but I wasn't in a position to dictate terms. I swiftly ordered a hundred cans, mixed contents. Thirty-six-hundred euros.

'It may take a few days to arrange a wire,' I said, pretending that I had the funds somewhere. I didn't, of course. I barely had five hundred in cash. But it was a plan. Or rather, it was the *start* of a plan.

'Listen,' said Lloyd, 'if you want to *earn* some food from me, I'll pay four cans of Ambrosia Creamed Rice for every new guest you can recruit.'

'Even winsomniacs?'

'*Especially* winsomniacs. I can bill their stay to the Winter Asylum Office. Deal?'

'Deal.'

He smiled and we shook on it.

'While we're speaking privately,' continued the porter, lowering his voice and shifting his weight uneasily, '*I know about her.*'

My heart missed a beat. Porters could always be bought – it was part of their job, pretty much – but continually keeping the information about Birgitta quiet would cost several busloads more than I could ever afford.

'How long have you known?' I asked.

'About half an hour.'

'You've been up to the ninth?'

'No, she came down here.'

'She did?' I said, looking around. 'Where is she now? Did you put her in the basement?'

'Look, I know it's none of my business,' he said, 'but can I offer you some advice of a fatherly nature?'

I swallowed nervously, visions of a declaration of disgust followed by an impossibly large bribe looming in my mind.

'Go on, then.'

'You seem a sensible person, but you must be out of your tiny mind to be bundling with Aurora, especially when you said you wouldn't. What will the Chief say when she finds out?'

I breathed a sigh of relief. Birgitta was, for the moment at least, safe.

'From yesterday?' I said, thinking he was referring to my lie. 'This is old news.'

'No, just now. I've been portering a while and I can recognise a jaunty step when I see one. She also told me to give you a double breakfast on her account and wasn't being subtle, so I'm not sure she's intending it to be a secret for long.'

'Nothing happened,' I said, 'she just dropped round to see how I was.'

'The head of HiberTech Security? Dropping round to see if a new Deputy is okay? C'mon, Charlie. It doesn't sound very plausible.'

He was right – it didn't. Aurora was playing me off against Toccata; perhaps forcing me to come and work for her – and pissing off her other self in the process.

'It's okay,' said Lloyd, laying a friendly hand on my shoulder. 'If this gets out – and it will, mark my words – it's not through me.'

I sighed. Sister Zygotia had once told me that lies begat lies: 'You start off by one small lie, then have to tell a larger one to cover that and before you know it, your whole life falls apart and there is nowhere to go but a downward spiral of self-loathing, despondency and despair.'

I told her that was wise counsel, and she responded by saying it was actually the format of the TV comedy *Fawlty Dormitorium* with Sybil and Basil and Polly and so forth – *'don't mention the Ottoman'* – but a sound life-lesson nonetheless.

Lloyd picked up a tea and a coffee pot and I followed him as he threaded his way between the tables. Fodder was already seated, reading an ancient copy of *Hollywood Stars* with a photo of Richard Burton on the cover. He nodded to me as I sat down, and I nodded in return, feeling oddly satisfied that he'd acknowledged me. At the third table sat Zsazsa, quite alone, a paperback copy of *Silver Dollar Amber Heart* propped against the milk jug in front of her.

I looked around. The cutlery shone brightly and smelled faintly of metal polish while a freshly-pressed white cloth was spread neatly across the table. Lloyd was making sure that table standards were scrupulously maintained, even if the food itself might be somewhat lacking in quality.

'Tea or coffee?' he asked.

'Which is better?'

'One's mostly chicory and the other scavenged tea bags blended with hay. Adding sugar, molasses, curry powder or peanut butter helps. Actually, adding anything helps.'

'Are either of them toxic?'

The porter had to think for a moment.

'In that regard the coffee is probably the wiser choice.'

'Coffee, then.'

The porter poured out a cup. It was dark and tarry and seemed to come out in lumps. He placed down the coffee jug and handed me a battered menu.

'Everything but the scrambled eggs is off.'

I stared at the menu anyway, a sumptuous array of culinary alternatives. While having no basis in reality, it was still an enjoyable read. If circumstance hadn't made choice redundant, I probably would have gone for the eggs Benedict, devilled mushrooms or kedgeree with mango chutney.

'I'll have the scrambled eggs,' I said, handing the menu back.

'A wise choice,' said Lloyd, and walked briskly away.

I looked outside. The sky was a sheet of drab off-white, the colour of boiled string, and the dull tone merged into the snow heaped upon the roofs so perfectly it was difficult to see where the roofline ended and the sky began. I could see a nightwalker wandering across the road about a hundred yards away, walking in an uncertain manner with a stick, yet wearing an impressive ballgown – with a distinctive fruit hat perched upon their head. If it was Carmen Miranda, Jonesy couldn't have thumped her hard enough.

'It's Charlie Worthing, isn't it?' came a familiar-sounding voice. I turned and found myself looking at Zsazsa. It was odd seeing her here and real and old, when I'd just seen her in my dream, younger, and as one of the classic Mrs Nesbits. I got to my feet as politeness dictates and before I could speak she'd pulled me into a Winter embrace. She smelled of inexpensive perfume and tolerably clean laundry – with just a hint of lemon marmalade.

She released me, smiled and sat down opposite without being asked. Her complexion was clear, her skin soft, but her conker-coloured eyes were dark-rimmed with lack of sleep and bore within them a sense of deep melancholy.

'Would you like some coffee?' I said. 'It's a little lumpy and not really coffee at all, but it's warm and dark coloured, and probably non-toxic.'

'Thank you,' she said, pushing an empty cup forward.

We fell silent for a moment or two.

'I've never met a Mrs Nesbit in the flesh before,' I said. 'In fact, I've never met a drowsy before.'

It seemed a stupid thing to say, but it was better than sitting there, struck dumb by awkwardness.

'Despite the stories, our honeyed words, extensive inventory of memorised poems and inspired lute-playing more often see to slumber than the intimate approach. Did you hear that the *Cambrensis* went cold?'

I nodded.

'The majority of residents were bed-swapped *en dormir*, but eighteen needed to be *eased* back down into the abyss. Most of them responded well to lullabies, but a few needed more intimate means. Men, women, other – in the fog of wake it doesn't really matter. You'd have to do it, if we didn't.'

I must have looked shocked, for she added:

'The Consul recruitment office doesn't shout about that part of the work; it puts people off, although given the horrors of the Winter, it's the least of one's worries. I like to see our Winter Easement work as an invaluable aid to the well-being of the Wintering community. And just so you know,' she continued, '"drowsy" is not really an appropriate term. It demeans the noble profession. *Sleepmaiden* or *Sleepmaster* is better, or if you're into your French, *Dormiselle* and *Dormonsieur*. Actually, even Sleepworker is more acceptable. Is it true you killed Lucky Ned?'

'Where did you hear that?'

'Lloyd.'

Perhaps telling him all about it might not have been such a good idea.

'I think the Winter took Ned,' I said.

She put her head on one side and stared at me for a few moments.

'The Winter takes a lot from everyone, and only ever returns meltwater and bodies.'

I mused on what she had said.

'Can I ask you a question?'

'The first is free, the second on account – the third, you pay cash.'

'You're living in the *Siddons*,' I said. 'Are you having any recurring dreams?'

She was about to take a sip of her coffee, but then stopped and raised an eyebrow.

'You mean the blue Buick dream that's blowing around the ninth floor like an unwelcome fart?'

'Yes,' I said, '*precisely* that sort of dream.'

She leaned forward.

'I live on the nineteenth floor – half of it, actually, sort of a penthouse – so I haven't had the dream, but I've heard all the details. And I know precisely how Mrs Nesbit got to be in it. I can sell you that information.'

'She's there because dreamers were *told* she's in it,' I said. 'The blue Buick, oak trees, hands, boulders, Mrs Nesbit. The dream was seeded by incautious gossip.'

She leaned forward and lowered her voice.

'Shimmery, was she? Looked as though she didn't belong there? Words and lip movements out of sync?'

'Look,' I said, now used to the reverse nature of my dream memory, 'I'm a touch narced and my memory is rebuilding retrospectively. All that stuff is in the dream because you said it just then.'

She frowned at me.

'I've never heard of *that* happening.'

'It's like being in a permanent state of déjà vu.'

Zsazsa looked around to make sure we were alone. Fodder was on the other side of the room and Lloyd nowhere to be seen.

'Do you have a pen and paper?'

I nodded and laid them on the table.

'The Mrs Nesbit in the dream, she said something, as she did to all the others. A sentence, a test line, a quote. We're both going to write it down. Okay?'

I agreed as there was nothing to lose, and wrote: '*We know of a remote farm in Lincolnshire where Mrs Buckley lives.*'

When we had both written, we swapped them over. Hers was the same as mine. *Word for word.* I stared at her, then at the sentence she'd written down.

'Trust in your memory, Charlie, trust in yourself. Now, here's the deal: I can tell you how Mrs Nesbit got to be in those dreams. But information has a price.'

I was still staring at her note. I felt hot and sweaty, and once more the image of the blue Buick started to bleed into the space around me. Soft and indistinct to begin with and then with the pile of rocks, more solid, more *defined*. The oak tree started to appear, too, as the dappled light began to play on the tables in the dining room. As the illusion unfolded I had the bewildering fear that the encroaching vision wouldn't stop, that it would wash over me and I would stay locked in the Dreamstate for ever. I gazed at what few scraps of reality remained – the table, the coffee pot, Zsazsa – and concentrated on them lest I lose them, too.

But to no avail.

Within a few seconds they had vanished and Mrs Nesbit had arrived, wanting to know where the cylinder was. She was shouting now, demanding, *coercing*. Louder and louder until I was about to draw my Bambi and attack her, when someone else appeared.

'Birgitta?'

She was right there in front of me, eternally unchanged, dressed in her dungarees and the man's shirt, holding the brushes, hair carelessly tied up. She smiled, told me she loved me, and I, in return, told her I loved her too. There was a pause, the waves crashed on the beach, and there was a gurgle of a child's laugh as the beach ball bounced past.

'Charlie? Are you okay?'

I looked at Birgitta and she suddenly appeared older, more care-worn, and in an instant she wasn't Birgitta at all but Zsazsa, and I was back in the dining room with the *Dormiselle* staring at me. My hand was still gripped around the butt of the Bambi, my thumb on the safety but thankfully I hadn't drawn the weapon – or worse. I had been seconds away from attacking an entirely imaginary foe. I carefully released my hold on the Bambi, palms damp with sweat.

'Shit,' I said, now knowing *precisely* what had taken Moody and Suzy. The blue Buick dream had swept over them, too, in a suffo-cating alternative reality, and they'd tried to kill the hectoring Mrs Nesbit, and been killed themselves. But I had a secret weapon: Birgitta. She'd just saved my life, and quite possibly Zsazsa's as well.

'Are you okay?' asked Zsazsa again.

'I'm fine,' I said, the return from the event almost as rapid as the descent.

I took a drink of water and stared at Zsazsa.

'So how did you know about Mrs Buckley and the remote farm in Lincolnshire?'

She cocked her head on one side and stared at me.

'Information has a price, my young friend. Two thousand euros.'

We haggled for almost five minutes, and settled on eight hundred euros, a dozen Snickers, three Cornettos and a Favour. We shook hands on it, and she began.

'It was when I was still a Mrs Nesbit, over thirty years ago. You're too young to remember.'

'True,' I said, 'but you're still familiar.'

'I'm glad of that. NesCorp Holdings gave a lot of funding to HiberTech in those days, so I often travelled over here for press junkets, announcing some new discovery or other. I was the face of Morphenox during its initial roll-out, and I was always treated very well.'

She looked around and lowered her voice.

'On one of these trips Don Hector took me aside and asked if I would assist with some high-level research work. I said I would — you don't turn down someone like Don Hector — so I signed reams and reams of non-disclosure contracts and they had me stand in a room. Lots of light, the air kind of alive with static — then they had me recite some of the usual Mrs Nesbit bullshit: products to buy, tips for the busy homemaker, how to balance your chores in the kitchen with wanting to be down the pub, advice on weight gain, that sort of stuff.'

'So?'

'Before we did all this, I'd been asked to do a sound check and I used the "remote farm in Lincolnshire" line as I always do. Ripple-dissolve thirty years on and Suzy Watson, Roscoe Smalls and Moody all had their dream with Mrs Nesbit saying the same thing — before the hectoring started in a voice that wasn't mine.'

She stopped talking. I'd had *exactly* the same thing.

'Did this high-level research project have a name?'

'It was part of something called *Dreamspace*.'

Shamanic Bob had mentioned something by that name, but hadn't gone into any detail.

'What was Dreamspace meant to do?'

'I've no idea, but the technician said I was going to be their first "Dream Avatar", whatever that is. And that's my lot. I'll expect payment as soon as you have it.'

She stood up as Lloyd approached the table, thanked me for the coffee and moved back to her table.

The porter placed my scrambled eggs in front of me and then left. I tried the eggs. The low points were colour, taste and consistency, with warmth the only redeeming feature. True to Aurora's demand, it was a double portion, which given the low quality of the food was not quite as good a deal as I'd hoped. But my mind, as usual, was on other matters. I reread the piece of paper Zsazsa had given me.

We know of a remote farm in Lincolnshire where Mrs Buckley lives.

This was, I realised, the first piece of true evidence that there *was* a viral dream. But quite why it was featuring a line of dialogue from a decades-old sound test, I had no idea. I was still as much in the dark now as I was when I arrived – in fact, I was probably *more* confused.

'Hey,' came a voice close behind.

Jonesy

'… The temperature during a Welsh Winter fluctuated between a few degrees above zero and polar snaps that could freeze the mercury in the thermometers. The lowest temperature recorded in Wales was at Llandudno in 1976 – a marrow-freezing minus 78C …'

– *Handbook of Winterology*, 4th edition, Hodder & Stoughton

Jonesy sat down opposite and sniffed the coffee pot gingerly.

'By St Etienne,' she said, pulling a face, 'what they say about the *Siddons* coffee is true. Kip well?'

'Yes,' I said, 'on the whole, yes, I think so.'

'Good. What's that you're eating?'

'It's an indeterminate foodstuff masquerading as scrambled egg.'

Jonesy picked up a spoon and prodded the grey mass gingerly. It wobbled as though irritated by the intrusion. She pulled a face, but helped herself to a spoonful anyway.

'I bumped into Aurora on the way over,' she murmured.

'Oh dear,' I said.

'Are you insane?' she said. 'Truly, I mean, out-of-your-head insane? Toccata's going to have your tongue out.'

'We didn't,' I said.

'Then why did she tell me you did?'

'She's using it to annoy the Chief.'

Jonesy stared at me for a while, unsure if I was telling the truth or not.

'Let's get to work,' she said finally, 'and look, I don't care one way or the other if the big A is using you to scratch an itch, but think very carefully of *actions*, Wonky. They have a dismaying tendency to be followed by consequences, and sometimes quite bad ones.'

I followed her out of the Winterlounge and, once booted and suited, we stepped outside and walked to her Sno-Trac. The temperature had fallen since the previous evening and the air was as crisp as a wafer. There was barely a breath of wind, the sky was a deep azure and ice crystals on the snow glistened like diamonds in the sunshine.

'I thought there was a storm coming in,' I said.

'There is. Six hours from now you won't be able to see your hand in front of your face.'

I started the Sno-Trac and drove off in the direction of the Consulate.

'We've got a problem,' said Jonesy. 'How many people did you tell about Lucky Ned?'

My heart sank.

'I might have ... mentioned something to Lloyd.'

'Here's some advice: if you've got a secret that you want everyone to know about, confide in a porter. There are just over seventy porters in the sector looking after nearly two hundred Dormitoria, who are now so familiar with *Bonanza*, *Dynasty* and *Crossroads* that they act them out in their spare time for fun. When they're not doing that, they're on the Open Network, gossiping, and last night you were the hot topic. Half think that you're an idiot to kill Ned, as retribution will surely rain upon all our heads, a little under half think that you did the right thing but were out of your tiny stupid mind, and of the remainder, three people couldn't give a toss so long as Gaer Brills comes last in *The Great Albion Sleep Off* – and one was convinced that the Gronk has returned to feed on the shame of the unworthy.'

'Was the last one Jim Treacle?'

'Good try. No. It was Laura. How can one Novice get into so much trouble so quickly? When I began in the mobile infantry nothing exciting happened to me for weeks.'

'Then what?'

'I lost sixty soldiers under my command.'

'Your fault?' I asked.

'No, but they were all my responsibility, so it amounts to the same thing.'

She fell silent and wiped off some condensation that had formed on the interior of her window.

'Aurora was asking me where Glitzy Tiara and Eddie Tangiers ended up,' I said. 'She said she checked the night pit and they weren't there.'

Jonesy stared at me.

'They're in the snow at the back of the car park. I couldn't be arsed to walk them to the night pit. What does she *think* I did with them?'

'She's of the opinion that you and the Chief are running some sort of farming scam that used to include Logan.'

'I'm glad you brought that to me,' she said, after staring at me in silence for a while, 'and in return, here's something that might interest you.'

She dug a sheet of notepaper out of her top pocket and passed it across. I read it briefly while driving along. On the paper were six names, but the only one I recognised was Charles Webster.

'What's this?' I asked.

'I was bored and in the records office. It turns out that Webster wasn't the only employee from HiberTech who went missing at that time – every single name on that list ended up either redeployed or vanished. And get this: all had been working at the Sleep Sciences Division. Interesting?'

'Kind of,' I said. 'What's your explanation?'

'Not sure. A purge, perhaps – they suspected someone of industrial espionage but didn't know who it was, so went through the lot. I'll bet good money Hooke was involved.'

'Why?'

'You heard Hooke was chucked out of the intelligence services for overenthusiastic interrogation?'

I nodded.

'The story goes that he spearheaded the military wing of HiberTech's Dreamspace-Derived Information Extraction Technique. Quite effective, apparently, going in to people's dreaming minds to extract intel, but with a downside: the subjects were rendered little better than nightwalkers by the process.'

'And you think he did this to Webster and the others?'

'HiberTech are not a pleasant company, Wonky. If they're employing people like Hooke, trebly unpleasant. You were interested in Webster, so I thought you should know.'

I thanked her and we drove past the Ashbrook advertising hoarding and then the *Cambrensis*. Jonesy's story would make a lot of sense if my dreams were real: HiberTech didn't know who Don Hector gave the cylinder to, so they interrogated everyone they suspected. I shivered, and pushed the thoughts to the back of my mind. Dream *then* reality; not the other way round.

I parked the Sno-Trac next to the statue of Howell Harris and Jonesy told me to keep the engine running.

'You're to go on patrol with Fod,' said Jonesy. 'Wait here.'

She climbed out the back of the Sno-Trac and went to have a word with Fodder, who was standing outside the Consulate. While I waited I fiddled with all the controls on the dashboard. The main headlamps, H4S radar, hydraulic snowplough. Most of my Sno-Trac time was on simulators, but it wasn't as if driving a Trac was hard – the controls were identical to those of every other road vehicle, from car to tank to coach to lorry to the biggest dumper truck. SkillZero protocols insisted upon it. 'Drive one, drive all' was the slogan.

'Don't like these things,' said Fodder as he climbed aboard, chucking a large black holdall on the seats behind, 'but we've got some distance to cover.'

His eye was badly bloodshot from the thump the previous day, but otherwise he seemed in good spirits.

'What's in the bag?' I said.

'A surprise.'

'I like surprises.'

'I'd hold off judgement in this particular case.'

We moved off with a low rumble from the engine and a shudder from the transmission.

'Take it out of town past the jammed truck,' he said, 'but be careful.'

I did as he requested and we edged slowly across the bridge.

'Before you ask,' I said, 'nothing happened between me and Aurora. She's just causing trouble.'

'Whether you did or didn't,' he said, 'it'd still be a good idea to stay out of Toccata's hair until this afternoon. She's pretty grouchy in the first hour after coming on shift. We'll take the road west out of town; the *Frances Hoggan* hasn't checked in for the past three weeks, so we need to take a look.'

The *Frances Hoggan*, I learned, was the sole Dormitorium in a village to the west of here, and as we headed over, the Sno-Trac making easy work of the deep snow, Fodder explained procedure: all Dormitoria were required to call the Consulate on a designated day.

'The *Hoggan* hasn't checked in for the past three Wednesdays,' he said, 'so Winter Best Practice demands that we have a look.'

I followed Fodder's directions while he described points of interest, of which there were many but all covered in snow, so it was mainly an exercise in imagining what was beneath the large drifts.

The day was quite beautiful, and the trip out to the *Hoggan* a break from Birgitta and the dream, both of which were dominating my thoughts. Fodder tired of being a tour guide after a half-hour or so and we fell to chatting about the Summer, of which my memory was as fresh as his was hazy. I told him about the warmth, and the breeze, and the harvest, and the freshness of the food. He said that this was the bit he missed the most.

'I haven't seen a banana for over six years,' he said almost dreamily, 'and I'd give my left foot for a fresh pineapple.'

No one who got cold and dirty in the Winter was ever truly welcome in the Summer. The citizenry didn't know or care what the Consuls did during the cold to keep them safe, they just wanted to wake alive in the Spring, same as always. For many people, the Winter didn't really exist except in an abstract sort of way, and by consequence, neither did we.

'You and Jonesy serve together?' I asked, recalling that she'd said that she and he 'went back a ways'.

'Camp Firebrand,' said Fodder, 'second Ottoman campaign.'

'I heard it was *seriously* hot out there.'

'Our real enemy was adequate hydration. We lost more soldiers to desiccation than to enemy action. Bodies out in the sun reduced to less than one per cent moisture in forty-eight hours. You could snap off a Souther's ear and grind it to dust in your fingers. Jonesy's lost more comrades than you and I have had hot dinners. It's what makes her a good Consul, especially out here – not afraid to die, and may even welcome it.'

I slowed down as we entered the village, although to the untrained eye it was simply a series of large, snow-covered lumps. Unlike Talgarth, Llangorse was a 'sleeper' town where no one ventured out, and the only overwinterers were the porters.

'Go through the town and you'll see the *Hoggan*. It's on the lake.'

I followed Fodder's directions and we were soon within sight of a circular tower sitting upon a small island within the smooth unbroken white of the frozen water. From the outside little looked remiss. The doorway was snowed in, and the thermal exhaust ports that ran in a ring beneath the top floor were clear of ice and snow, so from here all looked okay. I mentioned this to Fodder but he simply nodded.

'Pull over anywhere in the car park, then shut down.'

I did as he asked, and he grabbed the holdall on the way out. I followed him and we walked to the front of the Sno-Trac, the sun warming our faces. There was now a slight breeze, but little else to suggest the impending storm.

'Give me your Bambi, Wonk.'

'Why?'

'Do you trust me?' he asked.

'Yes.'

'Then give me your Bambi.'

I handed it over, not understanding, but then saw the movement of someone in the spinney. There was another person to the right of us, then a third by one of the snow-covered cars. They were dressed in the much-mended patchwork clothes typical of womads, scavengers or cold-hermits – but they weren't any of these: they were Villains.

And not any Villains. This was the family of the Earl of Farnesworth.

The Farnesworths

'… Pulse weapons come in many sizes. From the Plinker used to stun rats and squirrels to the hand-held Bambis and Bumpers, the two-handed Thumper, Stubby, Cowpuncher and Big Bopper, then up to the shoulder-mounted Schtumperschreck. Various-sized Airwitzers are chassis-based, the TerraNewton Highrollers mounted on railway flatbeds …'

– *Handbook of Winterology*, 1st edition, Hodder & Stoughton

'What the——?' I asked, and Fodder looked down at me with his empty dark eyes. My heart fell. There were no issues at the *Frances Hoggan*. We were out here for one reason and one reason only: to make amends for the loss of Lucky Ned Farnesworth and to try to broker a peace. And there was one big bargaining chip in all of this: me.

'You shouldn't have told Lloyd,' said Fodder as the Villains approached. 'News like that travels across the Sector like wildfire.'

'Frightfully sporting of you to drop by,' said the eldest of the Villains, a middle-aged woman with a wind-blown complexion who wore a faded twinset and pearls on the *outside* of her parka, 'although I have to confess I thought you'd pass up on the invitation.'

'And miss the finest cakes Mid-Wales has to offer?' replied Fodder in perfect English. 'Not a chance.'

There were eight of them, and they formed a wary half-circle about fifteen feet away. Half were armed with Thumpers, the other half with the short stabbing spear favoured by those who wish to leave no barometric fingerprint. Two were carrying cumbersome knapsacks, and one seemed to have some furniture on his back, secured by what looked like silk curtain-ties. The son we had seen the day before was there, his eyes badly bloodshot. They all looked in far worse health than the Winter alone might suggest. Fodder was taller by at least a foot, and more powerfully built than all of them put together.

'His Lordship and his son broke the truce, ma'am,' said Fodder, 'and we retaliated in self-defence.'

'I always knew stamp collecting would get them into trouble,' said the woman, who I assumed was the 13th Earl's widow, 'but look here, they were only doing a harmless spot of thieving — and it *was* the 2d Lloyd–George Mauve.'

'With the Anglesey cancellation,' said a man off to our right.

'Only one in the world,' said another.

'Stealing is stealing,' said Fodder, 'and they were in the town. Off-limits, as per the truce.'

They stared at one another for a few moments.

'Will you take tea?' asked Lady Farnesworth. 'I always find it so terribly, *terribly* uncivilised doing deals on matters of life and death just standing in the snow.'

'I'll take tea,' said Fodder.

The piece of furniture that one of the group was carrying turned out to be a gate-leg table and two folding chairs. These were soon set up, along with a tablecloth, cups and saucers and a cake stand with fresh Victoria sponge cake. Another member of the group had set up a small Primus stove and was heating the water.

'I do so abhor tea from a thermos,' said the countess, inviting Fodder to sit and then sitting herself, 'it *always* tastes stewed.'

She turned to the man heating the water and reminded him to warm the pot.

'It is so hard to get reliable staff these days,' she said to Fodder, 'which is why we have to resort to kidnapping and the occasional murder. Help yourself to some cake, why don't you?'

Fodder did so, while I stood there uneasily. Beneath the politeness was real menace.

'So,' said Lady Farnesworth, 'how is Aurora these days?'

'Pretty well, I think.'

'Is she still doing that thing where she's two people?'

'Yes.'

'She always loved to be centre stage,' said Lady Farnesworth, 'ever since we were little. I liked her, despite that. Would be happy to kill her now, of course, but with regret. So: how do we know you've not got my husband prisoner, with that reptilian Agent Hooke scouring his dreaming mind for intel? I know what you lot get up to at HiberTech.'

'We're Consuls,' said Fodder, 'not HiberTech, and we've no real idea what goes on there.'

'Nonsense,' scoffed the countess, 'you Welsh are as thick as thieves and I don't trust a single one of you. Ah, Chuck, bless you.'

The man boiling the water had brought a Meissen teapot to the table and laid it on a mat.

'I'm sorry to have to tell you,' said Fodder, 'that the 13th Earl speaks only to the Winter.'

He unzipped the holdall that he'd laid at his feet, removed Lucky Ned's head and placed it on the table along with a large gold signet ring. The 13th Earl was blue-white and frozen solid, and his expression seemed to be one of, well, *surprise*.

Everyone stared at it, as though sizing up a goose's suitability for the pre-winter feast.

'We thank you kindly for returning what is ours,' said Lady Farnesworth after staring at the head for a few moments. 'You know what this makes me?'

'Angry?' suggested Fodder. 'Vengeful?'

'No,' she said, passing the gold signet ring to her son, 'this makes me the Dowager Countess Farnesworth and my son the 14th Earl.'

We all looked at the earl's son, who tried not to look as though he was pleased. There was a ripple of applause and someone blew a party hooter, but in a dispirited manner. To the Villains, it seemed that death was neither something to become sad over, nor particularly unusual.

'Marigolds, please, Chuck,' said the Lady Dowager, and once he'd passed her the yellow washing-up gloves, she removed the late earl's head and placed it in the picnic hamper with a gingham cloth on top. She then patted it in an affectionate manner, and returned to the table.

'One lump or two?' asked the Lady Dowager, pouring the tea.

'Two, please,' said Fodder.

'Well, then,' she said, pushing the cup and saucer across the table to him, 'is this the Novice that killed my husband?'

She looked at me directly for the first time, and my heart thumped nervously.

'It is indeed,' said Fodder.

'Looks a mite scrawny to have taken His Lordship in single combat,' she said, peering at me through a lorgnette. 'You wouldn't be trying to palm us off with a sacrificial patsy, now, would you? The disposable runt of the litter?'

'Tell them you did it,' said Fodder.

'Are you kidding?'

'Tell them.'

I could feel my hands trembling and wanted to put them in my pockets, but thought that might appear threatening, so simply pressed them against the side of my coat.

'I was there when Lucky Ned— I mean, His Lordship was taken,' I said, forcibly trying not to let my voice crack. 'One moment he was about to kidnap me, the next he was gone.'

'Don't try to tell us it was the Gronk,' said the Lady Dowager, 'trying to wriggle out of your responsibilities by invoking the Wintervolk is beneath contempt.'

'It might have been me,' I conceded, 'but I have no recollection.'

The Dowager Countess took a sip of tea and gathered her thoughts.

'I don't want this to escalate to war any more than you do, Mr Fodder, so we'll accept reparations for our loss – your Novice there, for a ten-year servitude. Agree and the truce is kept as though it were not broken, nor even bruised.'

Fodder took a sip of tea, and they all stared at him, waiting to see what he would say.

'I came to bargain,' said Fodder, 'not to hand over one of ours. We will parley some more.'

'Then we'll take the stamp instead,' she said, 'the 2d Lloyd-George Mauve.'

'With the Anglesey cancellation,' said the same man off to our right.

'The only one in the world,' I said, when no one else had chimed in.

'We have no ownership of the collections,' said Fodder, 'you know that.'

'Then it's the Novice.'

'We'll bargain some more.'

'No, Mr Fodder, we shall not. It's the Novice, the stamp, or nothing. And think wisely and fast, my friend, for I'm of a mind to take you as well. Don't be upsetting a widow on her day of grieving.'

One of the small group drew out a large hunting knife and they all took a step forward, but Fodder simply reached down and pulled a dark cylindrical object the size of a rugby ball from the holdall. It was a Golgotha. Even if they started running now, Fodder could wait ten seconds before pulling the pin and they'd still be shredded. There was a sharp intake of breath from the assembled Villains. A mix of fear, respect and curiosity. Everyone had heard of a Golgotha, but few had seen one detonate. It is said the multiple shock waves are quite lovely to behold as they tumble and spiral outwards like a Romanesco cauliflower.

'No one moves,' said Fodder, who had a finger hooked around the detonation pin, 'or we all go. You get nothing from this, and I get my long-deserved peace.'

'I *so* love your style,' said the Lady Dowager with a chuckle. 'No fear or compromise. You'd make a fine Villain. We'll talk some more. What will you be putting on the table, Mr Fodder? And don't say the 2/6d Dylan Thomas Parcel Post red, because we've already got one – in mint condition, too.'

'The Novice remains free,' said Fodder, 'and in return we offer you six gross of Snicker bars, two Favours and a Debt.'

'A fig for your chocolate and promises,' said the Lady Dowager. 'No, you can pull the pin and know that the 15th, 16th and 17th Earls will all take vengeance upon your people from now until the end of time.'

This could be going a lot better than it was.

'Death suits none of us,' said Fodder, 'but we will find a trade. I offer you ... a healthy infant.'

Up until that moment most of the eight had been swapping random and irrelevant quotes to one another in Latin but they soon fell quiet as the idea found favour. I could easily see why. The gene pool was narrow in the groups living at the glaciated fringes of Albion, and an injection of genetic variation could mean a huge improvement in their long-term health prospects.

'I'm listening,' said the Lady Dowager, 'but we don't want any runts. A strong baby, genetically first tier. Make that so and you'll have the truce you seek, Mr Fodder.'

I couldn't see how resorting to child theft would be a healthier alternative to offering me up for a decade. Besides, I couldn't allow it.

'I'll take the ten,' I said. 'We'll not be taking anyone out of the Nursitorium.'

The Lady Dowager looked at me and smiled.

'Your Novice has grit,' she said, 'probably make a fine servant.'

'We offer more than that,' said Fodder, ignoring me. 'We offer a first-tier confinement sired by a Farnesworth for you to nurture and love.'

'Oh yes?' said the Lady Dowager. 'And which surrogate will you offer? We won't be wanting madwoman Jonesy, and Aurora would never let Toccata get past the first nine weeks. The one named Laura Strowger would be admirable, but only when she's of age. One does not approve of child with child.'

'No,' said Fodder, 'not Jonesy, not Toccata – *definitely* not Laura. I offer up ... *myself.*'

There was silence, and several of the Villains looked at one another and began to laugh.

'We aren't short of seed, we need a healthy plant pot to grow it in. Twenty-four carat as yours might be,' she added, looking up and down at his impressive physique. 'Your deal is no deal. Come, pull that pin and let the Winter embrace us all – or hand over the Strowger girl when she's ready, or the Novice for our dishes. We are all done talking.'

But Fodder didn't waver for an instant. I stared at him, wondering where he was going with this. He passed me the Golgotha.

'If anyone tries anything, pull the pin.'

'Sure,' I said, and I meant it. Ten years is a long time, and given previous cases of forced domestic service, in reality it meant a lifetime. You'd struggle until your third year, be reconciled to your lot by the fifth. By the end of the eighth you'd be assimilated and by the tenth you'd be loyal through and through, probably with family and responsibilities. Abductees rarely made it back.

'You've a right to view the goods you're trading for,' said Fodder, and began to unbutton his jacket.

We were on the road again in five minutes, the Golgotha made safe and in the holdall, the Farnesworths happy, the wax from the signet still warm on the hastily-scribbled agreement.

'It's always better to grab the vixen by the tail and broker a peace,' explained Fodder. 'The Winter is all about ensuring the most favourable outcome is enjoyed by the majority – but in a good way, of course.'

'You could have given me up.'

He turned to look at me.

'No,' he said, 'we don't do that. You're young and you're new and confused and need all the help you can get.'

I couldn't deny it; I think he'd summed me up pretty well.

'I'm in your debt,' I said, 'but you're going to bear and then give up your child – to Villains. Are you okay with that?'

'I'm sixth-generation Pool,' said Fodder. 'My people haven't known their biologicals for over two centuries. Villains are hideously class-conscious and English to boot, but good parents – my child will improve the health of their dynasty for generations. The truce gets to hold, and you don't get to work in the scullery. It's the Code of the Winter.'

Fodder had my back. It was a good feeling, but carried with it an awesome responsibility. In time, I would have to risk everything for another, and so on, down an unbroken chain of Winter camaraderie for centuries to come, as had been the case for centuries before us. In that moment, I realised what being a Winter Consul was all about, and I knew then that I'd never want to be anything else.

We drove on in silence for a few minutes.

'Does anyone else know?' I asked.

'No one around here, and you're not going to tell. I'll take two years' leave of absence until she's born. Money will be short but, well, heigh-ho.'

There was another pause.

'Can I ask why?'

'Why what?'

'Why you're something you're not.'

'We're all something we're not,' he said. 'Every one of us is stuck between the person we want to be and the person we can be. And there doesn't have to be a why. All things have to do is feel right.'

'I understand,' I said, 'and thank you.'

He didn't need to tell me to keep his secret. I'd carry it to the grave. I spent the rest of the journey thinking about the Farnesworths' incredulous expressions as they gazed upon Fodder's naked body, there in the snow and the sun: bold, muscular, athletic, Snowdonian in stature and physically at variance with the gender with which he felt most at home – but with the rare and highly desirable tiger stripes picked out in auburn on his blond winterdown.

Dreamspace

'... The Great Salt Marsh that stretches from Portland in the west and all the way round to the Dogger massif in the north-east opposite Hull represented a warmer period in the Earth's history, when less water was locked up in glaciers and the ice-caps. Although it is still relatively impassable other than by the east and west causeways, drainage plans are in hand and could convert the land to much-needed agriculture within the next century ...'

– *The Albion Peninsula*, by Roger Vanguard

'I'm guessing the trip was a success,' said Jonesy, who was lubricating the offside front drive sprocket of her Sno-Trac with a grease gun the size of her arm.

'My charm won the day,' said Fodder, 'that and a few Debts, Favours and fifty kilograms of banana Nesquik – plus the implicit threat engendered by a Golgotha.'

'The only live Golgothas we have are the ones in the museum,' said Jonesy. 'You used the dummy practice one?'

Fodder shrugged.

'Big promise is the secret of every campaign.'

Fodder went inside to report everything to Toccata and I stood there for a moment with Jonesy.

'Was it really just Debts and Nesquik that clinched the deal?' she asked.

'Yup,' I replied. 'Debts and Nesquik. Fodder's a fine negotiator. Where did you find Ned's body?'

'Pretty close to where we found his clothes. He'd been buried under the snow, and aside from the surprised look on his face we couldn't see how he died. Oh, and your theory about it being Gronk looks to be correct – his little finger was missing. Unless you removed it yourself. Did you?'

'No, I didn't. So you *do* believe in the Gronk?'

She thought for a moment.

'I believe there's something dreamy and inexplicable in the air, and if Gronk is the best way to describe it, then Gronk it is. Look,' she added, 'Toccata's not going to be in a great mood, so why don't you make yourself scarce for an hour?'

I took her advice and, deep in thought, walked across to the Wincarnis, where the snow had blown up against the door. Exterior doors were always double-hinged; outwards for fire, inwards for drift. There were early snows once at St Granata's, and when we tried to get out there was merely a wall of snow facing us – with an impression of the front door in minutely fine detail. That sort of thing really sticks in your mind.

The winsomniacs had just lunched on spaghetti that looked as though it had been bulked up with string, and were settling down for a busy afternoon wholly committed to the fine art of not doing very much. Given the vivid nature of my dreams I wanted to speak at greater length to Shamanic Bob and I found him reading a book next to the unlit fire. There was paper and kindling and logs but they had so far failed to assemble themselves into anything useful. I knelt down and started to lay the fire.

'Well, now,' said Shambob when he saw me, 'you've kinda been making a name for yourself. Killing Lucky Ned and you and Aurora a thing. Wow. Just … *wow*. Never would have thought it. Not of you. Hey, don't let her fall asleep halfway through – she'd wake up as Toccata. That could take one whole heap of explaining.'

'World-class awkward,' I agreed, 'but I didn't kill Lucky Ned, and Aurora and me aren't a thing.'

'It doesn't matter if it's true or not,' he said, 'it's what everyone believes that's important. Come to help us get seriously dreamed up?'

'Another time.'

'Fair enough,' said Shamanic Bob cheerfully, 'we've got a hiccup in supply anyway, but that will soon be sorted. So, what can I do for you?'

I struck a match and the newspaper flared as it caught.

'When we last met, you told me Don Hector's initial quest was not for us to dream less, but to dream *better.* I was wondering what you meant by that?'

He looked at me and narrowed his eyes.

'You been dreaming, Newbie?'

'Nope.'

'Truthfully?'

'Okay, a little.'

He smiled and moistened his lips.

'I meant what I said. Don Hector's initial research was not to find a way to stop us dreaming, but to help us do it better – and more productively.'

I said nothing, just waited for him to continue. He peered at me conspiratorially and looked around to ensure we were not overheard, which we were – the room was full of the sleep-shy. But there you go. Winsomniacs are like that.

'Did I mention Dreamspace?'

'Yes, but without details.'

Zsazsa had also mentioned Dreamspace when she was explaining about Mrs Buckley and the remote farm in Lincolnshire. Shamanic Bob laboured to sit upright and beckoned me closer.

'It's not common knowledge, but the original breakthrough drug at HiberTech was a powerful dream enhancer named E-28. It was synthesised during Don Hector's early attempts to make hibernation more useful through something known as Active Control Dreaming.'

'I've not heard of that,' I said, suddenly even more interested. The last time I was in the Birgitta and Buick dreams, I was in control – making decisions for myself, guiding the narrative.

'Few have. HiberTech guard their secrets closely. Active Control was designed so that we could carry on our lives during the Winter. But not out here, burning fat and victim to the hunger, cold and vermin predation, but in here.'

He tapped his temple.

'Cosy, safe and happy in a personalised dreaming environment where one would have sovereignty, a place where you could do what you wanted while still remaining fully aware, fully in control of your actions – yet fully asleep.'

'Okay,' I said, 'but wouldn't Active Control be as lonely as staying up over the Winter? Worse, perhaps?'

He smiled.

'This is where it gets good. The idea was that you could *share* the Dreamspace. It was going to become a place to meet, a place to socialise, a place to work and remain productive. There were plans to found the first Hiberversity. A degree in anything you chose – while you slumbered, deep in the abyss of hibernation. Education for the masses. There was even talk,' he added, laughing, I think, at the audacity of the idea, 'of implanting Dream Avatars in the sleeping mind in order to establish a link with the outside world. News and views as you slept, perhaps even live entertainment – and also establish a potential revenue stream by suggesting goods and services to the sleeping individual.'

'Seriously?'

'Yup.' Shamanic Bob grinned. 'They wanted to monetise the Dreamstate by selling entertainment and advertising space. Is nothing sacred? What's the matter? You look kind of ... shocked.'

'It's nothing,' I said, but it was. If what he and Zsazsa said was true, then it would explain how Mrs Nesbit got into my dreams. But they weren't trying to entertain me, sell me thermal socks or double glazing, they were demanding information. I had another thought, this time more unpleasant – about Agent Hooke and his in-dream interrogation techniques.

'This Dreamspace idea,' I said, 'did it ever work?'

'Not really. Twenty-one years and thirty billion euros later there was still one vast and wholly intractable problem: did you just learn about Charlotte Brontë, or did you *dream* you learned something? The person you just met in the Dreamspace. Did they really say what you thought they said, or was that just an invention? You are invited to have an affair in the Dreamspace. Does that make it adultery? Or even consensual? And if it wasn't consensual, then what was it? Business deals: legally binding or not? The point is, there would be no easy way of knowing whether what happened in the

Dreamspace was real, and what was imagined. Ten per cent? Eighty per cent? None?'

'I see the problem.'

'Right,' said Shamanic Bob, 'because when you merge the real and the fantasy, you can never quite define the boundaries. Dreamspace was a wonderful concept, but owing to the quirky nature of a sleeping mind prone to tangential invention, doomed to failure.'

He sighed wistfully, as though this was the greatest disappointment he could imagine. A world of permanent dreaming, navigating your own way through fantastic worlds of your own creation.

'Dreams are the one true freedom,' continued Shamanic Bob, 'the place where you can be yourself; do anything, be anything. The mind set free.'

'So long as it's Active Control,' I said, 'or you're just a passenger, right?'

'Guilty as charged,' said Shamanic Bob with a sad smile, 'and *that's* the Night Grail we seek: a dream indistinguishable from real life. A dream where you can lose yourself, a dream where you can be anyone you want, and do anything you wish, at your own choosing.'

'Could you dream yourself a principled and confident leading member of the Campaign for Real Sleep?' I asked. 'Deep undercover on a dangerous mission with the girl of your dreams?'

'Sure,' he said, 'if that's your thing. Me, I want to fly. But not like a pilot – like a bird. High on the wing above the hushed nation, chasing the spirit of freedom. Or maybe a saxophonist,' he added, 'playing for Holroyd Wilson, there at his last gig, before the Winter took him. Or maybe I could dream myself popular,' he said, 'or even respected. Or *normal*. That would be nice.'

Shamanic Bob came over all dreamy and his eyelids began to droop. I wasn't sure if it was hushed reverence because we were talking about dreams, or simply because he had dozed off. Winsomniacs doze off a lot.

'Ever dream of the blue Buick?' I asked.

Shamanic Bob was suddenly wide awake, and a second later his bony fingers had grasped my jacket and pulled me close.

'*That's why so many of us are scabbing*[58] *in the Twelve, friend.* We heard there was this dream that was more real than real, so vivid you were there, shielding your eyes against the sun, smelling the Summer, tasting the dust on your lips. Active Control, the Night Grail we seek. Where is it? Somewhere close? Which Dormitorium?'

I had to think about this for a few moments before speaking again.

'I've one last question,' I said. 'Can the memory of dreams ever unfold in your head retrospectively, influenced by later experiences?'

'I've not experienced such a thing *myself,*' he said after a moment's thought, 'nor heard of anyone who has – but narcosis can throw up an interesting-shaped bone from time to time. Are you sure you don't want to get all dream–faced with us?'

'I'm sure.'

I walked to the door, then turned. Our conversation had been followed by every winsomniac in the room. They were all watching me, dark-rimmed, wide eyes, blinking like owls.

'Understand this,' I said to the room in general, 'there is no blue Buick dream, it's definitely not Active Control, and it's certainly not at the *Sarah Siddons.*'

The winsomniacs all smiled faintly and nodded their heads in a languid manner. Lloyd had said I could have four tins of Ambrosia Creamed Rice for each winsomniac I got into the *Siddons.* For every one that arrived, Birgitta was four hours closer to Springrise, and four hours farther from cannibalism. Ambrosia Creamed Rice, good at the best of times, had never seemed more attractive.

---

58. I think it meant 'scrounging food in the Winter' but I never did find out for sure.

Fired & filing

'... The Winter Consul Service was barely four centuries old, and had changed little in that time. The origins of both porters and Consuls was the nightwatchman, a word often used to describe either trade. Life expectancy as a Consul was not high, but promotion prospects and extra cash always ensured there were more than enough recruits. There needed to be ...'

– from *Seventeen Winters*, by Consul Lance Jones

The sky had lowered while I'd been in the Wincarnis, and a stiff breeze was now stirring the snow into a cloud of flakes that swirled randomly in the air without settling. The visibility was still at least fair, although I don't think anyone expected it to stay that way for long: Jonesy had attached a fixed line from her Sno-Trac to the large brass ring fixed to the outside of the Consulate, so she could find either if things got bad.

As I entered, there seemed to be a sense of unhurried languor inside, as though everyone were getting ready for a damp Sunday indoors. Treacle was typing out a form on a large typewriter in an unhurried manner, and Jonesy was reading a report while leaning on the desk. Fodder was standing next to the coffee machine, lost in his own thoughts, staring off into the middle distance. Probably thinking about babies. Or maybe some military defeat he'd been involved in. Or a love lost. Or steak pie with peas and chips. Actually, I had no idea. The way he looked, impossible to tell.

I heard Toccata swearing at someone down the telephone from the comfort of her office, but now that I'd become accustomed to the idiosyncratic ways of Sector Twelve, the whole Aurora/Toccata issue hardly seemed unusual at all, and I could see why none of the crew saw any of it as particularly weird.

'The Chief said she wants to see you,' said Jonesy, looking up.

'Now?'

'Yes, now. She saw you come in, so it's too late to sneak away. Good luck.'

I walked slowly up to Toccata's office door, straightened my jacket and knocked politely. She bade me enter and I pushed open the door.

She was standing behind her desk, leaning on the chair-back.

'Close the door,' she said, and I did so.

'Sit down.'

I did that, too.

'You acquitted yourself well yesterday,' she said. 'Killing Ned Farnesworth was a foolish and impetuous move, but luckily, owing to Fodder's considerable negotiating skills, the truce is holding.'

'I didn't kill him.'

She nodded quietly to herself and then held up a gold-edged gift certificate with a lot of zeros on it.

'Then you won't want the ten-thousand-euro reward?'

I felt, all of a sudden, conflicted. It would pay for Birgitta to see Springrise, but it somehow didn't seem right taking it. I had an idea.

'Can we assign it to Fodder? I think he wants to take a couple of years' sabbatical and doesn't have a lot of cash.'

Toccata stared at me for a while.

'It wasn't Debts and Nesquik that carried the truce, was it?'

'No, ma'am.'

She pushed the certificate across the desk.

'Sign it on the back.'

I did so and my obligation to Fodder, I felt, was at least partly resolved.

'Now,' said Toccata, 'I suppose you're wondering why I'm being so nice to you?'

To be honest, I hadn't actually noticed.

'It's because you don't work for us any more. I'm only hideously offensive to my own.'

I thought this might be about Aurora having completed my job application without my say-so, but it wasn't.

'Here,' she said, passing me a fax. 'Looks like your Acting Sector Chief has requested me to return you to Cardiff. They're short staffed there, too. Unpaid leave can commence immediately; you can sit out this storm in the safety of the *Siddons* and once the weather breaks Jonesy will run you into Hereford and you can ride the Railplane home.'

I read the fax. It was from Vice-Consul Pryce and made reference to Logan's death 'at Aurora's hands in the defence of Novice Worthing', so at least I wasn't being held to account for that.

'Goodbye, Worthing. I'd like to say it's been a pleasure – but I can't.'

I paused. Sure, this was a far riskier place than Cardiff what with volatile Chief Consuls, homicidal HiberTech agents, Wintervolk and the subzero temperatures. But I couldn't think of anywhere I'd rather be. Besides, there was Birgitta. Sure, she might be only three jam doughnuts from turning cannibal, but she was still my responsibility.

'I'd like to stay, ma'am.'

Toccata's eyebrow twitched.

'You don't want to be in Sector Twelve, *I* don't want you in Sector Twelve. You're a liability and a wild card and trouble seems to follow you like a homesick spaniel. *And* you're bundling with Aurora, and no one who ever did that came to anything but grief.'

'No, really, I feel at home here. First time since leaving the Pool. First time *ever*.'

'You're breaking my heart. Okay, let me spell it out: you're fired. You've been lucky so far, but that's going to run out, and when it does you'll be taking good agents with you.'

She sat in her chair and stared up at me with her good eye, while the other contorted in its socket.

'You're done. We're done. Go.'

I walked to the door, the heady buzz of comradeship I'd felt so strongly that morning now cracked and forlorn.

But I had an idea, and turned back.

'You're still here,' she said, not looking up from her desk.

'I think you should know,' I said, 'I was offered a job at HiberTech this morning.'

She slowly looked up at me and a red flush spread rapidly across her neck and cheeks. Any last vestige of friendliness she might have had seemed to vanish.

'You wonky-faced piece of crap. You're kidding me, right?'

'No,' I said, as innocently as I could. 'Two-year contract, cash signing bonus, free puddings, apartment facing the quad – and a Cadbury's Fruit & Nut allocation.'

'I don't know why they want you there, but it's not for your charm, looks or experience. They'll use you, spit you out spent. Working for HiberTech would be the worst career move you'll ever make – and the last.'

'You're right,' I replied, somewhat daringly, 'I don't want to work there. I want to stay in Sector Twelve, but if that's the only option open to me, I'll take it.'

Toccata put her pen down, leaned back in her chair and stared at me.

'Well, I'll be,' she said, 'you just played me. No one has *ever* dared play me.' She looked almost impressed. 'Okay, have it your own way: you've got a job. Filing duties for the next ninety-one days, *inside* the Consulate – and demoted from Deputy to Novice. There'll be latrine duty in it somewhere, and you can do everyone's washing and ironing. Pretty soon you'll beg to go and work for Dowager Farnesworth. Okay, now piss off. Hang on, wait, one more thing.'

She got up, walked around the desk and punched me in the eye.

'*That's* for lying earlier.'

I got to my feet and she punched me a second time in the same place.

'And *that's* for bundling this morning with Aurora when you said you wouldn't.'

I left the office, head spinning, but at least clear on two points: firstly, that I was getting better at dealing with the Winter, and secondly, that the tongue-coming-out warning had indeed been an empty threat.

'How did that go?' asked Jonesy when she found me holding a cold compress to my eye in the washrooms.

'I was told to leave, said I didn't want to, was fired, reinstated then demoted to Novice. But I played her so I think she now respects me.'

'Is that why she punched you in the eye?'

'No, that was for lying and bundling with Aurora.'

'That's true, then?'

'*No.*'

'You'll be fine,' she said, patting me on the arm and chuckling. 'Toccata beat me so hard with a broom handle when I first arrived that I had concussion for a week. It's just kind of her thing.'

'I wish she would find some other thing.'

I went to look for Laura in the filing room, and when she saw me she offered me a seat at one of the desks.

'So, tell me about the Gronk,' she said excitedly, drawing up a chair herself. 'Did you actually see her?'

I repeated the story with as much detail as I could, which wasn't much. I'd been unconscious from the moment she arrived to the moment she left. Laura made notes, and nodded vigorously at the smallest detail, but when I'd finished she looked disappointed. It wasn't the slam dunk she'd been hoping for.

'So no pictures?' she asked.

'Not a single one.'

'Treacle has already dismissed it as Hibernational Narcosis,' she said with a sigh, '*yours*. He thinks you killed Lucky Ned and are now blanking it from your mind.'

'Do I look like the sort of person who would bite off a finger?'

'You bit off Gary Findlay's ear.'

'You heard about that?'

'No secrets in the Twelve.'

'So I've realised.'

She fell silent for a moment and stared at the floor. I looked around the room. My accelerated course at the Academy hadn't included filing duties.

'How does this work?' I asked.

Laura, who seemed not to be able to feel down for more than a few moments, told me she *loved* filing owing to its 'simple elegance' and instructed me, with a worryingly high level of enthusiasm, how things should be done. Not the best or most logical way, but the SkillZero way – simple enough for everyone to use, yet complex enough to function efficiently as a usable database – and easily understandable by anyone with a pass in General Skills.

'Shamanic Bob mentioned something called Active Control Dreaming,' I said while we were laboriously updating minor details to the individual cards, and by a complicated series of notches and holes, allowing them to be cross-referenced in an ingenious manner.

'Active Control is like Zebricorns and the missing 14th Ottoman,' said Laura. 'Myths with their roots in reality. Sure, Don Hector and HiberTech were looking into dreams you can control, but it's difficult to gauge what success they had. After all, it's possible you only dreamed you were controlling them.'

'And Dreamspace?' I asked.

'Meeting inside dreams? Even *more* far-fetched. Anecdotally there were a few successes mixed heavily with an abundance of failure, but it's a difficult area of research. Messing around with the hibernatory subconscious was never a risk-free occupation. There were stories of psychotic episodes, spontaneous sleepdeath, people supposedly trapped in the Dreamstate, stuff like that. *Fortean Times* talked about little else in the seventies.'

'Trapped in the Dreamspace?' I asked, and Laura looked at me, then shrugged.

'It's never been explained how the mind can return from deep hibernation; some say that the personality goes elsewhere. To a Dreamstate somewhere *outside* the body, perhaps – absorbed into the walls and furniture and plants.'

'A state of displaced consciousness,' I said, repeating what I'd heard Don Hector say in my dream. He'd been dead for two years, yet I felt part of his personality in me, alive.

'Ghosts could be explained this way,' said Laura, 'and Wintervolk. An orphaned consciousness returning periodically using the power of another sleeper's thoughts.'

At any other time I would have dismissed this as utter nonsense.

'Lloyd thought the Gronk might be somehow related to Ichabod's murdered daughter,' I said.

'I heard that too. Want to see a picture of her?'

'Sure.'

She pulled open a filing cabinet, rummaged for a moment and then drew out a file. She flicked through the contents, eventually showing me a family photograph. It was of Rhosilli beach in the Gower, the *Argentinian Queen* behind, recently wrecked. A man, thin and weaselly and with a sour, cruel face, a woman, bluff and optimistic. And Gretl, the daughter, holding a beach ball. I felt a cold chill run up my back. Yesterday – even this morning – I would have dismissed it all as a retrospective memory remapping, but now I wasn't so sure. It was the same child as the one in the Birgitta dream, the child with the gurgle of laughter. The same gurgle of laughter I'd heard before Lucky Ned was taken.

'What's the matter?' asked Laura. 'You look kind of … ill.'

'The Gronk's real,' I said.

'Yes, I know,' said Laura, 'that's why I gave you the camera. To take a picture of her. The wager was always sound; it was only the evidence that was going to be a problem.'

'I think she's in my mind,' I said quietly. 'I saw her in the Dreamstate.'

'That could mean she's either protecting or stalking you,' said Laura. 'Don't take this the wrong way, but there are plenty more unworthy than you. She'll pluck the ripest fruit first. You may want to whistle "Some Enchanted Evening"[59] when she makes landfall, just to be safe.'

'Good tip. Thanks,' I said sarcastically.

'You're welcome.'

Laura tidied away the picture and made to leave as Fodder had said he'd take her around to look at some of the folded linen traps she'd set up. She gave me a cheery wave, told me to keep the Instamatic camera close by at all times, and departed.

I sat for a long time considering the Gronk, then went and made a cup of tea, sat with it until it grew cold, and searched the Sector Twelve Residents filing cabinet until I found Birgitta's personnel file. Attached were her Spring & Autumn identity mug shots and the usual guff about hibernational intentions, National Insurance records

59. Track 4, Side 1, *South Pacific* original cast recording

and employment status – in her case 'freelance'. Aside from a hefty fine for failing to properly register with OffPop and an ongoing investigation for potential childbearing evasion, there was little of note. And there was no mention of marriage, nor any link to Webster.

I replaced the file, had a thought, then pulled Webster's file and stared at the contents curiously. Jonesy had pointed out that he and five others had either vanished or been made into nightwalkers, potentially because one of them was conducting some form of industrial espionage. And that got me to thinking that if one of them *was* claiming to be someone they weren't, then their file – the one used to conduct background checks – would be fraudulent.

Webster's name would have come back clean, but if he was an impostor, his *likeness* might very well show up a different result.

I unclipped the photograph from his file, attached it to a sheet of paper, wrote a request that purported to be from Toccata using a signature on another document I'd found, and sent it via fax to Central Records in Aber. I watched as the paper was slowly drawn into the machine. Sixty miles and a short time lag away it would be doing the same thing, only coming out.

As soon as it had vanished, a cold panic seized me. *What was I doing?* There was nothing to link Webster to, well, *anything*. A traitorous Don Hector mixed up with deep-cover Campaign for Real Sleep operatives battling to retrieve a missing wax cylinder existed only in my imagination. They were dreams. Fancies. Nonsense. *Narcosis.*

And even more stupidly, I'd just forged the Chief's signature on an information request. A felony during the Summer, potential Frigicution in the Winter. I stared at the dormant fax machine forlornly, wondering how I could have been so stupid. I considered sending another fax countermanding the first, but thought that would probably make it worse.

But, I told myself optimistically, it was entirely possible Central Records were busy, and checking photographs could take days.

It took all of eight minutes. And I only knew that because I got a personal visit from Toccata, who arrived with Jonesy into the filing room. Toccata didn't look very happy, but then she never looked very happy.

'Well, Gronk's dung in a piss-pot,' said Toccata as soon as she saw me moving in a guilty fashion away from the fax machine, 'I should have known it was you.'

I defaulted to stout denial, as Sister Placentia had done when eighteen empty gin bottles were found under her bed.

'I have no idea at all what you're talking about.'

Toccata raised an eyebrow. Oddly, over her non-seeing eye.

'Then let me enlighten you: I just got a call from Central Records, thanking me for the very interesting picture I sent to be identified. I was surprised about the call, Wonky. Do you know *why* I was surprised?'

'I've got a feeling you're going to tell me.'

'Because I never sent any picture ID request, and that must be me having a serious memory lapse, because it had my signature on it.'

'Oh,' I said, 'really?'

'Yes, really. Then they asked me who the man in the picture identified himself as, because they've been after him for twelve years and he's on their Campaign for Real Sleep watch list. And you know what?'

'What?'

'I couldn't answer that question, either. Because I hadn't sent it and didn't know what they were talking about. Isn't that totally weird?'

'Very weird – but I still have no idea what you're talking about.'

Jonesy picked up the actual fax that I had carelessly left on my desk and showed it to Toccata, then to me.

'You are *so* busted,' said Jonesy with a smile. 'I think you'd better tell us everything.'

Charlie Webster

'... The *Josephine III* was built on the Clyde and launched in 1936. After a long career plying the North Atlantic route she was sold to a Southern shipping line and renamed the *Argentinian Queen*. Captured while blockade-running in 1974, she was consigned to Newport to be scrapped in 1982. Her tow parted during delivery and she was swept onto Rhosilli beach ...'

— *Wrecks of the Gower* — Welsh Tourist Office

'So before I even *start* getting to work on you,' said Toccata, 'whose details are about to come back via the fax?'

There didn't seem much point in lying – they'd find out soon enough.

'You'll know him as Charles Webster.'

'Webster the orderly at HiberTech?'

I nodded, and Jonesy and Toccata looked at one another. They were surprised, or perhaps shocked, or perhaps both. I could feel my eye start to puff up where Toccata had hit me earlier, but resisted the urge to touch it.

The fax machine began to hum and we waited without speaking until the message had fed out of the printer. Jonesy picked it up before I could see and showed it to Toccata.

'How did those idiots at HiberTech Security miss this?' said Toccata. 'They let a known RealSleep agent right into the heart of their organisation.'

'That's actually quite amusing,' said Jonesy.

'Yes, it is,' agreed Toccata, and they both stared at me for some time in silence.

'Can you feel that empty pause, Wonky?' said Toccata. 'It's where you tell us *why* you were investigating Charles Webster. How you knew he wasn't who he said he was. Let's hear it.'

It felt like I was in front of Mother Fallopia, being harangued about some dumb prank we'd played back at the Pool. I knew one thing, though: I couldn't tell them I'd seen it all in a dream.

'Because,' I began, 'Birgitta had said she was married to someone named Charlie and I was trying to figure out … figure out … think, think … *probate*.'

'Probate?'

'Yes, probate. Who to give all her paintings to when she died.'

Toccata stared at me, her one eye unblinking. It was a heavy stare like treacle, which seemed to pour heavily down my neck and pool in my armpits.

'What are you, her executor or something?'

'It's a hobby,' I said, 'sort of like that TV programme where they look for relatives who have been left stuff. What's it called?'

'*Heir Hunters?*'

'That's the one. *Heir Hunters.*'

'You're lying again,' said Toccata, 'but I've no idea why. Birgitta married to Webster, you say?'

'Yes,' I replied, flushing a deep shade of crimson.

Jonesy had pulled her file as I had been stammering out my pathetic attempt to extricate myself from the jam.

'If they were,' she said, 'it was off grid – which might point towards her being Campaign for Real Sleep, too. He must have been made of pretty stern stuff to not give her up, and Hooke must have gone seriously to town to reduce him to little more than a nightwalker.'

'Hooke's an animal,' agreed Toccata. 'No one I know has ever withstood a prolonged Dreamspace attack.'

I think I knew that, too, through the memory I shared with Webster: that Birgitta had been RealSleep too, and that, yes, Webster didn't give her up and instead of legging it off-sector she had stayed, her cover burned, in a scuzzy out-of-the-way corner of nowhere, waiting for an instruction that might never come out of loyalty to the cause she loved. Hoping, perhaps, to make a difference if the need arose.

'Okay, then,' said Jonesy, turning to Toccata, 'but what do we do?'

Toccata sucked her lip and tapped the fax that had just come in.

'They'll probably have cc-ed this to HiberTech Security,' she said, 'but unlike us, they don't know Webster's connection to Birgitta.'

'We should check her room,' said Jonesy, 'in case there is anything incriminating to be found there.'

The words didn't register at first. I had to ask her to say them again.

'I said,' she repeated in a testy fashion, 'that we should check Birgitta's room. It might throw up something of interest.'

It would throw up a lot more than just something of interest. It would throw up Birgitta, exactly where I'd left her: clean and tidy and fed and oh-so-obviously harboured.

'Any objections, Wonky?'

I tried to look like the sort of person who wasn't about to be professionally, legally and socially destroyed before the hour was out.

'Me? None at all.'

'I can't make up my mind about you,' said Toccata, staring at me intently, head on one side, her lone eye unblinking. 'Most Novices we get are either burned-out ex-military with a thousand-yard stare, gung-ho idiots or saddos who might as well have *Kill Me Now* printed on their forehead. You're not any of those. But I can't figure out if you're a clever person pretending to be thick, a thick person pretending to be clever, or just a chancer stumbling through the Winter without any sort of plan or thought at all.'

'Can I vote for option "C"?' I asked, trying to lighten the mood.

'But one thing we do know,' added Toccata, ignoring me, 'is that we can't let you out of our sight.'

'Ah,' I said; my only plan – running away when their backs were turned, but details not yet worked out – was now tattered and broken. 'Can I ask a question?'

'A question?' said Toccata. 'Of *course* – actually, no. Be quiet and do as you're told or I'll make good on the tongue-coming-out promise. Don't think I've forgotten.'

In less than a minute I was driving Jonesy towards the *Siddons* in the falling snow, Toccata having elected to stay in the Consulate. The light was muted by the coming storm, and aside from the occasional street light that glowed a yellowy-orange, the sky had an angry blackness about it. I was fifteen minutes away from arrest, and no amount of talking would get me out of the charges that would undoubtedly follow.

'After all those years we spent together,' said Jonesy, finally finding something to say as we drove past the wrought-iron gates to the museum, 'you might have taken me into your confidence. Just shows that even when you pretend to think you know someone, you actually don't pretend to know them at all.'

'Can we have a break on the whole invented histories deal?' I asked.

'Absolutely not. For one thing the only way through the Winter is continuity, and for the other, I don't back out of a long and happy make-believe union just when things start getting rocky.'

A squall hit the Sno-Trac and the vehicle seemed to shake down to its smallest rivets. I instinctively throttled back to a slow crawl, and increased the speed of the wipers.

'This is nasty,' I said, attempting to distract myself from Birgitta's impending discovery, 'a blizzard.'

'This isn't a blizzard,' she replied, 'this is just crystallised water with a smattering of wind. When you open the door and know that going out is certain death, *that's* a blizzard.'

We continued on, the weather steadily worsening until by the time we had pulled up outside the *Siddons*, the visibility was down to less than ten yards.

'Are we in a blizzard now?'

'Nope,' said Jonesy, 'but we take precautions as if we were. You're leading.'

I broke a light-stick, clipped it to my coat, then moved to the back of the Sno-Trac and grasped one end of a steel cable that fed off a drum mounted near the rear exit and attached it to the loop on my belt. I pulled down my goggles and opened the door, allowing the wind and weather to blow inside. I paused and climbed out but it wasn't a time to dally; I let go of the vehicle and stepped out into the blinding void.

I'd practised this many times in a fog chamber – there was one the size of two football pitches at the Academy – but doing it for real was quite different: the noise and wind-blown snow added a raucous hostility that I hadn't expected, and despite the lack of visibility in a fog chamber, it doesn't have the disorientating effect of the snow constantly moving about you. I held my hand out in front of me and walked in the direction in which I hoped the *Siddons* would lie.

It took thirty-two-and-a-half paces to reach one of the statues that adorned the entrance. I was close enough to see it was a sleep-nymph, and I moved to the right until I found the door, then transferred the cable to the hefty eyelet bolted to the masonry. I tugged the cable twice, waited for Jonesy to emerge from the swirling emptiness, and once we were inside I shut the front door against the blizzard. The noise and wind ceased abruptly and the snowflakes, released from their wind-borne activity, floated gently to the floor.

Porter Lloyd and two cadaverous-looking winsomniacs were holding blankets and mugs of hot chocolate when we opened the inner door. Only they weren't waiting for us.

'Oh,' said Lloyd, 'Worthing. Thanks for the custom. Most grateful.'

'Custom?'

He pointed to the door of the Winterlounge, where I could see several winsomniacs warming themselves around the coal fire. Shamanic Bob was amongst them and waved a weak greeting. They must have left almost the moment I told them about the blue Buick dream.

'How many?'

'Eight have checked in out of the thirty-two who left the Wincarnis,' replied Lloyd, 'and the way things are looking, I won't expect many more. That was quite ruthless, if you don't mind me saying, sir. Didn't expect it of you.'

It was a surprise to me, too.

'I never expected them to move across in *this*.'

Jonesy, however, was not in a stop-and-chat sort of mood.

'Consulate business, Mr Lloyd. We'll see ourselves up.'

She headed off towards the paternoster lift. I thought of waiting in the lobby, but other than stealing her Sno-Trac and running off into the blizzard – again, details not yet fully worked out – I couldn't see any plan of action. Perhaps I could brazen it out.

'You're a dark horse,' said Jonesy as the lift took us slowly upwards, the pipes gurgling ominously. 'You've just ethically thinned twenty-four winsomniacs. Happy with yourself?'

'No, not really – but I thought everyone hated them?'

'We do,' she said, 'or we say we do. But a life's a life, and all this bunch want to do is dream away their years in relative happiness. It's not criminal, it's a mental sleep issue. How did you get them to move?'

'I told Shamanic Bob about the Active Control blue Buick dream washing around the *Siddons*.'

She turned and stared at me, brows knitted.

'Who said the Buick dream was Active Control?'

'Dunno,' I said, suddenly realising I'd said too much, 'I just heard.'

She stared at me some more, and her manner seemed to change.

'I don't know whether you're lying or not, Wonky. But if there's any Active Control dreaming going on in the *Siddons*, that changes everything.'

'It does?'

'Yes,' she said, 'it does. Active Control can only be initiated by HiberTech using a Somnagraph, and the only reason they'd want to undertake dream control experiments in the *Siddons* is ... well, nothing good.'

We stepped off the paternoster at the ninth and walked along the corridor, the only illumination the glimmer that seeped down the light wells, while outside the storm heaved and sighed around the building.

Jonesy unlocked the door to Birgitta's apartment and stepped inside, sweeping her flashlight around the room. I remained outside, heavy with nausea. I'd reconciled myself to Birgitta's discovery by now, and my thumping heart had been replaced by a hot sense of utter dejection.

Jonesy popped her head back outside the door.

'Come and help me search,' she said. 'There's nothing unusual in here that I can see.'

'There isn't?' I asked, quickly adding, in a less surprised voice: 'I mean, there isn't?'

'No. Why, what were you expecting me to find?'

'Nothing,' I replied, wondering if Birgitta had escaped, been taken by Lloyd or – outside chance – had simply been a hallucination, part of the narcosis. Intrigued, I followed her into Birgitta's apartment.

'Oh, hang on a mo,' said Jonesy, 'I lied when I said there was nothing unusual in here. There's Birgitta. And she's alive, missing a thumb. Care to explain?'

There was a sudden, nasty, hollow silence. Birgitta was sitting on the bed, staring blankly around, her food finished, several sketches lying on the bed. I couldn't see what they were at this distance. Perhaps more of my – our – dream. Don't know. Didn't matter. Not any more.

'Good Lord,' I said with inexpertly wrought mock-surprise. 'That's … incredible. She must have – I don't know – escaped from the pit behind the *Siddons*.'

'Oh, *please*,' said Jonesy. 'Can't you see the game's up? You're making things worse, if that's possible – which it isn't.'

'It happened once down at the Pool,' I said, still in some sort of continuous denial feedback loop. 'Sister Oesterious. They didn't hit her hard enough. Covered in fish heads when she came back, she was – and the same with Carmen Miranda, of course.'

It was an off-the-cuff remark as I didn't have a strategy, I was just flanneling wildly in the vague hope that providence would deliver me from my current dilemma.

Which it kind of did.

'Carmen Miranda?' said Jonesy, suddenly looking concerned.

'Yes,' I said, seizing on the initiative. 'You said you'd thumped her, but I saw her wandering down the road. She had a fruit hat on and a gown and everything.'

'Always a star,' mused Jonesy, 'when did you see her?'

'This morning.'

'Well,' she said, looking out of the window, where there was little to see but a wall of whirling snowflakes, 'perhaps her homing instincts will have kicked in. Now: I want your badge and your Bambi.'

'Look,' I said, handing them over, 'if we're talking due process: yes, I thought I'd retired Birgitta, but if Miranda's still alive then this sort of thing happens. Besides, what evidence do you have that I am anything but an innocent party in all this?'

'Let me see,' said Jonesy. 'First, you're an exceptionally bad liar. I mean *exceptionally*. Transparent, almost. Second, you— no, we'll skip reasons two to seven, because reason eight is quite enough all on its own: Birgitta drew this of you.'

She held up one of Birgitta's sketches. It was me, with her, here in the bathroom of her apartment. She had drawn it from memory, but it might easily have been from life. The picture was of me washing her hair while she sat naked in the tub, just before I'd given up her long black tresses as a lost cause and cut them off. In the picture, Birgitta didn't look vacant, she looked frustrated. Perhaps that's what her inner emotion was right now.

I felt my eyes well up as the true and utter uselessness of the position became clear, and how poorly I had fared in my efforts to keep her safe. I'd protected her for the grand total of nineteen hours and seventeen minutes.

Not even a single day.

'Can you explain this?' said Jonesy, showing me the sketch again.

'It's not what it looks like.'

'No?'

'No.'

'You know what it looks like to me?' she said. 'It looks like someone tending to someone else's needs. Someone who can't look after themselves. It looks a lot like empathy, Wonky. What say you?'

'What?'

'Empathy. Big on empathy, are you?'

'Yes,' I said, surprised by her understanding, 'that's exactly what it is. Empathy.'

'I love you, Charlie,' said Birgitta.

'She's not dead,' I said with a sigh. 'I couldn't kill her because she's still in there. It's not a neural collapse brought on by Morphenox – which, yes, I did supply her with – it's a state of displaced consciousness. She can process memories.'

320

'I can see that,' said Jonesy, staring at the sketches, 'and it's not the first I've seen.'

'I love you, Charlie.'

'I have to answer or she repeats herself,' I said. 'I love you, Birgitta.'

Birgitta relaxed, and began to sketch again. Jonesy looked at me, then at Birgitta.

'How long were you thinking of keeping her?'

I shrugged.

'I don't know. Until Springrise, I guess. I didn't really have a plan, more an objective. Events move fast in the Winter,' I added, remembering what Logan had told me, 'and you need flexibility to ensure the plan doesn't get in the way of the goal. Am I under arrest?'

'You are,' she said, 'in order to remain under our protection.'

'Is that important?'

'It's crucial. I don't know of a single Tricksy nightwalker who can do what Birgitta can do. The Notable Goodnight will be *especially* interested.'

'So that's why we're taking her to HiberTech?'

'No, that's why we're *not* taking her to HiberTech.'

'You're going to thump her?'

'No, we don't do that.'

'What about your sixty-three nightwalker retirements? What about Glitzy Tiara and Eddie Tangiers?'

'Smoke and mirrors, Wonk. Nothing is what it seems in the Douzey. Does Lloyd know about Baggy? Put it this way: has he tried to blackmail you?'

'No.'

'Then we'll assume not. Anyone else know about her?'

I shook my head.

'We keep it that way. Feed her these so she stays quiet, and say and do nothing while I have a look around.'

She handed me two Tunnock's Tea Cakes from her jacket pocket and I fed Birgitta while Jonesy searched the room. She took a half-hour to do so, and was beyond thorough. If Birgitta was smart, she wouldn't have left any evidence connecting her to Webster. She *was* smart, but like Charles, she couldn't bring herself to dispose of the only picture of them together. Jonesy found it inside the hem of a curtain, the stitching unpicked and replaced by Velcro.

'Bingo,' she said, and showed it to me. It was the Polaroid, the same as the one from my dream, the one the photographer had taken all those years ago, the one that Birgitta had admonished Charles for keeping, the one she'd said she'd destroy. I stared at the picture stupidly, trying once again to reconcile the real with the imagined.

'It's Rhosilli beach on the Gower,' I said, swallowing down a sense of rising confusion. 'The picture was taken when Birgitta and Charles spent a weekend together, cocooned in the flat above the garage at her mother's in Oxwich. They fed heartily upon the love they felt for one another, and on the way home they stopped for cockles and laver bread at Mumbles Pier, the wireless playing "Groove Me" as a lifeboat was retrieved. They said they loved one another, and they meant it: A tightening in the chest; a sense of euphoric oneness.'

'How can you know all that?' asked Jonesy.

I held my head as the frustration welled up inside me.

'I don't know how I know it,' I said, 'don't know if I dreamt the Polaroid, or if I'm placing it in my memory now, or ... dreaming about something I couldn't know about. Look over there.'

I pointed to Birgitta's painting on the wall, the one of the beach in the Gower, with the wreck, and the orange-and-red parasol of spectacular size and splendour, below which were the two figures.

'I dreamt I was there as Charles, with Birgitta, just as you see in that painting. But then details in the dream come true, and I can't tell if I can see stuff that happened to other people or if I'm patching holes in my memories with whatever is to hand.'

I could feel myself shaking and wanted all this to be over — in whatever fashion it could. Roscoe Smalls had taken the Cold Way Out when the blue Buick came calling. He hadn't been supremely brave or a miserable coward. He'd just wanted out of it, in any way he could.

She asked me to outline the dreams, which I did as quickly as I could.

'So let me get this straight,' she said when I'd finished. 'You met Don Hector in the blue Buick dream?'

'I *was* him in the blue Buick. He had a rattle in his chest, his vision felt faded, and there was a sense of a numbness down his left-hand side. He spoke French more naturally than he spoke English, and he found solace in a place he used to go with the Buick: an oak tree with the trunk piled high with stones. When they came to take him he told them they'd get nothing even if they tried to get into his dreams. He'd relinquish only the blue Buick moment and said he'd leave a night terror – hundreds of disembodied hands – to put anyone off trying to read him.'

'Nasty. Anything else?'

'Yes – Don Hector gave the cylinder to Webster.'

'The *cylinder*? Webster was given the *cylinder*?'

I nodded.

'And you know this because—?'

'Of my dream, yes.'

'Daughter of a dog,' she said, leaning against the door frame, 'we thought the Buick was just another Sub-beta recurring night terror. Not actually *active*. And you said that there was a Mrs Nesbit dream-avatar with The Notable Goodnight's voice demanding you find the cylinder?'

'Yes,' I said, 'what does it mean?'

'It means,' she murmured, 'they don't yet have it.'

She looked at me and thought for a second or two. 'What room you in?'

I pointed to the other side of the Dormitorium. '901.'

'Who lives next door to you?'

'On one side, Moody – until he got thumped. The other side is unused.'

'It won't be. There'll be a large box, a flight case or a—'

'—steamer trunk?'

'Yeah,' she said, 'a steamer trunk would do it. This is what we're doing: you're telling no one what you just told me, no one except Toccata. Understand?'

'I don't understand at all, but yes, I agree.'

'Good.'

She pocketed the Polaroid of Birgitta and Charles, then picked up the phone, speed-dialled the Consulate and asked to be put through to the Chief.

'It's Jonesy,' she said after a pause. 'The Buick dream was active, Wonky has been third-person Don Hector and get this: Webster was given the cylinder – and the nasties over at HiberTech don't have it yet.'

She listened for a moment, then stared at me.

'Because Wonky *dreamt* it – and much else besides.'

There was a pause. Jonesy said we'd be back in half an hour, put the phone down and then turned to me with some urgency.

'We're leaving now.'

'And Birgitta?'

'I know a safe place she can go; we'll drop her off on the way. Congratulations: you've just been promoted from liability to asset.'

'Because I harboured Birgitta?'

'Because you're dreaming the right dream. Because you've been in the Dreamspace, because Aurora thinks she owns you, because you're going to continue to make her think that. But you're not, because you're on our side now.'

'Which side is that?'

'The *right* side. Once we get back to the office, we'll tell you everything.'

'You'll tell me why I've been having these dreams?'

'*Everything.*'

Thumped

'... Winter Consuls never really felt comfortable with the Summer. It wasn't the warmth, thronging masses, or the general sense of euphoria that went with the knowledge that they had cheated the Winter. It was more the sense that come Autumn, when they headed back to their allotted Consulate, they would be facing the darkness, loneliness and the cold and doing it all over again. They loved it ...'

– from Seventeen Winters, by Winter Consul Lance Jones

We came down by way of the stairs, a circular descending journey that ran around the interior wall of the central heat-well like a helix. Lloyd was in the lobby with two of the winsomniacs, still standing by with blankets and hot drinks in case another of their compatriots made it through – an act of kindness liberally laced with deluded hope. I'd seen the blizzard, and doubted anyone could navigate the three changes on the fixed line to get here, even if it was less than two miles. Others would have either sought refuge in other Kipshops en route, got lost, or just given up. Winsomniacs had few energy reserves. Even blinking was an effort.

'What in—' began Lloyd when he saw me leading Birgitta by the hand.

'Harbouring,' said Jonesy. 'Worthing is *so* under arrest right now.'

The front door opened. But it wasn't a confused and very cold yet navigationally astute winsomniac, it was someone considerably less welcome – Mr Hooke. He was accompanied by Lucy Knapp, wrapped up tight in a duvet jacket and large woolly hat. She smiled when she saw me, but looked nervous, too.

'Safe Haven?' asked Hooke, the traditional request for unconditional shelter in the Winter. 'Staff transfer between facilities and we got lost.'

'Safe Haven,' said Lloyd, acknowledging the request.

'My first blizzard,' said Lucy to me, pulling off her parka. 'A little more excitement than I'd bargained for.'

'It's good to see you,' I said, with a sense of relief.

'And you,' she said, and we tapped fists.

'Good afternoon, Deputy Jones,' said Hooke.

'Good afternoon,' said Jonesy, without breaking her pace to the coat rack and now almost pushing Birgitta in front of her.

'It would be safer to stay inside,' said Hooke. 'Going out in this is foolhardy at best, and irresponsible at worst.'

'And yet you are yourself a new arrival,' retorted Jonesy, pulling on her boots and then rummaging for a spare parka for Birgitta.

'Safe Havening,' he replied, 'as you heard. We expect to be here until it eases – what's your reason for you venturing out? Something pretty important, I should imagine?'

He looked from me to Jonesy as he spoke.

'Consulate business,' said Jonesy, handing me my coat, 'and of an urgent and pressing nature.'

'With a nightwalker and a Novice?'

'Consulate business,' she repeated, smiling but without humour.

'That's as may be,' said Hooke, taking a step closer, 'but my orders are to ensure Worthing remains free to join us at HiberTech.'

And then, with the pretext of moving his arm to straighten his tie, Hooke pushed his coat back to allow easier access to the Bambi on his hip. The gesture did not go unnoticed by Jonesy. He wasn't there to Safe Haven, he'd been likely ordered to interrupt his journey to come over here and stop us from leaving. HiberTech had been tipped off – by Lloyd, most probably.

'We take recruitment seriously,' continued Hooke, 'and the Chief has made a personal investment that she doesn't want to see bruised.'

'Charlie's a Consul, not a piece of overripe fruit, and right now, under arrest – our prisoner, our jurisdiction.'

I opened my mouth to say something, but Jonesy pressed her fingers on my mouth to keep me silent.

'You've charged Worthing with harbouring?' asked Hooke.

'Yes.'

Hooke looked at Birgitta, who was still staring blankly around the lobby and freaking out the winsomniacs, who were studiously avoiding her blank gaze.

'Worthing was looking after this nightwalker at our request,' said Hooke. 'We'll swear to that in an affidavit. There has been no crime. Now, release the prisoner from your custody and this can end without recrimination.'

'Irrespective, Charlie is still a Consul,' said Jonesy.

'Deputy Worthing could resign,' said Hooke, 'here and now.'

Jonesy stared at him coldly.

'Charlie's not resigning. Wonky, you're not resigning.'

'Only Charlie can make that decision.'

It was Lucy Knapp who'd spoken. She looked at me and smiled.

'Charlie, listen to me. The Consul Service are not your friends. I've seen stuff and know stuff and at HiberTech we're on the cusp of introducing something quite new and wonderful to the world. For purely personal reasons and an intense dislike of Aurora, Toccata is trying to throw a spanner in the works. But we need to move forward without let or hindrance: it's a game changer.'

'Project Lazarus?'

'Ten years in the preparation. It's a winner, any way you want to look at it. And HiberTech needs your help to ensure the most satisfactory outcome is enjoyed by the majority.'

'What's on the cylinder?'

'I don't know, Hooke doesn't know, and I'm willing to bet Miss Jones doesn't know.'

I looked at Jonesy, who didn't deny it.

'Why me?' I asked. 'What's so special about me that only I can help?'

'Aurora sees something special in you,' she said, 'a gift that can be nurtured until it becomes a skill that will set you head and shoulders above any potential career with the Consuls. Working for HiberTech will be the best decision you'll ever make.'

'She's lying,' said Jonesy, 'whoever she is – sorry, we weren't introduced.'

'Lucy Knapp,' said Lucy, holding out a hand, which Jonesy shook.

'Miss Knapp's lying,' continued Jonesy, slowly moving her hand to where her Bambi was holstered. 'HiberTech look out only for themselves. They'll take what they want from you and the next thing you know you'll be driving a golf cart around the facility. Only you won't know that, because you won't be able to.'

'Jonesy exaggerates wildly like the outspoken fool I now realise she is,' said Lucy, her voice rising, 'but she has no cogent arguments, merely slander. It's a bona fide career. How about it?'

'There will always be the Gower.'

It was Birgitta. She'd interrupted the conversation and was momentarily distracting – something that Hooke and Jonesy both exploited.

Whu–whump

They'd drawn and fired their weapons almost simultaneously. Concussive vortex rings do strange things in restricted spaces, but *opposing* thumps do even stranger things – and like weather systems, Arctic badgers and Sister Contractia, they are difficult to predict. The two pulses met with the sound of a log being split, then ran around each other before stabilising in a tight vertical dust devil that sucked up anything not nailed down – dust, paper, hats, gloves, books. We watched the vortex grow darker and heavier and had to hold onto furniture and each other to avoid being swept off our feet, until the maelstrom explosively lost cohesion and knocked us all off our feet. Hooke drew his second Bambi but Jonesy's back-up weapon caught him on the chest and cannoned him backwards into a plaster wall, which buckled under the impact, and Hooke fell forwards in a cloud of dust.

Jonesy dropped the spent thermalite from the Bambi and swiftly replaced it with another.

'We'll laugh about this later,' she said to me, advancing upon Hooke, who was struggling to get up, still dazed, 'in that cosy retirement we promised ourselves.'

Whump

There was another ear-popping concussion and Jonesy was lifted off her feet and thrown backwards through two chairs, a standard lamp and out through one of the front windows by way of the heavy drapes. The snow and wind swirled into the room, the cold air replacing the hot in an instant. I turned. Lucy Knapp was holding a Thumper and had a look of steely determination about her. Lucy had lied: she was HiberTech first, friend second. When you accept a corporate fast track, you have to leave a part of yourself behind.

I pushed my way past the tattered curtains, which were flapping wildly in the gale, and waded through the snow to where Jonesy was lying. She wasn't dead, but it wouldn't be long. Her face was a fine mesh of broken capillaries. Her eyelids were sunken and closed and I knew that her sockets were empty underneath. She was breathing in short gasps, and a small amount of blood frothed from the side of her mouth. Her lips were moving and I leaned closer.

'It's Charlie,' I said.

Her cheek twitched into a half-smile.

'We had a good life together, didn't we?' she whispered.

'The best,' I replied, 'I have no regrets.'

She smiled again and pressed something unseen into my palm which I knew was the Polaroid of Birgitta and Webster, and after that, she moved her hand in an uncertain manner up towards her chest. I didn't see at first what she was trying to do, but then noticed her thumb was out, and guessing her intent, I hooked her thumb into the D-ring of the pulse mortar on her chest. She patted my hand and twitched me another smile.

'Move away from her,' said Lucy and I trudged back through the snow into the lobby. Already, Porter Lloyd was fetching emergency shutters of folded canvas on bamboo while the winsomniacs all made themselves scarce, just not very quickly.

'I'm sorry if you liked her,' said Lucy, 'but Project Lazarus brings a whole new meaning to the word importance.'

Hooke picked himself up, touched a finger to his bleeding nose, shook his head and then found his weapon. He reloaded it and looked at Lucy and me in turn, then outside at Jonesy, who was still moving weakly on her back in the snow.

'Put her out of her misery,' said Lucy. 'We'd expect the same courtesy from her.'

'It's time you were blooded,' said Hooke. 'Do it yourself if you've the stomach.'

She glared at him.

'Oh, I've the stomach,' said Lucy, and took Hooke's Bambi from him.

I started to say something. A warning, I think. Lucy noticed, stopped and stared at me.

'What is it?'

I stared back at her for a moment.

'It's nothing.'

She strode across to where Jonesy's form was lying in the snow outside, then leaned over and placed the Bambi to Jonesy's head. I turned away as Jonesy detonated the pulse charge, a heavy concussion that blew the snow and tattered remnants of the curtains back into the lobby. When I looked back outside, there was only a refrozen circle of clear ice on the ground, about the size of an ornamental fountain.

'Well, *shit*,' said Hooke, following my gaze, 'that's a loss.'

'I liked her,' I said, referring to both of them, I think.

'No,' retorted Hooke, 'I was talking about my staff protection bonus.'

He then looked at me, and presumably misconstrued my lack of decisive action or intervention in any of this as tacit approval of his intentions to take me to HiberTech.

'Well now, Worthing,' he said, switching his attention to Birgitta, 'wouldn't have marked you as a harbourer. Porter, put this deadhead somewhere safe, and make sure she's looked after.'

I asked Hooke in something of a daze if we should wait until the blizzard had abated, but he told me that the sooner I was safe inside HiberTech, the better it would be for him. He walked away and I, in a confused and shocked daze, followed.

H4S radar

'... Limited-vision navigation is more than simply being blind within a snowstorm. The wind, swirling snow and lack of visual cues all conspire to disorientate the unwary traveller. Even seasoned professionals became lost, and only the advent of modern navigational aids made going out in a blizzard anything other than for the morbidly foolhardy ...'

— Basic Blind Driving Techniques for Overwinterers

I followed Hooke behind the line he had strung from his Sno-Trac and we climbed aboard, all the while buffeted by the blizzard. The wind had risen, the snowfall was heavier, and the temperature was dropping by the minute. It was dark by now and in every other circumstance, we would not be venturing out.

Hooke wound in the cable, shut the rear door then climbed past me and started up the engine. But instead of troubling with the high beams which would have been useless in the blizzard, he instead switched on the H4S and waited while the screen warmed up. The outside temperature gauge was now indicating minus twenty-four Celsius and still falling. Any porter worth his salt right now would be going Full Rods Out on the HotPots.

'Lucy killed Jonesy,' I said in a quiet voice.

'Other way round, kiddo – Jonesy killed Knapp. But the good news is we lost one each, so at least Pinky and Perky will have less to squabble over.'

'Where are you taking me?'

'To safety,' he said. 'Recent events have proved that you're not safe in Sector Twelve with Toccata kicking around. Once you're with us, we can figure out what's going on, and if you want, you can accept that job Aurora was talking about.'

'So I'm not a prisoner?'

'Goodness me, no,' he replied with perhaps not *quite* the tone of veracity in his voice he'd hoped for, 'you can leave whenever you want.'

I looked outside at the cold and the snow. Somehow leaving wasn't really an option right now.

The circular H4S screen in the centre of the Trac's panel was now glowing an unearthly shade of green; the radar returns from the surrounding topography displayed as green specks on the screen, refreshed every second by the sweep of the scanner. It would give us more than enough information to navigate, although at greatly reduced speed. Clearly visible was the Dormitorium exit road, part of the *Siddons* and, closest of all, Jonesy's Sno-Trac. I could see the shape of the vehicle less than twenty feet away on the screen, but when I looked outside there was nothing but a wall of swirling snow.

Hooke said something vague about 'returning to base with Worthing' on the shortwave, then popped the Sno-Trac into gear and we moved off. I was annoyed with myself because Jonesy had been a far better friend than I realised. She'd had answers, and so had Toccata, whom I'd also underestimated. I briefly thought of opening the rear door of the Sno-Trac and making a run for it, but going out in blizzards was like consorting with drowsies, borrowing from bondsmen or poking an already-enraged mammoth with a sharpened stick: don't. Just *don't*. But despite everything, there was a plus point: HiberTech had placed some sort of value on me. As long as I had value, I was safe. And if I was safe, then so was Birgitta. Sort of.

The odd thing was, I didn't feel anything about Lucy at all. It wasn't that our friendship meant nothing, nor did I feel that I had, by omission, led her to her death. There was just a certain numbness, as though I'd known all along that she really only looked after herself. Mother Fallopia and the Sisterhood would be distraught, but phil-osophical. People die in the Winter; it's what it's there for.

Hooke concentrated on the journey, the route clear on the glowing H4S, while outside the storm buffeted the small vehicle. In this way we passed slowly back down the drive from the *Siddons*, took a left, then after what seemed like an age, the right turn at the billboard.

'So,' I said, thinking about Hooke's reputed enthusiasm for invasive interrogation techniques, 'I heard you used to be with military intelligence.'

'Regretfully not,' he said, 'more's the pity. I would have liked to have served my country in that manner, but no. We put it about that it was me, but it was actually Aurora.'

I should have been more surprised than I was.

'Until her retirement, she was the best they had. Just went into the dreaming subject's mind and took what she wanted. I was her assistant for a time and had a go at dream incursions, but it's hard to know what's real and what isn't. I left it up to her. We all did.'

'What's on this cylinder?' I asked.

'I don't know,' he said, 'but if I were to hazard a guess, about the most impor—'

The Sno-Trac lurched to a halt. I looked up and could see nothing but blizzard through the windscreen. Hooke flicked the ranging knob on the H4S and adjusted the gain.

'What is it?' I whispered.

'There,' he said, pointing at the glowing dots on the screen. Not more than ten yards away in the middle of the road was a strong radar return. Something that shouldn't be there. I'd driven this way with Jonesy an hour before, and the road had been clear.

'Winsomniacs on the move ... but now *not* moving?' I suggested.

Hooke shook his head.

'They're lazy, not stupid.'

'Could be womads who got caught out.'

This was unlikely, but possible. Winter Nomads had been known to move in clutches of twenty or more to conserve heat, usually covered by a yurt with caribou skirts to stop the outer walkers' legs from freezing. If things got bad they just downed the yurt with them in it, lit the fire, wrapped themselves in skins and huddled.

'Possibly. Still, can't be helped.'

He lowered the snow plough and moved forward. But as he did so, the trace moved away from us. Hooke stopped, and the trace shifted on for a few yards, stopped, paused, then approached us again. A squall of wind hit the Sno-Trac and the vehicle shook. The anemometer on the roof was reading gusts of sixty miles per hour, but the whatever-it-was on the H4S seemed unaffected.

There was silence in the cab for a moment and then, with a slowness that denoted clear deliberation, the radar trace started moving towards us.

'After a scrap, are you?' said Hooke, and took the Cowpuncher off the rack behind him. He pushed four D-Cell thermalites into the magazine and racked the first into the battery chamber. The Cowpuncher was not the subtlest of weapons – it was actually intended for herding dairy mammoths rather than fighting – but was the close-quarter weapon of choice when you weren't big on subtlety and hostility was getting right in your face.

Hooke slid back the window and held the weapon outside while we both stared at the H4S screen, the trace moving ever closer. When it was at the ten-yard range, Hooke let fly.

The pressure wave momentarily turned the snow to rain and should have revealed whatever it was in the blizzard, but there was nothing to be seen except the side of the road and one half of a horse trough. Within a second the blizzard had once more closed in and by the time we looked back at the H4S screen, the radar return had gone.

'Must have been a glitch,' said Hooke.

'No,' I said, pointing at the bottom of the screen, 'I think it's behind us.'

The H4S scanner was mounted on the top of the Sno-Trac and gave a 360-degree view of the surroundings. It was now picking up a trace directly behind, and moving slowly left to right.

'I've had enough of this,' said Hooke, and drove backwards as fast as he could. I felt a thump and then a judder as we hit something, and he stopped.

'We got it, whatever it was. Bear, I think.'

'Why would a bear not hibernate? That never happens.'

'First time for everything. I'm—'

He'd stopped talking because the electrical power in the Sno-Trac had died, and with it the lights, H4S and engine. The only thing still working was the AM wireless, the dial a dull orange. It was tuned to the Winter Network, and now the engine was off we could hear the music — a crackly rendering of 'Getting to Know You'. The implication of a Rodgers and Hammerstein track wasn't lost on Hooke, and he went to switch the wireless off, but the knob broke off in his fingers.

'The plastic must have been fatigued by the cold,' I said, but if I thought this situation was in any way good, I was mistaken. The auxiliary heater had died with the power outage and Sno-Tracs were not well insulated. Without heating they'd match the exterior temperature in less than ten minutes.

'Bad time to have a breakdown,' said Hooke, checking all the trips. After cracking a light-stick, he pressed the starter and the compressed air turned the engine but without a restart, and that's when we felt the vehicle lurch violently to one side. We exchanged looks.

'It's dragging us backwards,' I said. 'You must have snagged her.'

'Not for long,' he replied, his temper up. He selected low reverse, let out the clutch and then pressed the air starter. The compressed air hissed into the engine, turned the motor over without a start but it moved the Sno-Trac regardless, jerkily, and in reverse; he was attempting to run over what was pulling us. There was another lurch, the vehicle lifted as it went over an obstruction, then fell to the ground again and stopped hard; we'd struck a wall or something. Hooke pushed the gear selector into first and pressed the starter again but there was only a faint hiss as the compressed air tank ran out — we were going nowhere.

'Stay here,' said Hooke, grabbing the Cowpuncher. 'Me and it need to get some face time.'

He opened the rear door and the cab was suddenly full of wind-borne snow.

'Safety line,' I reminded him, shivering with the sudden cold, and he nodded, grabbed the safety cable, clipped it to his belt and dropped out of the cab and into the blizzard.

Once the door had shut, the snowflakes that had blown into the cab settled and turned to water in the warm interior. The ratchet on the steel safety reel began to pay out, matching Hooke's cautious walking speed. After about a half-minute it stopped. And then, softened by the storm, there was a distant thud – Hooke had deployed the Cowpuncher. A second or two later and there was a howl of noise as the safety reel paid out at a furious rate. Within ten seconds the entire fifty-yard length had gone and the reel came to a juddering halt. The tensioned wire bit into the drum and door surround, bent the mounting spindle and jerked the entire Sno-Trac sideways. The cable stayed taut for a second, then went slack.

I sat there for a few minutes with the wind buffeting the Sno-Trac, the temperature falling. My breath was now showing white in the chill air, and the moisture in the cab was beginning to freeze on the inside of the windscreen and instrument panel. This was not good news: in the rush to leave the *Siddons*, I'd left my heavy coat, gloves, hat and overboots behind. If I didn't do anything, in a couple of hours I'd be solid until the thaw.

Just as I was trying to figure out my best option the lights flickered back on as electrical power returned. I jumped into the driver's seat, checked the Trac was in neutral, turned on the ignition and then pushed the air starter. Nothing. The H4S had powered up again, and the creature was visible only as a whispering collection of greenish spots on the screen in front of me, reinforced by every sweep of the scanner. The trace moved, took a pace forward, then stopped, and by the time the scanner came around again, it had gone. There was just me, the blizzard and an immobile Sno-Trac.

I shivered again and realised that notwithstanding the apparent safety of the vehicle, I needed to make a move now while I was still warm enough to do so. I rummaged in the back of the Sno-Trac and found a pair of socks, a flat cap and a spare woncho. I put the woncho over my head and pulled the hat down as far as I could, then slipped the woolly socks on my hands to use as gloves. I took the emergency lantern from its place on the bulkhead, pushed in a thermalite and switched it on. There was a soft fizz and the cabin was flooded by a warm orange glow. I looked at the temperature gauge and wind speed, and figured I had perhaps ten minutes to find shelter or I'd be next in line for a multiple finger transplant. Leave it twenty minutes and I could upgrade the loss to that of a foot, nose or hand. Half an hour and I'd probably be dead.

I popped the door release and was once more buffeted by the wind and the snow. I lowered myself to the ground, the wind tugging at the woncho and cutting into my cheeks, while small flakes of snow sneaked through my clothing to thaw on my warm flesh. The ground yielded soft underfoot; there was about eighteen inches of snow. The lantern made little headway in the blizzard so in the absence of any better ideas I wrapped Hooke's safety cable in the crook of my arm and followed it away from the Sno-Trac. Now in the full force of the wind, I crouched lower as I walked to minimise the effect of the gale, which at every step threatened to push me off balance.

I followed the cable for thirty or so paces and was relieved to see a flicker of light, but it turned out to be only a street lamp, the small gas flame battling to stay alight. Another minute of slow trudge took me to the end of the cable, which was attached to Hooke's over-trousers, which were neatly folded in a pile along with everything else he'd been wearing, his boots placed on top. Hooke was close by, his head twisted around to the left and a lump showing through on his neck where it had been broken. He wore a look of surprise on his rapidly chilling features, his eyes and mouth wide open. Like Lucky Ned, his little finger was missing. It was the Gronk, and she was taking souvenirs.

I put his parka over my woncho, then pulled on his gloves and hat. I turned and my foot knocked against Hooke's Cowpuncher, so I picked it up and racked a fresh thermalite into the battery chamber. I paused for a moment, and felt a tug on the safety wire, as though someone was testing the line. And then, with a sudden jerk, the cable was pulled violently from my hand.

I dropped to my knees, and while scrabbling with increasing desperation in the snow for the safety line, I heard a child's laughter through the swirling whiteness. It had taken Hooke but was still hungry for the unworthy and I, having done nothing to prevent my friend Lucy's demise and with the loss of Logan and twenty-four winsomniacs still weighing on my conscience, had the strongest conviction that I would be next. I very slowly took Laura's camera out of my bag and held it on top of the Cowpuncher. I paused, waited until I heard another giggle, then fired and pressed the shutter a moment later.

A momentary funnel of wet air opened in the snowstorm, briefly illuminated by the camera flash. I could see all the way to the trees behind a fence swaying in the wind and part of a parked car, and in the foreground I could see, or thought I could see, a *beach ball*. I think I yelled, then racked the fourth and final thermalite into the chamber, rewound the camera and fired again. This time there was nothing extra to be seen and the snowstorm once more closed in upon me. I knelt there, taking in great gulping mouthfuls of air, trying to relax, trying to stop my heart from pounding. Despite the cold I could feel sweat prickling down my back even though my lips, cheeks, fingers and feet were beginning to feel the hard nip of impending frostbite. I dropped the now-empty Cowpuncher and attempted to find the cable once more but my hands were numb, and scrabbling in the snow gave them less feeling, not more.

There was nothing to do but walk in any direction and hope to find a wall with a fixed line on it. I stumbled forward for ten or so paces but didn't find a wall – I found a door. Old, Gothic, belted steel on oak. I wiped the snow off the signboard with my forearm.

It was the *Geraldus Cambrensis*.

The Geraldus Cambrensis

'... Night lights were these days low-consumption LEDs, but many porters clung to the obsolete but more satisfying bioluminescent tubes. The light would often move from greeny-blue to yellowy-orange depending on the plankton's mood and temperature. They needed fortnightly feeding and this could be time-consuming in a large Dormitorium, but many porters thought it worth the extra work ...'

– *The Elegant Simplicity of WinterTech*, by Emma Llewelyn WiEng

The lock turned easily against my Omnikey and I pushed open the heavy door, squeezed inside and then heaved it shut. As the latch clicked, the storm dramatically subsided to a humming rush of wind. I opened the inner door and stepped inside. I'd expected the interior of the *Cambrensis* to be cold and dark, as everyone had told me the HotPot had been shut down, but it hadn't and it wasn't. The temperature inside was a healthy eighteen degrees – the internal heating system was working perfectly. I pulled the socks from my hands, kicked off my shoes and sank both hands and feet into the tepid water of the defrost basin. I could feel my extremities ache as the blood returned to circulation, and within twenty minutes the tingling had stopped and I knew I was in the clear. I put on some dry socks and a pair of house slippers, then held up my lantern so I could see.

I'd seen the lobby before. It was the one that I'd seen in my dream, when I was bouncing around in Webster's Dreamstate. Stairs behind, the remains of sofas on the lobby floor, central reception desk. I moved forward and noted that empty food cans and wooden crates were lying around. Probably in the rush to abandon the place, although now, given the safe temperature in here, I couldn't see *why* it had been abandoned. I had a sudden and very worrying thought that there might be a radiation leak that no one was 'fessing up to, but the large Geiger counter behind the reception desk was indicating a level that, while broadly safe, would probably require that residents were Winter only and above the age of thirty, just in case.

The house lights were off and, although gloomy, it was not pitch black. Someone had taken the time to feed the plankton in the tubes and a thin blue-green bioluminescence suffused the interior of the building.

There was a noise from upstairs. Like something being knocked over.

'Hello?'

My voice sounded timid in the silence, and the dryness of my throat caught me off guard. I was more on edge than I'd imagined. No one answered and I figured it was probably hiburnal rodents. From the smell in the air, there might be a long-dead resident or two for them to feed on. I took the stairs cautiously to the first floor, as I had done in my dream – and experienced the most curious feeling of double déjà vu. It all looked extremely familiar, as if I'd walked this way many times before. The corridor, the decor, the heavy woven wall-hangings, *everything*.

I heard another noise, this time behind me, the soft drag-clump-drag-clump of a nightwalker.

'Hello?'

In reply there was a faint whisper and the creak of a board above my head. I held my breath as a figure entered the periphery of the soft glow from my lantern, perhaps ten yards down the corridor. It was the nightwalker Eddie Tangiers, dressed in light blue overalls, shambling towards me. Jonesy hadn't retired him at all. Annoyingly, this was also the precise moment the battery in my lantern ran out and plunged me into darkness. With my eyes not yet accustomed to the meagre glow afforded by the tubes, I was effectively blind. I quickly fitted a second thermalite but was not overly worried. The drag-clump-drag-clump had not altered pace.

When the light began to illuminate the scene I almost yelled as I found myself face to face with *another* nightwalker whom I'd not heard approach. She was staring at me with a single milky eye and her face was old and lined, with high arched eyebrows and a large mouth. But it was the fruit hat, now dented and worn and missing most of its bananas that gave her away.

'Chicka-chicka-boom-chic,' she said, her voice a husky monotone.

'I've seen you looking better, Ms Miranda,' I replied.

She seemed to gaze at me for some moments, then moved her hips left and right, and shambled off to follow the first nightwalker along the corridor and back beyond the periphery of the light. She and Tangiers wore matching overalls and were either not hungry or had not yet discovered cannibalism.

'When I love, I love,' came Miranda's voice from the darkness, then silence. I moved off down the corridor, now guided by nothing more than the memory of Webster's dream. I found room 106, paused, then pushed open the door. The room had the same pine linenfold panelling, the same single bay window with a fire escape, the same large chimney. On the wall was a lighter patch of faded wallpaper in the shape of a star – the place where the wall-clock had once hung, again, as in Charles' dream.

I felt hot and sweaty and confused and tired but half suspected, despite all the evidence to the contrary, that all of this could still be explained as my memory unfolding simultaneously as I walked, like a locomotive laying its own tracks. But there was one test I could perform, something that would decide once and for all if I was dreaming my own dreams, or dreaming someone else's.

I stepped forward and reached up the chimney as far as I could. At first I felt nothing, but then the lip of a ledge, and inside that my fingers touched something that yielded, and after some squirming and stretching – Webster had been almost four inches taller than me – I removed a cylindrical cardboard tube that was dusty and stained. I opened the tube and pulled out a shiny blue-black hard wax cylinder, the fine grooves shining in the light. I stared at it for a moment, not knowing what to think. Happy or sad? Didn't know. All I knew was that it had been placed there by Charles Webster, was valuable enough for HiberTech to destroy six people for, and Don Hector, through Charles, had been trying to get it out to Kiki and RealSleep for at least three years.

I replaced it in the tube and, my curiosity aroused, decided that it would be best to play it back and see what was on it. I needed a phonograph so retraced my steps, and passed the nightwalker Glitzy Tiara on the landing as I headed towards the porter's lodge on the lower ground floor. There were more nightwalkers in the lobby and I moved cautiously amongst them. Some of them whispered words and phrases, one of them was constantly shuffling a pack of cards, and a fifth was holding two Rubik's cubes: with her left hand she scrambled, with her right hand she solved. The crates and cans of food littered around also indicated to me that they were being harboured, almost certainly by Jonesy and Toccata, and on an industrial scale. Jonesy had indicated that she, too, thought nightwalkers were still sentient and it was likely Toccata thought the same. Despite my feeling vindicated, the notion flew in the face of conventional medical and scientific thought. Rigorous tests had been run and the conclusion had been unanimous: nightwalkers were irrecoverably brain dead. But if their consciousness *was* complete yet displaced to somewhere impossible to detect, and HiberTech knew about it, then the current nightwalker policy of redeployment, retirement and then being parted out for spares would be murder. No, wait, considerably *worse* than murder.

As I was passing the reception desk my lantern went out a second time. I had one thermalite remaining so instead simply waited for my eyes to become accustomed to the darkness.

The cylinder was key. RealSleep desperately wanted it, and HiberTech would do anything to stop them getting it. I started to see vague shapes as my eyes became used to the darkness, and while they did I could hear the nightwalkers walking past me in the gloom, whispering as they did so, which is a truly unnerving experience. Once, one brushed against me and nibbled me on the arm, and I suddenly wondered how often anyone fed them, and how long they would have to *not* be fed before they started to feed on one another – or me. The answer, I soon realised, was right about now. I hadn't fully been aware as my eyes became used to the dim light, but they had grouped around me in the semi-dark and I felt their hands touching me. I tried to push them away but as soon as I moved past two and wrested myself from the grip of a third, another three or four pairs of hands grabbed me and I felt a sharp pain as one of them bit me hard on the side of my head. I yelped, but the noise only invigorated them, and I felt them grip me tighter. I gave up on the soft approach and struggled, shoved and punched, but their numbers were too great and I was pushed to the ground, the nightwalkers murmuring and groaning in an increasingly aggressive fashion in the dim greeny-blue light. This was, I knew, how it worked. An attack began slowly, then rapidly escalated in aggression to a frenzy. I felt several bony fingers try to lift up my shirt to get at my stomach. I was beyond shouting, and just kicked and struggled as hard as I could, the sound of their hungry murmurings growing in my ears. I had come so far, and ultimately – for nothing. The cylinder, worthless to the nightwalkers, would pass to whoever stumbled upon my remains.

Uselessly, I pulled my shoulder bag closer to me and closed into a ball, then had an idea. I ignored the bites and scratches, reached into my bag and pulled out Laura's camera. I pointed it in their general direction and pressed the shutter.

The flashbulb fired, and in the stagnant gloom of the lobby it was as though a door had momentarily been opened into the Summer. The effect was impressive, and instantaneous. The nightwalkers paused, their minds momentarily scrambled. This wasn't a trick I'd learned in the Academy, this was a trick I'd learned from Lloyd, two days before.

The nightwalker's confusion was short lived but long enough for me to wind on the camera and fire the flash again. In the bright white light I could see their bewildered expressions and wasted no time in pushing my way through the tangle of confused bodies. I ran down the steps to the lower ground floor, found the porter's lodge and slammed and bolted the door after me, my heart racing, my hands shaking.

Every hour I was experiencing something new, every hour I was wishing I wasn't.

The cylinder

'… The wax cylinder was the first true sound recording and playback device, and had survived over a hundred years owing to its ubiquity and the fact that it did not require electricity to operate. Given that academics often stayed up in the Winter to finish their work, it was not unusual for a secretary to be confronted with up to a hundred cylinders waiting for them at Springrise, all to be transcribed and then skimmed for reuse …'

— *The Elegant Simplicity of WinterTech*, by Emma Llewelyn WiEng

I clicked on the emergency light and went straight through to the bathroom, rummaged through the medicine cabinet for some iodine and then dabbed it on the bite marks, of which I had many. I'd been lucky that their hunger had come on relatively slowly. If they'd attacked me en masse as I'd walked in, I'd have been too tired and cold to defend myself. Whilst I self-administered as best as I could, I heard unpleasant noises from the lobby, where it sounded as if their hunger had been appeased on one of their own. If they'd eaten the weighty Eddie Tangiers, they'd be quiet maybe eight hours. Glitzy Tiara, ninety minutes, tops.

Still sore but having found no bites to be life-threatening, I walked back into the porter's living area and looked around. The walls were covered with bookshelves and display cases that contained numerous specimens from the animal and plant kingdoms. Porters were never simply glorified hoteliers, they were generally people who welcomed a monk-like existence, and spent their spare hours on contemplation or studies.

There was a salt-water hippo skull hanging from the ceiling and a baby glyptodon skeleton in the process of being articulated. There was also a Dictaphone, all brass and rosewood with a large copper horn for playback. I switched on the desk lamp, wound the clockwork motor fully and slipped the cylinder onto the machine. I flicked the lever, waited for the cylinder to spin up and then gently placed the needle on the groove, half expecting to hear Don Hector's voice, and a long explanation of what he'd found, and every single one of my questions answered.

I didn't. Not even a tiniest bit. It was Don Hector's voice all right, but what he was saying made no sense at all – a long and seemingly random collection of apparently unconnected words interspersed with numbers and Greek letters, all spoken in an even monotone. It lasted five and three quarter minutes and was, I presumed, some kind of code. It was only after the discordant collection of words had faded that I heard *another* noise – a gentle murmur from outside. I walked over and quietly opened the door a couple of inches. As I'd suspected, there was a nightwalker outside. It was Rubik's Cube Girl, but she'd stopped doing the puzzle and was standing stock still in apparent Torpor. She wasn't the only one. They were all there, perhaps thirty or so, filling the entire corridor. All standing still, unblinking, tightly yet equally spaced from each other, all missing a thumb. I was about to close the door when the nightwalker blinked, and that was unusual. Firstly because nightwalkers in Torpor don't blink, and secondly, because they'd *all* blinked – in unison.

I cautiously reached my arm out through the door and pushed her hard on the sternum. She took a step back to steady herself. If she'd been in Torpor, she would have fallen over, knocked the next and they'd all be over, one after the other in a comedy fashion, like skittles. But the thing was, they *all* took a steadying step backwards.

'Why are you doing this?' I asked, and they whispered back in unison, like a lispy echo: *'Why are you doing this?'*

'What's going on?'

'What's going on?'

'Simple Simone says,' I said slowly, '"Put your hands on your head".'

They all obediently put their hands on their head.

'Simple Simone says: "Put your hands by your side".'

They all put them down again.

'Stand on one leg.'

They ignored the order. Simple Simone hadn't told them to, see. I smiled, for the first time in a while.

'Simple Simone says: "Tell me your name".'

They answered as one, but each with their own. I only heard a few in the mass of different words. Rubik's Cube Girl was Rebecca and Glitzy Tiara, positioned off to her right, was Betty, who now had tears rolling softly down her cheeks.

'How are you feeling right now?' I asked, and there followed a mix of responses – frustrated, trapped, lost, adrift.

They stood there for a moment longer, but then the magic faded, and they moved out of the trance and drifted off down the corridor, as vacant as ever. I had no idea of the meaning of Don Hector's words on the cylinder, but whatever it was, it had an effect on nightwalkers. The recording might not retrieve the nightwalkers, but it was a step in the right direction.

I went into the kitchenette, mixed some muesli with long-life milk and a large spoonful of peanut butter and walked to the window. I could hear the wind whipping around the building outside, rattling the shutters and trying to find a chink in the building's Winter armour. I needed a plan, and after some careful thought figured one out: I'd go and see Hugo Foulnap, who was on duty at the museum. The reason was simple. Aurora had suggested he was Campaign for Real Sleep and if this was true and he was hiding as Danny Pockets in Sector Twelve, then I could make two assumptions: that there was an ongoing RealSleep operation and he, Jonesy, Toccata and the shambling occupants of the *Cambrensis* were a big part of it.

I found some fresh warm clothes in the wardrobe, replaced the flashcube on the camera so I was armed with more flashes, then cautiously opened the apartment door and peered out into the empty corridor. I crept back upstairs without being molested, found a heavy parka, pulled on some snow boots, shoved the camera in my bag and consulted the fixed line schematic that was screwed to the wall between the inner and outer doors of the *Cambrensis*. The museum was on the other side of the road and about a quarter of a mile away. In daylight and without weather, about a five-minute stroll. I would have to do it in less than thirty and not lose my way if I wanted to keep all my fingers and toes.

I took a deep breath, then opened the outer door.

If I thought the weather had been bad before it was twice as bad now. The icy wind was howling past the door, the view a mass of angry swirling snow. I fired up the lamp with the last thermalite, then clipped myself onto the fixed line. I paused to tell myself that this was the best course of action, Gronk or no Gronk, and set off into the storm. My lantern afforded me really only moral support but by staying close to the wall I could minimise the buffeting from the wind, and although the snow was now almost three feet deep in drifts and the going slow, I made progress. Within ten minutes I was at the bridge, from where I would have to cross the road without the fixed line. I was less cautious than perhaps I should have been; after leaving the line and taking two paces towards the opposite parapet, the full force of the wind lifted me off my feet.

I think I remember tumbling for a while, then being wedged head first in the snow. To make matters worse the snow guard inside my parka then ripped, and the wind-blown snow rushed up inside the back of my coat and wrapped itself around my neck and chest. I momentarily stopped breathing with the sudden chill and could actually feel myself begin to lose core temperature. It started with an uncontrollable shiver, then a chattering of teeth, then a sense of calm mixed with resignation, loss and waste. I wanted badly to dream, to be back on the beach in the Gower, beneath the orange-and-red parasol of spectacular size and splendour with Birgitta being Birgitta and me being Charles. But I couldn't, and slowly, with an annoying drab certainty, I felt myself slipping away.

But I didn't die. Not yet.

Night in the museum

'... The Minister for Culture had to threaten to slit his own throat on the steps of Parliament House before the Regional Antiquities Repatriation Act was made into law. Simply put, it allowed for centralised collections to be returned to the region, village or hamlet where they were discovered. It was localisation at its very best ...'

– *Museums Quarterly*, November 1973 edition

'What kind of dopey halfwit goes out in weather like this?'

It was Hugo Foulnap. He was staring at me with the same sort of look you afford someone who has been repeatedly told not to play with lighter fuel and matches, and who has just set themselves on fire. He was out of the shock-suit – probably because invasion during the storm was unlikely – and was staring at me with a sense of curious fascination. We were in a white-tiled warmroom, presumably within the museum, although according to my last memory I had yet to even get to the wrought-iron gates. I was completely naked and immersed in a roll-top bath filled with warm water.

'This kind of dopey halfwit,' I said, pointing at myself.

'Run into a spot of bother?'

He indicated my body, which was covered with all the bruises, scratches and tooth marks I'd gained when I was nearly nightwalker lunch, all now stained by dabs of iodine on my pale wintercoat, which made me look a little like a purple Dalmatian. I pointed to the bite mark on my face.

'See that?'

'Yes.'

'Carmen Miranda.'

'Is that how she does autographs these days?'

'Pretty much. She was at the *Cambrensis*.'

'Ah,' said Foulnap. 'Cold in there? Empty and shuttered?'

'No,' I said after a pause, 'no, it's not.'

We stared at one another for a while.

'How are the toes?' he asked, and I stared at them uneasily. They had a marzipanish look to them and were hurting badly, so I thought probably not that good.

'I may lose one or two.'

'To match your finger?'

I looked down and noticed for the first time that my right pinky had vanished below the knuckle, the wound hardly bleeding and the exposed fleshy part looking like a cut of uncooked silverside. I felt underwhelmed as I stared at the loss – it was as though this were somehow inevitable. I thought for a moment. Outside, in the snowdrift, upside down, as I was slipping away, I'd heard the laugh of a young girl.

'Where did you find me?'

'I heard a thump on the outer door,' replied Foulnap, 'and there you were. Your finger must have caught in the wire when you fell. They come off surprisingly easily in the cold.'

'It was the Gronk.'

'Yes; assisted by unicorns, the tooth fairy and the ghost of Owain Glyndwr, I shouldn't wonder. Here.'

He handed me a large mug of tea laced with condensed milk and Nutella.[60] If you'd offered it to me in the Summer I'd only have drunk it as a dare, but right here and now I thought it was the best thing I'd ever tasted. Within half an hour I was warm enough to climb out of the bath and get dressed.

'The Open Network has been chattering constantly for the past hour,' said Foulnap, hanging up my damp towel. 'We heard you'd been harbouring Birgitta, Jonesy was bumped off by a mystery girl from HiberTech who was then herself killed – and you'd been taken off to HiberTech. Is that anywhere near correct?'

I told him yes – and that Hooke had been taken by the Gronk on the way to HiberTech while I'd sought refuge out in the *Cambrensis*.

60. Ferrero Rocher tried to market this drink in the Summer as *Teatella*, but it never caught on.

'A lot of Gronk this evening. Who was the mystery girl from HiberTech?'

'An old friend of mine from the Pool back in Swansea. She was on one of HiberTech's Fast Track Management schemes. It didn't work out for her.'

'They rarely do.'

Foulnap stared at me for a moment, deep in thought.

'Why did you leave the *Cambrensis* in this weather, Worthing?'

'To come and see you.'

'For?'

'Answers.'

He stared at me again, trying to make up his mind.

'That's the hardest thing about all this,' he said, 'knowing who to trust. Can I trust you?'

'Can I trust *you*?' I said in return. 'When we met in Cardiff you were attempting to farm a nightwalker.'

'Were we? Were we really?'

'Yes, I ...'

My voice trailed off. I'd been so convinced of that particular narrative I'd never for one moment stopped to reappraise the situation. About Mrs Tiffen, and Foulnap not wanting her to go to HiberTech, then Jack Logan cajoling and threatening me to simply drop it.

They weren't going to farm Mrs Tiffen at all – they were trying to *protect* her. My legs suddenly felt so weak I had to sit on a handy chair. Logan had told me to forget all about Mrs Tiffen, and I, the naive fool that I was, drunk on good intentions, ignored him – and he died. Not at my hand, but certainly because of my intransigent stupidity. I closed my eyes and felt the heavy burden of guilt fall across my shoulders. I had a feeling it wouldn't lift for a long time, if at all. The Gronk had been circling me for a while now. If Ned Farnesworth and Hooke were the starter and main, I was to be the dessert. Perhaps she'd spared me so I could discover my unworthiness all on my own, and self-season my soul with the tangy taste of guilt. Perhaps the Gronk took my finger to mark me out, like choosing lobsters in a tank. Perhaps that's what Gronks do.

'Was Logan going to kill me?' I asked. 'When he was walking me out of the *John Edward Jones* back in the fire valleys?'

Foulnap sat down next to me and laid a hand on my arm.

'He would've explained it all to you on the train to Sector Twelve, and trusted you'd come across. No one who figures out HiberTech's criminality ever stays long with the status quo. It was just our dumb luck that Aurora chanced along when she did.'

'So Logan was RealSleep?'

'More than that – he was Kiki.'

'*Shit.*'

'It's annoying and tragic and a waste,' said Foulnap once I'd digested this particular nugget, 'but you don't come out so bad in all of this – you were simply trying to do the right thing with an incomplete understanding of the situation.'

'That's very generous, but I should have listened to you both.'

'Agreed,' said Foulnap, 'but perhaps we should have seen you for what you were earlier, and brought you into our confidence. We just don't know who to trust.'

I ran my fingers through my hair. Sector Twelve had lived up to its reputation.

'So,' I said finally, 'what would you have done with Mrs Tiffen if not farmed her?'

'The more complex tricks they can do, the less complete the neural collapse, the easier it might be to effect a retrieval. We've not managed it yet, but it can be done.'

I asked him how he knew and he showed me his left thumb, or rather, he didn't show me his thumb – it was missing.

'For five weeks I was a nightwalker,' he said. 'I returned because I'd been dumped, but against HiberTech's strict policy, I'd not been thumped. I woke up with a spade of lime over me in the landfill. I think we live inside our deepest memories when hibernating, with cyclical returns to the upper Dreamstate to maintain a connection with the mind. Morphenox suppresses this link and, on rare occasions, damages it so severely that it locks the victim in the lower Dreamstate. When I was a nightwalker the only thing I really felt were the *dreams*. Loud, expansive, overpowering, like I was trapped in deep memory loops – with the real world appearing to me as vague and nebulous as long-forgotten dreams in the real world. I didn't remember anything too specific as regards what I'd been doing when a deadhead, but I have a pretty good idea: I passed a human tooth two days after waking, complete with a gold filling. First time I'd ever turned a profit taking a dump.'

He paused.

'But that's enough about me. Why do HiberTech want you so badly?'

He'd trusted me, so it was time for me to trust him.

'Because I've been Active Control first person – both Don Hector *and* Webster – and I know where the cylinder is.'

Foulnap raised an eyebrow.

'You're shitting me?'

'No, I am certainly not shitting you.'

'Then you'd better come with me.'

We walked out of the warmroom and down the corridor towards the central atrium, where the Airwitzer was for the moment abandoned. I could hear the storm rattling the heavy shutters, and a low moan was emanating from where the wind blew across the downpipes on the roof. We took the main stairs upwards, then a left on the top corridor towards a sign marked 'conservation'. Foulnap stopped at a door, rapped twice, muttered the password *'Fresh Water Walrus'* and I heard a draw-bolt pulled back.

I recognised the man who opened the door. It was the medic from back at the *John Edward Jones* in Merthyr, the one who wore scrubs and smelled of antiseptic and whose aunt wasn't his aunt. He looked at me and raised an eyebrow.

'Charlie is a friendly,' said Foulnap.

'Yeah? Last time we met a good man died.'

'A misunderstanding. Charlie's been Active Control first person.'

'You're kidding?' said the medic, his manner abruptly changing from suspicion to curiosity.

'Nope,' said Foulnap. 'Don Hector *and* Webster.'

The medic stepped closer and peered at me intently.

'We don't know anyone who's been Active Control and is still sane,' he said. 'What was it like?'

'More real than real,' I said, 'all the senses ramped up to eleven. I can see why the dreamers want it. Better than life. Or at least, better than *their* life.'

The medic mouthed 'wow' and stared at me some more.

'This is Dr Theophilus Gwynne,' said Foulnap, stepping in. 'He was, until his tragic, untimely and very faked death three years ago, a junior member of HiberTech's Sleep Sciences Division.'

'Then you know all about Project Lazarus?'

'Actually, I was *very* junior,' he admitted, 'logging data mostly, equipment maintenance, tea, bit of laundry, cooking, that sort of thing.'

'We found out about Project Lazarus yesterday,' said Foulnap, 'and quite by chance.'

'So, what is it?'

'One moment,' said Dr Gwynne, making safe a booby-trap detonation device on the door that was attached to not a single Golgotha but *two*. Unlike Fodder's, these looked to be live.

Dr Gwynne and I Winter embraced; he smelled of burned-out electric motors, pear drops and solder. Once we'd parted I took a step inside the room and looked around. The ceiling was ornate plaster, and the wooden panelling and glass-fronted cabinets suggested use as a library in days gone by. There was a fireplace at one end, long disused, and most of the floor space was taken up by machines liberally festooned with blinking lights, knobs, dials and switches. Sitting on a bar stool in the middle of it all was a nightwalker doing probably the most complex tricks I'd ever seen with a yo-yo. She looked vacant enough, but was connected to the machine by a series of wires glued to pads on her head. When she yo-yoed, the trace on the oscilloscopes jumped and danced.

'That's Wendy,' said Dr Gwynne, indicating the nightwalker. 'She's helping me with my nightwalker retrieval experiments.'

'How's that working out?' I asked.

'Somewhere between frustratingly slow and fiendishly elusive,' replied Dr Gwynne. 'Have you met Josh? He's a recent acquisition.'

I turned, and sitting on a wicker chair was the receptionist from HiberTech. He was reading a book and chuckling occasionally.

'Josh defected from HiberTech,' said Foulnap, 'and brought Wendy with him. Coffee?'

I said that would be very welcome and he told me to have a look around, so I walked over to Josh.

'Oh, hullo, Worthing,' he said in a cheery manner. 'How are things?'

'Outlook stormy with a chance of scattered death moving in randomly from all points of the compass.'

He laughed, told me that weather forecasts were often wrong, and showed me a pencil that was sharpened on both ends.

'I call it the "Twincil",' he said. 'Always a problem breaking the lead, right? Now all you have to do is turn it around and – bam – keep on drawing.'

'It's kind of useful having an eraser on the other end.'

'I thought of that too,' he said, producing a pencil with the eraser on both ends. 'This is the "Biraser". You can make twice as many mistakes, and unlike a conventional pencil, it never gets any shorter. What do you think?'

'Wouldn't it be easier to just have two pencils?'

He stared at me for a moment, blinked twice then handed me an after-dinner mint.

'What do you make of this?'

'It tastes just like an After Eight mint,' I said, suddenly realising how hungry I was.

'To the casual observer, yes. But in reality it's an after-dinner mint mint – to eat *after* you've eaten your after-dinner mint. I call it an After After Eight.'

'Do people like after-dinner mints that much?'

Josh looked thoughtful for a moment, then said quite simply: 'I do.'

'Here,' said Foulnap, handing me a coffee and a plate of shortbread, which I ate hungrily.

'So, Josh,' said Dr Gwynne, 'tell Worthing here what you told us.'

'Not much to tell,' he said, 'and I don't know the precise details, only that Project Lazarus aims to have everyone on Morphenox.'

'That's been a stated aim for over thirty years,' I said.

'This goes one step beyond. Morphenox-B will be marketed as a slightly cheaper alternative, but carries a higher-than-normal propensity for sleepers to become nightwalkers. Quite aside from the greatly increased revenue on drug sales, there will be a large resource ready to be redeployed and rented out as a hugely profitable and uncomplaining workforce. Nightwalkers will be collected directly from Dormitoria and taken straight to redeployment centres so there can be no chance the truth will come out.'

We were all silent for a few moments.

'How do you know this?' I asked.

'Receptionists know *everything*,' he said simply, 'and d'you know, all of this is so fundamentally *wrong*. I have little expectation that I'll live to see the Spring, but if I can help bring down Greedy Pharma, I'm *so* going to take it.'

He fell silent, then suddenly piped up: 'Might this make me RealSleep's Employee of the Week? I've been the EOTW for sixty-two weeks running, and it would be a shame to break my record.'

Foulnap said he would see to it personally, and we left Josh to his somewhat eclectic thought processes. We settled in another part of the room, while outside the wind blew around the museum's rotunda with low moans, whistles and shrieks.

'So,' said Foulnap once we were seated, 'I know you don't have the cylinder on you, so we need to formulate a plan to retrieve it. But first: tell us your story from the very beginning.'

'I'm not sure I know where to start.'

'You'll know the beginning easily enough; it's when it all started going weird.'

Night in the museum 2

'... The invention of the Somnagraph by Thomas Edison would not have been possible without the Somnaécritaphone, invented thirty years previously by M. Gaston Tournesol. With Tournesol's device, the content of a dream could be logged as a series of dots on a sheet of carbon-coated tin. Tournesol was working on a method to read the dots when he died in the harsh Winter of 1898 ...'

– *Early Dream Tech*, by Emma Llewelyn WiEng

It took me almost forty minutes to tell my story, and throughout that time Foulnap and Dr Gwynne stared at me, nodding quietly. When I'd finished they paused for a while, gathering their thoughts.

'Tell us what happened when you played the cylinder again?' asked Dr Gwynne.

I repeated how I had seen the gathered nightwalkers' partial retrieval in the *Cambrensis*. The doctor was fascinated by the notion that retrieval could be accomplished by a collection of well-chosen words.

'Did they rhyme?' he asked.

'They *sort* of rhymed,' I said.

'Then I think chosen not for their actual meaning,' said Dr Gwynne, 'but for their rhythm, cadence and associative function – a subconscious therapy. It explains the partial recovery you observed.'

'We might need a Somnagraph to effect a full retrieval,' said Foulnap.

'Wait, wait, wait,' I said, now realising that Shamanic Bob and his wild conspiracy theories didn't actually go far *enough*. 'Why were my dreams identical each time?'

'The Somnagraph is a device that records dreams on a wax cylinder,' said Dr Gwynne, 'and was originally devised by Thomas Edison in an odd collaboration with Sigmund Freud. Edison famously recorded a woman dreaming of a cat in 1904 and then played it back to a drowsy audience of politicians and the military, who were astounded. As you saw, it's not just the pictures and sounds but an entire sense of being. You take on their character, remember their memories, feel their passion, their hate, their fears, their frustration.'

'I felt the love Webster felt for Birgitta,' I said slowly, 'and through him, the love that she felt back.'

'Do you still feel it?'

'Yes.'

'And that's the problem with continued overexposure to Somnagraph-induced dreams: the emotional memories have a way of flooding into your waking hours, causing reality confusion until you have no idea what's real and what isn't.'

'Moody, Roscoe and Suzy Watson,' I murmured. 'They had it night after night. And then nearly me.'

'Bingo. People go insane in the Winter, and yelling about hands and Mrs Nesbit is random enough to not raise any suspicions. HiberTech recorded Don Hector's dreams and then used the residents of the ninth floor of the *Siddons* as disposable assets to try and figure out what he did with the cylinder. And by using Dream Avatar technology in the form of Mrs Nesbit to communicate, there was no risk to HiberTech, and every risk to the subject.'

'But all without much luck, right?'

'Right,' said Foulnap, 'because Don Hector trained himself to dream only the one dream – and spiked it with a nightmare to dissuade anyone from poking around.'

'The hands.'

'Yes, the hands.'

'From the scraps of information available to us,' continued Foulnap, 'we think Don Hector discovered an *improved* Morphenox-C that didn't generate nightwalkers at all. By then, the redeployment and transplant industries were booming, and HiberTech management really weren't interested. We figure he decided to go public with what he knew, recorded nightwalker extraction protocols on the cylinder and was trying to get it out until his death – and beyond.'

We all fell silent. If Don Hector had tried and failed to make all this public, I wasn't sure how any of us lesser mortals could do it.

'So HiberTech beamed Don Hector's dream into our heads to try and find out what he did with the cylinder?'

'That's about the tune of it.'

'So where did the Birgitta dream come from?'

They scratched their heads.

'We're really not sure. Dream induction is more of an art than a science. Even Thomas Edison was a little confused by it – and it was also professionally devastating for him, as he couldn't find a useful way to bring the invention to market.'

'One last question,' I said, my head beginning to spin. 'Where does Dreamspace come into all of this?'

Foulnap and Dr Gwynne exchanged looks, but it was Foulnap who spoke.

'To initiate a Dreamspace, you must record a target dream on a Somnagraph and then play it back simultaneously to as many people as you wish to interact within that target dream.'

'It would be like finding yourself in the Mrs Nesbit tearoom scene during the movie *Brief Encounter*,' said Dr Gwynne, 'and while Trevor Howard and Celia Johnson bang on about how frightfully, frightfully hard it is to justify their feelings for one another, you interact with all the other Dreamspacers in the tearooms. But Howard and Johnson's dialogue carries on unchanging in a continuous repetitive loop.'[61]

'Shamanic Bob said the problem was about knowing what was real and what wasn't,' I said, 'because when you merge the real and the fantasy, you can never quite define the boundaries.'

'That's true,' said Dr Gwynne, 'but Dreamspace was also highly dangerous. Psychotic episodes, reality distortions, paranoia, death.'

'Far too dangerous for civilians,' added Foulnap, 'but the risk wasn't an issue when used militarily. If detainees suffered a devastating neural collapse after interrogation, the official line was "so what?"'

---

61. A cylinder only has enough capacity for eight minutes of dreams, but you can double the duration if you run the Somnagraph at half-speed – but the detail is never as fine, and the voices sound muffled.

'Hooke told me that it was Aurora who was the expert at in-dream interrogation, but was keeping it quiet.'

'Too true,' said Foulnap. 'She likes to pretend she's the moderating influence at HiberTech, but she's actually the opposite. Aurora enthusiastically embraced the intelligence-gathering possibilities like no other, and was by far and away the best at manipulating the Dreamspace. Could go into anyone's head and take what she wanted. Go off-piste, so they said, and take the dream to wherever she wanted it to go. She could invoke nightmares, read your thoughts, delve into your emotions – anything. She's extracted more secrets from sleeping suspects than anyone else alive, and has caused neurological damage to thousands. It was eventually her undoing.'

'What do you mean?'

'The story goes,' said Dr Gwynne, 'that fourteen years ago she suffered a moral conflict during a dream interrogation, where the last vestiges of her decent self struggled with what she was doing. Unable to reconcile the dissent within her own mind she split into two people: one containing the very worst bits of her, and the other with the ... well, faintly tolerable. They retired her from the military, put it about she was a Halfer and placed her in charge of HiberTech security. They thought all would be fine with the "faintly okay angels of her nature" side of her working behind the bar in the Wincarnis. Trouble was, Toccata wanted a career for herself and took a job as a Consul. Within ten years she was head of Sector Twelve's Consul Service.'

'Couldn't HiberTech have just locked Toccata up or something?' I asked.

'It's complicated,' said Dr Gwynne, 'because Aurora views her as a slightly loathsome younger sister who needs to be continuously looked after. Aurora has actually *helped* Toccata, put her in a position where they are in real-world conflict – part of their ongoing resolution and healing process, we think.'

'Can they remerge?' I asked, and they both shrugged.

'The best neuroscientists are as confused as anyone over it,' said Foulnap. 'The simple answer is: no one knows. But this conflict you see out here in the real world? It's probably ten times worse on the inside.'

I mused on this for a moment. It kind of made sense.

'So … what's the plan?' I asked.

'We secure the cylinder,' said Foulnap, 'and find a Somnagraph to play it to the nightwalkers. We wake as many as possible, get them to Springrise and cause the biggest upset you're ever likely to see.'

'It sounds so simple when you say it like that,' I said.

'It's more wishful thinking than plan,' agreed Foulnap, 'and more hope than objective. So: where's the cylinder?'

'At the *Cambrensis*.'

'Good. We'll need that – and a Somnagraph.'

I told them the ninth-floor device was most likely hidden in a steamer trunk in the room next to mine, and after discussing tactics, Foulnap said he should call Toccata.

'She'll only be on shift for another three hours,' he said as he got to his feet, 'and if we miss this opportunity we'll be without Toccata for eleven hours – and have the added burden of Aurora to contend with.'

Dr Gwynne also departed, saying he had to take Wendy back to her quarters, a converted janitor's cupboard on the fourth floor, just below the rotunda. I sat there trying to make sense of how my situation had changed so dramatically, and in just a few hours. Last night I was dreaming I was working for RealSleep in a life-or-death struggle against a pharmaceutical corporation with only the slenderest grasp of morality – and now I was doing the very same thing, for *real*.

'Hey,' said Josh as he was walking past, I think to his quarters somewhere.

'Hey,' I said, 'what happens to you now?'

'I get to stay in Sector Twelve until Springrise then try and make it back to Canada without HiberTech noticing.'

He gave me his hand and I shook it gratefully.

'May the Spring embrace you,' I said.

'And embrace you,' he replied, then smiled, and moved off.

I watched him go, then felt hungry and rummaged in my shoulder bag for my spare Snickers, while at the same time wondering if the feelings I held for Birgitta were actually mine at all, and not simply

Webster's, projected into my subconscious by the Somnagraph. I opened the bag as I couldn't find the Snickers, and took out my purse, spare pants, paracetamol, the Polaroid of Birgitta and Charles and Laura's Instamatic camera. No sign of the Snickers. The Gronk must have taken that, too. I looked at the camera again and frowned. All four flashes had been fired, even though I had replaced the flashcube after the attack by the nightwalkers. I looked at the back of the camera; the window showed I'd taken eight pictures but I could only remember taking four.

Out there on the way over, when I was upside down in the snow and cooling rapidly, I must have taken four pictures of something.

And that something may have been the Gronk.

White-out

'... Although the shock-suit wouldn't protect the wearer against the kinetic effects of a thump, it would negate the primary effects to the lungs, sinuses and Eustachian tubes, and greatly reduce secondary effects such as capillary rupture, internal bleeds and axonal shearing. The more modern suits have H4S, cooling and wireless, with a power pack to give ten hours' survival down to minus forty ...'

— *The Elegant Simplicity of WinterTech*, by Emma Llewelyn WiEng

It was half an hour before we were ready to leave, and we talked continually as we prepared. Toccata had been roped in to assist, despite her often erratic behaviour, which explained amongst other things why there were so many nightwalkers in the *Cambrensis*: she'd decided one day that no more would be retired or deployed, so had falsified the HotPot overheat to clear out the *Cambrensis* to make room. Quite how long they could be held there was never discussed, nor if this was a practical or well-thought-out policy – which it clearly wasn't. But if it was a gut decision like the one I made about Birgitta, I totally got it.

Dr Gwynne was not coming with us. He viewed himself as being possessed of 'Fortitude Lite'[62] but was good at technical support.

'Good luck,' he said as we were preparing to leave.

I thanked him and passed over a scribbled note.

'I know this is a long shot,' I said, 'and the weather's bad and everything, but I have a suggestion as to how you could redeploy at least one of the Golgothas to greater effect.'

He looked at the note and nodded slowly, then patted me on the shoulder, told me to take care, and we parted.

'The plan is simple,' said Foulnap as we walked down to the

---

62. More simply put, a coward.

museum's basement. 'We go to the *Siddons* and retrieve the Somnagraph, then head to the *Cambrensis* for the cylinder. If anyone tries to stop us, we thump them.'

'It has the benefit of simplicity.'

'The best plans always do.'

The museum basement was used mostly for storage and contained a fairground ride, an entire Railplane tractor unit and half-scale educational models of a HotPot, both the closed thermosiphon and sintered hotplate version. There was also a collection of the now unfashionable hyperbaric deep-sleep chambers and a moth-eaten animatronic giant tree sloth, which had been doing the rounds as they were on the brink of extinction. More relevant to us there was a Welsh licence-built Sno-Trac branded a Griffin V, which looked as though it had just been pulled off display.

Foulnap instructed me to start her up and drive her out so I climbed in, my shock-suit more restricting than cumbersome. I hadn't actually wanted to wear the one functioning suit, but Foulnap argued that since I was the most valuable, I should be the one inside it.

I settled into the Griffin, switched on the electrical systems, then pressed the air start and the engine hissed into life. Once Foulnap had opened and closed the double shock-doors, he joined me in the cab. It was now pitch black outside. The on-board anemometer registered gusts of sixty; the temperature was at minus forty, the only view from the headlights a bank of constantly moving snow.

I drove out through the wrought-iron gates and crept up the road, around the bridge, then past the *Cambrensis* – all courtesy of the topography revealed on the H4S screen. There was even a radar return from Hooke's abandoned Sno-Trac, a good deal farther on than where I'd guessed, but no sign whatever of the Gronk. While I navigated beyond the *Cambrensis* and towards the *Sarah Siddons* at a slow crawl, Foulnap sat beside me, his eyes fixed on the glowing green dots of the H4S, refreshed and updated by every sweep of the scanner.

'So,' I said, unable to keep quiet lest my nerves actually snapped with an audible twang, 'who's the current Kiki now Logan's dead?'

'It's safer not to know,' he said, 'with the threat of Aurora and her interrogative use of Dreamspace. Webster worked to Logan's instructions but never knew who he was, so couldn't give him up. Hold it here.'

I pulled up and Foulnap pointed to a cluster of returns on the H4S.

'We're about forty yards behind another Sno-Trac. They're waiting for us on the corner near the billboard.'

'Can't they see us if we can see them?'

'With a bit of luck they'll think we're a friendly; I'm squawking a HiberTech ident on the IFF.'

'You're what?'

'Just boring techy stuff,'[63] he said, making for the rear door. 'I'm going to look for Toccata. If I'm not back in twenty minutes, assume own initiative—'

He'd stopped talking because in front of us there was a soft glow of orange light from within the snowstorm.

'Cancel that,' said Foulnap, 'I think we've just found her.'

The snow was instantly cleared from the air, revealing a flaming Sno-Trac, the fire burning in concentric rings as the fuel mixture in the compressed parts of the torus ignited more brightly. It was a spectacle that was both beautiful and alarming – and short lived. For a fleeting glimpse I saw Toccata holding a Schtumperschreck twenty feet in front of us, and then, once the pressure had equalised, the water condensed back into ice and all was dark once more.

Within a few minutes the rear door opened and Toccata jumped in.

'Raising overkill to an art form?' asked Foulnap.

'As dead as the Winter and good luck to them,' she said with a look that seemed mildly unhinged. 'It was payback for Jonesy. Actually, no, that was just the *interest* on the payback for Jonesy. Open Network says it was Hooke and a HiberTech newbie who killed her.'

'The newbie died,' I said, suddenly thinking that Lucy didn't have to be named again, not ever.

'Good,' said Toccata. 'Where's Hooke now?'

---

63. He was right, it was. I found out later that IFF meant 'Identification Friend or Foe', but it didn't improve my life knowing it.

'Taken by the Gronk,' I said. 'He was … unworthy.'

She stared at me for a moment.

'If you say so. Now, Hugo,' she began, reloading the massive weapon with a thermalite the size of a baked-bean tin, 'where are we headed?'

'The *Siddons*,' he said, 'to pick up a Somnagraph from room 902.'

'Game on. Will Aurora be there?'

'I can almost guarantee not.'

Within fifteen minutes we were parked just short of the *Siddons* by about ten yards. Foulnap went out first into the blizzard, trailing a safety line, and we both followed and caught up with him outside the Dormitorium. We all entered the lobby one by one, weapons at the ready. I had my Bambi, but also a Cowpuncher slung around my shoulder, which every single training manual ever written said shouldn't be discharged indoors unless 'there was *absolutely* no alternative'.

The windows had been hastily repaired with layers of canvas and pieces of wood, but they still rattled and shook with the buffeting of the wind. The Winterlounge looked empty, and we could see Laura Strowger sitting behind the desk in the porter's lodge.

'I'm sorry about Jonesy,' said Laura to Toccata. 'I gathered up what I could find of her and put it all in the cold store. These were her personal things. Her Silver Storks and stuff.'

She gave Toccata a clear plastic bag. Toccata took it without speaking and shoved the bundle into her jacket.

'They took Birgitta to HiberTech,' said Laura, 'and Lloyd said he was going to take a … walk outside. He was only in his shirt sleeves so I don't think he's coming back.'

He must have known about the abuses happening on the ninth floor. He probably tipped off Hooke, too. Perhaps the Cold Way Out was the best thing for him.

'Is there anyone from HiberTech still in the building?'

'I don't know,' said Laura, 'but I expect so – be careful.'

'You stay in the lobby,' said Foulnap to Toccata. 'Charlie, with me.'

Toccata nodded, then moved back into a defensive position where she could control all possible entrances to the lobby.

'Here,' I said, handing Laura the Instamatic camera, 'I think I might have got something.'

'Such as?'

I showed her my missing little finger.[64]

'Oh,' she said, 'right.'

I then ran up the stairs after Foulnap.

'Does Toccata really eat nightwalkers with mint sauce?' I asked as we reached the first landing and started towards the second.

'No, that's just a story she puts around to intimidate people.'

'It works.'

We made it to the ninth floor without encountering any HiberTech operatives, then padded silently along the corridor and stopped outside room 902. I carefully unlocked the door and let it swing open, half expecting an agent to be inside, but it was empty aside from the steamer trunk. Foulnap produced a large screwdriver from his coat and levered off the lock.

The trunk was empty.

It was too much to hope they'd leave something as valuable as a Somnagraph once they'd been rumbled.

'That was disappointing,' said Foulnap in a masterful display of understatement, and I asked him what the plan was now.

'I don't know,' he said in a dispirited fashion, 'this was pretty much it. Default is to get all assets to a safe house and rethink the situation.'

'You have a safe house?'

'Actually, no,' he said, 'but it was high on my to-do list. To be honest, given the size and quantity of RealSleep's assets right now, this steamer trunk would probably suffice. Let's go.'

I stayed in the room while he walked out into the corridor. He turned to me once there, opened his mouth to say something and was then blasted off his feet with a concussive thud that catapulted him off down the corridor and out of sight.

There *were* HiberTech agents in the building. I stayed silent, flipped down my visor and powered up the shock-suit, which crackled as it inflated. I pulled out my Bambi, changed my mind and instead

64. The Mk III shock-suits still had elasticated cuffs, rather than gloves. Users often walked away from a heavy thump intact, their hands livid purple with bruising. Hence the expression 'caught red handed'.

carefully removed the Cowpuncher from where it was hanging around my shoulders. I knelt down, flicked off the safety and aimed it at the open door.

'Is that Worthing?' came a voice. 'I saw two people going in, so I know the room's not empty.'

'I'm in here,' I confirmed.

'Then best come out.'

My hands tightened on the Puncher. I'd never fired a weapon at anyone, with either lethal or non-lethal intent. But I was ready to do so now.

'I choose not to surrender,' I said. 'Do your worst.'

'As you wish.'

There was a pause and two puck-shaped pulse grenades rolled in. One went under the steamer trunk but the other described a languid circle in the middle of the floor before coming to rest. They would have been designed only to concuss and disorientate; they wanted me alive. If the shock-suit ever needed a test, this was it. The grenade detonated, but all I felt was a momentary sense of increased pressure on my body, like being softly squeezed by a large hand. Almost immediately a single figure – no one I recognised, but dressed in the HiberTech Security uniform – came running through the doorway. I didn't hesitate for a moment and pulled the trigger. He was thrown backwards in the direction of the corridor behind, but as he passed through the door, the pressure wave that had carried him off *also* tried to get through the door, and had to accelerate rapidly to compress itself to fit through the aperture, then expanded with a devastatingly explosive effect on Foulnap's assailant, along with a very audible *pop*.

I wiped the drops of blood and tissue from the visor, then walked cautiously to the door and peered out. I stepped gingerly over the body parts that were strewn along the corridor to look at the man who I had known as Hugo Foulnap or Danny Pockets, although that too was probably an alias. He was quite dead, and looked utterly peaceful. I told him I was sorry for not listening to his sound advice back at the *John Edward Jones*, paused for a moment to dignify his departure, then trotted down the stairs to rejoin Toccata. Quite where this left us all, I wasn't sure. No Foulnap, no Somnagraph, no plan, no Birgitta, *nothing*.

'What was that?' asked Toccata as soon as I was back down in the lobby. Laura, it seemed, had legged it for safety.

'Foulnap's dead,' I replied.

'That is *definitely* an arse.'

'But I got the fella who killed him.'

'An arse with a silver lining. What now?'

'I was hoping you'd tell me.'

'I'm on a RealSleep need-to-know kind of deal – not sure why,' she said, swinging the Schtumper back and forth, covering the main entrance, then the door to the basement, then the Winterlounge, 'and I work only to Hugo or Jonesy's orders. They're both dead, so according to Hydra principles, that makes you the new Kiki. Congratulations. You're now head of the Campaign for Real Sleep, with full control of all assets and supreme command of policy, both strategic and tactical. You're also one of only two people ever sentenced to death *in absentia* by the Northern Fed's Supreme Council. Consider yourself honoured they think you that important.'

This took a moment or two to sink in.

'Foulnap was Kiki?'

'Yup, but don't be too impressed. The size of RealSleep has been dwindling recently and I think you and me are now pretty much it. In the absence of any known command structure and my "need to know just follow orders" status, that makes you the big cheese.'

I thought this might have been her quirky sense of humour, but she was deadly serious.

'I'm not sure I'm qualified.'

'If you can tell right from wrong and have a pulse, you're qualified. And from what I've heard from Foulnap about you and Birgitta, you know right from wrong. I'm only sorry we didn't know this earlier. You could have been on board all along instead of dancing around the periphery like a ninny.'

My face fell.

'You're not going to bail, are you?' she asked. 'We've gone too far and lost too many and risked too much for that. Bringing down

HiberTech and Aurora isn't just a good idea, it's a moral imperative. And,' she added, 'dealing with Aurora once and for all would be hugely enjoyable.'

I thought about what Dr Gwynne and Foulnap had said about Aurora and Toccata's inner conflict. They couldn't play it out internally, so it was being played out here, in the real world.

'No,' I said, thinking of Birgitta and the other nightwalkers, 'I'm not going to bail.'

'There's no uniform or medal or hat or anything to being Kiki,' continued Toccata, 'and if you and I get killed it's entirely possible that no one will ever know you *were* Kiki. But I know, and I salute you for your fearlessness and steadfast adherence to duty.'

And she dipped her head in respect.

'I'll … try not to let you down.'

'It's not me you don't want to let down,' she said, 'but broader society — and all the nightwalkers murdered and parted out in the past. No pressure, mind. So,' she added in a more upbeat tone, 'what's our next move, Chief?'

It was kind of galling that the first time I was head of anything it would be a banned disruptionist organisation and carried a mandatory death sentence. If anything I'd hoped to work my way up to Desk Sergeant-Consul via Head of Records and the vehicle pool. But that was the thing about the Hydra principle: you could be zero to hero and back again in less time than it takes to blink.

But oddly, I wasn't panicking. I was actually thinking quite clearly. I could retrieve the cylinder, sure, but I didn't have a Somnagraph and the Spring was a long way away. I could fall back and consider my next move, but that would give HiberTech more time to figure out *their* next move — and they had more and better minds on this than I.

No, I'd have to go on the offensive right now, and hope that providence and a few aces up my sleeve would win the day. I took out my Bambi, flicked it to the lowest setting and pointed it at Toccata.

'Wonky?' she said. 'What are you doing?'

'It's … on a need-to-know basis.'

She looked at me, then at the Bambi, then back to me.

'Bring it on,' she said, 'you're the Kiki.'

I pulled the trigger and Toccata went over like a ninepin. It was an audacious plan, sure, but right now I didn't see any alternative. I needed to get us both into HiberTech to meet them head on, and there was only one person who could get us there. I swiftly climbed out of the shock-suit and then stared at Toccata with a sense of morbid fascination as she changed from one person to the other. Her unseeing right eye moved violently around in its socket, then, after some jerks, a quivering foot and some swearing, her eyes swapped: the *left* eye became the unseeing eye, and her *right* popped open.

'Charlie?' said Aurora, sitting up and looking around. 'Is that you?'

'It's me.'

'Where are we?'

'The *Siddons*,' I said, feigning a quivering lip. 'Thank goodness you're here. Hugo Foulnap and his RealSleep nutjobs tried to kidnap me – I think they killed one of your agents up on the ninth.' I gave out an award-winning sob. 'You've *got* to help me.'

'Everything's all right now,' she said in a soothing tone, taking my hand in hers. 'I promise.'

Orientation

'... The HiberTech facility was originally designed to alleviate the long-term suffering brought on by the occasional side effects of hibernation, before medical science began to get a handle on potential cures. Hibernational Narcosis sufferers constituted the majority of patients, and those with emaciatory muscle loss and calcium migration equal close second ...'

– *HiberTech: A Short History*, by Ronald Fudge

It was lucky I did what I did when I did it. Six more HiberTech Security agents were through the door of the *Siddons* within a minute of Toccata turning into Aurora. She seemed curiously accepting of the fact that she was in different clothes in a strange place, but presumably she was used to this by now. While the HiberTech Security agents went up to the ninth floor to investigate, Aurora sat me down and quizzed me on what was going on.

'Hooke and I were ambushed when he was taking me to safety at HiberTech,' I explained, trying to make it all sound plausible. 'He goes out in the Winter and vanishes, and I go to look for him and I find him, dead, but then I lose the line and make it to the – um – *museum*, and Danny Pockets is there, who is actually Hugo Foulnap, and he gives me all this bullshit about needing a cylinder and the dreams being projected into my head and we go to the *Siddons* because he's convinced there's a dream machine in 902 but then one of your agents killed Foulnap who is then killed in turn by ... Toccata.'

Aurora looked around nervously.

'She's here?'

'No,' I said, 'she left just before you arrived.'

Aurora frowned and her unseeing eye twisted and turned in its socket.

'She *keeps* on doing that. Why does she keep on doing that?'

The last part of her sentence she delivered in an angry, almost frightened tone, and she gripped my arm so tightly it was painful.

'I don't know.'

'Toccata's up to something,' she continued. 'She wants to bring me down. Why would she want to bring me down?'

She glared at me dangerously.

'I still don't know.'

She stared at me some more and then seemed to relax.

'Tell me more about the cylinder that Foulnap mentioned.'

'I don't know anything. He didn't elaborate.'

One of her agents came downstairs and whispered in her ear.

'So the Foulnap part of your story is correct,' she said. 'Do you know what he was doing in Sector Twelve? Something to do with RealSleep?'

I decided to just play dumb.

'That's above my intellect and pay grade,' I said simply, staring at my feet. 'I'm just a stranded Novice with narcosis, having bizarre dreams that I'm remembering backwards.'

She stared at me for a while longer.

'Okay, then,' she said, getting to her feet, 'we'll debrief more at our leisure. The job at HiberTech still stands. Light duties until the narcosis clears. Up for it?'

I said I was, and after being checked for weapons I was ushered into a waiting Sno-Trac and driven across to HiberTech, the storm still raging, the small vehicle buffeted by a wind that on occasions seemed to blow in all directions at once. I sat in the back without a plan of any sort – I'd seen too many plans come to naught recently to have any hope that if I made one, all would be well. But if I'd learned anything from Logan, it was that plans often get in the way of a fast-moving incident-rich landscape, so better to have on-the-hoof flexibility – and objectives.

I *so* had objectives. And, as I said earlier, a couple of spare aces up my sleeve.

We bumped down the entrance slope to the underground car park and through the shock-gates to park, then made our way into the building by way of a service elevator and along a corridor.

'This is the way to the Project Lazarus labs,' I said, suddenly recalling the route. 'What about the apartment facing the quad with the generous rations, abundant hot water and a nightwalker valet?'

'All in good time,' said Aurora. 'There's someone who needs to speak to you before you start to work for us. Orientation, I think HR call it.'

We moved through the door marked *Project Lazarus*, the lab unchanged since I'd been here last. We took several lefts and rights and walked through some swing doors, then found ourselves back in the circular room with eight corridors leading off towards the cells.

'Wait here,' said Aurora, and moved away.

I stood there for perhaps ten minutes, then, thinking that Birgitta might be somewhere near, started to look around. My eye caught sight of the door with the glass panel, behind which was the room that contained the barber's chair and the copper device the shape of a traffic cone.

'Curiosity doesn't kill cats at all,' came a familiar voice, 'curiosity is the very bedrock upon which this institution is founded. You want to see more? Come and have a look.'

It was the Notable Charlotte Goodnight, and she appeared quite friendly. She opened the door and stepped inside, beckoning both me and Aurora to follow. Slightly wary, I complied. When I'd seen the room last, there had been a nightwalker on the table, but now the room was empty, the machine switched off and dead.

'This is a Mk IX Somnagraph,' explained Goodnight. 'It can both record and play back dreams.'

'You can record dreams?' I asked, trying to sound surprised.

'Indeed we can. There are five hundred of these in a converted dormitory down the hall. I'll spare you the technical details, but we use them to redeploy nightwalkers by inducing simple dreams to overwrite their limited skills. The more Tricksy the nightwalker, the more complex the duties we can get them to do.'

'If this is company orientation,' I said, 'it's kind of a steep learning curve – shouldn't you start with the photocopier and where the milk is kept?'

373

Jasper Fforde

'I don't appreciate impertinence,' said The Notable Goodnight, 'but you are young, so I will overlook it this once. Where was I? Oh yes: while we have every confidence you will become a productive member of the company, we need to ensure that you understand what we do here, and how best policy can be implemented while still maintaining a morally correct framework.'

I didn't say anything. Not much I could say, really.

'We're all small cogs, Charlie,' continued Aurora, 'even The Notable Goodnight here, but we only work in the big machine by meshing perfectly. And when I say big machine, I don't mean the Ferch Llewelyn Dynasty, Europia or the Northern Fed, I mean the advancement of the human race. This is *real* progress, Worthing, above politics and corporate stock value. Do you understand?'

'I think so, ma'am, yes.'

'Good. So why were you harbouring Birgitta? And don't tell me simply because she can draw. We're beyond all that now.'

I stared at her for a moment. When you're in the hornet's nest it's probably better to act like another hornet, or, if you can, a bigger one. Dealing with Gary Findlay had taught me that.

'I believe she's still alive in there,' I said, 'processing thoughts and memories while trapped in a Dreamstate so deep it can't be detected. I've heard of others, too,' I added, 'anecdotal stories that were enough to convince me.'

Goodnight and Aurora looked at one another.

'You're a keen observer,' said the Notable, 'which we like. And you're right – we've known that for a long time. But muse on this: at the last count, Morphenox has saved over fifty million lives in Europia alone, yet created only twenty-five-thousand quasi-sentient nightwalkers. You're too young to remember pre-Morphenox days, but life was a constant cycle of death, loss and stalled societal and technical development. This was never a war against the Winter, but against *wastage* – the lives that couldn't and shouldn't be lost. For the massive benefits of Morphenox, there would have to be victims.'

Aurora picked up the story.

'We saw them more as the unsung heroes of the hibernatory revolution, unknowingly brave foot-soldiers, spearheading the fight

374

against the horrors of the Winter to bring us victorious into the Spring. Those citizens, those nightwalkers, died honourably to make a better place for all of us.'

It was an understandable point, just not a very ethical one. The victims, the Nightwalkers, had no choice in the matter.

'And Morphenox-B?' I asked. 'What about that?'

'*Much* more exciting,' said Aurora. 'The expense in manufacture was predicated on drug purity so nightwalker numbers were kept to an absolute minimum. But we were seeing it arse about face. *More* nightwalkers actually works for us. Cut a few corners in the manu-facturing process and instead of a one-in-two-thousand likelihood of walking, Morphenox-B will give us one in every five hundred.'

'With those figures, the nightwalker economy could be worth 4.2 billion euros to us within five years,' continued Goodnight, 'and will also be socially transformative: tedious and repetitive tasks will be given to workers who don't know or care what they do and can work sixteen uncomplaining hours a day. Productivity will rise, costs will fall, food production will increase. And once their year is done, they get to be parted out and add immeasurable quality of life to thousands. True vertical integration, Worthing – *everything of use but the yawn*. I made up that slogan,' she added proudly. 'Sums it up well, doesn't it?'

'Best of all,' said Aurora, 'is that when Winter wastage falls, places like your joyous St Granata's will actually cease to exist; the burden of endless childbearing a thing of the past. It's win–win all the way down the line. But,' she continued, 'there is a very small fly in our very large ointment. The venerable Don Hector discovered a way to retrieve nightwalkers. He's dead now, thank goodness, but he encoded it all on a cylinder which he then gave to someone connected to RealSleep. While that cylinder is at large, we are exposed, and we don't like being exposed.'

They fell silent and stared at me expectantly.

'You want me to agree with you,' I said, 'but I can't. *Nightwalkers are alive*. And while they are, you have to do what you can to bring them back. And you can't murder them, nor part them out. Not for *any* reason, no matter how noble you think it is.'

'It's so easy to be judgemental,' said Goodnight in a patronising tone, 'but you must understand that we've done too much good for too long to have our work sacrificed on the altar of short-term, wishy-washy, woolly-headed egalitarianism. The benefits of Morphenox-B far, *far* outweigh the drawbacks and we are here to ensure the most—'

'—favourable outcome is enjoyed by the majority,' I said. 'I know. I hear that a lot. What about this: "If you can't have change without injustice, then there should be no change".'

'Who said that?'

'I can't remember. Someone important. It's annoying when that happens.'

'The idealism of youth,' she said with a dismissive snort. 'We can't fail, not now. We're too big, too integrated into society. All that we've done. All that we can do. All that we *will* do.'

They stared at me without speaking for some moments.

'So what do you want from me?' I asked.

Goodnight stared at me for a moment, and then walked from the small room, beckoning us to follow.

'I want you to meet someone.'

She led me across to cell 4-H. I guessed who was in there but looked through the peephole anyway. Birgitta was lying on the bed staring up at the ceiling. Her hands were drawing circles in the air; pretend pens on pretend paper.

'What are you going to do with her?'

'Nothing for the moment, but she's a good candidate for retrieval, and we do conduct tests from time to time. How about if we were to retrieve Birgitta right now? In exchange for the cylinder? She'd never know anything had ever happened. She'd be missing a thumb, of course, but that could be explained away as rats or mould or something.'

I had to think very carefully on this one. I could have given them the cylinder, but I had a pretty strong feeling that once the cylinder was secured, anyone remotely attached to it would end up in the night pit covered by a spadeful of lime.

'I don't know where the cylinder is.'

The Notable Goodnight cocked her head on one side.

'Then we could redeploy Birgitta instead,' she said, 'next on the list. She's very Tricksy so might be able to manage simple data entry. The problem is, one in every hundred do not survive the redeployment procedure. I can't say it will be Birgitta, but we might have some bad luck.'

The implication wasn't lost on me. I was to play ball – or Birgitta died. But again, I had no guarantee that wouldn't happen anyway.

'I don't know what you want me to say,' I said, 'but I don't have the cylinder.'

The Notable Goodnight stared at me again for a few moments.

'You wouldn't lie to me, would you?'

'I probably would, actually,' I said, 'about some things – y'know, like personal stuff. But not about this.'

'Sure?'

'Yes.'

'And that's perfectly acceptable and understandable,' replied Goodnight, suddenly coming over all sunny, 'we just had to be sure, that's all.'

She gave me a smile and then, the 'orientation' over, asked Aurora to show me where I would be staying.

It wasn't too far from the labs, no more than a flight of stairs and along a corridor. The proximity, I guessed, was not so much based on convenience, but on technology. If they wanted to try to coerce me into the Dreamspace in order to use more invasive methods, they would need a few machines to do so.

Aurora showed me into the room and told me to make myself comfortable, and how I'd have to remain here until my security clearance was established.

'We can't have anyone from RealSleep infiltrating the facility, now, can we?' she said with a laugh, 'Reporting back to Kiki and whatnot.'

I told her no, of course not, that would be silly.

She wished me goodnight, the door closed and I heard a bolt being slid across. I stood for a moment, listening to her footsteps retreat on the polished wooden floor outside, then chucked my jacket over a chair-back and looked around.

The apartment was spacious, warm and in good order. Two rooms, carpeted, all mod cons. Oddly, I kind of missed Clytemnestra and the charming grottiness of *Siddons* 901. I went into the bathroom, turned on the shower and checked my collection of bite marks in the mirror, only one of which seemed to have an infection. I squeezed the pus from the wound, cleaned it with some vodka I'd found in the mini-bar and then changed all the dressings. I had a shower, found a bathrobe, climbed into bed and considered my position. The default plan was to simply stay awake as long as I could and deny HiberTech my sleeping mind, but on reflection that might not be the best strategy. I would eventually fall asleep after two days or more, but I'd be in a poor state to resist what they had planned. The best idea would be to go to sleep *now*, while I was still strong, my mind unmuddied by fatigue.

So I switched off the light and stared at the ceiling, trying to get to sleep. It took an hour to do so. I felt the room darken, there were a couple of flashes, an all-consuming glossy darkness, and—

Dreamspace

'... Dreams are nothing more than the random and wasteful firings of the brain, a mesh of thoughts and memories giving narrative to the sleeping mind by a cortex eager to make order out of chaos. A waste of energy, a waste of processing power, a drain on the life-fat that promises to deliver one from the darkness ...'

— *Press release from HiberTech. Morphenox launch, July 1975*

I heard the gulls cackle before I saw them, punctuated by the boom of the incoming tide and a wind that whistled through the cable-stays that secured the funnels of the *Argentinian Queen*. I inhaled deeply of the salt-laden air, the freshness of the breeze, the gently rotting seaweed on the storm-shore. I opened my eyes and was back on Rhosilli beach in the Gower, the wreck before me, high and dry on the huge expanse of sand. The dream was *exactly* the same as it had been for the past few nights.

More real than real, but for one thing: I wasn't Birgitta's Charlie, I was *me* Charlie, still in my bathrobe, covered in bite marks, dotted with blobs of iodine. It was the same dream, but instead of being first person Active Control, I was *third* person Active Control – this, I presumed, was Dreamspace.

Charles and Birgitta were beneath the parasol talking in low voices, and every now and again they would laugh, and touch one another, and kiss. I can't pretend that I didn't feel some sort of jealousy, for I did – a dull ache in my chest.

There was a gurgle of laughter and the young girl chased her beach ball, while Birgitta and Charlie exchanged their vows of affection, as before, as always, again.

'I love you, Charlie,' said Birgitta.

'I love you, Birgitta,' said Charlie.

A voice broke into my thoughts.

'Where is this place?'

I turned to find Aurora staring at me. She was dressed in a flowery blouse and a white skirt over a stripy swimming costume. She looked tanned and well, with longer hair less streaked with grey and a fuller body which made her look a good deal healthier than the lean overwinterer I had come to know. I guess in Dreamspace you can idealise yourself. She was still armed, a Bambi at her hip, while her unseeing left eye flicked around in its socket.

Aurora looked around curiously, as though she'd blundered into a newly undiscovered cupboard in her kitchen, and was trying to figure out its function.

'The Gower Peninsula,' I said, 'a glorious weekend, fondly recalled. A place to visit when in pensive mood, an escape from the real world, something to flash upon the inward eye.'

'Very romantic,' replied Aurora. 'I remember that parasol. This is a dream from one of the orderlies we interrogated after the cylinder went missing. What was his name again?'

'Charles Webster.'

She clicked her fingers.

'Right. Webster. Nothing came of it, I recall. So why are we here?'

'This is the dream you've been projecting into my sleeping mind these past few nights at the *Sarah Siddons*,' I said, 'through the wall from 902.'

'Nope, you got a fresh Don Hector dream recording all to yourself,' she replied. 'We replace them because they wear out after five or six playings – tend to get scratched and lose their detail.'

I shrugged.

'All I know is that I dreamt I was Webster in the Gower, then went to the blue Buick from here.'

She frowned, then a flash of understanding moved across her face.

'With a jump and a tear?'

'Yes,' I said, 'with a jump and a tear.'

'That's a first,' she said, genuinely impressed. 'We record dreams on wax cylinder because Edison's invention has never really been improved upon. But there is another, more practical reason. Do you want to try and guess what it is?'

'I have no idea.'

'It's this: each cylinder records about eight minutes of dream. A single night's recording can produce upwards of twenty cylinders. We kept Don Hector's – there are about seven hundred dreams of his in storage – but we can't keep them all, so the dreams we record from people of no consequence are—'

'—erased,' I said.

'Yes indeed,' said Aurora. 'Whoever was on erasing duty that day didn't do such a good job and left the remains of one of Webster's dreams on the start of the cylinder.'

I understood, then. Everything I knew of Birgitta and Charles I'd gained from a half-inch of shiny blue grooves at the head of a single wax cylinder. Without random chance to bring me and this cylinder together, meeting Birgitta under the car would have been only intriguing, at best, and I'd likely not have intervened when Aurora was going to retire her. Without her becoming my dream-woman, she'd be dead.

'I'll make sure this cylinder is trashed once we're done,' said Aurora. 'Now, you know why I'm here?'

'You want to know where the cylinder is.'

'Full marks. Are you going to tell me?'

'I don't know where it is.'

'You're a bad liar, Charlie. I've been working the Dreamspace since before you were squirted out of the turkey baster, and I'm good at it. When dreams are your own, you have agency over them, but right now we're equal actors in another's dream. I can mould it the way I want it to go, I can mould *you* the way I want you to go. I can pull something from your subconscious that you don't want revealed, and I can even have your mind sweated out of you, so you end up like that dopey orderly, no better than a nightwalker. What was his name again?'

'Webster.'

'Thank you. So ... Where was I?'

'Something about sweating my mind out of me so I ended up like Webster?'

'Yes – good only for driving a golf cart. So, here's the deal: tell us where the cylinder is and we'll retrieve Birgitta and you get to go back to the land of the living. How about it?'

I looked around at the beach, the *Argentinian Queen* and the parasol of spectacular size and splendour.

'If I didn't take the deal when offered by Goodnight, what makes you think I'll take it with you? Besides, I don't know about any cylinder.'

There was a sudden gust of cold wind, and a flurry of snowflakes drifted around the beach. The photographer had just arrived and was offering his services to Birgitta and Charles, just as before.

'You see?' said Aurora. 'A subconscious clue. You *will* tell me. It's hard not to think about stuff when asked. Out in the cold somewhere?'

'I don't know.'

Aurora took a step closer, and all of a sudden she was three times larger. I felt my chest tighten and for a fleeting instant I thought I would wake and be safely away from this, but Aurora took my ear between finger and thumb and squeezed so tightly I yelped.

'Now,' she said, 'before I *really* get to work on you, last chance: tell me where the cylinder is.'

She drew closer and her teeth seemed to sharpen into points. I was suddenly reminded of Sister Contractia, who filed her teeth for fun until Mother Fallopia told her not to.

Despite the pain, I closed my eyes, concentrated, and shifted away from Aurora, away from the beach, away from the dream. I could feel myself momentarily aware of the apartment at HiberTech with two technicians looming over me, and then I was standing next to the blue Buick under the azure sky, the picnic laid out beside me, the oak tree around which the stones were piled. And sitting on top of them, Don Hector. Old, grizzled, tired. There were no hands around except his and mine, nor was there any Aurora. She'd have to find me.

The old man caught my eye and I walked over, the sun feeling warm against my skin. He was eating a sandwich, and a glass of freshly poured Champagne stood on a nearby boulder, the fizz rising in the liquid. The detail was all there. Every texture, every smell, every sound.

'Your dream or mine?' he asked, waving a hand about him.

'Yours,' I said, 'with maybe a hint of mine.'

He smiled and patted the stones he was seated upon.

'Do you know *why* these boulders are heaped around the tree?'

'I've been wondering that for a while.'

'Farmers ploughing their fields,' he replied. 'Whenever they snagged a boulder it was pulled up and discarded. Usually deposited to the side of the field, but if there was a tree, that would become the place. The heap of stones represents toil; a lichen-encrusted palimpsest of an agricultural way of life before mechanisation.'

'I have the cylinder,' I said, 'but I need to know what to do with it.'

'You have to get it to Kiki.'

'I *am* Kiki.'

'Then my mission is complete, my work is done.'

'Yes, but what do *I* do now?' I asked, 'very little is clear to me right now.'

He stared at me for a moment, then smiled.

'Bring them all back,' he said, 'bring them home.'

'Okay—but how?'

'I think you already know. Good luck, Charlie.'

Whump

Don Hector was knocked violently from the pile of rocks and to the ground, where he lay quite still. I turned around to find Aurora holding a Thumper. She didn't look very happy. No, wait, scrub that: she looked *seriously* pissed off.

'Think I've never been in the Dreamspace before? Think you can outwit me? I have over fourteen hundred hours' dreamtime, Wonky, and I've prised bigger secrets from stronger people's heads than yours.'

I wasn't worried. I'd escaped from her once, I could escape from her again.

'You killed Don Hector out in the real world, didn't you?'

'He'd lost sight of the good work we were doing,' said Aurora with a half-smile, 'and we felt he had swung from asset to liability. Asset good, liability bad,' she added, in case I'd missed the main thrust of her argument.

'Nightwalker retrieval was only the beginning,' I said. 'He'd perfected a risk-free Morphenox that could be synthesised cheaply and easily. He was going to go public. No secrets, Morphenox a universal right. Sub-beta, the Ottoman, the emerging Southern Alliance – everyone. A global hibernating village, equal in sleep, equal in dignity.'

She stared at me for a few seconds before speaking.

'So what? With no one to tell, it's the same as you never finding out. Now, where's the cylinder?'

I concentrated hard and shifted again – this time to the abandoned Morpheleum, all mould and decay, stone arches, dirt and windblown leaves. Webster was in his orderly's outfit, and Don Hector, back again, looked at me oddly, as though I shouldn't be there. In truth, I wasn't. I was actually on my own; all this was my invention. I was dreaming the dream, dancing my own steps. First person Active Control but no longer tied to a target dream. *Freestyle*.

'Hullo, Wonky,' said Webster cheerfully, 'I hear you've been helping out Birgitta.'

'I could have done a better job.'

'You and me both.'

He suddenly looked around, saw Don Hector, and a look of panic crossed his face.

'No, no, no,' said Webster. 'This is just what Aurora wants. Connecting Don Hector to me. Move somewhere else or wake up. Go, now, *go!*'

But I was too late. Aurora was standing in the shaft of light that emerged through the roof above the altar, and looked oddly magisterial.

'So it *was* Webster after all,' said Aurora, looking at them both, then me. I tried to shift again, but Aurora had grabbed me by the arm and twisted it around so she had my wrist in a swan-neck. It was a trick to keep someone anchored, I guessed – flood their mind with pain so they couldn't concentrate.

'I'm impressed,' she said. 'You have a natural talent for dreaming; it took me years to do what you're doing.'

Aurora then lifted her head and spoke. Inter-dream operatives like

her worked in pairs, I guessed – one in the Dreamstate and a monitor
to listen to their sleeptalkings. I imagined Aurora on a bed somewhere close to me at HiberTech, mumbling in her sleep.

'Don Hector's contact was Webster after all,' she said. 'Find out
where he lived and get someone over there.'

I wriggled out of her hold; with the pain gone I could concentrate, and in an instant the small naked hands started to flood in
through the open door, tossing, squirming and falling over one
another in their haste to gain entry. They rushed towards Aurora but
she took one look at them and they all melted into dry autumn
leaves.

'What's this? Amateur hour? Now, before I start to bring all manner
of horrors to bear: where – did – Webster – hide – the – cylinder?'

'Don't go there, Wonky,' said Charles, but try as I might, I couldn't
help myself. I was suddenly in the lobby of the *Cambrensis*, sitting
on the sofa, opposite Zsazsa, who looked at me suspiciously.

'We know of a remote farm in Lincolnshire,' she began, 'where
Mrs Buckley lives—'

'Yeah, I know,' I said, 'and in July, peas grow there.'

I heard the front door opening. It was Webster again. Different
clothes, same face. It was all the dreams I'd had, jumbling into one
another.

'Don't let Aurora find the cylinder,' he said, looking around nervously, 'don't even think about it. In fact, *don't even think about thinking
about it*. Think *Bonanza*.'

'*Bonanza?*'

'Or *Rawhide*. It doesn't matter. A brick wall, a prawn, Ed Reardon,
Mott the Hoople, *Green Rye*, Yorkminster. Anything to block her
out.'

Aurora walked into the lobby, talking to her unseen monitor: 'It's
the *Cambrensis*. The twisty-headed frostwit is leading us straight to
it. This is my twenty-seven-hundredth incursion,' she added, marching
up to me. 'You get to spot the runaways, the misdirectors, the
randomisers, even the world-builders, shape-shifters and tangential
digressers. You're none of those. You're just bouncing around, leaving
a trail so broad an amateur could follow. Now: where's the cylinder?'

'The laundry room.'

'You gave that up *way* too easily. Again: where's the cylinder?'

It's hard not to think of the thing you're trying hard not to think about. I tried to take us elsewhere – back to the Gower, the Wincarnis, the Ponderosa ranch, the last Fat Thursday at the Pool, but it wasn't easy, and a moment later we were inside Charlie Webster's old room.

'You see?' said Aurora. 'This could all be so painless. And you know what? I don't even need you to tell me where it is. All you have to do is think it. And you will, eventually. Room 106,' she said to her monitor, 'get the team over there.'

I concentrated hard on the first random thought that came into my head in order to block her out: the time Billy DeFroid found the nightwalker in the orchard back at the Pool. The apple trees were still without leaves, the dry-stone wall had partially collapsed under the weight of the drifts, and the remnants of snowmen, always the last to thaw, were still on the ground. The nightwalker was a man, middle-aged, close to starvation and mumbling.

'Hidden up the chimney?' said Aurora with a smile as the information popped annoyingly into my head. 'Which side? Doesn't matter, you've just thought it.'

She relayed the intel to her monitor: 'Up the chimney, left—'

She stopped talking, looked at me, then took a step forwards and stared deeply into my eyes.

'—cancel that. It's in the ticket office to the funfair just behind the museum.'

A second later and we were in the ticket office, the dusty floor strewn with fliers from last year's attractions, the temperature minus twenty and only a meagre light reaching us through the snow-covered windows.

'Bottom drawer of the desk,' said Aurora with a smirk. I leant against the wall near the door, then slid down until I was sitting on the floor, arms around head.

'I could be bluffing,' I said in a despondent tone, shivering in the cold, my breath showing white, 'perhaps it's not there at all.'

'It was a good try,' she conceded, 'I almost went with your

Cambrensis story. That's when experience counts. To know instinctively when someone is lying.'

She laughed, relaxed, then sat on a handy chair. Out in the real world, HiberTech agents would be battling through the blizzard to converge on the ticket office.

She pulled a hip flask from her pocket and took a swig.

'I don't drink out there any more,' she explained, 'but in here I can do as I wish. You don't get drunk in dreams, not properly, more's the pity.'

She offered the flask to me but I shook my head and she replaced it in her pocket.

'You'd have made a good dream analyst,' she said in a quiet, conversational manner. 'Your technique is clumsy and impetuous, but with a genuine flair.'

'If I agree to work for you,' I said, 'will you retrieve Birgitta?'

'I think that particular ship has sailed, Bucko. You should have negotiated when you had the chance. But heigh-ho, life's full of disappointments. Or rather, *your* life is full of disappointments. Mine's been unusually rich.'

'What about Toccata?' I asked, and Aurora's unseeing left eye twisted around in its socket to stare at me.

'What about her?'

'Do you think you'll ever reconcile yourselves to the fact that you're actually one person?'

Both of her eyes suddenly glared at me in a dangerous manner, which gave the odd impression that she was staring at me in a completely normal manner. But then her left eye wandered off to stare at the ceiling, and she was back to her old self.

'You need to stop listening to Shamanic Bob's conspiracy theories,' she scoffed. 'Toccata and I the same person? Ridiculous.'

I could see she was rattled, though.

'When was the last time you saw her in the flesh?' I persisted. 'In fact, have you *ever* seen her in the flesh?'

'No, but by that reasoning,' she said slowly, 'anyone who I've never met in the flesh might actually be me. There would be millions. What about you? Have you ever met Carmen Miranda? In the flesh, I mean?'

Jasper Fforde

'Well, yes, I have actually.'
'Okay, that was a bad example. How about Dylan Thomas?'
'No.'
'Then why couldn't you be him as well as being yourself?'
'Because he's dead?'
'Okay, maybe that's also a bad example. Look, it's not my fault Toccata is such a coward that she avoids me at every—'
She was interrupted by a knock at the ticket office door. Aurora narrowed her eyes.
'Don't try anything stupid, Wonky.'
'It's nothing to do with me,' I said, and it wasn't – it was the shimmery Mrs Nesbit. But she wasn't here to sell us targeted advertising, she was here to bring news from the outside world, and I already knew what it was. I'd asked Dr Gwynne to donate one of his Golgotha demolition charges to the ticket office, the firing pin booby-trapped to the lower drawer of the desk.
'Three dead, one missing and that's the second Sno-Trac destroyed this evening,' said Goodnight through Mrs Nesbit. 'We need to up the ante; if you don't think you can handle it, instigate 110B. Everyone talks after that.'
I turned to face Aurora, who, like all powerful people, was more annoyed about being outmanoeuvred than just losing. All of a sudden this wasn't about a cylinder, it was about winning, and that made it personal.
'I told you it wasn't there,' I said.
'You *fooled* me,' she said, 'led me on that merry dance to the *Cambrensis* so I wouldn't see that you were spinning a false narrative. I take it back: you're very good. But this only delays the outcome, not changes it. We still need that cylinder, and now we play hardball. Ever wanted to know what it's like to be eaten alive by nightwalkers?'
'I'd have to answer no to that.'
'They push their nails into the flesh of your stomach,' she said, 'and disembowel you while you're still alive. It has a visceral terror to it that is quite unlike any other; we call it Night Terror 110b. This is how it works: I'll have you eaten alive on the hour every hour, night after night, week after week for as long as it takes.

You know what the record is? The most that anyone has ever endured?'

'Twelve?'

'Forty-seven. But we figured they didn't know anything. It was that orderly. What was his name again?'

'Webster.'

'Right. He must have been made of fairly tough material to withstand *that*. We don't often miss one. So, are you ready?'

She didn't wait for a reply and all of a sudden my feet were anchored to the ground by two blocks of clear ice. I saw a shadow move past the window of the ticket office, then another. I could hear the nightwalkers outside making soft whispering noises, the rattle of a Rubik's cube, the soft murmur of Glitzy Tiara running through a shopping list for a meal she'd never make. I had felt the same when they had attacked me for real in the *Cambrensis*, a sort of dull, helpless terror that makes you hot and sweaty and nauseous. I shivered as the nightwalkers began to creep in through the door, some of them across the walls and one along the ceiling.

'I'll make a deal,' I said.

'We're done negotiating, Charlie. The sooner you tell us where the cylinder is, the sooner this can all be over. And I mean over. There's one of my agents waiting next door to smother your worthless wonky head with a grubby pillow as soon as I wake up and give the order. It won't be quick, but it'll be final. And you *will* tell us. They all do.'

'Except Webster,' I said.

'Yes, okay, *except* Webster,' she agreed in a tetchy manner. 'We'll up it to a hundred repeats in the future. Live and learn. So: be eaten alive once, twice, thirty times – you'll still be dead at the end of it and we will have the cylinder. Your choice.'

The nightwalkers started to move in again with unpleasant slathering noises and in a slow, calculated fashion. I tried to jump out to the fire valleys but I couldn't. I'd overlooked that I was thin, and tired, and slightly narced. Aurora, by contrast, was about as fit as she could be. The first nightwalker was barely a couple of feet from me, all nails and teeth and hunger, when The Notable Goodnight spoke again.

'Something's happened,' she said through the medium of the shimmering Mrs Nesbit, and Aurora held up her hand. The night-walkers stopped abruptly but continued to stare at me hungrily.

'We've got a crew inside the *Cambrensis* and the HotPot hadn't been shut down at all,' said Mrs Nesbit. 'There's also about thirty nightwalkers inside.'

Aurora looked at me.

'Jonesy and Toccata,' she said, reading my thoughts perfectly. 'Pull out the nightwalkers and send them for immediate redeployment. No, wait. Safer to simply retire them – along with Birgitta and Webster. We can't risk any of them being retrieved.'

And in that moment, I broke. I thought about what I'd done with the cylinder, and Aurora picked up on it immediately.

'Porter's lodge, lower ground floor,' she said in a triumphant tone, 'behind the vermin grid on the ventilation duct.'

She relayed the information to Goodnight, and Mrs Nesbit acknowledged the message, then asked Aurora if she was going to come out, retire Worthing and then get some rest.

'I'll see this through,' she said. 'I want Wonky to know what happens to people who annoy me. Besides, it will be fun. I'll see you later.'

Goodnight agreed, and the shimmery Mrs Nesbit vanished.

'Well now,' said Aurora, 'that wasn't so very hard, was it? If you'd told us earlier you might still be alive. Driving a golf cart and brain dead, but alive.'

'Even if I lived another thousand years,' I said, 'I'd never come across a more obnoxious person than you.'

'That's a hard call to make,' she said cheerily. 'HiberTech is a big place, and I'm really only the muscle, the one who does the shitty jobs that need to be done. Who's worse? The monster who does, or the monster who guides policy and gives the orders?'

I was probably past caring at this point. Tears of frustration were running down my cheeks and freezing before they hit the ground. I'd failed – *again*. I looked up, and the nightwalkers continued their slow advance. There were about ten of them, and they all licked their dry lips as they stared at me. Some were missing body parts, all were in rags, and the stench of decaying flesh mixed with body odour and excrement was overpowering. I struggled to free my feet but couldn't, and the nearest nightwalker lifted my bathrobe and placed a dirty fingernail on my stomach. I thumped it hard on the head, but it was like striking a bowling ball, and I did little except hurt my hand.

I closed my eyes and awaited my fate. If Webster could take it, so could I.

I braced myself, but nothing happened. After a few moments I opened a wary eye to see that the ticket office was no longer there; we were standing on an unbroken white carpet of undulating deep snow, the sound deadened, a dull empty whiteness in all directions. The nightwalkers were paying me no heed as they had been startled by something within the blizzard, like a pack of carrion-wolves disturbed by hunters. Within a few seconds they had all scuttled away into the white of the snowstorm and Aurora and I were left completely alone.

'Another of your tricks, Worthing?'

'No,' I said, equally confused, 'this isn't me, I swear.'

We both stared into the empty drab whiteness all around but there was nothing to be seen aside from the smooth snow and softly falling flakes. I took a step back – the ice around my feet had melted.

Aurora drew her Bambi but it was pulled from her hands and went whirling off into the whiteness. She stared at me, and I back at her, and then, from the depthless emptiness, there was the soft chuckle of a child.

'What's that?' demanded Aurora, as a sudden gust of wind sent the falling snow into a flurry.

'It's the Gronk,' I said simply.

'There is no Gronk, Worthing.'

'I thought so too, at first,' I said, 'but I've learned a few things while I've been here. The Wintervolk have a free pass during our dreaming times, moving from one to another as mice move around a house behind the wainscotting. Dreams nourish them, dreams give them life. They wait, they bide their time, then they make landfall briefly to do what is right to those who do what is wrong.'

She glared at me but I think she knew I was telling the truth.

'We can fight it together,' she said, 'the combined strength of us two will defeat her.'

'I don't need to defeat her,' I said, 'she doesn't want me, *never* wanted me. She's come for you: the juiciest morsel on the whole Sector Twelve platter.'

Aurora looked at me, then out at the steadily falling snow. There was another gurgle of laughter and the Winter opened up, ready to be nourished with the shame of the unworthy. I felt a shard of ice pierce my heart as the Winter welcomed me into its darkness, then watched as Aurora had the burdens of her sins drawn from her, as heat might be extracted from a hapless traveller. Every murder, every lie, every interrogation. Her face went from fear to realisation, then to sorrow, contrition, guilt, then ... *shame*.

'Oh sweet mercy,' she whispered, hand over her mouth, *'what have I done?'*

And once she'd become fully aware of the enormity of her sins, she was gone. All was quiet once more, the snow gently falling, the air fresh, calm.

I wasn't alone for long. I felt a small hand clasp mine and I looked down. There was a young girl grinning up at me, dressed in a swimming costume and holding a beach ball, the snow melting on her cheeks as it settled.

'Hey, Gretl,' I said.

'Hey, Charlie,' she replied. 'She was unworthy, you know.'

'I know.'

She squeezed my hand again.

'You are noble and wise beyond your understanding, Charlie. It's important you know that.'

'Thank you,' I said, 'but I don't feel it. HiberTech are about to retire all the nightwalkers from the *Cambrensis*, including Birgitta and Webster. I'm due to be murdered in my sleep as soon as it's noted Aurora is missing or dead or however it works out there, and my nightwalker retrieval plan counted on me actually staying alive.'

'We might be able to do something about that,' said Gretl. 'I have

a feeling that Aurora might not be quite as dead as you suppose. ·
There's a reason I didn't take her clothes, or her finger. She still
needs them. Here she is.'

A figure was walking out of the snow towards us. I recognised
her not by her features, but by her demeanour. She looked scared
and a little confused. Actually, a *lot* confused.

'I feel kind of odd,' said Toccata, with both her eyes looking
straight at me, 'like I'm waking up from a very wild and implausible
dream.'

'Not yet you're not,' I said, 'but soon. And there's one or two
urgent things I'd like you to do for us.'

She tilted her head on one side.

'Does it involve bringing down HiberTech?'

'It does.'

'Then let's hear them.'

The Awakening

The Kiki (n.): From Mid-Wales hibernatory mythology. A benign Winter spirit that manifests itself during the hibernational Dreamstate, and is generally thought to keep the inexperienced sleeper from falling too far into the abyss of deep hibernation. (See also Legends: Gronk; Slink; Dorweevil; Thermalovaur.)

In a desperate alliterative bid to be the first to coin a phrase, the press variously dubbed it: 'The Wonder of Wales', 'The Miracle of the Marches' and 'The Sensation of Sector Twelve'. Ultimately, to no avail. Historically and medically it became known simply as 'The Awakening'.

All told, there were sixty-one nightwalkers across Sector Twelve who suddenly found themselves awake, one after the other, at five and three-quarter minute intervals, continually over the space of six hours. Of those, five were being harboured at different locations in the Sector, eight were still wandering around outside, an unreliable twelve were reported from HeberTech's Redeployment labs, and an impressive thirty-six were, for no clearly explained reason or purpose, all gathered at the *Cambrensis* Dormitorium.

'One moment I was curling up for sleep at Port Talbot,' explained one, 'and the next I'm wandering around the icy wastes of Sector Twelve, wrapped in gold Dralon curtains.' One woke up on a slab about to be parted out, and another said that she had been, as far as she was aware, 'asleep for five years, and in that time was looked after by my husband until he was drowned in a HotPot overheat. I knew nothing of this,' she added, 'until I came to be seated in a golf cart at HiberTech.'

There were many physical marks of their time walking: myriad scratches, frostbite, missing fingers and in some cases malnutrition or even wrongnutrition: a nightwalker who didn't want to be named had two pounds of carpet underlay removed from their stomach, along with parts of a car tyre, seventeen buttons – all blue – and the partially digested skulls of three cats. But of psychological after-effects, there seemed to be mercifully few: almost all of the awakees described the experience as akin to hibernation, which is technically what it was, but with vague, half-forgotten dreams of what they might have been doing, and a lingering affection for raw tripe and undercooked pork.

The most notable awakee was the singing and dancing star Carmen Miranda who despite her advanced years, would go on to spearhead the campaign for a government inquiry into the potentially dangerous side effects of Morphenox.

'Despite considerable research, we've *absolutely* no idea how and why this occurred,' said The Notable Goodnight in a rare television appearance four weeks after the Awakening, 'and although we may theorise that historically other nightwalkers may also have been poten-tially recoverable, we have no evidence one way or the other. Obviously, we are delighted by this unprecedented event, are currently conducting considerable research into the issue, will be cooperating fully with the inquiry and have withdrawn Morphenox from the marketplace.'

It was pretty much as expected, really.

The numbers were too great for HiberTech to hide what had happened. As it was, well-engineered corporate surprise, orchestrated bafflement, faux delight, suitable soul-searching and feigned contri-tion won the day. The story dominated the headlines at Springrise for almost a month before they moved on to more pressing matters, such as updated wastage targets, chilling new evidence for a planet-wide runaway climatic 'snowball' effect and, of course, the *Albion's Got Talent* odds-on favourite: a pug dressed as a clown who can bark 'The Lambeth Waltz'.

I met up with Toccata at the Wincarnis three days after Aurora was taken by the Gronk. She'd already tendered her resignation as both head of the Consul Service and HiberTech Security.

'I can't pretend to be two people for ever,' she said, 'and it's impossible to hide the fact that I do now actually need to sleep.'

'What's that like?' I asked.

'It's ... *glorious.*'

Unable to feign the curious eye movements of her previously split personality, Toccata had taken to wearing an eyepatch that she simply switched when she took on a different persona.

'Do you think anyone suspects anything?' I asked.

She shook her head.

'Too much going on. And although it could be beneficial for me to stay on at HiberTech from a RealSleep espionage point of view, I have no recollection of anything Aurora got up to, so it would only be a matter of time before I was rumbled. I'm putting it about that I need to retire on mental health grounds. I don't think anyone's surprised, and quite a few people are actually quite relieved.'

Shamanic Bob brought our coffees and we waited until he had departed before continuing our conversation. Toccata had woken that night over at HiberTech, and while feigning to be Aurora, specifically ordered that I not be killed as I had 'helped out considerably' and that the nightwalkers were no longer scheduled for retirement. She got me out of HiberTech the following morning when the storm had abated, but not before I had gone to sleep again – and dreamed, big time.

The thing is, you don't need a Somnagraph when you have a helpful entity like the Gronk to take you into the deep dreams of nightwalkers, don't need a cylinder from Don Hector when you came second in the Swansea Town Memory Bee with six hundred and forty-eight random words – taking precisely six minutes to recite – memorised after only two readings. Back in the *Cambrensis*, before I went to see Foulnap in the museum, I played the cylinder twelve times to memorise it, each time with the nightwalkers gathering behind the door. I kind of figured HiberTech would squeeze the location of the cylinder out of me, and it's always good to have a back-up, just in case. I'll never know for sure, but I think Jack Logan had planned something like this all along. Perhaps not with the Gronk, but certainly regarding my memory.

'Where will you go?' I asked Toccata. 'In retirement, I mean.'

'I have a house on the Gower,' she said. 'I'd like you to visit me every year. Last two weeks in August. I don't have many friends.'

'Neither do I.'

So I did, every year until she died eighteen years later, of natural causes. Sometimes we walked to the abandoned lighthouse at the end of Whiteford Sands, sometimes to Oxwich Point, where we paused at the oddly shaped tree before we made our way down to the sea and then along the coastal path to Port Eynon for fish and chips. On the last day I spent with her every year we made a point of going to the Mumbles Pier for cockles and laver bread on toast with thick-cut bacon and a large mug of tea, all consumed outside, the gulls scavenging for scraps.[65]

We sometimes saw Birgitta and Charles down at Port Eynon, where they now live. She paints and he looks after their daughters. I only spoke to Birgitta once, two weeks after Springrise when they were both preparing to leave Sector Twelve for good.

'Hello, Deputy Worthing,' she said when I opened my door one morning. I'd stayed in the *Siddons*. I kind of liked it there and had formed an attachment to Clytemnestra.

'It's Charlie,' I said, trying hard not to stare. The return of Charles had lifted the melancholy I had seen in her earlier. I was still in love with her and would remain so for many years, but I think that was Webster's love, carried over from his dream. If I was getting only half of what he felt, they would be happy as none other.

She asked me if I still had the painting she did of me, and could she have it back. I said that was fine, which saved me five hundred euros, and when she came in to fetch it, I asked her if she recalled anything from when she was a nightwalker.

'I remember being under a car,' she said, thinking hard, 'and in the tub having my hair cut off. Other than that, zilch.'

She stared at me with her penetrating violet eyes, then held up her hand with the missing thumb.

'I was reported retired, but someone decided I was worth keeping and spared me. I was also looked after in my room at the *Siddons*. I owe a Debt to someone. Do you know anything about that?'

65. I strongly recommend that you do, too.

I wanted to tell her what I felt, and what I'd done, and what I'd risked to keep her safe and just how close it had all been, but that would have only complicated matters. And to be honest the love that had kept her safe was her husband's, channelled through me. It was his triumph as much as anyone's.

'I shouldn't tell you this,' I said, 'but your thumb was entered into the books by Jonesy. She's no longer with us, but I have a feeling that she might have had something to do with it. We all owe her a lot. I found this in her stuff. I guess it belongs to you.'

I handed her the Polaroid of her and Charles on the beach at Rhossilli and she gazed at the faded photo intently.

'Those were happy days.'

'For me, too', I said, 'there'll always be the Gower.'

'Yes,' she said thoughtfully, 'there'll always be the Gower.'

She then smiled, kissed me on the cheek, and looked at her watch. 'We've a train to catch. Cheerio, Charlie – and thank you.'

And that was it, although I think she might have remembered more as the years went on, as I suddenly started receiving *cartes de bon hiber* from her and Charles and the girls about five years later. I keep them in a shoebox under the bed to this day. Seven years later she and Charles let it be known through appropriate channels that they would be happy to work for RealSleep again, but I had a message sent that they had both discharged their duties in an exemplary manner, that the Global Hibernating Village was in part due to them, and no further contribution was needed.

Laura Strowger had to wait until the labs were open after Springrise to get the film developed, and the evidence, whilst certainly unusual and compelling, could also be open to interpretation. Not that it mattered; she retained her child option rights fully, without let or hindrance.

'I think HiberTech had become such a toxic brand that they wanted to avoid all controversies,' she told me at Summer Solstice celebrations, when Sector Twelve was green and verdant, a far cry from its Winter drabness, 'and purchasing collateralised child options didn't sit well with their improved corporate image.'

'What about Treacle?' I asked.

'To him it's all just profit and loss. Win some, lose some. He's okay about it.'

Laura stayed in Sector Twelve and became a part of the team, along with Fodder, once he had completed his two-year sabbatical. We had no more trouble from the Farnesworths, and Laura went on to save my life two years later when I became trapped under a Sno-Trac near Llanigon, for which she was highly commended.

As for me, I carried on at the Sector Twelve Winter Consul's office, and within five years I was made Chief Consul, the youngest ever. Sister Zygotia was extremely proud, and when I visited St Granata's on Fat Thursday, even Mother Fallopia offered me a grudging comment of admiration and a box of Maltesers.

'To share,' she added.

To this day my washing is always mysteriously folded overnight.

'It's a courtesy,' Gretl told me when we met a Springrise Plus Two, the Consuls disbanded, the snow and ice thawed, the population returned to life, hungry and skinny and confused. We'd replaced Moody and Roscoe and Suzy with a new RailTech team, and the first Spring train left the platform at Talgarth only 5.6 seconds late – impressive but only enough to come twelfth in the Mid-Wales Springrise Punctuality Championships.

Without Morphenox, everyone went back to dreaming from the next season, and the general consensus felt that it was better this way. Winter Wastage is up, but there are no more Nightwalkers, and the government is investing heavily in sound nutritional strategies to aid weight gain in the run up to Winter. HiberTech still conduct research into a side-effect free version of Morphenox, but so far nothing. Don Hector guarded his work well and he kept the secret only in his dreaming mind, something that is now shared with me.

I will have to consider carefully what I do with the knowledge.

Gretl is always there ahead of me when I dream myself onto Rhosilli beach, playing with her beach ball accompanied by the familiar gurgle of a laugh now firmly etched into my mind as I sit near an orange-and-red parasol of spectacular size and splendour.

These days, there is no one beneath it – the previous incumbents now happy enough not to dream of times when they were.

'All that I am is now within you,' said Gretl as we watched the sun set over Worm's Head, the waves beating the hull of the *Argentinian Queen* like a drum, 'don't be dying on me or anything – finding an agreeable host is harder than you might imagine.'

'I'll do my best.'

'Good,' said Gretl, 'now: what did you learn in your first Winter?'

I paused for thought.

'I could talk about loyalty and the cold, Tunnocks Teacakes and the desolate beauty. Of the code that glues us winterers together, or the loneliness of the souls who call it home. But I think the one thing that struck me is that the Winter isn't a season – it's a calling.'

'I concur,' said Gretl with a smile, and the sun set over the Gower. Again.

Acknowledgements

My thanks firstly to you, dear sweet reader, for sticking with me during what I now call my creative hiatus of 2014–2016. That you are still here now (and have presumably finished the book if you are reading this) is testament to your loyalty, for which I am immensely grateful. I can only apologise profusely that it happened (I'm still trying to figure out why) and hope to return to the year-on-year books that I managed to do in the past.

Thanks also go to the estimable Carolyn Mays at Hodder, who never lost faith in my ability to one day deliver another book, and was a pillar of strength throughout. Similar thanks also to Andrea Schulz and Allison Lorentzen at Penguin, and special gratitude indeed belongs to the ever-supportive Will Francis, ably assisted by the team at Janklow & Nesbit.

John Wooten once again agreed to my: 'yes, Jasper, it's vaguely plausible' fact-checking regime and offered vital help and assistance with the theoretical functioning of the HotPots and Vortex Cannon.

Josh Landy in the book is actually a real person, and a jolly splendid one too. The part of 'Josh' was auctioned off in the book to support our local school and the Hay and Talgarth Refugees group, of which many thanks for his generosity. I wanted Josh to be recognisable as such rather than simply 'Your Name Here' and he entered into the spirit of the exercise with all due gusto, and much of the dialogue and descriptive prose attached to Josh's character is his – my thanks for making it all so easy.

The frontispiece was done by Bill Mudron and Dylan Meconis, and a jolly fine job was done, as usual, and at lightning speed – they can be contacted at www.billmudron.com and www.dylanmeconis.com and are open for commissions. My thanks also to Catherine Affleck for undertaking the infinitely subtle job of designing logos for HiberTech and the Consul service. More of her work and contact details can be found at www.catherineruthdesign.com.

It only remains for me to thank Simon for our Thursday lunches, all my children for the never ending joy they continue to bring me, and Ozzy, whose sharply focused and never-ending enthusiasm for stick fetching has been a source of huge inspiration.

Jasper Fforde
March 2018

Look after the ones that look after you

Support the WinterConsul Service

THE WELSH GIRL

FOR ALL YOUR WONCHO NEEDS

WWW.THEWELSHGIRL.COM
OR VISIT OUR SHOWROOMS AT HAY-ON-WYE

The
GOWER
Peninsula

Sand + Surf + Sea
What are you waiting for?

Call your local Welsh
Tourist Office now!
Visa no longer required

CHOOSE
TALGARTH
FOR YOUR MAMMOTH WATCHING HOLIDAY

* WELDED STEEL OBSERVATION HIDES
* TRY YOUR HAND AT MILKING*
* FUN FOR ALL AGES
* NO EXPERIENCE NECESSARY
* PETTING ZOO*
* RIDES*

*LIABILITY WAIVER REQUIRED. 38% RISK OF DEATH OR SERIOUS INJURY. NO REFUNDS POSSIBLE, SORRY.

ADOPT A CALF TODAY!

CALL YOUR LOCAL WELSH TOURIST OFFICE FOR DETAILS

INSOMNIAC?

Have difficulty slipping down into the Hib?
Reruns of BONANZA and CROSSROADS not enough?
Then why not try:

A BORING BOOK?

By government mandate all libraries
and bookshops MUST have a 'dull'
section by July 2003

Suggested Titles:

"The regulatory
framework for
the importation
of carrots"

"The non-pictorial
complete history of
doorhandles"

"Moby Dick"

"The story of gingham"

"Farmall tractor
carburettor options
of 1932"

'I was awake until Slumber-
down +6 until I started to
read PAMELA. Thank you,
Ministry of Sleep!'
—Ms D, Bristol

This Message Brought To You By The
MINISTRY OF SLEEP